JUNGLE SHIFTERS

GW01406564

Under YOUR SKIN

KAT TURNER

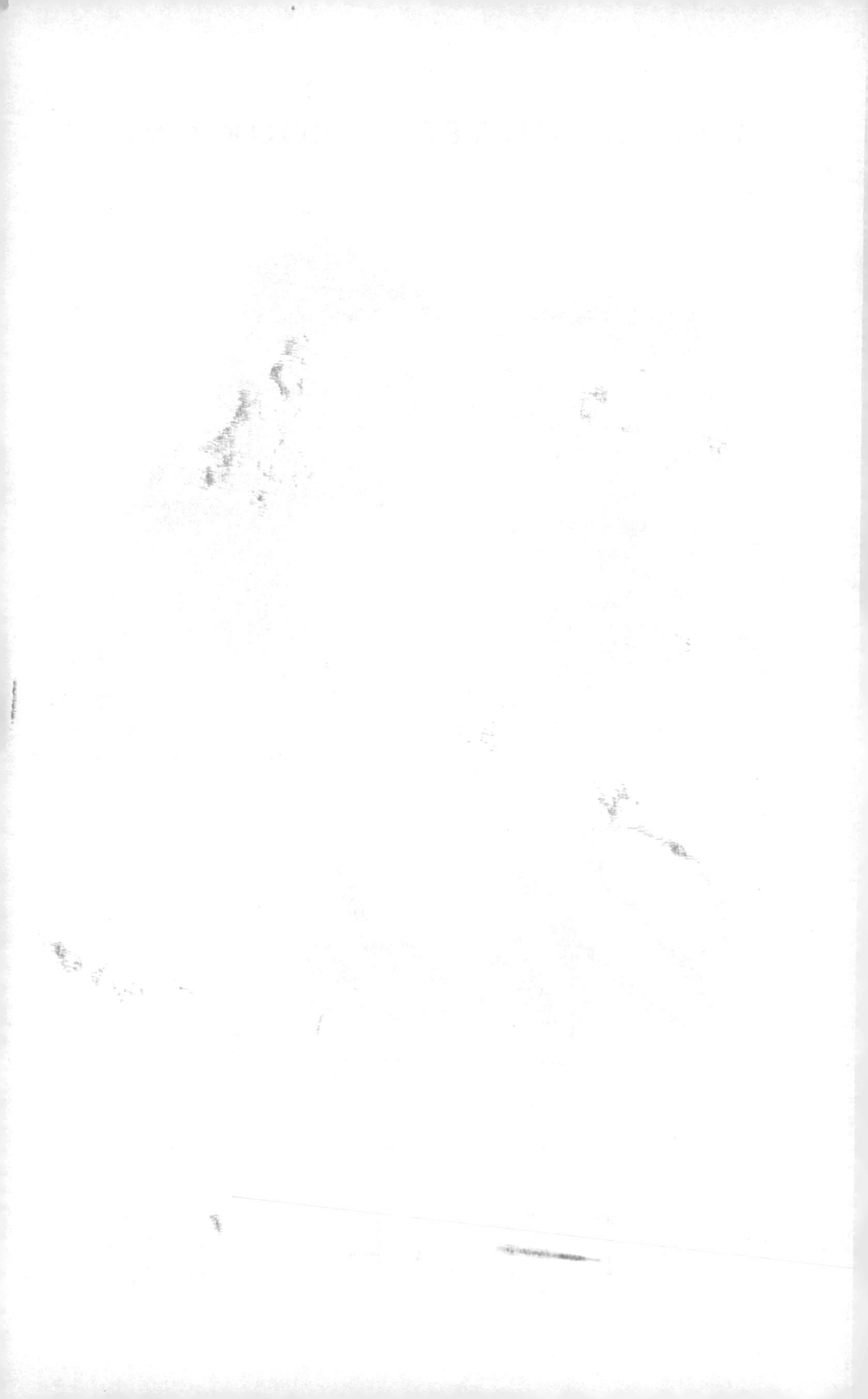

UNDER YOUR SKIN

KAT TURNER

CITY OWL
PRESS

This book is a work of fiction. Names, characters, places, and incidents either are products of the author's imagination or are used fictitiously. Any resemblance to actual events or locales or persons, living or dead, is entirely coincidental and not intended by the author.

UNDER YOUR SKIN
Jungle Shifters, Book 1

CITY OWL PRESS
www.cityowlpress.com

All Rights reserved. Except as permitted under the U.S. Copyright Act of 1976, no part of this publication may be reproduced, distributed, or transmitted in any form or by any means, or stored in a database or retrieval system, without the prior consent and permission of the publisher.

Copyright © 2025 by Kat Turner

Cover Design by MiblArt. All stock photos licensed appropriately.

Edited by Tee Tate.

For information on subsidiary rights, please contact the publisher at info@cityowlpress.com.

Print Edition ISBN: 978-1-64898-489-1

Digital Edition ISBN: 978-1-64898-490-7

Printed in the United States of America

PRAISE FOR KAT TURNER

"A fledgling witch finds love with a mature rock star in the midst of occult danger in Turner's magic-heavy debut and series launch. Turner sets up a promising world that readers will be pleased to return to in subsequent installments. Paranormal fans should check this out." – _Publisher's Weekly_

"_Hex, Love, and Rock & Roll_ is clever, witty, and captivating from chapter one. Helen and Brian pull you into their world and refuse to let you go. It is utterly a bewitching love story that has it all: chemistry, mystery, _love,_ but most of all– rock and roll." – _Jaqueline Snowe, author of the Shut Up and Kiss Me series_

"In _Blood Sugar_, readers can expect Turner's trademark snark mixed with magical and metaphysical mysteries, a well-paced plot full of unexpected twists, and two layered and complex characters winning their happily ever after." – _Janet Walden-West, author of Salt + Stilettos_

"I adore Cynthia and Raven! The chemistry between them is off the charts and they are both such badasses. _Fallen Angel_ is pure paranormal joy. From the scintillating opening scene to the satisfying ending, it grabbed me and didn't let me go. Kat Turner has not only provided readers with a fascinating new addition to her series, she's given them a story and characters that feel distinct and fresh. I loved every moment of it." – _Rosanna Leo, author of Darke Passion_

"_Song of Virgo_ is an intense and perfect combination of magic, mystery, and love!" – _Jaqueline Snowe, author of the Shut Up and Kiss Me series_

"Absolute magic. _Hex, Love, and Rock & Roll_ delivers thrilling suspense, steamy chemistry, and a sexy British front man. Anyone who's ever had a crush on a rock musician or wished on a star will fall in love with this debut." – _Mary Ann Marlowe, author of Some Kind of Magic_

ALSO BY KAT TURNER

COVEN DAUGHTERS

Hex, Love, and Rock and Roll

Blood Sugar

Song of Virgo

Fallen Angel

Inferno

Dark Heart

✷

COVEN DAUGHTERS ORIGINS

Embers

For Austin

ONE

THE RUSTLE OF CHEERS, GROANS, AND CURSES FROM HER CLASSMATES surrounded Taylor McClure as she clutched her rolled-up economics exam and exited the lecture hall. A long exhale failed to banish her jittery nerves. She stepped into the foyer on shaky legs. Her stomach clenched, heart slamming.

If she flunked the first big test in the toughest upper-level econ seminar at the University of Texas, Austin, she'd fail the class and likely lose her Wall Street internship.

She unfurled the tube, her sweaty palm sticking to the paper, and peeked at her grade.

Relief crashed over her in a cooling waterfall. Her throat swelled with the threat of tears.

An A, penned in a red capital letter, beamed from the middle of a circle. She hadn't mixed up a single equation despite her math-related learning disability, dyscalculia. She pumped a fist in the air and told a fellow econ major walking past, "Nailed it."

The guy wore a polo shirt and had a dark look of envy in his eyes, his own test crushed in his fist. "Congrats."

She assumed her place at the end of a line of students waiting for java service from the coffee cart by the side exit. The aroma of roasted beans centered her until she routed her focus to the next task.

Would her dad dismiss or downplay her accomplishment yet again? Earning the approval of her genius physicist-turned-senator father was so challenging. Being good enough was consistently out of reach.

Without the support of Senator Jeff McClure's Manhattan connections, though, she'd be just another anonymous girl in the big city, vulnerable to sabotage by her ruthless colleagues.

Get it over with. Rip of the proverbial sticky bandage.

As she fumbled in the side pocket of her backpack to grab her phone, hot pain flared in the crook of her elbow. A thick haze clouded her mind while a sensation similar to déjà vu but twice as disorienting swallowed her whole.

Stretching pressure pulled on the tips of her ears. Caught in a state of trapped paralysis, she stared at the spot where the hem of her shorts met her thigh. What was happening? Did lack of sleep cause severe reactions like this?

One red blotch glimmered in the air right above her knee. She could make out a glowing handprint, its fingers twisted into crooked claws.

Numb with disbelief, Taylor squeezed her eyes shut and opened them.

The handprint was still there.

Air left her lungs. Vertigo pulled her perception in and out. Her lips parted, and she looked left to right. The symbol moved with her. What the fuck? She was seeing things. This could not be real.

But it was. The red stamp with the broken fingers morphed into an upside-down triangle.

What did that mean? Stunned, all she could do was gape.

It took another five seconds for the vision to fade and vanish. She blinked, unable to shake the weirdest experience of her entire life.

"Ms. McClure?" The authoritative voice of Dr. Sanchez, her economics professor, ripped her from her stupor. "Are you okay?"

She snapped her head up to see Sanchez standing by the coffee line, his bushy eyebrows drawn together in a frown. "Fine," she croaked the word out of a dry mouth.

Not like she could indulge in a freak-out or confess what she'd seen.

Even if he believed her, he'd blame exhaustion or stress, which could jeopardize her standing in the class.

One less-than-effusive recommendation from a professor could cost her the internship at Bull Gordon Investment Bank, who might check her references again before she graduated in December and moved to New York.

A lucrative Wall Street career was the only way to both nuke the six-figure debt her family had accrued during her dad's run for office and kill her student loans.

"Are you sure?" Sanchez cocked his head.

"My hair snagged on my earring. Hurt like hell."

The instant the lie flew out of her mouth, a breeze of cold air slid over the back of Taylor's neck. She'd gotten a brand-new pixie cut over Labor Day weekend a few days ago in a begrudging concession to the never-ending Central Texas summer.

Sanchez scrunched his face into a portrait of skepticism, but at least he ambled off without another word.

Still frazzled by her apparent hallucination, Taylor found herself next in line. She ordered an iced latte, nearly dropping her wallet as she fumbled for her credit card.

Sucking down ice-cold caffeine and sugar, she attempted to clear her mind of the red weirdness. Human brains did odd, inexplicable stuff now and then. Hers used to insist that one plus one equaled three while classmates laughed at her.

The bottom line was that Taylor had bigger things to think about. Maybe the lecture hall was having a technology malfunction, or a student was playing with a new kind of laser pointer. She got out of there fast, crossed the street, and unlocked her car with a chirp of the key fob. Her dad had leased the BMW for her as a birthday present, and with a twist of guilt, she remembered to call him.

Even though her parents were supposed to be paying off credit cards and not splurging, he insisted that she drive in luxury in order to help maintain the illusion of family wealth. After firing up the ignition and cranking the air conditioning, she texted him.

Aced the test!!!!

Her phone vibrated a second later, making her sit bolt upright. Jeff

McClure *never* replied immediately. He'd explained once that forcing others to wait was a strong power play. Yet he'd texted right back: *Congrats. Told Jay Stearns about your position today. He said they'll be lucky to have you on board.*

This Stearns intel was awesome news. Her dad was using his status to put her name in the ears of New York's best financiers. She'd need the support of those top Wall Street dogs. Her dad was coming through for her. So what if he'd spent her college fund wooing potential campaign donors, forcing her to borrow heavily for school? It was just business, a cold economic calculation.

Thanks. There's a three-month probationary period that I have to beat, so I need to be on top of my game.

Another super quick reply came. She read his words twice to make sure that she'd seen them correctly: *Heads up. Big stuff is starting to happen, really huge, so stay alert. Gotta run. Love you.*

Taylor touched her heart, buoyed by lightness. Her dad had never told her that he loved her, though she'd been battling to win those words for years. Each math trophy or ribbon, every clobbered test, brought her one step closer to earning those three words. After twenty-two years on the planet, she'd fulfilled some final, mysterious condition and now held the precious words like diamonds in her palm.

Euphoria running through her in streaks, she slid the gear shift into drive in a single, triumphant thrust. A twenty-minute drive on the Interstate landed her at the South Austin Branch Library, where her tutor client Kirk preferred to meet. Inconvenient for her, but she respected the guy's dedication to passing his classes and heeded his wishes.

The parking lot was empty save for a rusted green pickup and one other sensible car glazed with the golden rays of sunset. The library sat at the edge of cracked concrete, chunky and brown like two squished cardboard boxes stacked on top of each other. A bit of a sad sight, but one she'd come to like thanks to the fulfilment of helping Kirk succeed.

Once inside, a pulpy-sweet smell of old books and glue washed over her, carrying memories of the summer STEM camp where her dad used to take her.

Kirk wasn't in his favorite chair, though. Nor was he crashed on the couch by the wall of gleaming donor plaques or having a sip of water from the fountain next to the looming fake tree.

She ducked between two stacks, their heights towering above her five-five frame, and took her phone out of her backpack. Before she could text Kirk, a message from him that must've come through while she was driving got her attention.

Stuck at practice, had 2 sneak off just 2 text u. Coach is busting our balls. Sorry.

Your macroeconomics test is next week, and you need to study. HARD.

I can take the loss this time.

With a huff of defeat, she put the phone away. There was only so much she could do.

"Unbelievable." The word came in a male voice with a slight accent involving extra vowel emphasis, the pitch as deep and warm as logs on the campfire.

She peeked out from her hiding spot, chancing a glance at the row of tables lining the back wall. People watching: free and fun.

A dark-haired man sat at a scuffed wooden table covered in books and newspapers, his head bent down in concentration.

Though not a man who would normally ping her "hot guy" radar, this guy was, without a doubt, handsome in an unconventional way. A thick ponytail, its hue so black it edged toward indigo, sailed past broad shoulders. His simple white t-shirt wrapped the heft of his muscles perfectly. His strong, angular nose drew her gaze to lush eyelashes resting above pronounced cheekbones.

He cut quite the striking profile from the side.

A half-dozen books, the colors of their covers shades of brown close to his complexion, lay strewn across the table surface. He turned the page of a leather-bound tome. The soft, fluttery sound that followed his leafing complemented the pleasurable sight of his intellectual contemplation.

The longer Taylor stared, the more she felt like she was living in a dream. The man with the stunning bone structure was uncanny. She'd seen him before, but where?

Throbs of agony seized the crook of her elbow, followed by a buzzing sensation like a hive of bees teemed under her skin. This was new. New and bad. What was wrong with her, a brain tumor? She pressed both of her palms into the sides of her head.

The symbol popped up, hanging in the air like before. First, the red handprint. Then the triangle. They cycled back and forth at a pace that made her queasy.

Pressure gripped the tips of her ears, an invisible force pulling them upward like it did in the coffee line. She rubbed her ears as her mind spun.

Discomfort abated as quickly as it had arrived, a jolt of force that made her gasp. She clutched the sore area on her arm, legs wobbling, and fumbled for support. The effort failed, and she smacked her hand against the shelving before biffing face-first onto carpet that probably hadn't been steam cleaned in years. Her flailing knocked a few books off the shelves, the hardbacks thumping on the carpet in mockery.

Two thick legs, clad in jeans ending in cowboy boots capped with shiny golden tips, appeared. The bearer of the legs crouched in front of her.

"I've got you." A man's voice came in a soothing rumble. He extended a big hand, and she grabbed on to his warm strength and staggered into an upright position.

Lucid again, Taylor slapped a palm to her clammy forehead. The attractive man that she'd spotted a minute ago studied her with luscious eyes the color of dark sable. The deep quality of his stare betrayed concern for her well-being.

He wore his jeans and t-shirt like most men wore a tailored suit, with proud posture and confident ease. His bulky physique was neither overweight nor as carved as a gym rat's, and he had a swaggering presence that expanded to fill the room. Not that she was scoping him out. Her ears rang, and the sharp tang of her sweat floated up to her nostrils. She was a mess and in no state to flirt.

An embarrassed laugh burst from her lips. No reason to admit her newfound crazy to this random guy, as caring as he seemed. "Thanks. I guess those all-nighters finally caught up with me." Their hands still clasped in a bind of inconvenient intimacy, she said, "I'm Taylor."

He firmed up their grip and made confident eye contact. As if leading a dance, he moved their joined arms up and down once, twice. "Julian Nez."

The sound of his hot name in that cool voice of his sent off a flurry of traitorous flutters near her bikini line. She lost the battle to dismiss how his massive, silver belt buckle caught winks of light and seduced the eye to travel below his waist.

She returned his intense stare and attempted her own self-assured shake as warmth pooled in her center despite her best efforts not to think scandalous thoughts. A man with a good handshake likely wielded practiced, capable hands in...more personal ways.

He broke the clasp and led Taylor to his table with a stabilizing hold on her upper arm. She rubbed her temples and lowered herself into a chair.

"How are you feeling?" He took his own seat.

"Better." No point in subjecting him to her brain tumor fears.

Her gaze focused on one spot as she worked to stabilize her blurred vision, Taylor caught sight of a newspaper on the end of the table. The paper advertised its tabloid nature with a salacious headline: *Real-Life X-Files Starring Good Old Boy Texas Senator.*

A lump lodged in Taylor's throat. She could hazard a damn good guess as to who was being accused, and the first paragraph of the accompanying text confirmed her suspicion.

Texas Senator Jeff McClure's sinister dealings in genetic mutation and mind control are about to be revealed. Anonymous whistleblower spills the truth on a covert military initiative to rip the fabric of space time apart at the seams, enabling the identification and movement of shape-shifters to top-secret locations. Senator McClure has no qualms about turning to the paranormal to achieve his ambitions —y'all heard that right. Shape-shifters exist. Paranormal entities are REAL. McClure's even going as far as to participate in the use of shape-shifters for warfare.

She laughed and shook her head. Paranormal creatures weren't real, and the notion that her dad was embroiled in some conspiracy involving them was ludicrous. Her dad didn't deserve a smear job in some hack rag because he held a public office. She cut her stare from the paper to Julian. "Why are you reading this?"

A stony expression guarded his reaction. "Not that it's any of your business, but I'm reading it because I'm a concerned citizen with an open mind."

"Concerned about what?"

He leaned forward. She pretended to ignore his bulging biceps and the jagged edge of his black tattoo peeking out of his sleeve. Pretended to ignore a fantasy about him picking her up and throwing her over his shoulder. He totally could too. Not like she wanted that. She swallowed like the motion would bury the thought.

"The truth," he said.

She rose from her chair, unwilling to deal with some truther wacko. Of course Mr. Hot had to be Mr. Crazy. No wonder he wasn't wearing a wedding ring. "You're looking for truth in the wrong place."

"A week ago, I would have agreed with you." He slid the paper at her. "Everyone needs to see this. Read on."

She caught the trail of his scent, a mixture of leather, smoke, and pine. Damn this guy. He was a nutjob who possibly believed in the existence of freaking Bigfoot and therefore not allowed to be sexy. "No thanks. I'm good."

"I don't think any of us are good as long as this is going on."

Red flags were popping up around this guy for sure, yet Taylor didn't feel afraid or even turned off. He was so earnest. Not sketchy at all. She considered herself a good judge of character with a reliable intuition, and this was the most interesting interaction she'd had with another person in a long time. Still, it didn't hurt to keep her guard up. "Why do you care about my opinion on this?"

He tipped one of his shoulders in a slight shrug. "Despite your best efforts to come across as otherwise, you seem open-minded. I hate to turn down a conversation with an interesting person."

She could have gotten up and left right then, yet she chose to stay, halfway hooked by this stranger's luscious eyes, weird ideas, and first impression as someone who was somehow both aloof and inviting. "Fine. What's your theory?"

Did Julian know who she was? Was that why he'd helped her? She had to figure out what this guy's deal was.

Julian continued, "I really think there's some merit in this story. I never figured politicians to be more than a bunch of crooks, but now I'm not so sure this McClure character isn't perpetrating some evil shenanigans. And if what's being printed here is true, or even partially true, we're all in for a shock with consequences we can't even begin to contemplate."

Loyalty and curiosity waged a war in her mind. "If there was any truth to these allegations, they'd be in a mainstream paper."

He quirked one eyebrow. "Can you really see the *Times* running a story about shape-shifters in secret locations?"

"Yeah, okay, that's valid, I guess." Interest eclipsing irritation, Taylor turned her attention to the rest of the items crowding Julian's tabletop. Book titles etched on broken spines indicated esoteric subject matter: *Lycanthropy; Demonology from Pre-Christianity to Present; Witchcraft Lore in the American Southwest and Mexico; Encyclopedia of the Paranormal.*

She could, at least, attempt to deduce *why* he might believe the paper's claim that paranormal stuff was real. A bit more info might help her figure out if she actually remembered him from somewhere. "Are you studying paranormal phenomena for a research project?"

She didn't peg Julian as a typical college guy, the light lines at the corners of his eyes suggested he was in his thirties, but he could be a graduate student or professor studying conspiracy theories. Or a nontraditional student.

"In a sense," he said.

She found herself startled by how much she wanted to hear him say more, both to listen to the sound of his voice and catch a glimpse of the workings of his hidden mind. This circumspect aloofness of his was a surprising turn on. So many of the guys she met were supposed to be simple creatures, easier to read than magazines. This man, however, had in the span of a few minutes turned her expectations and preconceived notions upside down. "In what sense?"

"Long story." He opened a book and leafed through pages. "I suggest that you keep researching. That's what I'll be doing."

His response hit her as a kind rejection would, polite yet distanced. Whatever. Time to go take a nap. Not before opening a door to more interaction, though. She slipped a business card from her wallet and laid it on top of one of his books. "I do a lot of tutoring, so if you ever need help with research or a paper, give me a call."

His mouth tilted into a crooked smile. He slid the card off the book and tucked it in the front pocket of his jeans. "I'll hang on to this."

Taylor had made it to the sliding doors marking the exit when buzzing hit her ears. Panic raced in, her pulse accelerating.

A throb in her arm expanded and contracted like a muscle cramp. She ground her molars and powered through the hurt as she raced into the vestibule. Equilibrium off, she bumped into a wall.

"Down here, Taylor. Help. Help!" She jerked her head in both directions, but there was nobody around. The words came from inside her own damn mind. Nausea bore down. She shook her head in a feeble attempt to ward off the madness, but her resistance was useless.

Images rushed through her mind at breakneck speed. Waves nibbling a rocky shoreline. Shackles bolted to concrete walls. Her father pushing buttons. Peoples' faces and bodies contorting and stretching into all sorts of unnatural positions. Wolf heads on human torsos. Hands morphing into claw-capped paws.

Sweat stung Taylor's eyes while she ran through the parking lot, seeking a bit of solace in her car even though she struggled to see through the rush of imagery. Baby blue triangles, upside-down and the same size as the red one, dropped over her field of vision. They scrolled and scrolled, endless triangles. So many triangles.

Images flickered among integers every half second. Underground tunnels. An emaciated man, seven feet tall with endless arms and legs like stilts, prowled some kind of dungeon. No sound, then screams. Tortured screams.

"Help us, Taylor," a chorus shouted. "You know how."

The tall man stalked his chamber, hunched and pallid. He stopped and glowered with eyes as red as hot coals straight out of hell. She strangled a scream in her throat.

Her world a mess of senseless nightmare fuel, she fumbled in her backpack and managed to scoop out her keys. Her sweaty palm slid over the scalding metal handle of her car door before she finally got the damn thing open.

The discomfort at the tops of her ears returned, yanking like some invisible sadist wanted to rip them off. She dumped herself into the driver's seat, tossed her backpack on the floor, and sucked down big breaths until her head finally cleared and the pain stopped.

Smashing her forehead into the steering wheel, she scrabbled at vanishing scraps of reason. "I need a doctor."

Movement in her peripheral vision prompted her to look out her driver's side window. In the parking place next to hers, Julian unlocked the green pickup. Lazy breezes animating a few loose strands of his hair, he watched her watch him, a cryptic, knowing expression on his face.

Julian tipped his chin at her once before getting inside with a slam of the door.

She got a strange case of chills mixed with more déjà vu, and knew, deep in her intuition, that she was connected to this man and had to figure out how.

No way was she going to let him leave.

TWO

As Julian Nez fired up his trusty old beater, his ultra-sensitive nose savored lingering notes of licorice, vanilla, and the far more personal and delectable smell of a woman. The unique scent of Taylor.

Deep inside, his wolf heart beat alongside his own. The beast who shared his spirit wanted to be with someone as badly as Julian did. With all his free time consumed by researching whether or not shifters like him lived in South America, Julian hadn't been with anyone in months.

Three knocks struck his passenger side window. He glanced to the right and spotted Taylor. A tight-lipped, narrow-eyed look set her pretty face in stern resolve. Her diamond earrings glimmered icy-hot in the dying sun, fiery like what little he'd gleaned of her personality.

He couldn't help but entertain a fleeting thought of what she was like in bed, the ferocious blonde with her wolfish ears and keen eyes the color of wild Texas bluebonnets.

Damn, those ears of hers, tapered to pointed tips, like she was starting to shift. Ears so pronounced he allowed himself to fantasize not only about sex, but that, after many lonely years, a she-wolf had finally found him. He'd sure as hell felt a powerful charge in the library, and when they'd locked gazes a moment ago.

Could the lore be true, the legends about fated mates crossing paths at the most inconvenient possible time? Fate's mischievous, trickster nature worked that way. Allegedly.

Impossible. As far as he knew from meticulous research, all shifters lived secreted away deep in the Peruvian jungle. He'd never run across *anyone* else like him, so it made no sense that Taylor might be a shifter.

"I need to talk to you." The curt impact of her statement kicked her Southern drawl up a notch and switched his thoughts from found shifter family to a certain someone's smooth skin and fit curves.

Julian leaned across the front seat and opened the door. The plastic storage containers full of copied articles about his Peru lead poked him in the hip. He had to call his contact during their agreed upon time frame or risk losing the man's goodwill by coming off as unreliable. No way would Julian blow his shot at finally fitting in. But Taylor needed him. And she fascinated him. "Okay, I've got a few minutes."

To his surprise, she hopped right in to the cab of his truck, picked up the box, and set it in her lap. He stole a quick glance at her body. Assertive was the understatement of the century when it came to Taylor. Big attitude in a compact package.

"Why did you happen to be at this library today reading a kooky story about my father? And what was up with the cryptic remark about evil and all those books?"

Well, small talk sure wasn't happening, but that didn't mean he could open his mouth and blab the entire unfiltered truth, either. *Nice to meet you. I can shift my shape into a wolf and might have found others who can too.* No way to finesse those bombshells, and he hadn't built enough of a rapport with Taylor to trust her. Especially knowing now that she was Jeff McClure's daughter.

Julian rotated the keepsake turquoise ring on his index finger and hazarded a truthful yet guarded answer. "I've been seeing things that corroborate some of the claims made in the story," he said.

"What do you mean, seeing things?"

A distant howl sounded in the recesses of his consciousness, followed by hidden claws pushing sharp against the insides of his fingertips. His inner wolf got agitated over women now and again, but never this intensely. He forced himself not to glimpse at her small breasts or toned legs. They weren't here to flirt or mate.

"Are you going to tell me?" Taylor drummed her trimmed nails on the lid of the box.

Julian simultaneously pressed his feet against the clutch and brake and turned the key in the ignition. A grinding roar filled the cabin along with a blast of tepid air conditioning that offered a bit of respite from the punishing climate. Whew. His truck sure had heated up. "Are you sure you want to know? It's going to sound nuts."

She pinned him in an intense stare. "I can take it. Try me."

Since she seemed to have at least a tentative interest in accepting paranormal phenomena and didn't appear to be playing him, he let his guard down some. "I've had run-ins with an entity. At first, I thought that someone put a curse on me. I started my investigation by reading about Navajo witches and paranormal activity. Next thing I know, I've got that article about your father in my hands."

Her mouth stretched open. "You think my father is connected to a curse on you? That's absurd."

"I realize it doesn't make sense. I don't have lines connecting all the dots, either. But this thing that's been visiting me matches the description of a creature that some of these conspiracy types associate with your father and whatever he's up to."

"He's not up to anything," Taylor snapped, though pain trembled under her flash of temper and made him feel bad for her. Denial was a helluva drug.

Julian put his hands in the air. "I don't mean to offend you. I'm just relaying what I've read."

She closed her eyes and leaned back, resting the back of her head against the top of her seat. "Yeah, I know. Have you read anything about symbols flashing before a person's eyes along with lots of pain?"

He sure hadn't heard of that, but from the way she spoke, it sounded significant. And disturbing. "I have not. Is that what happened to you in there?" He gestured to the library.

Taylor let go of a weighty sigh before she abruptly changed course. "Can I ask you a personal question? If it's intrusive in any way, go ahead and tell me to fuck off."

He chuckled, unable to deny the allure of the rough cuss word in her sweet voice. "Sure."

Taylor opened her eyes and slid him a sidelong glance, the memory of a smile tilting one side of her mouth. "I'm not usually this open with people, but I feel like there's something connecting us that's more than a coincidence, and we need to get to the bottom of it for closure. There's nobody else I can tell who won't think I'm crazy. I guess sometimes it's easier to talk to strangers than friends and family, huh?"

Julian smiled back at her as unspoken vibes passed between them, an invisible energy he could not name bringing them into mysterious communion. They weren't strangers, not really, though he wasn't sure what exactly they shared. "Come on, now. Lay it on me."

She ran a hand through her cropped hair. "Do you have a personal connection to these legends through your history or heritage? Since, as you say, you began your research there."

It had been twenty years since he'd left the rez on a motorcycle at age fifteen, taken off on a cross-country pilgrimage in search of others who could shift their shapes. He'd settled in Texas, but the Navajo Nation with its red rocks, frybread, and painted Arizona sunsets would always be his home, tribe, and people. Even once he set off for Peru, where shifters of all races, religions, and identities supposedly lived in utopian harmony.

"Yeah. I'm Navajo and Comanche. Mostly Comanche I think, but the Navajo claimed me." He laid a hand on her shoulder and wished he hadn't because the yielding feel of her flesh made him crave a whole lot more. "I don't mind talking about my heritage. Why did you ask, though?"

She pressed fingertips to her lips and spoke through the gaps. "I'm trying to get to the bottom of a really scary thing that happened to me. That continues to happen to me."

"Share as much or as little as you need, and I'll do my best to help."

"You mentioned a run-in with an entity and how at first you thought it was connected to your culture, but now maybe not so much. Have you ever seen symbols that had had a really dark, scary energy surrounding them?"

Taylor's words had a chilling effect. What she was describing sounded like black magic, which he wanted no part of. Was his entity sighting tied to the sinister insignia that she was describing? There were many ways that the Jeff McClure supernatural link could be binding him and Taylor, and none of them were good. As much as she interested him, this was getting weirder by the second, and he'd best keep a bit of emotional distance while he figured things out. "I can't say I've experienced events like you're describing."

"But you said you saw an entity, right? So did I. I think I had a vision right as I was leaving the library. There were the symbols that I've been seeing today. This monster with spindly arms and legs was in there, and so were underground tunnels and people crying out to me to help them. Ah, forget it." Her voice shook. She reached for the handle and pushed open the door.

"Wait." Julian cupped Taylor's elbow, protectiveness swelling inside his chest. He hated seeing a woman in distress, and so did his beast. She needed help, and if he could offer it he would.

Maybe the same curse had targeted them both. Maybe they could beat it together. On the flipside, it was possible that Taylor was bad news. He'd figure it out.

The hard and glassy sheen in her eye softened. "Does any of what I described sound familiar?"

Julian ground the heel of his boot into a worn patch in the floorboard. Time slowed to an eerie drag, and his guts knotted as he recalled the worst of the incident. She seemed so vulnerable. Telling her what had happened wasn't inherently dangerous. Even if she was lying or playing him, there wasn't much she could do with the information. "Yeah. The one time I got a good look at whatever this thing is, he looked like your description, inhumanly tall with noodle arms and long legs. Like an apparition, though, not fully there. Blinking in and out. He appeared on my property and tried to grab me, but his hands passed through as a ghost's would."

Seeing this thing in his special ceremonial space scared the shit out of him, but projecting strength might help her remain calm.

Her knuckles went white as she squeezed the edges of the plastic box, tendons and blue veins bulging against her pale skin. "So we saw the same creature. What's happening?"

"I don't know. Hence the books and newspaper and anything else relevant that's printed on paper or available through an Internet search."

She turned her face away from him and to the windshield, a blank, somber look falling over her profile. "I have to leave."

A sinking sensation dropped like a stone into his shoes. "Are you sure? Maybe we could go back inside and look at some of the books together. Figure out what lines up—"

"No, thanks. I probably just need to make a doctor's appointment." Taylor got out of his truck and set the box on the seat, a flare of fear in her eyes. She slammed his door with more force than he would have guessed she had in her.

The motor of her car started with a purr. Tires screeched as she peeled out of the parking lot. Resigned, Julian her go.

If they were meant to cross paths again, they would. Pursuing her could backfire if his efforts edged into stalker territory, and besides, chasing a college girl didn't fit with his moving plans.

He checked his watch. Two hours left in the time frame his Peru contact had given him to call and discuss the logistics of a visit, meaning he had enough time to make a quick pit stop and attempt to decompress after his tense, confounding encounter with Taylor.

Gravel kicked up under his wheels and clattered against the metal. Julian hung a left out of the parking lot and took off down the country road, passing a scruffy swath of sunbaked land and a shallow ravine ending in a dried-up creek bed.

As he turned onto the one-lane highway by an old family farm speckled with a pack of grazing goats, he pushed the radio dial and then the scan button. Pop songs cycled, and, in the midst of them, Julian caught the ranting of a notorious conspiracy theorist shouting in his signature, deep rumble.

His throat constricted as he debated whether or not to listen. He pressed the scan button, stopping on the talk radio program. Of course he was going to listen.

"Jeff McClure folks, a real piece of work. As dirty as it gets. He'll announce his White House run any day now. And if he wins? Expect techno fascism. Every man, woman, and child in this country outfitted with an RFID tracking chip to watch our every move and squash dissent. And speaking of microchips, I have it on good authority that he's doing even weirder stuff with implants. We're talking covertly putting them in people's bodies. This guy is literally casting spells to modify their DNA and enlisting them in his agenda of capturing and training genetically modified super soldiers. Black magic and science, a lethal combination. Wanna hear just how bad it is? Be right back after the break."

The program cut to a commercial, and Julian's memory lingered on the wild accusations and their implications. What was the deal with super soldiers and DNA implants? Could it tie in with the whereabouts of more shifters?

He muttered a dismissive noise for his own benefit. Falling deeper down the conspiracy rabbit hole wouldn't help him get a fix on kinfolk, but calling Tim in Peru would. He turned off the radio.

Julian drove into Giddy Up's lot and snagged a parking spot near the redbrick shack of a dive bar's entrance. A stocky man in a cowboy hat stood between the "no loitering" sign on the side of the building and one of the blacked-out windows, smoking.

Julian turned off his truck, palmed his cell phone off its spot between the two seats, and pushed the speed dial button for Tim. Why wait? Might as well get the phone call over with and then he could relax.

The phone rang twice. Jitters surged within him as he imagined Tim saying nah, never mind, we vetted you and thanks but no thanks. Taking risks never got easier, and that went double when it came to looking for those like him. He'd run after too many false leads to get caught up in optimism anymore. Maybe he was the only animal shifter, the last of his kind.

A click came through the line. Julian's mouth dried. He rummaged in the center console, unwrapped a stick of cinnamon gum, and smashed it between his teeth. Spicy sweetness zinged his taste buds and burned away the crap in his head.

"Jules my man." The younger guy shouted with excitement. Honking horns and squawking chickens made a noisy background cacophony. "I'm at the market. You'd love it. Iquitos, Peru, the only place on Earth where you can buy a pound of fish, a bundle of mystical herbs, and a Coke in the same location. Talk about one-stop shopping."

After three phone calls and as many emails, nobody had so much as uttered the word "shifter" or talked about anything esoteric. Which was fine, they were still in the mundane, trust-building phase. Best to keep his thoughts positive, though. The polite chats were going well.

"Sounds convenient as hell. Look, man, I wanted to talk to you about finalizing plans for that visit. Sales have been solid lately, and I think it would be a good time for me to take off for a week."

"Yeah, yeah." Tim's voice cut out, the crackle and fizz of a shoddy connection making it difficult to read his tone.

Julian scratched the back of his neck and ground the rubbery gum between his teeth, extracting the last of the spicy juices. His belly teemed with nerves.

Tim went on, "We do a special thing for the autumnal equinox that you'll want to be a part of. I'd love to get you down here for that so you can see what we're about."

A soaring sensation carried him high. "See what we're all about" could be code for come out as shifters. "Sounds perfect."

"Great. I'd love it if you arrived a few days before, to get settled in and meet everyone."

"I think I can make it happen." The bar's animated sign danced a familiar show as Julian spoke. Rendered in neon loops the hue of orange sherbet, a silhouette of a cowboy on a horse tossed a lasso around the cursive curves of Giddy Up's name.

Colorful energy brighter than the sign's illumination fed his soul. Even as a painter, he'd never noticed the kitschy, techno-dream beauty of neon before. He might have to do an acrylic or watercolor portrait of Giddy Up before he left. Commemorate the moment.

"Cool. Later." Tim hung up, and Julian followed suit.

Anxiety skated over his sternum as he left his car and walked to the joint's front door, where fliers for local bands plastered scuffed wood. It was a big risk, heading to Peru in hopes of finding a clan. At thirty-five, he might be getting too old to chase dreams.

He pulled on the handle, country music pouring out of the dim bar and bringing with it a rush of earthy tobacco smoke and stale beer. Ten or so patrons, typical for the late afternoon crowd, sat at some of the center tables and booths and shot the shit over pints or playing cards.

An impressive collection of plug-in beer brand signs covered the walls of the ratty place and lit up outdated wooden paneling in a bright array of all-American primary colors.

Julian eyed a sign for a Mexican beer, the aesthetic generically tropical with a parrot and a palm tree. Maybe this Peru thing was a mistake, a fool's errand. He'd done pretty well as a loner all these years, more or less given up on the idea of fitting in on a deeper level. He was too damn different from everyone else, so best to keep friendships and relationships superficial.

Enough brooding. Time for a palate and mind-clearing drink before heading home and studying his research papers some more.

Julian walked up to the bar, passing a cluster of six bearded leather-clad bikers armed with pool cue spears as they stood around the old table with ripped felt the color of a cheap drugstore rose. Balls cracked, and a groan followed.

He pulled out a stool and sat next to Dave, a fellow townie. A rough fifty, Dave wore a stained Hawaiian shirt, and his graying hair sported its usual fork-in-a-light-socket style. The two exchanged friendly nods.

"What's the latest, J?"

"Not much. You?" Julian scanned the length of the bar. Near the end of the rows of liquor bottles, Roxy the bartender poured draught beer, foam sliding over the chunky silver rings on her fingers.

"Cowboys won." Dave took a drink from his pint glass. "I got fifty bucks."

"Congrats." Julian's mind wandered. He fantasized about more meaningful relationships and conversations, what they might be like.

Roxy sauntered over, her mane of dyed-black hair threaded with feather extensions swishing as she wiped her hands on a bar towel. She stopped in front of Julian and bent into a deep lean, causing her ample cleavage to swell beneath a tank top. A silver charm disappeared into her bosom, drowning in flesh.

"If it isn't my favorite customer, the old-time warrior walking the Earth. I thought you moved or something." Desire thickened her already smoky voice.

"I might be." His pulse leapt. Even placing the moving subject in the realm of definite possibility juiced it up with a thrilling sense of realness.

UNDER YOUR SKIN   21

"That's a damn shame." Roxy snagged a bottle of his preferred beer from the mini-fridge and cracked it open on the counter. "We still haven't gotten to know each other very well." She slid a suggestive, green-eyed gaze to the janitorial closet where people hooked up.

"Give it a rest, Rox." Dave slugged a big gulp. "If he wanted a hooker, he'd go on Craigslist."

Roxy slashed Dave her best murderbitch glare. "Keep talkin' and you're cut off for the rest of your alcoholic life, old man. Scoot."

Dave muttered something incomprehensible. Roxy glowered and flapped her hand.

The old drunk picked up his glass and moved a few seats down the bar, grunting the whole way.

She leaned in close, her breath hot against Julian's ear, and whispered, "What do you say? You, me, and some real close quarters. You won't be sorry."

He managed an awkward laugh. Yeah, he could have Roxy. But why? Casual sex wasn't for him, as using a woman's body to get his rocks off when he didn't care about her as a person struck him as a dick move. He was old-fashioned like that.

Besides, he couldn't be bothered wasting his time with women who couldn't accept him, wolf and all. Which ruled out both meaningless romps and serious dating. Lucky for him, single life and the intimate company of his right hand suited him fine. "You know that's not my style, Rox."

She backed off and wiped down the bar with her rag. "You aren't easy, that's for sure. Makes you even hotter."

He lifted his glass. "Thanks."

She toasted him with an invisible glass, a rueful and strange smile encroaching onto her scarlet lips. "Just as well. Suze and Rusty went back there the other week and say they saw something really nuts."

Julian's skin crawled. He cooled his throat with a fast drink of skunky, bitter brew. "Nuts how?"

Roxy shrugged. "I dunno. Maybe they were just fucking with me."

"Tell me anyway." He picked at his beer label as if repetitive motion would keep impending dread at bay.

"You believe in ghosts?" Roxy hummed *The X-Files*'s theme tune.

"I'm not sure." He swallowed past a lump in his throat. Surety he wouldn't commit to, not yet, but evidence of paranormal meddling kept stacking up. "Why, what's the story?"

This time, when she looked at the hookup room, her face paled to a putty hue. She chewed a fake nail. "It was after last call, and they were closing. The only people in here. Suze says they're going at it, getting hot and heavy, when some kind of spirit starts blinking in and out. Moving its mouth like it's trying to say shit."

Blinking in and out. Behavior consistent with what he'd seen. Didn't make sense why the apparition would be lurking around Giddy Up. "Did it say specific words?"

"No. But that's where the story gets weird."

He was both interested in the details and reluctant to learn them but couldn't look away. "Weird how?"

Roxy squinted like her brain struggled to categorize whatever she'd heard. "Both Suze and Rusty say they started seeing visuals when the creeper was in there with them, and they swore they weren't tripping on acid or mushrooms. They saw underground tunnels, a torture dungeon, and some kind of metal chair. Suze said, she said..."

"What did Suze say?" Underground tunnels fit with Taylor's account, as did the phenomenon of seeing visuals in this entity's presence.

"Suze said she saw you being led through one of those tunnels."

Chills threaded up Julian's back. His world shrunk to a void of fear. So this thing was connected to him in some way, latched on. Possibly a trace of his energy had attracted it to Giddy Up. The specifics eluded him, but he better not finalize travel plans just yet. No way would he risk dragging some curse or poltergeist along with him to Peru, no way would he risk alienating his potential new community by rolling up to their doorstep with nefarious baggage in tow.

Meaning he needed to figure out what the hell was amiss with this haunting and how to exorcize the fiend. He might be able to tap into the stuff he'd learned from the tribe's medicine man.

Julian pushed back his bar stool and stood. "Thanks, Rox, you've been a big help."

An incredulous laugh from the bartender followed. "With what?"

"I'm not sure." He laid a five dollar bill on the table and made haste out of the bar. Time to figure out how to kick a flickering spirit to the curb.

THREE

Taylor stepped to the threshold of her dad's home office, a room tucked in a secluded corner of the third floor of the McClure estate, with a clear directive. She wiped her palms on her skirt, looking through the sliver of office space revealed by the ajar door. The gap offered a peep at a bookcase full of texts on political theory and economics, her dad's preferred reading material.

She reviewed her mental list of tidy, straightforward goals. In a manner as casual as the context would allow, she'd chat with him about the internship and rule out his involvement in any of the strange happenings she'd discussed with Julian.

Once she removed her dad from the list of suspects, she could look into other causes and sources for the symbols. The best course of action was to find a mundane explanation for the odd happenings in her life and get her plans back on track instead of following the sexy but possibly insane man from the library down his rabbit hole of conspiracy theories.

She didn't need Julian. Didn't need the element of temptation he introduced and certainly didn't need his chaos. She had goals to pursue, tangible and practical ones.

"Come on in, Taylor," her father called from inside his workspace. "No need to act like you're in trouble."

Acid bubbled in her stomach, abdominal muscles closing in on the few bites of bagel she'd eaten earlier. He'd sensed her presence and disarmed her right out of the gate, deploying his power through humor.

She'd built this up too much. All she was doing was hanging out with her dad, for Christ's sakes. No need to put some Sun Tzu *Art of War* narrative around their interaction.

She pushed open the door to her dad's prestige den and confronted the splendor. Turkish throw rugs, built-in bookcases filled to capacity and covering every wall, and a big window overlooking the sprawling slopes of Texas Hill country boasted wealth and hid debt.

Her dad sat behind his desk, the oak polished to a stately gleam. A subtle scent of cherries and bourbon perfumed crisp air.

Yet amidst the tasteful signifiers of money, she sensed an ominous presence. Corrupt and invisible, a bloodstain painted over but not removed. Shivers needled her arms. Something unseemly was up with him. Likely not as sinister as the speculations in the paper would surmise, but dark nonetheless.

He paused from leafing through a three-ring binder to regard her with a warm smile that crinkled the corners of his pale blue eyes. Shards of sunlight highlighted the streaks of dignified gray peppering his sandy blond hair. "How's my future Wall Street tycoon?"

Guilt sloshing around her middle, she sat in the leather office chair across from him and found an appreciative yet demure expression fit for a good girl Texas debutante.

Her dad had done so much for her. What the hell was wrong with her, questioning his integrity and morals? Yet she couldn't shake the gnawing, irritating sensation at the back of her mind, the little nagging voice.

He's behind this somehow, the voice whispered. *You won't rule him out.*

"I'm okay, but I need to talk to you." Her world contracted to the words she spoke. They hung suspended in the space in front of her like the stupid hallucinatory text.

Like always, his poker face gave away zilch. He closed his binder and said, "Of course."

She had one viable way to play this, one move she could make and not risk coming off as accusatory, mistrustful, or irrational. "I read some pretty disturbing stuff written about you in that fringe paper those libertarians like. Ugly. You might want to consider suing them for libel."

He leaned deep into the cocoa leather of his chair and stroked his tie, his facial expression a sealed vault. "I taught you better than to believe everything you read, Taylor Bree."

The sound of her middle name in his stern, paternal voice worked like a fast-acting shrinking potion. She flinched and knew he saw her cringe, which made her want to smack herself.

"I didn't say I believed it, I said that there are hack reporters out there smearing you, and you might want to try and stop their onslaught before they do some real damage to your good name." Her words squeaked out in a humiliating upswing, unsure and childish. Traitorous heat climbed from her neck to the roots of her hair. She was bombing.

"While I appreciate your concern, rest assured that this matter does not pertain to you. Focus on your schoolwork and then your new job." It didn't last long, but for a hot second, her dad's façade cracked in the wake of his brusque rejoinder. A tentacle of anxiety sneaked through as a subtle, sharp smell and a twitch of his nose and lips.

Plus, this matter? What matter? Though now unsure of which way was up, Taylor made a move for the upper hand. "I'm starting to think it does pertain to me though, that I'm implicated. And it would help if I knew some specifics about the matter in question."

Her father nursed a pause, his stare drifting a million miles away. He reached for a glass carafe resting on a golden platter and poured water into two tumblers, the glug glug sound thrumming in her ears. "Ionized water. Your mother got me started on this shit. At first, I thought it was another one of her snake oil obsessions, but now I'm hooked. I can taste the purity."

He handed her a glass, and she wrapped her palm around the smooth surface. She swirled the liquid, impossibly confused.

"Cheers." Her dad made a move to clink.

Taylor pulled back her glass before his could touch it. "It's bad luck to toast with water."

"I don't believe in luck any more than I believe in Santa Claus. Neither should you. You know that we make our own luck through our conscious choices, just like you knew from the age of two who was really putting those presents under the tree."

She brought the glass to her lips but didn't allow the liquid to breach her mouth. Of course he would never try to poison her, but the energy was weird, wrong, off. Her dad didn't play hide the ball with her, he preferred a straightforward and blunt approach to communication.

It was like she'd been cast into some other role, framed as one of his political rivals or a business acquaintance, someone he had to hold at a formal distance and outmaneuver. She couldn't ignore the pain lancing through her in light of that observation, nor could she disregard the feeling of his "I love you" slipping through her fingers.

Taylor set her glass on the gilt tray, where it came to rest with a soft clink.

Her father's eyes remained bottomless; his expression as neutral as a rubber mask. God, it was worse than being heckled for breaking a test curve, looking into that Tabula Rasa. Like drowning in social quicksand, and the longer they stayed locked in a stare-down, the deeper she sunk.

She rose, walked to a shelf, and pulled out a book on algorithms she'd lent him. A flash of metal behind the book caught her eye. A keypad with numbered buttons, like those on an ATM machine. Her pulse increased in rhythm as her muscles heated and gripped the bones.

Secrets, and something to bank for later, winked coyly behind the books. Taylor approached the desk again and flipped pages, staying on her feet. This way, she towered above her seated father's Napoleonic height. A placebo effect of an advantage, maybe, but better than floundering. "Do you think that genius toes the line of insanity?"

"Sure. Some say Einstein was a bit of a madman."

"I'm seeing numbers and equations everywhere now. Formulas and theorems. In my dreams. Moving through the world." A white lie, but with any luck, mention of visions would pique his interest if he was entangled in the paranormal. She glanced up from the text, met a stare that would unnerve a professional adversary at the Vegas poker tables, and went for broke. "I'm having waking visions, as a matter of fact."

His body tightened up in a ghost of a tell. "Interesting."

"Yes." She set the book on his desk next to his precious water. "Could it, in any way, apply to the matter that you say doesn't concern me?"

A brick wall of inaccessibility faced her. "Are numbers the only thing you remember?"

Memories of the handprint played in a haunting loop. "Yes."

Tension left the man in a subtle relaxation of his arms, a loosening of his jaw. Physical reactions so subtle, a stranger would have missed them, didn't escape Taylor's watch.

"You have nothing to worry about, Taylor. If I were you, I'd write down those equations and formulas. Hell, I wouldn't put it past you to make a mathematical breakthrough or solve the Theory of Everything with that brain of yours."

She spackled on her best daddy's princess smile and pretended to eat up the ass-kissing as if she didn't see through his attempt to deflect through flattery. His plan must've been for her to forget all the weird stuff, plunge the symbols into her subconscious. Noted. "You're biased."

"I know a good investment when I see one, and with you, I'm damn sure I backed the right horse. Now get out of here and go rule the world, kiddo. I love you."

Those three words she'd treasured a day ago now curdled in her gut like spoiled food. "I love you, too."

"We're good?" Tone clipped and businesslike, her dad returned to his binder.

The bitter taste of bile rose up Taylor's throat. "We're good."

With that, he was back to perusing his paperwork. She'd been dismissed. The visit wasn't a bust, though, not by a long shot. She left his office and closed the door with a quiet click. Her dad was implicated in something big and horrible, and so was she. Something big and horrible that she wasn't supposed to remember, but for whatever reason lingered in her awareness anyway.

Footfalls silent on carpet, she wove through the second floor of the estate and past the Medieval suit of armor standing vigil in the corner where the hallway opened up to the formal dining room. Taylor paused before the hollow knight.

As she looked up into Tin Man's empty metal sockets, a familiar dull cramp birthed an old memory. Her mother had picked up the imposing decoration during one of the many McClure family trips to Switzerland, the summer Taylor turned thirteen. The night had ended with her parents screaming and crying and smashing the boutique inn's fine china in one of their routine marital blowouts.

Taylor had slept on the deck that night, seeking a lullaby in the Italian Rivera and wishing on a star for her batshit crazy family to turn normal. So many trips to Switzerland, all of them poisoned by animosity and tension shot through with mystery. Why all the negativity? She might not have explanations at the moment, but she had the seeds of strategies and would get answers growing in the crevices of her brain.

She traversed the dining room and went down the staircase leading to the main kitchen, her mother's favorite room in the house.

Sure enough, Diana McClure putzed around with a machine that looked like it belonged on *Star Trek* with its plethora of spouts and spigots and knobs forged in reflective stainless steel.

Some expensive stylist had coiffed her blonde bob to shiny perfection, and a tennis skirt and white tank top showed off the size-zero figure she'd devoted her life to maintaining.

At the sight of her starved, shiny mother in her element, hurt and resentment bubbled.

Would have been nice if her mother had made some effort to broaden her world beyond vanity and lust for pricey home furnishings, at least taken a stab at strengthening her mind or fostering love and empathy in her heart.

Alas, though, the roles of loving or wise mother exceeded Diana's range by miles. "Hi," Taylor said.

"One of the help taught me how to make an absolutely fabulous smoothie." An affected, baby girl voice sniped from reality television socialites carried the breathy, almost aroused timbre reserved for talk of diets or high-end objects. She measured powder from a giant blue tub and dumped it in her gadget. "Are you caught up in the acai berry craze yet, Taylor? It's a miracle fruit. Consuming it turns the metabolism into a furnace."

Mechanical whirrs filled the kitchen, and a florid magenta concoction spun within the confines of its transparent plastic repository.

"Mom, can I talk to you about something serious?" Uttering the word "mom" twisted Taylor's tongue, the texture of that one syllable as unnatural as verbalizing a wrong answer in class.

Diana approached her daughters as rivals and took great pleasure in cutting Taylor down to size in true mean girl fashion. Mealtimes were tense, little more than an excuse to dole out emotional abuse and flaunt her status as the thinnest woman at the table. Clothes shopping was worse.

Before then, she hadn't been much more to Diana than a doll to dress in designer labels and show off to the other competitive housewives.

All for the sake of illusion. Anyone even tangentially connected to the Texas society gossip circuit knew that Diana McClure, heiress to a sizable mayonnaise fortune, had wasted her inheritance with alarming devotion. Celebrity weight loss gurus and soul healing retreats in Nepalese ashrams weren't cheap, and now American Express and Visa footed those bills while ensuring that the senator's wife kept up appearances of obscene, endless wealth.

Oh well. Not everyone scored a nurturing mother overflowing with unconditional love, so Taylor found other ways to fill her heart. Worked out fine. Besides, she wasn't here to brood or mope.

Diana shut off her juicer and turned to Taylor, blue eyes sliding a frosty appraisal over her body. "Instead of those fatty lattes you love, try putting a pat of butter in your afternoon coffee to kill the midday sugar cravings."

"I'm a healthy weight for my height, and I won't let you use that subject to hurt me anymore. Can we go sit down?"

"Yes, of course." Diana opened a cupboard, got down a child's sippy cup, and poured a measure of her beverage into a vessel decorated with cartoon characters. So fucking weird, and weirder still that this sort of self-infantilizing fell within the spectrum of Diana's normal lexicon of behaviors.

"Try some?" Diana bared a bright set of veneers.

"No thanks." Taylor led the way through the granite and stainless cocoon fit for a professional chef and took a seat at the dining room table in the adjacent room.

Chair legs scraped against marble tile as Diana joined, crossing her legs high on the thigh. She tipped her toddler cup and sucked goo from the spout. "Nummy," she said in her Kim Kardashian voice.

Stepford wifery was fucking wild. At the moment, though, Taylor lacked the time or patience to psychoanalyze her mother's cluster of pathologies. "I have a few questions."

Widening her eyes, Diana hunched her shoulders and pressed her arms against her breast implants, a pose she struck to make herself appear smaller.

"What's going on? School troubles? Boy troubles?" She drawled out the "o" in boy, her delivery as canned and fake as a bad actress reading a script for a miscast part.

"Why did we take so many trips to Switzerland when I was younger? And why were they always so stressful and full of you guys fighting?"

They never did any tourist things, either, no museums or skiing. Everyone just hung around the bed and breakfast. Now and again, Taylor would tag along on her father's visits to one lab or another and observe his work as a theoretical physicist. Lots of fussing with massive machines and meetings with men in white lab coats while she played with dolls or listened to music in the corner.

A heady, liquid sensation swelled in Taylor and ushered in the gauzy remnants of a memory. Doctors and crying and sterile rooms of antiseptic and pain. Her left arm itched, then a twinge of sharp pain bit.

Taylor rubbed the pad of her thumb over the spot, brushing up against something hard and raised and square-shaped. Her heart kicked into her throat. She traced the chunk. Something was in there. Under her skin. Her perception wobbled with fear, but she forced herself to stay cool.

Diana blinked like a stunned deer and clutched her baby cup in two hands. "We traveled extensively for your father's work. He was an important scientist, making big deals with important people."

Her mother could have been underwater, a million miles away. Taylor pinched the area below the crease of her elbow. Something was embedded in her body. Horror razed her universe into a barren hellscape of menace and unknown. She swallowed an excess of saliva and ventured, "What kind of big deals? Medical deals?"

More doe-eyed gawking. "Medical deals?" Diana asked like a kid who didn't understand a teacher's instructions.

"Did he ever talk about, or did you guys ever argue about, genetic experimentation or DNA modification? Could there have been anything shady going on in those labs?"

Did the experiments mix anything more sinister in with scientific experimentation? Could the conspiracy paper be *correct*?

Diana sucked a bottom lip injected with hefty doses of fillers. "There was his Eyes Project. Between you and me, I found that rather gauche and uncouth."

Taylor sat up straighter. "Tell me all about it."

A wince twisted Diana's face, enough to breach her Botox and groove lines into her forehead. She pressed three manicured fingers to one of her temples. "Brain freeze. Owie."

The answer was close, dangling in the air, teasing her with proximity but still too far out of reach. "Mom. What was the Eyes Project?"

Diana's tarantulas of false eyelashes fluttered. "We stayed in a marvelous villa once, right on the Italian border. There was a cat who'd come by the door every night, begging for fish. He was white, with the cutest little black feet. I called him Socks." Diana giggled and meowed.

Taylor's blood ran frigid. It was like her mother had been mind-wiped. "Mom. Tell me about the Eyes Project. This is really, really important. I might be in danger. Tell me everything you remember about it."

Diana raised her hand and curled it like a claw. "Meow."

"What the hell is wrong with you?" She waved a hand in front of her mother's face, but the woman didn't react. Nobody home except this abject cat girl persona.

"Master? Kitty needs her whip. Naughty, naughty. Can I wear the pretty diamond collar this time, pwetty pwease?"

"Stop this cat thing right now!" Taylor's guts plummeted. She clamped her hands on her mother's upper arms and shook her twice.

"Their eyes see you." One of Diana's eyelids drooped and stayed down, stuck like a plastic doll's. "They see right through you."

She itched all over, physically miserable from the effects of an emotion related to shame. The grotesque spectacle of her mother behaving like a sex slave disgusted her more than she'd thought possible. "Mom, wake up." Taylor's throat closed up. Tears stung the inside of her nose. She felt tiny and hollow. She shook Diana again. "Mom, I know you're in there."

Her mother wasn't perfect, but she'd give anything to have her back and get rid of whatever intervention had swooped in and reprogrammed her mother, tinkered with her mind.

Who were the eyes, and what was the Eyes Project? What did they see?

The implications of this were terrifying.

"Bad, bad, bad. Bad kitty needs a spanking." Diana made a scratching gesture at Taylor, then hissed. She pushed out her lips into a pout and sat mute, a stupefied glaze clouding her eyes.

Taylor backed away from Diana, her legs so wobbly that she whacked her calf against the leg of a chair. Pain bloomed below her knee but failed to break the spell of her shock. Her ears rang. Her stomach did backflips. She had to find out what had happened in Switzerland.

"Can you tell me," Taylor hissed out in a hoarse whisper, "what the hell is going on with my arm and why I'm seeing occult symbols?"

Diana pointed at her closed eyelid. "Inside you. Watching." Her voice didn't sound like her own, not completely, but at least the cat thing had waned.

Desperate for answers, Taylor locked in with her mother's vacant stare. "Who is inside me watching? Do the Switzerland trips tie in with this? With the symbols?" She swallowed hard and pushed past a wave of pain in her chest to force out the next question. "Does Dad?"

Diana twitched. Blinked each lid in that creepy doll fashion. "Your dad..."

"He's what?" Taylor was on the edge. The verge. She had to know. The pieces were so close to connecting. Her heartbeat slammed against her ribs. "He's what, Mom?"

"He went too..."

"Say more." She could barely speak. Her voice was filled with concrete. Dread submerged her inch by inch. Her world contracted to the pinprick that was this bizarre interaction with her mind-controlled mother. Diana was half-in, half-out, and Taylor could feel herself losing her. "He went somewhere? Where?"

"Too far." Another spasm wracked Diana, and whatever light had been forcing its way through her eyes dimmed. "Meow."

That was it. No more rational explanations, rationalizations, or forays into denial would suffice anymore.

Her mother might be gone, but there was someone who Taylor could bring this crazy to. Someone who would listen to her and maybe even help. There was nowhere else to go except into the realm of the outlandish. She was already there, spinning her wheels, stuck in a funhouse of frustration and no closer to answers.

That was about to change.

Taylor left the mansion as fast as her feet would fly. Following a stint on the Interstate, she reached South Austin Branch Library and ripped into the parking lot. No rusty green pickup. Fuck!

She ran inside and to the checkout desk, where a brunette librarian checked in books with a chunky radar gun. The device flashed a red line over bar codes. Red, like the handprint symbol.

She needed the person who'd first aroused her suspicions. Needed to join forces with the mysterious man who knew too much and said too little.

No time to waste. Taylor splayed her palms flat on the woman's desk and leaned forward. The name tag on the librarian's blouse read Beth. "Hi, Beth. I need the phone number for a patron named Julian. Tall, long black hair, checks out lots of paranormal books."

The librarian shook her head. "I know who you mean, but I can't give out our members' contact information."

Taylor rummaged in her purse, slipped out her wallet, and withdrew a fifty. With its magical problem-solving powers, king cash reigned. She laid the crisp note down and said, "Can you make an exception today?"

Beth eyed the bill like it was a dead bird, then sent a panoramic gaze around the ceiling. "Attempting to bribe a city employee is a federal offense."

"How about we say I'm a generous patron of literacy and you furnished the information out of concern for his safety." Taylor whipped out a one-hundred and laid it over the fifty.

Beth sucked in a puff of wind. "Is Julian okay?"

"I'm trying to figure that out, but standing here haggling with you isn't helping."

Beth nodded, swiveled her stool, and typed on her keyboard. Taylor's pulse ticked in time with each clack on a key, calming when Beth pulled a pad and pen from a drawer and wrote down an address.

"I appreciate it." She stuck the slip in her back pocket and scooted to her car.

If Julian was so informed, it was time that he came clean with what he knew, because she was going to solve this puzzle one way or another.

FOUR

FLAT ON HIS BACK UNDER DAVE'S STATION WAGON, JULIAN UNSCREWED the cap on the oil drain plug.

Brown liquid flowed out and hit the pan in a succession of gurgles and splats. Thick and gooey as mud, the ooze conjured up a hazy image of the Amazon River's soggy banks. He needed to buy a sturdy pair of rubber boots for mucking through the jungle. Every mundane life detail got him daydreaming about Peru these days.

He bounced a restless leg and finished changing his neighbor's oil, going over the steps for his Enemy Way ceremony. He'd be damned if he let some spirit interfere with his moving plans. Of course he didn't have any hard data yet on what this thing was or what it wanted, but he'd address those factors if they arose. Bottom line: The fucker was malevolent and needed to go.

But first, he'd take care of this automotive favor. Julian's mama taught him that a decent man saw to the needs of his community, his people, by sharing his skills and abilities.

"You're all set." Julian slid out and stood up, grabbing a rag from his work bench and wiping off his hands.

"Thanks, man." Dave sucked on a cigarette and scratched his ass. He'd done up the buttons of his shirt wrong, the resulting gap revealing a belly button as deep as a bullet wound and a couple of bruises.

Dull pain moved within Julian as he threw the dirty towel on the bench. His buddy was in bad shape. Judging from how a pensive expression cut his wrinkles deep, Dave wanted to ask for some additional help. If the guy needed money, Julian would have to deflect until he sold another large painting.

The older dude dropped a sheepish stare to the garage's concrete floor. "There is one other thing."

Julian's ability to read people rendered most folks transparent. Adaptability and people-pleasing became his superpowers during the cross-country travels decades ago. When the need arose to depend on the kindness of others, flirting and flattery and being everyone's best pal worked. "Yeah. Shoot."

"I've been feeling kinda dizzy lately and throwing up in the morning. This quack I went to doesn't know shit, just wants to push pills. I want holistic and natural. Organic. Can you do traditional healing spells out back in the teepee? You know, authentic medicine?" An inflection in Dave's tone came off as patronizing, as if implying that Julian's traditional practices were quirky or backwards.

Half the time he spent in the white and sheltered Texas boonies, Julian couldn't pinpoint if people were putting him down subtly or if he was being touchy and imagining things. Either way, having to think about crap like that junked up his brain.

With any luck, some more Indigenous folks would live among the shifters in South America. Folks who understood his culture and traditions and approached them with a certain degree of wisdom and sensitivity that his crusty old neighbors and bar buds lacked.

"It's a hogan. Only the Great Plains and prairie people had *tipis*." He could qualify for Dave that he could use a tipi owning to his Comanche blood, but introducing such a specific degree of tribal distinction would be lost on the guy.

"Oh, sorry. Hogan. So, uh, can you?"

"I don't have enough training as a medicine man to feel comfortable performing a healing ceremony. All I can tell you is go on the wagon. Taper, though, or you'll get nasty detox symptoms."

Alcoholics Anonymous was probably a better fit for Dave anyway. Maybe he'd meet some folks in there who could help him get sober. What a jackpot that would be—both Julian and Dave moving on and making new friends.

The gentle hum of a well-maintained car engine sang with the wind, a pleasing, feline murmur out of place with the usual grinds and rattles of failing transmissions and shot-out mufflers.

A rich person car, some high-end brand with the kind of flashy hood ornaments that the bored kids he once hung out with used to steal, rolled into the driveway.

As recognition set in, chemicals juiced up his system and set off a series of jumps in his stomach. Julian laid a hand on his midsection, an involuntary pleasure grunt popping from his throat when a familiar blonde stepped out of the vehicle. Fated mate fantasy aside, Taylor exerted an undeniable pull over him, that was for sure.

When she moved into his perceptual field, his awareness narrowed to a tunnel leading to her. All other surroundings damn near vanished until only she remained. To say the infatuation floored him was an understatement. Julian wasn't one to go all dumb over feminine wiles, and Taylor wasn't even playing the seduction game. This automatic yet mighty quality to his attraction practically had him reeling. Something was up between the two of them. A force that warranted examination.

"Hot mama," Dave muttered while Taylor, still out of earshot, made her way toward them. "I'd like to—"

Julian whacked Dave's upper arm, hard enough to shut him up before he said something crude. Nobody but Julian got to have fantasies about the fierce angel in their midst.

Dave shot Julian a crusty look and rubbed his bicep. "What the fuck, man? She your girlfriend?"

A glow trespassed into the space between Julian's ribs, not unpleasant, but all kinds of inconvenient. If he wasn't laying the groundwork to move, he might ask Taylor out, but in this case, the condition following the "if" trumped any and all hypotheticals.

Bummer about the crap timing, but dating and relationships didn't fit right now. "No. I don't like hearing that bullshit sexist talk about women is all."

Dave snorted. "You better go pick up those tampons now, or you'll be late for your Women's Studies class."

"How about you leave instead and go sign up for a comedy class? Cause you're banned from trying to tell any more jokes until you take one."

Taylor strode into the garage, the polka dot skirt hem swishing right below her knees. A welcome anomaly in his dirty workspace with its wall of wrenches and vehicle fluid stains on the floor. A feminine presence was missing from his life, no doubt about that.

What threw him was the ache caused by his realization, the extent to which he now insisted on understanding it as a lack. Didn't his life plan matter more than finding a partner?

Julian flinched at the sight of dirt under his nails and hid his hands behind his back.

"Hey, Taylor. What's up?" He almost didn't recognize the soft and throaty cadence in his voice. Absurd, though, because judging by the grimace on her face she wasn't in a soft mindset.

"I need to talk to you." After addressing Julian, she turned to Dave and said, "Can you excuse us for a moment?"

Dave saluted Taylor. "Yes, ma'am." He winked at Julian, a hokey and over the top gesture far too obvious to come off as sly. "Good luck, man."

"Good luck with what?" Taylor bounced a suspicious appraisal between the two men.

Dave winked again and waggled his brows, the blatant and ongoing nature of it all making a blend of annoyance and embarrassment squirm in Julian. The older man got in his car and drove off, ending his mortifying role in the interaction after what felt like an eternity.

"Ignore him," Julian muttered, embarrassed that he didn't associate with higher-caliber friends.

Residual aggravation from Dave's bullshit ruined any attempt Julian might have made to act charming or smooth. He tried to clean one nail by picking it with another nail. Not like he planned to touch Taylor.

She let off a hard laugh. "What, do you want to fuck me? Is that what you two were talking about?"

Ah, shit, her words put images in his mind. Taylor naked on his bed.

The taste of her. Taylor on top of him. Him gripping her hips from behind. His cock jerked. Yes, he wanted Taylor.

More than her sexual parts, though, he craved her personality in those intimate moments. Her attitude and voice, dirty talk in her mouth telling him what to do. Higher, slower, harder, don't stop. Yes, yes, yes.

Tense heat swirled through his lower belly, and his pants tightened. He turned his back to her and went to the sink in the corner, where he scrubbed his hands under icy water and attacked gunk until it ran black down the drain. What was wrong with him? Julian was more mature than this. He'd long since left behind the horny, hormonal teenager driven by urges.

"No, we weren't talking about you. Just batting around senseless banter. He's kind of a jerk, but he's harmless. Sorry if he offended you."

Her aroma, floral and powdery, signaled her presence beside him at the sink. The aura she exuded softened the entire atmosphere in a disarming way that he liked. New and novel. The familiar humdrum of grease and grit dissolved in the field of her shining gloss.

Water ran black over his hands, somehow cleaning him on the inside as well as the outside. The afternoon sun glazed his workbench in buttery tones. He hadn't noticed the sunshine, really noticed it, until this moment in the day. Already, this was so much lighter than all the dumb stuff with Dave. He could use a little more of Taylor in his life.

"It's fine. And I'm sorry. I get snappy when I'm stressed or tense, and I shouldn't have lashed out at you." A drag on her tone underscored the stress and tension in question.

Wiping palms on his jeans, Julian angled himself to face Taylor. A troublesome look, the frightened glint of a prey animal under siege, sharpened her stare. Her lips twitched the longer she looked at him, and her chin trembled. The whites of her eyes reddened and pooled with liquid.

"Oh, no," Julian's speech fell to a whisper. The sight of a woman crying or close to tears wrecked him. "What's wrong?"

At least he managed not to call her baby or honey. His arms ached with the instinct to pull her close and hold her until all distress left her beautiful face, but he prevented himself.

They weren't on touching terms. Fuck if he knew what terms they were on, or even what the terms were. When it came to Taylor and her blunt, prickly ways, Julian lacked much of an understanding of the ground on which they stood. It could be made of firm soil, jelly, or shark-infested water.

"It makes me sick to say this." She rubbed her cheek and closed her eyelids, and when she blinked them open, the familiar tough glare had chased away sadness. "But I think you might be right."

Discomfort kicked into Julian's chest, followed by a shrinking feeling. The peek of vulnerability she offered stirred in him a desire to deliver tenderness, but now, the gentle quiver was gone. *Just as well.* He repeated the mantra three times, figuring he *should* be more interested in the problem she was talking about than the yearning for skin-on-skin affection her presence bafflingly created.

"Right about what?" Though he asked out of good faith, he could hazard a damn good guess as to which subject haunted her mind. Because that exact same subject haunted his nightmares, both sleeping and waking.

She stuck her hands on her hips, the gesture highlighting both her figure and her bossy personality, and looked him dead in the eye. "I think..."

He licked his teeth as she trailed off, allowing a rogue gaze to roam over those ears of hers. What a woman. Tough. Protective. Loyal. Like an alpha female who'd kill to protect her pack. One who might demonstrate the capability for downright mercenary actions if she deemed them fit to achieve her goals. But her complexities didn't matter, and these she-wolf fantasies he indulged in were stupid.

"Go on." He pushed his drifting thoughts aside.

"I think." The brittle crispness with which she spoke created a distancing effect. "I think."

Taylor surrendered her intimidating stance and fidgeted with a scrub brush laying on the side of the wash basin, rolling its bristles between the pads of slender fingers suited to playing the piano. Or to stroking his jaw and neck, tracing the tattoos on his chest as they ventured down.

When she targeted him with that stare of hers, her eyes lacked any trace of predatory aggression. As the pause played and a breeze slid by, starting up the tinkling tune of his wind chimes, he searched behind her eyes for her deepest self. Behind the hardness, the armor, for the woman who neglected her gentler side. That woman fascinated him, stoked an impulse to coax her forth from the cave in which she hid.

Best not to come on too strong, though, as tension still flexed in the air between them. "You're in some kind of trouble, aren't you?"

Moisture curled the jagged edges of her cropped hair. Her throat moved as she swallowed. "Yeah." The word came out like a piece of broken glass.

Right about now, he should be making excuses to end their exchange and get her home safely. Women in serious trouble prompted Julian to back off, as they promised pure chaos.

With Taylor, though, he didn't read dramatic, histrionic, or destructive into her motives.

A power pulsed behind her eyes, daring him to get close, like she exuded a magnetic field. He didn't know her, yet he did. Some sixth sense picked up on her energy and enticed him to enter her radius. On some level, this made Taylor the most dangerous woman Julian had ever met, capable of throwing his ordered existence into disarray with nothing more than a silent glance.

He was the one in serious trouble, a daring, perfect, exhilarating sort of trouble. Danger he might have to court, even if all that did was burn the intrigue out of his system. Normally, he played it safe. But now? Screw safe.

Julian closed some space between them and permitted himself to stroke the inside of her wrist. "Tell me. Please."

A near-imperceptible forward tilt of her body betrayed interest in him, or at least attraction to his physical presence. "Can we look over those photocopied papers?"

Before answering, he drew in two lungs full of balmy air and exhaled. A pale line existed between risk-taking and recklessness, a line he best abide by. He didn't have a fix on the Senator McClure madness, what all the saga involved and how it implicated Taylor.

"What changed?" he asked.

"I had a weird exchange with my father. Followed by a horrifying one with my mother. I went over to their place to rule out the idea that he was mixed up in any of the stuff mentioned in that paper on your desk. I wanted to put my mind at ease, but I left more shocked and freaked out than I was before I walked in."

She scrubbed a hand over her face and caught her breath in a sharp slurp. "And I have these pieces, you know? An anecdote here, a reference there, how I was seeing things that I couldn't explain. More and more and more keep mounting, piling up, but I don't see how any of it fits together yet. So I have this jumble of creepy facts without any semblance of context to order them. You're the only person I can think of who's connected to this—the only one who seems earnest and trustworthy, at least."

He pursed his lips. If, *if* the senator was implicated in the kidnapping of shifters, no way could Taylor be involved. She came off as too earnest, a straight shooter.

This line of reasoning, though, didn't explain the images she'd seen, and whatever she'd seen or claimed she'd seen tied in with the article's claims about secret tunnels. Plus, Roxy's testimony about the couple in the closet brought this malevolent spirit, him, and Taylor into a common orbit.

Nefariously or not, Taylor was involved. And Julian had to figure out exactly how. He couldn't shake the idea that these runes or symbols or whatever had something to do with magic—and not the healing kind.

Bottom line was if Taylor trusted him, she'd talk, and the more she talked, the more he'd close in on an action plan for how to manage all the weird shit in his life before he split.

If she could offer information on the senator's misdeeds, he might gather a better sense of the accuracy of the claims made in the article. And if there were shifters imprisoned in top-secret locations, Julian would find them, with or without the help of the South American crew.

Hell, if he rolled down to Iquitos with insight into the location of their brethren, it could ingratiate him into the clan right away and set him up with a good ranking in any existing pack structure.

He didn't know the first thing about rival packs and clans, old grudges, or anything of the sort. But if shifters were suffering and imprisoned? That injustice would not stand. He'd approach all shifters in good faith until given a reason not to.

Lots of loose ends and unknowns, but it made more sense to keep Taylor close than to push her away.

Nothing romantic or sexual would happen between them, except for maybe the sharing of a good meal and a suggestive, lingering look or two before he hit the road. He was allowed to enjoy the company of a woman, however fleeting.

Julian stepped in front of Taylor and walked to the screen door joining his garage to the house. "Come on in. Let's take a look."

"Thank you." The sound of her unburdening came through as a rush.

He looked back as he opened the door leading to his mudroom. While she didn't quite smile, what she offered him was better, richer, so much more special. A glint of awareness in her eye sparkled while the light of the rising moon called attention to her voluptuous lips. Her whole essence glowed in the bath of blue-silver lunar coolness as if the disc in the sky illuminated her from the inside out.

Cicadas, crickets, and frogs at the nearby creek sang their chorus, a serenade of croaks and chirps. She stood still, a statuesque portrait of feminine strength with an aching, poetic, tender current beneath. A breeze animated her skirt, and the planets aligned.

Moonlight on a magic night. So scary and perfect and downright bewitching that he almost panted. Julian enveloped Taylor's hand in his and led her inside.

FIVE

UNDER DIFFERENT CIRCUMSTANCES, TAYLOR WOULD BE GAME FOR getting to know Julian a little better. A person's inner sanctuary revealed treasures about them, and his one-story ranch home was no exception.

Paintings set in carved frames decorated walls with splashes of color, everything from landscape sunsets to people working at looms and petting dogs. She would not have pegged him as the sort who would enjoy home aesthetics or interior design, but clearly intriguing layers lay below the guy's surface.

Seated at his rustic, wooden dining room table, she flipped another page of the conspiracy paper. The deeper the gist sunk in, the more the content weighed on her beleaguered brain. A deep breath inflated her with the scents of his home, sawdust and detergent perfumed with a touch of spicy aftershave.

She massaged a tweaked shoulder muscle. It sure would be nice to curl up on his big couch and watch a movie, pretend they were on a date.

A litany of unanswered questions spun a demented carousel in her head. What did all the symbols mean? Why did they appear, and why hadn't they returned? What the fuck was her mom talking about with the all-seeing eyes and their project?

What was her dad hiding?

"What are you thinking about?" Julian laid his palm on the top of her hand, his fingertips bringing comfort in the form of callused ruggedness contrasted against a soft touch.

Julian's caress soothed some of the unrest bouncing through her system. He exuded a natural, calming mojo. If only timing and circumstance were more ideal.

She pushed copied news articles aside and dragged the plastic box to her as if the cache of information was the problem. "I wish I could read Spanish."

Julian sighed like he had more to say.

"What's in these?" She picked up one of the international papers, flipped it over, and glimpsed at the back. More text she couldn't decipher washed over her in an unintelligible deluge, evoking an unsettling recollection of symbols lacking sense.

"I think it's time for us to get more honest with each other," he said.

This, she could get behind. The more Julian opened up, the more she could put the facts he shared to work on the next reconnaissance mission to her family estate.

An upcoming banquet to woo potential political donors promised ideal opportunities to sneak away and access the button panel. Until then, her objective on the parental front remained consistent. Accumulate as much knowledge as possible because information loaded her strategic guns with ammunition. "I'm all ears."

She swore he chuckled.

Her lips twitched. Julian was such a beautiful, perplexing weirdo. "What?"

"Ah, you know." He ran a finger over one dark eyebrow, the apple of his cheek plumping like he fought to keep a grin in check. His face wasn't all that expressive, which made studying him for subtle tells fun. Like the ability to read his emotions bestowed upon her a special, reserved privilege.

"I don't. Tell me."

He stroked the petal of a succulent in the middle of the table, his mouth set, though the webs branching from his eyes kept the score by revealing stubborn pleasure. "I've never found myself so attracted to a woman's ears before."

Warmth unspooled in her pelvis and dropped to the juncture between her legs. More than anything, she yearned to forget what had happened at her parents' house. The urge to escape pulsed within her. She was so damn weary, and escape was right in front of her. Escape to Julian and with him. "I've never found myself so attracted to a conspiracy theorist before. But you'd look hot in a tinfoil hat."

Julian flicked his gaze from the cactus and met her with an intense stare ablaze with certainty and incongruous with her attempt to flirt. "The more I hear and read and think about it, the more I'm convinced that it's no fantasy conspiracy theory."

The fever of arousal morphed to insidious chills. "Is this what we're about to get more honest about?"

"In part." His Adam's apple bobbed. His expression grew stony and serious. The game changed.

Moonlight from beyond his kitchen windows splashed the papers on the table, imbuing the evidence before them with uncanny hints. Secrets hid in plain sight.

Time folded into trippy swirls in her moments with Julian, speeding and slowing in one motion as past and present, truth versus fantasy, and mundane yet outlandish all blended together into a psychedelic yin yang.

He popped into sharp relief, a high-voltage contrast against the backdrop of a simple living room. Julian had a way, sexy though taboo, of presenting as anachronistic and even untouchable. An urge to crack the protective sealant at his center and access those parts he guarded, the fantastic and inaccessible, became close to unbearable.

Taylor floated beside herself, spacey, netted up in dissociation. If she believed in spirits and alternate realities, she'd swear unseen forces were attempting to communicate with her, slipping through as moon glow shadows.

When the drifting strangeness ebbed, she said in a tone that came out as an eerie murmur, "I'm listening."

Julian steepled hands beneath his chin. "The newspapers are from Peru. Long story short, they contain a collection of reports from farmers and others who claim to have seen people shifting into animals in the jungle. I read them to get a fix on the exact location."

People shifting into animals had cropped up in the library

hallucination. "What's your stake in this? All your talk of being honest with each other makes me think you aren't some hobbyist obsessed with the Loch Ness Monster."

"No. I'm not." He looked through her, not at her, a shadow passing over his eyes in a pensive flutter.

"So what are you?" No question she'd asked before in her life had ever felt so true, so blunt. Raw and uncut. Terrifying and thrilling at the same time, for she steered toward getting closer to Julian than she'd ever gotten to another person.

"I'm one of them." Each word in his deep voice fell like a domino, dense with gravity and gravitas.

She didn't need to ask a follow-up question, for the answer was obvious. They'd transcended. Sped beyond the borders of generic reactions. Freaking out, denying, or coming back with a barrage of responses to undermine his claim didn't apply. Those were amateur replies.

In this new realm, a form of intimacy arose that startled her with a shot of electric power. His special secret could be hers. She wanted him and could *have* him.

Taylor leaned forward, pushing the papers aside, and reached for Julian's forearm. "Show me."

Static electricity zapped her at the instant of their contact. Her entire body came alive, sensitive and present. Intuition pumped through her in flashes of incandescent light. This was right. True. Meant to be.

He rolled his bottom lip between his teeth and gave a subtle shake of his head. The teasing flick of a spell between them broke, and she clenched with frustration and yanked away her touch.

"I don't think I'm quite ready." He didn't physically retreat from her, though, and in fact deepened his lean and widened his legs. An invitation, or a tease. Perhaps even he didn't know.

With as much gentle tact as her personality could muster, she followed up, "What does it take to get ready?"

"Deep trust."

In the fallout of his unflinching words, connotations of a brutal admission, Taylor worked to regulate her breathing. "You don't trust me?"

"I'm not sure. I like you, but I don't have a handle on *your* stake in this. The whole thing with seeing symbols feels dark to me in a way that I can't explain. It doesn't make sense to me, and because of that, I'm apprehensive. Does that make sense?"

He sliced a deep cut, but she couldn't deny the legitimacy of his point. "Yes."

One of his shoulders shrugged, the effect edging toward shyness in a way that charmed her. "That's not to say we couldn't get to know each other a little better."

Time and space, surroundings, everything but his inviting form cloaked in luminescent night, fell away into irrelevance. Though he delivered his statement in a measured enough cadence as to leave meaning ambiguous, Taylor chose her preferred interpretation.

To the tune of her yearning heartbeat, animated by a strange desire impossible to ignore any longer, Taylor got out of her chair, walked to Julian, and straddled him.

Their forward momentum was moving. Happening. He might not trust her wholly due to the mystery of the symbols, but she'd make him forget. Make him forget the dark parts of what bound them and remember only the primal, inexplicable, elemental charge.

She felt it. He felt it. They had to see it through. This fact was beyond both of them, spiritual and preordained. Their connection would be the key to solving the mystery. Though this made no sense to her, she knew it to be true in the deepest place within herself, some other realm that she'd never touched before now.

He groaned when their bodies pressed into contact, a pained plea that made the fantasy of satisfying his urges feel like the most important thing in the world.

She hiked up her skirt and adjusted herself until their bodies rubbed together in the manner she craved, his bulge stiff against the cotton shielding her most intimate area.

A sudden seductress, she brushed her nose and lips against his neck and began to gyrate her hips and stroke his dick with her own clothed sex. Denim against cotton made warm, delicious friction and an inviting scratching sound.

"Get to know each other like this?" Her voice came out gruff and husky and without a shred of uncertainty or fake innocence. Perfect.

This had to be. Had to happen. Taylor never moved this fast, but the circumstances were extenuating. What was happening between them was more than sex. They were turning a prophetic key and unlocking mysteries that neither understood. A shadowy, supernatural cousin of virginity was being disavowed.

This wasn't a hookup, this was ritual.

Let the eyes look. Let them watch. Soon Taylor would know their secrets, the meaning of their symbols. She was too powerful for them to even begin to comprehend.

She was more than a simple human. Her intuition knew right then.

"There is no way in hell I'll be able to resist you." His low growl of male lust shot into her veins like lighter fluid.

He grabbed her ass in his big hands, kneading her flesh as he urged her to move back and forth. Telling her with his body what he wanted as he surrendered to her thrall. No point in denying the power trip his greed put her on.

She repaid his nonverbal request with quickened humping motions, her hands making a study of his thick arms and shoulders while she kissed his neck.

Together, they reformed the spell, a forbidden intoxication of night magic that would coax forth a breakthrough. Pull answers from the darkness and moonbeams teasing her with a secret garden of scrumptious delights.

"Don't resist me then." She moved her lips and teeth to his jaw, caught his earlobe in a bite, blew a breath on the sensitive spot behind his ear. His noises and scent told her everything she needed to know. Conquest was inevitable, the deal sealed.

"You're making me feel like a dirty old man."

"There isn't anything dirty about you, because I want to taste every inch of your body."

Ancient instinct pumped her up. Their coupling was good, right, the most natural and harmonious act. A solution.

Taylor changed her foreplay motions. Kisses and licks on his neck turned into nuzzling and rooting as her emergent primeval side stabbed hooks into her soul. She dug her nails into his biceps.

A snarl escaped her throat, flooding her with fright though it made her clit swell and lubrication flow down her channel. Control, decorum, and all other civilized aspects of her lost out to wild lust.

"Good God." With that, he stood, lifting her like her bones were made of air and paper. "It's you. It was always you."

She hung on with her arms and legs, desire igniting her flesh and blood with hot spurts. On impulse, she pierced her teeth into his neck. Hard. The tang of iron seeped onto her tongue.

"You bit me," he growled, kicking a door open as the dining room table faded into background. He walked them into a room with deer antlers mounted on the walls, sidestepping a dresser covered in framed photographs.

"You liked it."

He put his hands on her sides, hoisted her until she peeled off his body, and threw her on a bed. Taylor bounced on the mattress, her skirt flying to her waist. She drank in the sight of the man standing over her. He regarded her with equal intensity, shoulders square and back straight.

"I loved it." A sprinkle of disbelief trailed his breathless words.

His bedroom cocooned them in cool air and hot need. Julian's chest rose and fell. He reached behind his head, triceps flexing, and pulled off his shirt from behind.

When he threw the cloth to the ground in a gesture of confident sexual determination, the tension below her navel ratcheted. She tugged down her dress straps, baring her shoulders and a peek of bra.

"Wait." Julian dropped his knees to the bed and prowled up her body. He propped on his elbows and gazed into her eyes. "I want to undress you. I haven't even kissed you yet."

She ran slow hands up his chest, caressing smooth skin and hard muscle, catching glimpses of tattoos masked by darkness. Instead of waiting for him to make the move, she leaned in and crushed her mouth to his. His tongue came first, stiff and wet, intent on claiming.

Taylor wrapped her legs around his hips and rocked, grinding into his erection. She sucked his lips, tasted his flavor of mint and excitement.

Her tongue probed his mouth, and soon his fast, hot breath merged with hers until one began where the other ended.

With a gasp, she broke their molded lock and gripped his swollen length under his jeans. "Turn on the lights."

He obeyed, reaching over and flicking the switch on a bedside lamp. A soft white halo mingled with the offering of the moon, draping their exploration in gauze. Taylor emerged from herself, new and virginal in a way she couldn't explain. With Julian, every kiss and caress was a discovery.

When she kissed the tattoo wrapped around one of his pectoral muscles, a photorealistic portrayal of a black wolf with brown eyes whose magnificence she lost herself in, he shivered. A flare of goosebumps erupted across the hairless surface of him.

She kissed the inked portrait's nose and each ear. "Is this you?"

"It's me." His voice trembled, and he jerked above her.

Though not a person prone to give comfort, the peep of neediness shown by such a guarded man prompted her to move a hand to his cheek. He closed his eyes and sighed.

"Are you okay?" she asked.

With her thumb, she traced his bottom lip. He opened his mouth, giving her access to the wet part, and the submission of it resonated as an ache in her sex but also her heart. His concession symbolized the tentative gift of his trust, the initial unwrapping of a present she dared not squander.

"I'm great. Full disclosure: I haven't been with a woman in a while."

"Do you want to stop?"

A smirk she hadn't seen before bent his lips. Taylor took proud possession of this new detail. She owned his bedroom face, all rights reserved.

"Hell no."

She laughed, throwing her head back far enough to bare her throat. "There you are again."

He veered things back on track with efficiency, ridding her of her dress and bra as he toed off his boots. His heavy footwear plopped on the carpet with two muted thuds, sound signals confirming the forward movement to sweaty, animal inevitability.

Taylor arched her back as he kissed her neck, then her shoulders, then her breasts. He sucked one pebbled nipple into his mouth, and she gasped at the flurry of pleasure sparks set off by his licks and suction. With his free hand, he palmed her other breast and rolled its rosy point between two fingers.

By the time he switched breasts, she was straight-up mewling a goddamn keening wail.

"You're so beautiful. So sexy," he murmured, the mouthful of her flesh impeding his speech in a tender, personal way.

The stimulation overwhelmed her senses, her nerves, and she punched up her hips and ground into his stiffness. "Let's fuck now."

He trailed kisses down her abdomen. Each spot tingled in his wake. "You're not in a hurry, are you?"

"No, but I want to fuck."

Shocking words, but not due to the expletive. Taylor couldn't recall ever asking a guy to move things along, but she'd never before felt the passion she felt in Julian's bed. The times with her two ex-boyfriends had been unmemorable, not awful, but in no way worthy of distinction. Her utterance in and of itself propelled the night with Julian into first place against fuzzy memories of those basic bro college guys.

"You don't want me to give you oral first? I'm good at it." A teasing kiss fell on top of her underwear.

"No. I want you to put your dick in me. How's that for enthusiastic consent given?"

"Quite clear."

He moved up and knelt between her spread legs. Never taking his eyes off her, he unbuckled his belt and slid it through the loops with a titillating whoosh of leather zipping against denim.

She was on him before the accessory hit the ground, poised on all fours as she attacked his button and zipper and yanked his jeans to his knees.

His cock jutted upward in a long, proud curve. She looked him in the eye and stroked the velvet steel, rubbing him from root to tip, her haunches high in the air. If a second Julian materialized behind her, she'd take him too.

One kiss on the underside of his broad head, just to smell and taste his musk, turned into her licking and sucking and bobbing. After a minute or so, he rubbed her shoulder. "You said you wanted to fuck, but at this rate, I'm going to lose it in your mouth."

God, the word fuck in his silky-rough, accented voice made her pussy clench around emptiness. Pathetic, how her neglected sex had nothing but the air to stimulate.

With a wet pop, she freed his cock and flipped to her hands and knees, so her ass faced him. Taylor cast her best come hither look over her shoulder. Julian gripped his cock and fixed a hard stare on her backside.

The bed creaked as he closed in and grabbed her hips. "How'd you know my favorite position?"

"Lucky guess. We have at least one thing in common."

They had so much more than that one thing, she was sure of it, but the position was a gateway to discovery.

A surprise grin flashed straight white teeth. She smiled back at him, their nonverbal communion profound. Normally, this would be the time to remind herself that this was just sex. A stolen moment to forget about their shared debacle and indulge a whim, not the beginning of emotional entanglement. Except if she told herself that they were merely fooling around, she'd be lying.

"Ah, damn." He furrowed his brow and patted the side of her butt.

"What?"

"I don't have any protection in the house. You didn't bring a condom, did you?"

"No, but I'm on the birth control shot. STI-free." Hormonal contraception meant that Taylor could enjoy some relief from her painful, heavy periods, sexual activity or no.

"Squeaky clean over here." His blunt tip butted her opening. "Now where were we?"

"Right there." Taylor lowered to her elbows, then her chest, and stuck her ass up high. The thrill of submission took over, a welcome vacation from always being in charge. "We were right there."

He slid inside in a single stroke, the pressure and fullness of his flesh in her sleeve making her moan. Soon they moved together, picking up in tempo, while Julian held on tight.

Tension mounted in her core as he pounded, hitting her G-spot on every push. Wet skin slapped in a crudely glorious rhythm as his pelvis knocked into her. His grunts grew more frequent, his thrusts faster and interspersed with curses and utterances of her name. The wooden headboard thumped the wall, banging in time with their tempo.

"Rub your clit."

"Yes, sir." Her fingers brushed his slick, driving cock when she found her nub near the top of her hidden lips and stroked. Extreme pleasure surged fast.

"Julian," she gasped, the side of her face pressed to the bed. She rubbed herself faster and faster. The head of his cock worked her sensitive inner button while her first two fingers stimulated the outside bulge. Pleasure grew to bliss, then to base and unspeakable need as she rushed to the end. One more piece would set her off. "Julian. Talk dirty to me. Bossy."

"You're my fucking bitch." The hard words ground out in a growl. "How's that?"

Her heart jumped, and her eyes stretched wide. He spoke the sexiest words, the naughtiest words, the crudest and nastiest and *best* words. She smiled a stupefied grin.

Climax rolled in. Hot pressure cracked above her pubic floor. "Fuck yeah I am," she shouted with reverence and gratitude. "More."

"Say it." Slurping sounds of wet skin slapping fit a shameless order. His fingertips dug ten points of desperation into her flesh. He was getting off on this, hard.

"I'm your fucking bitch." She screamed the declaration, then unleashed a helpless cry as her world shattered into shards of ecstasy. Orgasmic blasts tore through her again and again, unmooring.

This went on forever, eternal, as Taylor became nothing but bucking hips and shouts of stunned release.

She still writhed and yelled at the apex of her peak when Julian howled. He pulled her butt to his pelvis and held her in place while he came. They cried out as one, then tapered to satisfied sighs.

He pulled out, leaving her wet and empty, and crashed to his side. She joined him, capable only of staring at the slackened satisfaction of his face while working to catch her breath.

"Wow." Julian laid a hand over his heart and kissed her forehead and the tip of her nose. "Intense."

"Intensely awesome." She planted a wet kiss of appreciation on his lips, and he kissed her back without a moment's hesitation.

Awesome afterglow followed, snuggles and the sighs of placated lust.

But then the inside of her elbow stung. Taylor's heart plummeted. She told herself a mosquito had bitten her and traced the hard, graceful curve of Julian's collarbone in a desperate grasp at distraction.

The pain returned, flaying her nerves in a scalding lash. She squeezed her eyes shut and sent a silent prayer to no God in particular to make it stop. To make the distress be something other than what she knew it was. To please, please, make the horrible stop happening so they could appreciate a nice post-coital minute or two.

Hope leaked out with the return of each familiar symptom. Buzzing. Disorientation. Agony radiating to her fingertips.

What she knew to be inevitable flickered into bright, wobbly existence. A red blob in the atmosphere shimmered a taunt as the handprint symbol appeared, this time encased in an upside-down triangle.

SIX

INTIMACY SHATTERED AS TAYLOR LEAPT FROM BED AND RAN NAKED into the kitchen.

"Do you have anything to write with?" Rummaging sounds followed her urgent question.

Julian's head swam. He pulled up his underwear and pants. Dealt with the zipper and button. Jumbled thoughts filled his brain. Sex with Taylor had felt so perfect, but maybe their indulgence had been wrong. An alarming reversal swung the pendulum before he'd even come down from the high of passion.

Fuck if he could make sense of the twisted funhouse his life had become, but he needed to try. Try to connect Taylor to the shifters. He couldn't let her go until he figured out how she was involved. She was, though, for sure. His intuition was a reliable compass.

He had to leave soon, but he didn't want to lose her when he'd just found her. Not that he wanted to be rid of her. Moments ago, all he'd wanted was to hold and kiss her, laugh and talk with her.

She muttered frantic gibberish to herself, tossed a salad of nonsense words. He pinched the corners of his eyes. Guilt and confusion hung a millstone around his neck. Maybe he ought to want to back away from her, from this. Pull up the stakes and haul ass to Peru. The spirit hadn't hassled him in days. Except he'd gone and had sex with Taylor, and Julian was no punk who bedded women and then discarded them.

He padded out of the bedroom and across cold tile, finding her nude and hunched over his countertop. Her hand moved in a furious frenzy, and she babbled as if aligning brain, speech, and writing presented a struggle.

"Taylor, tell me exactly what's happening."

He stood behind her and laid a hand on each of her silken shoulders. His lips divided at the sight of her writing. She'd damn near filled up the back of an old Chinese takeout menu with symbols and words. Some of the text looked foreign and ancient, words that he'd never seen before. He might have dropped out of high school, but he was pretty sure this language had been dead for generations. The words in English that he could make out were worse and sent an icy rush over his skin.

Witch. Prophecy. Other Place. Abyss.

"I'm receiving information right now. Some kind of channeling. The symbols, plus words from a book. I've never seen the book, but it's mine. My birthright." She blurted the sentences out like neither speech nor scribbles would come fast enough. "It's code. A key. Almost like an algorithm, but not mathematical in the sense that we commonly understand math. This is an ancient prophecy, and I'm one of six who will stop it. This download is giving me the instructions."

She tapped her pen against the granite counter and continued, "So this is where I move to venture that the Other Place could be space, insofar as frequency functions in space. Space, space, time, and space. The unfolding of this prophecy takes the shape of a hexagon and behaves similarly to a musical chord, though as we know, light can be both a wave and a particle. Einstein broke ground on the relationship between time and space. Tell me about space, people in my head! There could be bodies buried somewhere. Do I need these spells to unlock a door, or find a particular location? Am I a radio, is that how you're reaching me? Through some frequency? Stop screaming, dammit, and tell me where to go. We haven't even touched on the algorithm."

She shook the pen and wrote more, engaged with the drama in her mind.

Pain lanced through his chest. The woman he'd made love to was gone, and the person who'd replaced her frightened him with her looping, obsessive thoughts and blurred babble. But he would not show her his fear or turn away from her. She wasn't crazy, she was cursed. He'd seen a negative entity, too, and now whatever had found him was attached to her. That explanation had to be in the realm of possibility, but it didn't make him feel any better.

Feelings aside, he would be the strong one, the rock, the good guy. His values mattered.

Julian turned Taylor around to face him and pressed them chest to chest. He stroked her sweat-slicked hair. Her heartbeat pounded against him while ragged exhalations puffed from her lungs.

"I can't solve this unless I know how functions spread out in the time domain involve the frequency domain," she whispered, her breath choppy and hot against his wolf tattoo. "I need to decipher how to bend time and space, to interchange them. I need to mix mathematics and dark magic, like they've done."

"Taylor, stop." His throat clenched, and tears stung his nose.

He couldn't break down, wouldn't reject her. If only he didn't feel so helpless, if only he possessed the power to intervene in a meaningful manner or offer useful counsel.

"They're inside of me." She squirmed against him until she got loose. "Begging, crying, screaming. Showing me things. It's faster now, speeding up. I can't keep up. It's this thing they put inside me. It's letting in the magic."

Taylor undulated her spine in a serpentine curve. Her eyes stretched to discs of terror. She dropped to her knees on his kitchen floor, then fell to her back and writhed. "My organs and bones. I feel them shifting and merging, breaking and rearranging. I'm about to burst out of my skin. My DNA strands, I can see them as mating snakes. Forming and reforming. I'm inside my brain stem now, with my ancestors. There is so much we don't see, it's ancient and hidden."

A new possibility smacked him upside the head. He'd never gotten the chance to do his Enemy Way ceremony, and now Taylor was acting possessed. He'd better not rule out the possibility that the spirit got to her on a deep level. Invaded her. Which might explain why she'd been seeing things from the very beginning.

If his tagalong was a trickster entity, the malevolence could have afflicted her with visions of shifters to confuse him, keep him close to Taylor, tease him with the possibility that she knew about shifters or even was one. The spirit might have concocted an in-between step to possessing him.

Lots of unknowns and loose ends, but he couldn't afford to nix any possibilities. Nor could he cope with seeing someone he cared about gripped by suffering.

He knelt beside her, pulled her up by the arm until she sat, and cupped her face in both hands. Though he'd left his tribe before finishing the medicine man initiation, he might be able to stumble his way through a ceremony to bring her some peace.

No way was he going to stand by like a fool while she succumbed to this fit of psychosis.

Her mention of ancestors gave him a bit of data to work with. If he managed to stabilize her and keep her grounded, he could, in theory, enlist her help in comparing her reports to the other material from his research.

"I need you to come back to me now, Taylor. Look into my eyes and take a deep breath. Hold and release three times."

She offered a weak nod and sucked down a harsh inhale. Her breath left slower and more relaxed than it came in, a small improvement that lifted his hope and prompted him to continue.

"You are here in my home, on Earth, on the floor. Do you remember who I am? My name?"

A single tear rolled down her cheek. "Your name is Julian." She whispered his name like she held those three syllables in sacred regard. She blinked a few times, and her chest heaved. She looked and sounded more like herself. The worst of the fit had subsided.

He brushed his lips between her eyebrows. Some strange bond, perversely pleasurable with a terrible eccentricity reserved for the two of them, took hold in his heart and soul.

"Good. My name is Julian, and I'm here to take care of you and make sure you're all right. I think something nasty might've compromised you, and I'm going to try to help. Do you trust me?"

"Yes."

The resolute conviction with which she spoke burrowed into him. When he was able, he'd reciprocate her offering in kind. "Thank you."

"But I don't understand why any of this is going on. It doesn't feel like a demon or whatever inside of me, it feels like an attempt at communication. A cry for help."

He pulled back and held her hands. Their best bet was to address the most sinister and malevolent possibilities. Attack any intruders hovering at the boundary of her selfhood before they did irreparable damage to Taylor's spiritual health or mental faculties. Then they could explore alternatives, but her safety was paramount.

"You may be right. What concerns me is your description of the tall man with the red eyes because it's something I've also seen. If we can get that under control and get you well and both of us safe, then we can look into whatever's up with shifters and these red lights and blue numbers you see. But there's a ton going on, and if we don't tackle it in manageable pieces, I'm worried we'll fall apart."

"Oh God," she whimpered and closed her eyes. "I can see him right now. He's...he's eating people. There are people wearing animal skins killing wolves. No. No. No."

This was possession alright. Less theorizing, more action. He hauled Taylor to her feet. She looked up at him with wet eyes, a devastating plea etched across her face. A plea to save her. He had to. Somehow.

Julian ran to his storage closet and pulled down one of the woven blankets his mama sent him. While she wrapped herself in colorful wool, he fetched her sandals and his boots from the bedroom, walking backwards so she never left his sight.

Taylor slid on her shoes and asked, "Where are we going?"

He stepped in front of her and, with a scoop of his hand, motioned for her to follow. She trailed him through the mudroom and onto the concrete patio leading to his backyard, his two acres of land drenched in ebony sprinkled by the silver dollar of a full moon and a dusting of stars. Wind whistled through trees, livening up the late hour.

"See that?" Julian grabbed a flashlight off his washing machine and pointed it at the hogan. The round hut made of lumber loomed in the halogen glare. The ceremonial structure where he honored his traditions took on an ominous voltage given the circumstances. The squat doorway gaped like a dark portal.

"It's hard to miss. Is that where you're taking me?"

"Yeah." He resumed walking, crispy grass crunching under his boot heels.

"Not my typical first date experience, but neither is sex."

He permitted himself to smile and draped an arm around her shoulders, pulling her swaddled form closer while they walked in tandem. At least she was back to being herself, and he had to count every blessing he could snatch. "Nothing about us is typical, huh?"

Movement on the ground breached the barrier of illumination. A tan tube slunk across the grass, muscles flexing in a scaly body while the snake blazed a trail less than a foot in front of their shoes. Lance-shaped head, body as fat as a beer can. No mistaking a full-grown rattler.

Adrenaline shot to Julian's toes in a frying sizzle, but he remained still as a statue.

"Danger noodle alert." Taylor spoke each word slowly, though she kept her cool.

"You didn't scream. I'm impressed."

"I have a pet snake, so obviously I'm not phobic. Questionable omen, though, huh?"

The reptile kept on slithering, lost in its own snake world. He took the excuse offered by her dry humor to inject a bit more levity into the rapport. "I'm in a lose-lose situation here."

A tiny, though authentic, laugh from Taylor cut the tension like rainstorm to drought. "Why?"

"If I stomp on its head in a gallant effort to protect you, I'm a brute. But if I don't, I've shirked my manly responsibility to keep my woman safe, making me a coward."

"Nah, you're good. I think it's already wiggled under your fence." She chanced him a glance, a small smile bending her lips. Her eyes glittered like sapphires, beacons of hope on a bleak night. "I'll admit I liked the 'my woman' part."

He didn't dare tell her how good her admission made him feel. It wasn't time to get cozy and romantic yet, because they had serious work to do. "Tell you what. Let's kick this bad guy to the curb, then I'll make some food, and we'll put on a movie. Proper first date activities."

"Deal." She initiated the return to movement, and they finished the short trek to the hogan.

Taylor ducked to clear the doorway, and Julian followed. The moment he stepped foot in his spiritual haven, his energy aligned with the harmony of the planets above him.

Scents of smoke and sawdust from years of ritual had probed deep into the floor and walls, the smells of his heritage and culture. An opening at the top, positioned directly under the Sirius star, invited the penetration of radiant starlight.

He held Taylor and said, "Take a seat against a wall and get comfortable. If you meditate or pray, do that now."

She chose a spot across from the doorway and sat in a cross-legged position, tucking the blanket under her legs. "I've meditated. I can do that."

"I can try a traditional ceremony to purify you from any entities hanging around who don't have your best interests in mind."

Taylor picked at a thread on her blanket. "I don't feel right about that. I appreciate it, but I'm worried that my presence here, whatever came over me back there, will pollute the sacred ritual. I still feel a presence around me. Like residue."

He wasn't worried about that but didn't want to pressure out of her comfort zone, either. "Okay. I understand. Nothing formal, then. Just rest in here and meditate. There's good energy in this space. Relax and clear your head."

Taylor nodded and chewed on the tip of her finger before settling in to a still pose. She took deep breaths. This strategy was a placebo, mostly, and with any luck, she'd get centered enough to where they could begin to figure out how to tackle this problem. At the moment, he didn't have a clue.

Julian tried to meditate, too, hoping that clearing his mind would help him find answers. But he wasn't able to still his thoughts. He worried that the curse had started with Taylor and moved to him. That dark magic was stuck to him somehow. Dark magic was out of his depth, and he didn't want to be anywhere near it. The idea of witchcraft made his skin crawl.

Who was Taylor McClure, and who the hell was her father? Had Julian made a colossal mistake by getting closer to her?

His pulse quickened as he silently prayed for help and solutions.

The sound of her soft breathing filled the silence.

His own meditation deepened, and finally his thoughts fell away as he corralled his mind and focused on his breath.

"The coven daughter of water has found her target," a strange female voice whispered. *"The prophecy comes to you. Prepare for the Song of Virgo, shifter."*

Julian's pulse leapt, snapping him from his peace. His eyes popped open. There wasn't anyone else in the hogan with him except Taylor. He hadn't liked the sound of that voice one bit. It was malicious and threatening.

Taylor rocked in a gentle back and forth rhythm, eyes closed and face tranquil.

"Did you hear that?" Julian asked.

"Hmm?" Blissed out, she didn't open her eyes. Either she hadn't heard or wasn't sharing if she had.

All he could do was focus on positive energy to keep this negative force at bay, not give. He looked at the opening at the top of the hogan and took in the sight of the five-pointed diamond hanging high in the sky. In mystical moments such as these, he wondered if the stories were true, the ones that claimed his people traveled, long, long, ago, through a wormhole in space connecting Sirius to Earth's solar system. In homage to that possibility, he'd aligned the top of the hogan with the majestic star at the end of Orion's belt.

"We are the lost people of the stars," his *amá sání* had said once as she glanced out a kitchen window into the starlit night. It wasn't the traditional Navajo origin story, but as a boy, Julian loved her tale. Tribal lore was corrupted all to hell by colonialism anyway, so it was anyone's guess which legends were authentic.

Once he felt more centered, Julian said a quick, silent prayer to the Great Spirit and his ancestors who walked the road beyond.

"How are you feeling?" he asked.

Taylor's eyes opened; calm waters as blue as the sea. "I feel good. Normal."

A collection of phantom muscles unclenched deep in his core. He rubbed her outer arms and cherished the feel of her flesh beneath the scratch of his mama's blanket.

"Outstanding. Let's get inside and eat. I've got two deer steaks marinating in the fridge."

She'd opened her mouth to say something when her eyes and lips twisted into mortified contortions.

"Julian." Her voice shook, and her entire body followed. "Behind you."

Dread and denial joined forces to pull him into one tense, taut mass. He looked into Taylor's frightened eyes and clutched a dumb hope that she'd laugh and say gotcha and he'd pretend to be pissed that she'd pranked him.

"That snake's back, isn't he?" His instinct rebelled against the incorrect words he spoke, the crummy feeling of uttering a statement he knew to be wrong.

She clamped a hand over her mouth. "It's coming."

"I'll go inside and get a gun. Stand behind me."

"It's no snake," she whispered through the gaps in her fingers. "He found us. That thing found us. It's my fault."

His molars clamped, and blood roared in his head, but he chanced an apprehensive look.

Incandescent light spilled through the opening. With his forearm, he shielded his eyes from the worst of it and squinted against the pain.

He saw two pale feet. They levitated, descending downward to reveal endless, pasty legs. Stones of bulbous knee knobs appeared, then thighs and shriveled male genitals.

Julian held on tight to Taylor as the entity continued to float down from the hole. Two puffs of dust leapt into the air when the thing's soles met dirt.

And before Julian, there it stood, the color of boiled bones and as nude as a plucked chicken. Bald and hairless, gaunt and sunken. The fiend he'd seen before, the one Taylor described.

"The first Other One has been born to your world," cooed that unwholesome female voice. *"My baby, emerged Earthside through your portal like an infant from the womb."*

The only sound battering his eardrums was his own pulse and breathing.

Evil spirits were fabled to do crazy shit, but Julian didn't know the score with this one. He was so far out of his league he was trying to play hockey with a basketball.

The fever dream apparition advanced upon them, closing several feet of space with two ungainly steps. Flab wobbled beneath a protruding ribcage and hung near the bowl of a defined pelvis. Its jaw dropped, unhinging like a python ready to devour a mammal.

"Get out," Julian shouted, though he grasped at a dust speck in a tornado. "You aren't wanted here."

The disembodied voice laughed.

Red light spilled from the monster's sockets, mingling with the beam overhead. Julian's mental faculties blurred. The red light warmed him. All he could do was stare into those red lights and dissolve.

His hands dropped from Taylor's arms. Fur lined the inside of his empty skull. Thoughts dissipated. He floated.

Unintelligible, fast whisperings from Taylor bombarded his empty brain. A string of those arcane words. A red handprint with broken fingers flashed before his eyes.

He battled the stupor with every last shred of remaining strength, but his bones softened to mud. His mouth moved, but no words came. Next thing he knew, his cheek hit the dirt.

"Coven daughter of water." Taylor's speech slurred. "The Song of Virgo must occur. For the prophecy. For the Other Ones. For Folly!"

"Folly," the voice purred. *"The master and mother of all. Your coven mother of chaos."*

Two icy clamps circled Julian's ankles. He slid backwards on his belly. Groaning, fighting though pulled against his will, he cranked his neck and looked up at Taylor. Her stare vacant, she looked at the light.

Clicks reverberated deep in his marrow. It took more willpower than he thought he held, but he managed to grunt out a command to her.

"Look away from that light and write down any words that are coming to you."

His legs peeled off the ground, followed by his torso. Blood rushed to his brain, filling him with unbearable, ripe pressure. He hung upside down and floated to the gap.

Despair suffocated him along with the fluid pushing into his head. She rambled, and he flailed in the air, control gone and headed for the sky.

But then, she screamed, and her scream turned to a guttural roar. "No. No, no, no."

She slapped the heels of her hands to her eyes, tore them away, and volleyed her gaze to the ground. After glancing in both directions and gripping the sides of her head, Taylor began to scribble in the dust with a single finger.

Julian fell and hit solidness with a thud. Sharp pain dashed from his shoulder down his arm when his upper body took the brunt of the collision. Grimacing, he forced himself upright and ran to where Taylor wrote. The light left along with the creature, and Julian had never felt so overwhelmed with relief to be bathed in darkness.

"Capture phase," she muttered. A string of numbers appeared under the working of her makeshift writing. "It wanted you in here, wanted me in here. I'm a tool, a conduit, a device."

Nausea clamped his stomach. Though his knee-jerk reaction was to counter with some statement about how that made no sense, his instinct counter punched. It did make sense.

Taylor was connected to the capture of shifters. His heart collapsed into a dense and pained lump, but he maintained his wits. "Tell me everything you know. Now. If you care about me at all, it's time to come clean."

She looked up, and the raw grief and puzzlement on her face confessed the truth. She wasn't plotting, she was manipulated.

He wrapped her in the best bear hug he could, seeking comfort while giving her relief. Symbols and text surrounded them in a circle, a plethora of secrecy juiced up with a freakish, occult charge.

"I need to crack this algorithm. That has to be what this is. The patterns. The repetition." She jerked in his arms and craned her neck in the direction of a fresh scrawl. "The more I look at and think about everything else I'm seeing, and in light of what happened, the more I'm closing in on a guess."

"Which is?"

"Geographic coordinates."

SEVEN

TAYLOR YANKED ON HER DRESS, TUGGING SO HARD THAT A RIPPING noise tore through Julian's bedroom. A ragged tear along the side seam made her wince, but she had bigger problems than a ruined garment.

"Will you talk to me?" Julian said.

She pretended that she couldn't still smell him on her, pretended her heart didn't ache at the sound of his voice.

Instead of surrendering to emotion, Taylor triple-checked her purse. Chinese menu still in there, filled front and back with everything she saw and heard. As soon as possible, she'd chase this hunch about latitudes and longitudes in the algorithm. Her theory lined up with the suspicion that the distraught voices wanted to lead her to a precise location.

"I have to go. Now." The horrors witnessed in the hogan stayed branded on her brain, their traumas searing into the backs of her eyelids every time she blinked. But obsessing would accomplish all of zilch.

Time to act, somehow, and get to the bottom of the crazy before she fell to pieces. Not like she'd given up on school or her future job, but no way could she move through her days while in the grip of these visions.

Sliding her underwear up her legs, Taylor pinpointed a simple and specific goal. Purge the imagery and voices and go back to who she'd been prior to the nightmare. Attending the upcoming McClure donor banquet to hunt for intel might help her make strides in the right direction and provide a chance to put her geographic coordinates theory to the test. Perhaps she could ply some big shot with drinks until he blathered actionable information.

"Taylor, stay the night." Julian circled her upper arm in a gentle but decisive hold. "I'm worried about you."

The protective, territorial nature of his grasp coupled with his statement hurt her heart. Betrayal punched her middle. He had no right to pretend to care, to toy with her feelings when shoving her fear and pain aside demanded every ounce of her energy.

She wrestled with competing urges to slap him and fall into his arms and weep. Both stupid. She didn't mean much to Julian and vice versa, they were simply two people sucked into the same fiendish orbit who'd enjoyed some intensely passionate sex. Nothing more. Sex didn't equal love. She was smarter than to fall for that trap society sprung on women. Taylor didn't do warm fuzzies. She didn't do love. She had to keep telling herself all those things if she was to survive, and if Julian was to survive, in her new and terrifying life.

"I can't stay, we both know that." She looked away before gazing into those eyes of his could blast her defenses to smithereens.

"Yes, you can." He leaned down and slid a hand over her cheek, making a play for eye contact with a stare that dug deep. "I can't have you running out into the night alone when we have no idea what is happening. What if that freak from the hogan attacks again? What if you wreck your car?"

A poison spear lodged into the spaces between her ribs. The longer the arrow stayed, the more bitter brew invaded her system. Julian had no right to make her feel weak and small, needy. She summoned a glare.

"You aren't going to *have* me do anything one way or another, because you don't *have* a say in my choices. Understood?"

"I'm not trying to control you or pull some alpha male bullshit; I'm looking after you because I care. I know we haven't gotten a chance to get to know each other as much as we should have. I'm aware that we rushed things. But that doesn't mean you're nothing to me."

His words were too painful. He'd better not care. She was a danger to him. Her bones knew it. The voices in her head knew it, those whispering fiends put there by those who wanted to cause pain.

She left the room before she cried, doing her best to ignore the misery thrumming inside as she pulled on her sandals. "You don't know me." Her voice shook. Damn her voice, damn it straight to hell. "You don't know what's going on inside of me."

Each second spent in Julian's house siphoned off another layer of her wall and absorbed those defenses into the shadow-shifting theatre of mystery playing out in the rural landscape beyond his walls.

Every moment in his home, his presence, caused a mask she wasn't aware she'd been wearing to slip an inch lower. Which might be liberating if the slippage wasn't so scary. She refused to look into her own black hole and confront the abyss staring back at her.

He was behind her now, resting a firm palm against the curve where her spine met her bottom. She jerked, a knot of anger twisting in her abdomen. Beneath rage, emptiness and grief sobbed with a despair rivaling those voices in her head.

"Is that what this is about? You think you don't deserve to have someone who cares about you? Like you're broken or something? If that's the case, I assure you that you're not. Whatever is happening, you'll beat it. It doesn't define you. I'm here if you want my help."

She whipped around to look up into his face, finding a threatening tenderness in his expression. Because he was right about a painful truth. She hadn't done shit to earn his care and affection, and she knew full well that those things were earned. She'd never earned them. So why was he dangling the temptation in front of her nose? To lure her into a breakdown where she'd act helpless? Nope. Never would she deteriorate into some damsel in distress who enabled him to put on the big man routine.

"Shut up, Julian."

He snorted, though his countenance didn't morph to a mean and contemptuous grimace like a sick part of her hoped. No, he hadn't taken the bait. This failure on her part upset her even more but compounded her respect for Julian. The man was solid inside, a monument to the concept of integrity.

"Push me away if that's how you need to cope, I guess, but will you at least tell me what you want to accomplish? Because like it or not, I've got skin in this game. My own, in fact. Whatever is hassling you is also after me, meaning that we're connected. If you aren't ready to open up, I can accept that, but don't you think I could be an ally to you?"

While she hiked her purse strap on her shoulder, Taylor thought things over. She allowed the worst of her negativity to submit to logic and reason. "It's tempting to call bullshit on your claim to being a wolf shifter, but I can't unsee what I saw in the hogan. So there's that."

"Yeah." He offered her a dry smirk. "There's that. And since you might be brainwashed to capture me and have an inroad to the alleged mastermind of the whole plot, I'd say that gives me a pretty solid reason for wanting to keep you close. Given your intent to solving this mystery and extricate yourself from it, I'd wager that you ought to want to have me all over your radar as well. Agree?"

She took a few deep breaths. "I agree. And I'm sorry I snapped at you."

"No harm done. Now please stay the night and get some rest. All this crap will be waiting for us in the morning."

His choice of the word "us" flittered around her like a fairy, taunting her with the promise of stroking a wonderful thing she could never catch. With remorse, she let the sprite fly away. But she could show him that she, too, cared in her own way.

"I appreciate it, but no." Taylor brushed her fingers against Julian's. "I have to leave."

"Will you call me when you get home, at least? So I know you made it safe."

Mr. Chivalrous. She could get used to having a man like Julian in her life but had better not. Nothing was safe or certain at the moment.

Taylor got herself out of Julian's house, away from him and all his disarming qualities. She drove home numb, willing herself to neither think nor feel.

When she entered her condo's covered garage and parked in her spot, familiarity steered her mind back on track. Screw feelings, but she held plenty of space for thoughts. And chief among those was how to turn this upcoming donor banquet into a reconnaissance mission and generate some fucking answers.

A brief text to Julian in honor of her word: *I'm home safe.*

Her phone chirped a second later. *Good deal. Thank you. Talk soon.*

The sight of his short sentences, his voice shining through in written form, put a lightness to her step in spite of her attempts to snuff the glow. Keeping Julian Nez from embedding himself into her heart might prove more difficult than solving the paranormal mystery that had burrowed under her skin.

✳

TAYLOR WOKE AT ELEVEN FOLLOWING A SCUZZY, RESTLESS SLEEP. With a groan of protest against the glare streaming through her wall-sized bedroom windows, she hauled her body into a seated position and stared out over downtown Austin.

Nineteen stories below, Matchbox cars zipped down streets and people scurried like ants to weekend activities. No yoga or farmer's market for Taylor, though. The day was for strategizing, the night designated for investigating.

She probably would have felt better waking up next to Julian, but she wasn't allowed to think of him at the moment.

Time to get moving.

She brushed her teeth, showered, and changed into a sporty skirt and t-shirt. A walk to the corner bodega scored her a burner phone. Back home, she popped the SIM card out of her permanent cell, stuck the speck of a chip in a jewelry box, and called her sister Chloe on the replacement.

Not wise to rule out possibilities or avoid precautions. God knew what these creeps had bugged or otherwise put under surveillance.

Chloe answered, voice ragged from sleep and husky from smoking and drinking anything she could get her hands on. "Who the fuck is this? It's like, five in the morning. Whoever you are, I'm not holding."

Taylor sighed. Disappointment dragged her low, though she'd learned not to get her hopes up anymore. Chloe had blown through five private high schools and three rehab programs in a single year, and if she didn't start showing potential to pass eleventh grade, their parents would pack her off to boarding school. From the sounds of things, Chloe was facing her ultimatum with an extended middle finger and a sneer. Bigger problems than Chloe's predictable screwing up, however, loomed.

"It's me, and it's almost noon. Hang up and call me back on one of those druggie temp phones that I know you have." She rattled off her new number.

"Ugh, it's too early for an intervention. And hello, pot calling kettle black. Why do you of all people have a sketchy phone now? That area code is from, like, the moon."

"Hurry."

Taylor watered her five plants and pulled dead leaves out of the fern pot, busying her hands so she didn't bite her nails or second-guess her decision to involve Chloe. Her sister was cunning and savvy. She'd ace her role in the impending caper.

The line clicked dead, and a second later, Taylor's new phone trilled a foreign ring.

"Hey." She brushed crumbs off her countertop and tossed a Styrofoam takeout box in the trash. A mental blueprint of the McClure mansion's layout took shape. "I have a mission for you."

Chloe laughed her smoky laugh. "Hey, dork-o. What in the actual fuck is going on? You working for the CIA now or some shit?"

Agitated grasshoppers bounced around inside of her. "I need you to go to Dad's banquet tonight and help me with something."

Chloe scoffed. "Show up at one of his ass-kiss fests? Hard pass. And why would anyone want me there? You're the prize pony. You go and talk about how awesome you are or flaunt your golden crown or whatever it is you do. Imma chill."

The pain that wobbled just below Chloe's hardened voice resonated with Taylor. Too loud, too defiant, a rebel smarter than her own good and in all the wrong ways, Chloe never stood a chance in the McClure Court of Ice and Thorns.

At least Taylor's scheme would give Chloe a boost of pride in an accomplishment along with the excitement of flouting authority. The perfect opportunity for her. "Actually, I think you'll enjoy it."

While riding the pause that trailed behind her nugget of temptation, Taylor lifted the lid of Salazar's aquarium. Her ball python sat coiled under his rock, peeking his brown and tan-spotted head out of the opening. The gray fork of his tongue tasted the air in a quick probe of curiosity.

She lifted his hiding cubby and scooped his cool, muscular body into her palm.

Since freshman year in the dorms with her best friend Angie, Taylor's beloved pet had been a ride or die companion, her legless little buddy and the third prong of the Slytherin trio.

Most people preferred dogs and cats, but while wandering through a mall pet store one day, Taylor found herself enchanted by the snake's graceful movements. Dignified in his own way, he regarded the world with detachment through pebbles of ebony eyes.

"Why the fuck would I enjoy it?" Chloe yawned.

"I think Dad is up to something insane. I'm hoping you can help me slip away during the schmoozing so I can investigate his office." Salazar slithered a leathery path up Taylor's arm, warming to room temperature as he absorbed her body heat.

He reminded her of herself. Chilly, but capable of warming up in the right environment and company. A keen observer of the world who showed his vicious streak when ready to strike.

Snakes weren't evil, they were just using their unique tools and strengths to get by the only ways they knew how. A born hunter couldn't up and decide not to hunt, and cold-bloodedness was a natural fact that needn't come with a value judgment.

A deep laugh bellowed through the line. "Investigate his office? What are you talking about? Not that I'm not completely amused by this, because I am."

With Salazar's two-foot length looped around the back of her neck, Taylor dusted her bookshelves and tidied her desk. "You've never seen anything weird over there? Weirder than usual, I mean?"

Though Chloe was fairly checked out from home life and not on the lookout, in theory, she could have seen or overheard something of use to Taylor.

"Nope. But I take it you have."

"I met with Dad the other day, and when I pulled a book from a shelf, I saw a hidden panel of buttons. I think he has a secret chamber."

Chloe snorted. "Okay. So? I mean, I'll grant that's sketchy, but don't you think it's probably just like for a safe? I don't quite see where you're coming from."

Taylor swiveled a twitchy glance over her shoulder, aware for the first time how a burner phone might not be an ironclad line of defense. She ought to play this situation carefully at every level. "He's sucked me into some kind of scheme that I want no part of. I'll tell you more at the fundraiser."

"Ah, bribing me with juicy gossip. Well played, well played. I'm getting hooked. Why wouldn't you want to be part of his scheme, though? I thought you two were besties."

Taylor sat on her couch, stealing a taste of respite in the softness of the cushion. She peeled a dime-sized sheet of dead skin off Salazar's back and blew the translucent bit of shed into the air.

Perhaps a monster lurked beneath her father's polished veneer of designer suits and shrewd political acumen, and the man shed his human trappings like Salazar sloughed off his old sheaths.

Only a monster was capable of using his supposed favorite daughter in a clandestine mind control experiment.

"I think he's up to something with technology experiments. Weird and frightening. Really, really scary."

"Yeah, you sound legit scared."

"I am." Upon admitting it, Taylor released a shackle of manufactured toughness. Longing for support churned below her surface, pushing up and out through her pores. "I need you, Chloe."

In the absence of another person to touch, Taylor rubbed her bare feet together while waiting for Chloe's next words.

"You got it. What can I do?"

A quick mental rundown of Chloe's top skills and attributes yielded an answer. "Get the key to his office and have it handy to slip to me. When the time comes for the handoff, I'll give you the duck bill sign. As soon as you see it, stage some kind of ruse. A good distraction, so I can grab the key and slip away."

Old, sweet memories pierced Taylor. She and Chloe had been Lucky and Ducky during their childhood make believe games, two ducklings waiting on their real mother to swoop down from the sky as a bird and spirit them away to somewhere better, a true home full of nurturing and love.

As for swiping the key logistic, easy peasy. Chloe once hid a puppy in her bedroom for six months without their parents finding out.

"I got you. Are you gonna be okay alone tonight?"

"Yeah." Something clunked in the kitchen, and a sizzle of chemicals jolted Taylor's extremities. She jerked in the direction of the sound, rolling her eyes at herself and patting Salazar when her jumpy gaze landed on the dishwasher she'd forgotten she started. "I'll be fine."

"Later. See you at the freak show." Chloe hung up, and Taylor set her phone on the coffee table.

Taylor put Salazar in his cage and tried to study, but concentration proved impossible.

She stuck her pen in her textbook and paced, rubbing the goosebumps on her arms. Her emotional state inched toward the precipice of an anxiety attack. Memories of words and images danced in her memories like deranged clowns.

Never before had Taylor noticed how silence had its own unique sound, a texture. It teemed in a near-imperceptible hum and bent the atmosphere with a rise and fall of swells that mirrored her pulse. Noticing such nuance made her skin crawl and put her senses on high alert.

More backup for the event might help ease her mind. Her best friend Angie would think she was nuts and refuse to go, but it would make sense to invite Julian. She nodded at the rational, sensible thought. She was soliciting his help, not asking him out on a date.

After all, he cared about the whereabouts of shifters and would appreciate a first look at any evidence she found. Not like she needed a man's protection, but it might help her think straight to go to the banquet armed with the company of someone who not only believed her, but also had a stake in the outcome. Pure logic. Smart call.

She swiped her cell and pushed the phone icon next to his text, tapping her foot as a dial tone rang once, twice.

"Hey, what's going on?" The sound of his voice ushered her nerves away from the ledge and even hit her with a slight case of happiness. Which had to be a stress reaction—overvaluing the slightest morsel of positivity. Not like she pined for the guy. Taylor did *not* pine or moon over men. Romance was the farthest thing from her mind.

"Come with me to the donor banquet." She swallowed thickly at the sound of her own brusque order. If she wanted Julian to have any desire to keep hanging out with her, she'd better work on sanding down the sharpness of her edges. "Please. I need you there with me."

EIGHT

Normally, the grandiose and environmentally wasteful spectacle put on by the McClure estate would have left Taylor perturbed.

Light blasted from three stories of windows, presenting the generic mansion like it was a castle. Only the newest of new money tried so damn hard, but baby wealth in Texas lived to build spectacle. Everything was bigger there, yadda yadda.

Tonight, though, Taylor appreciated how the excessive illumination flattered Julian's chiseled profile and dark hair. On the doorstop next to her, he rocked on his boot heels and smoothed the gold tie cutting a clean line down the front of his dress shirt. No matter where he went, he owned the space and looked like he belonged. Nobody could miss how comfortable he was in his own skin.

His knot wasn't crooked in the slightest, yet she stood on her tiptoes and adjusted the twist of fabric.

"Thank you." He touched her upper arm, a nonverbal gesture confusingly ambiguous but understandable. Sure they'd had sex, but were they on hand-holding terms?

Their relationship lived in limbo, a purgatory of broken rules and flouted conventions. Together, they had confused any and all norms and rules of courtship. She'd accept the arrangement for what it was, inherent limitations and all.

"We should review the plan." One element of their mission was devoid of ambiguity or complex emotions, so it was best to focus on what they'd hashed out during the drive.

Julian nodded. "When your sister creates a distraction, you'll slip away first. As soon as everyone is caught up in her antics, I follow you up the grand staircase and through the second-floor hallway to the office. From there, we have ten to fifteen minutes to see if we can open whatever the keypad controls. If we're lucky enough to do it, we take pictures of what we find."

Her stomach fluttered, and she chuckled before she could halt the eruption. Tough to feel nervous or unsure with Julian around. "Your name's Bond. James Bond."

He winked. "Nah, I'm not that smooth. But I take direction well. Teachers said I was a good listener."

She stepped a little closer, glad their early arrival permitted them a few stolen minutes to talk. "What's your degree in? Wait. Let me guess. Journalism."

"I never went to college."

"Could have fooled me."

"Impossible." Julian lifted his chin, his eyes playful and kind.

Though tempted to grab his wrist, speed back into town, and drive them to a romantic restaurant, Taylor quashed the urge. They were here on a mission. Work.

"Ready?" she asked.

"Born that way."

"Let's do this." She pushed the doorbell button, and when a few tasteful notes of classical music played beyond the door, Julian tucked a piece of hair behind his ear.

A slight headache throbbed between her eyes, and she let her head droop. Sure would be nice if she had a regular, loving clan that she could be proud of, a nice family to introduce to Julian. But that wasn't why they were here. This wasn't a "meet the parents" visit.

Soft footfalls approached. Her cheeks burned. "Just so you know, you don't have to worry about impressing anyone."

"I figured a good first impression works like leverage." Yet a curve in the vowels of his pragmatic words belied hope for something that wasn't there and would never be there.

Sadness settled within, heavy and blue. Maybe she and Julian would find each other in the next lifetime and be able to have a nice, normal relationship.

The deadbolt turned with a click. Her breath hitched, but she forced her head up and shoulders back. The flight instinct kicked in and flooded her with chemicals begging her to flee.

But no. She had to deal with this. Solve the mystery, fix it, and get back to achieving her life goals. "My father can be really disarming. He's all charm and charisma, so if he gets to you, remember what you read in that paper in the library."

"Don't worry. I'm not losing sight of our purpose and going sentimental." The tone coating his statement, pensiveness seasoned with remorse, twisted the knife.

Sentimentality, longing for her family to change for the better, was a luxury she couldn't afford. Taylor had never thought of herself as someone who couldn't afford something she wanted. But maybe she was poor in all the ways that counted, shriveled emotionally and unable to love herself or others.

A year ago, she'd ended up in a therapist's office when an A-minus paper sent her spiraling into depression and anxiety. The kind woman offered insights, the profound nature of which were starting to land:

"Enmeshed, narcissistic parents assign golden child and scapegoat roles and reassign them according to their whims, with the golden child serving as an extension of the parent's ego. It's an understandable source of anxiety for the golden child, teetering on top of an unsteady pedestal. Try to remember that you are worthy not because of your achievements or your ability to please the narcissistic parents, but because of who you are."

Instead of staying and internalizing the lesson, she'd stormed out in a defensive fit. Bad move. If she'd been ready to hear the analysis, maybe she'd have fixed her multitude of flaws by now.

An uncontrolled moan popped out of her mouth when the door parted. "Help me stay on track."

Julian cupped her shoulder. "What's wrong?"

So much. Before she could hazard an acceptable response, the front door stretched to reveal Taylor's mother.

Diana wore a white bandage dress that hugged her bones and impossible stilettos matching the shade of burgundy painted on her pout. Dilated pupils absorbed her irises in black voids.

One nostril and upper lip corner ticked, the slightest twitch of animation on an otherwise immobile face topped by a lacquered blonde helmet.

"Welcome Taylor and distinguished guest," she said in monotone before stepping to the side. "Appetizers and champagne are circulating. Make yourselves comfortable. We will dine al Fresco in one hour. I'm glad you wore a cardigan, Taylor, or you, my darling daughter, would be dining al *chill*-o."

Following the apparent attempt at cute humor, Diana trilled her trademark giggle.

Julian looked at Taylor like he was drowning, and she held the raft. "Distinguished guest?" he whispered.

Taylor shrugged with palms up, laying on a performance of sarcasm while acid ate her stomach lining. It was what it was, so why pretend that the entire fracas was mortifying? Mortifying implied unexpected or shocking.

He caught her hand, interlaced their fingers, and looked her straight in the eye with an assured stare.

Bleak sludge drained out of Taylor as she returned his gaze with her own confident one. She'd never felt so understood, so seen, until now. He had become the raft when she'd started to sink, and the role reversal inspired the most glorious and freeing sense of respite.

I appreciate you.

The crooked tilt of his lips and warmth in his eyes further steeled her sense of security.

She could get used to a man like Julian in her life, even if only as a friend.

"Please, come in." Diana beckoned with one hand.

Julian at her side, Taylor stepped into the foyer and assessed the scene. Men in suits and women in gowns socialized and admired the family painting collection.

A graying guy who'd come around a lot back when Taylor's dad worked as a theoretical physicist played a piece of Beethoven on the piano while bystanders clapped. Waitstaff wearing standard penguin uniform milled about, carrying platters of champagne and appetizers.

Two coiffed, starving society wives came up on Taylor's left and headed straight for Diana.

A brunette began to prattle. "I didn't have a chance to tell you how fabulous you look. You must be a double zero. Are you macrobiotic? Juicing aggressively? Doing the extreme carb challenge?"

"I take a cutting-edge blend of elite supplements and ionized water," Diana gushed. "My husband is investing in some truly phenomenal pharmaceutical companies, and they are paying all sorts dividends, as you can see." Diana twirled for her audience.

"You can never be too rich or too thin." The other wife said in a squeaky voice.

Taylor paused from mapping a couple of different routes to the study. Second mention of ionized water in a week. Also, what pharmaceutical companies? Her dad always told her he invested in space travel. Not that she should take him at his word anymore.

"What's on your mind?" Julian leaned in close and whispered, his breath tickling the shell of her ear.

Before she could answer, Chloe sauntered into the living room. Dressed to provoke with her ripped fishnets and combat boots, she poked a proverbial finger into the legion of eyes regarding her with contempt and disdain.

"What's up, girly? Love how you brought a new guy to this shitshow. Get out while you can, bro." Chloe swept a hand through her riot of hot pink curls and pulled out a hairpin.

Chloe didn't do politeness or decorum and lived to take swipes at the people who'd called her a failure since she was old enough to speak her opinionated mind.

The sight of red squiggles in Chloe's eyes sucker punched Taylor. She would find a way to save the sister she adored before her lifestyle killed her. But tonight would not be the night.

"Chloe, Julian. Julian, Chloe."

"Nice to meet you." Julian offered his hand.

Chloe accepted his handshake. "Pleasure is all mine. You're insanely hot, so I hope you aren't an asshole. Treat my sister right or I'll drop by and leak a dirty pee in your coffee. She's a total cunt but a really good person."

Taylor rolled her eyes for banter purposes, though the compliment made her smile. Good person. Now there was a rare accolade she could get used to hearing. "The plan's still Ducky's sign, right?"

Chloe broke away from Julian and entered the social fray, walking toward a catering table stocked with liquor bottles and serving ware. Her wild hair bounced as she looked over her shoulder and said, "The plan is think fast, sissy."

Julian pressed his palm to Taylor and slipped her a hard object. Pieces clicked. Chloe hadn't taken a clip from her hair or greeted Julian with a simple handshake.

Chloe poured booze into a shot glass and slammed it. "Shit," she yelled loud enough to pierce the din of chatter. "Fuck. Call nine-one-one. Help."

Sputtering ragged cries, Chloe grabbed a fistful of tablecloth, pulling it to the ground with her as she fell. Bottles clattered against each other as they hit the carpet. A decanter split in two, and wine splashed crimson against ivory softness. Chloe twitched and jerked, her head shaking.

Party guests gasped, tittered, formed a circle around the ruined table. Piano music clashed to an abrupt halt.

Taylor's vision contracted to a single line leading to Chloe. She ran to her sister and crouched, blood roaring in her ears. "Stay with me. What have you taken tonight besides alcohol?"

Chloe flashed a joker's smile, her Harley Quinn hair making a parachute behind her head.

"This." She discreetly stuck a capsule in her mouth. Foam flowed out of lips and down her chin.

So the evening's ruse would come in the form of a bogus seizure.

"Help. Overdose. Need a doctor." Chloe bellowed her plea with Oscar-worthy pizzazz and performed a spasm that drew another round of gasps from the gawkers. A few onlookers took out phones and recorded.

The angry voice of Taylor's father intervened, "What the hell have you done this time? And tonight, of all nights. I'm through with your delinquent degeneracy in my home. You are vile and you repulse me, Chloe Ann." He rushed to the daughter he didn't love and roughly checked the pulse on her wrist.

Diana, mincing in a little high heel trot, joined the floor show.

"Is that blood? I feel faint." She fell into the arms of the two skinny women as Jeff shook Chloe's shoulders and peered in her eyes.

The pair of trophies fussed over Diana, supplying the attention she sought.

Everyone was distracted, but not indefinitely.

After lobbing Julian a "game on" look, Taylor cut through the study and ran up the grand staircase. By the time she reached her father's office, she'd calmed down enough to manage the door with steady hands. The key disengaged the lock with a snick, and she turned the knob and eased the barrier shut.

Jeff McClure's personal zone of corruption swallowed her in bad juju the moment she entered. Though she'd met with him in the room many times over the years, the space breathed with sinister vibes like never before. The scent of shoe polish and oranges, whose blend of chemical headiness and wholesome sweetness once inspired a sense of stately, old-fashioned mystique, now sickened her.

Gathering her nerve, she pinned an adversarial look on the row of book spines covering the panel and willed her body to walk over and get busy investigating what she didn't want to find. Any discovery was bound to be awful.

Two taps hit the door, followed by an assuring low voice. "It's me."

A phantom belt cutting off Taylor's breath loosened. At least she didn't have to do this alone. She let Julian in, closed the door, and led him to the area of interest.

The books she pulled free were heavy in her grasp, everything gravid with menacing significance. Behind the volumes, shiny metal winked. Her mouth sour, she handed the books to Julian. "Can you put these somewhere?"

He set the stack on an end table, where they rested next to a potted cactus. "It's going to work out fine. We're in this together."

She pulled a wan smile from a place inside of her that still sparkled despite so much darkness and decay. Sure he spoke a platitude, but with so little to hold on to, she clutched his reassurance tight. "Yeah. We are."

"Think you can crack the code?"

"I'll try." She pulled the Chinese menu from her purse and unfolded the paper, narrowing her focus to the highlighted portions of words where she'd caught meaningful repetitions of sequences. The number six was significant, but that was all she had so far. There were six witches, apparently.

First, she punched in the date of the upcoming election. A light flashed red, and nothing happened. Next, her birthday. Nope. Then a set of suspected coordinates. Nope. The address to the house. Nope.

From far off came three muffled clomps. Julian glanced at the door. "Might be someone on the staircase." Tension wound his cadence taut.

She poked keys. Her dad's birthday. Nope. Entering a few of the unknown, possible addresses earned a blink from that stupid red light she wanted to shatter. "Come on."

More thuds landed, then quieted. Anxiety infected her, and her pulse spiked. After a couple more fails, the tiny dome turned green. A metallic clunk gave way to a long mechanical groan.

"What did it?" Julian slipped to the office door and rattled the knob. "It's locked. But I bet there's more than one key, yeah?"

"Probably, but it buys us a bit of time while he figures that out and goes to get it." She swallowed a big gulp. "My social security number worked."

She didn't get much time to analyze the significance of the victorious combination, because the bookcase parted down the middle. Each half pushed forward and moved to the side, coming to rest in front of an adjacent part of the built-in.

"What the hell?" Julian drew out each word.

Taylor shared his dumbfounded sentiment. The secret room behind the bookcase housed an assortment of objects and furnishings so strange and out of place that the sight of them made for a garish display carrying a frightening institutional charge.

A panel of screens covered one wall, and a huge table of knobs and buttons occupied floor space in front of the monitors. Several file cabinets rested against the opposite wall.

The weirdest furnishing, by far, was in the center of the floor. It looked like a clear plastic booth, the sort of soundproof structure musicians used to record. Except instead of a microphone, a metal chair occupied the middle. Fat wires in a variety of primary colors flowed out of the legs and connected to a shoebox-sized piece of electronic equipment on the ground.

Her vision blurred. Her legs and feet grew heavy and cold. A sense of dissociation blew through her mind, and a dream or memory surfaced. In the scenario, she lay on a cot while several doctors peered down at her. They spoke German, and a needle pierced her arm.

The sound of footsteps and agitated voices whipped her back to lucidity.

"We need to hurry." Julian went to the dummy wall and ran his hands over metal plating. "And figure out how to close this in case someone comes in."

"Right. You work on that and then look through the file cabinets. Take pictures of as much stuff as you can. I'll handle these monitors."

She found a marked "on" switch and flipped it, causing the flat screens to spark to life. Black and white imagery sans sound flooded the dim, cool space.

The dummy wall groaned shut, and soon after came the sounds of metal drawers creaking, papers rustling, and a cell phone camera clicking.

"Good work, J."

"I like the nickname. Wait until you see what I'm capturing over here." Shock offset the victory lilt in his tone. His camera snapped and snapped.

Her attention, though, stayed with the monitors. Her stare swept over a few dozen screens. They all showed what looked like real-time security footage of various locations. Sea foam licked a stretch of sand. A cabana or beach house, flanked by palm trees. Tennis court. Huge pool abutting rocky shoreline. A gold-domed temple on a hill.

The footsteps and voices got closer. Her heart slammed, and surroundings came into clear, sharp focus. She took her phone out of her purse, turned off the flash, and nabbed picture after picture of the content on the televisions. Security cameras captured what appeared to be the main building, a single-story home with an airy exterior layout, snapped from multiple angles.

"It's some kind of mansion on an island, but there are multiple structures," she whispered mostly to herself as Julian worked.

There was creepy stuff amidst fancy vacation-style buildings too. A giant, circular sundial ringed by benches. A dirt mound the size of a football field.

Creepy, yet senseless. She couldn't pinpoint any internal logic—why would anyone want to form a seated circle around a sundial? What was up with the dirt mound and temple? Most importantly, how did all these elements fit together?

She stepped to the side and evaluated the next group of screens. This batch showed interior footage. Bedrooms, bathrooms, fancy rec room decked out with artwork and a pool table. Cigar humidor, wine cellar.

What looked like the interior of the temple, empty but for checkerboard flooring and a glass elevator, shimmered with an occult suggestion. She shuddered despite the warm air.

"We need to wrap it up. I think whoever is coming is in the hallway." Julian's voice dropped to an urgent whisper.

"Just a minute." She matched his tone and kept taking shots.

When she moved to photograph the next set of screens, the hairs on her neck stood on end. She could tell by the lack of windows, the drab walls, and the uncarpeted floor that the security footage was filmed in an underground area. A staircase led down and opened to a network of corridors. Basement tunnels.

Some led to doors, others to more tunnels. An entire labyrinth.

Taylor was clicking away when she came face to face with her own image. She gasped, a hollow sound that sucked the wind from her lungs.

It was like looking into a mirror, except she was staring at one of the black and white monitors.

She lowered her phone and met her own horrified eyes. The image on the screen moved with her.

The office door opened and brought two male voices. Taylor bit down on her tongue. The file cabinet doors closed with quiet whines.

"You must have toed it under the door when you saw me coming. Get down on that carpet and find the damn key." This from Taylor's dad in a furious yell.

"I don't have it. I thought I did, but it's not on my key ring." Her brother Donnie spoke in his nasally whine.

"So you admit you stole the spare key. Where is it? Who did you give it to?"

"I don't know. Nobody. And I don't get why I'm not allowed to have the spare anymore. I told you, what happened will never happen again. I went there by myself once. *Once*, and for the purpose of mingling with high-powered clientele. I wasn't being selfish. I was thinking of our partnership. You were always telling me to be more proactive in going after what I wanted. I thought I was acting with bold decisiveness."

"You have irreparably damaged relationships with some very important people," Jeff shouted. "Blabbing and name-dropping to your stupid frat house buddies, violating the privacy of men who have indicated in no uncertain terms their desire to keep their trips discreet. Partnership, my ass."

Heavy feet approached the bookcase. Taylor slapped a hand over her mouth and cast Julian a desperate look. She dropped to her knees and crawled under the control panel, where he joined her. Crappy hiding place, but it was all they had.

"I'm not going to stand here and listen to you berate me when I was only ever representing us. And now that you've got your precious princess gathering product for them, I'd say you're back in their good graces."

A crash followed, and Donnie groaned.

"Don't you ever, *ever* speak of your sister ever again. You do not deserve the honor of mentioning her even in passing. It was supposed to be dormant. I *never* wanted to activate that program, and then you had to go and screw everything up and give them leverage over me."

Donnie laughed without mirth. "Keep blaming me all you want. Everyone knows Stearns has some juicy blackmail on you that has nothing to do with what I did. What is it? Drugs? Underage girls? Boys? What's so bad that you pulled the trigger on pimping out your favorite kid to Scarab? And was her getting railed from behind by that wolf man part of them calling in a favor?"

The sickening sound of flesh yielding to bone and vice versa carried through the walls.

Tangy sweat laced with the astringent bite of fear invaded Taylor's nostrils. Her underarms dampened. She kept her hand in place and looked at Julian. He gazed back with a knowing, troubled stare.

"You know nothing," Jeff screamed. "You know less than nothing, and you *are* nothing but a petty white-collar criminal who is unfit to lick dog shit off Bernie Madoff's shoe. Moral nightmare aside, do you know how much of our investors' money you lost? How many of them will never touch us again, and rightly so? Can you fathom the extent of your error?"

"I invested. I was making moves to expand the operation."

"Expand the operation? You let yourself slide into the enabling of complete and utter perversion. Canned hunts? Ritual sacrifice and cannibalism? Conjuring and trapping a fucking bloodthirsty demon? That shit is so far beyond the pale, I can't believe I even have to speak of it."

"That's what the guys at the top wanted, and you know it. They needed perks. Incentives. No-holds-barred entertainment that nobody but them has access to. You think they wanted to fly all the way to that island to discuss military strategy? Or jerk off to your pie in the sky fantasies of flying a rocket ship to Mars? Will they throw their money into long-term unknowns? Nope. Like it or not, I was luring new investors who were looking for thrills without limits. And guess what? They're still going. Still spending. If you want to keep reaping the rewards of this, I'd try a little harder to keep your phony moralizing in check."

"There is nothing phony about my rejection of torture and murder for sport."

"Because sending those shapeshifters to fight in pointless corporate wars is so much better."

"That is protecting our troops. Saving front line human life."

"They change into people. How do you justify your condoning of the program considering that inconvenient truth? Hm?"

"I've had it with you. If I catch you sneaking over here again or hear that you took another unauthorized jaunt to Scarab Island, you will regret it for the rest of your miserable life. Understood?"

Donnie snorted. "Whatever. Sure."

"Good. Now give me the key."

"I swear I don't have it. It's gone."

A little more senseless bickering, and both her father and brother left the office and shut the door.

Taylor took her hand off her mouth and huffed a giant exhale. "Shit just got real."

"Wait until you see what I got in here." Julian held up his phone.

"Ditto."

Taylor pinched the hard chunk under her skin. Did the mystery lump have anything to do with the monitor showing her viewpoint? If it was an implant or other foreign object, it needed to come out, pronto. Then she could study the invading device and determine exactly how she was being used.

What sorts of atrocities happened on the island? From the sounds of things, not only were shifters suffering under ghastly conditions, but Julian was at risk. A risk that she posed to him that she better figure out how to curtail.

Shit had just gotten real indeed.

NINE

Taylor had been in the bathroom for quite a while. A coil inside Julian wound tighter with each passing second. It was dispiriting how one mundane observation about restroom use insinuated all sorts of unpleasant significance.

"You okay?" Stationed at her dining room table, he called down the hall while shaking a restless leg.

"Yep. Just a sec." Of course her tone sounded normal, if irritated.

Christ, he ought to calm down. "Take your time. Sorry to bother you."

Yet he could not back off the edge that anxiety put him on. The frightening cache of documents that he'd pulled from those file cabinets wasn't helping. Mind control experiments and top-secret plans to enlist brainwashed shifters in warfare. If such horrors were true, how would he stop them?

Julian rubbed his forehead. Printouts from their investigation lay strewn across the tabletop, blueprints and redacted memos rendered doubly sinister by their grainy, difficult to read appearance. That paper at the library was a children's picture book compared to all this. He'd officially gone too far down the rabbit hole. He knew too much.

In the living room of the open floor plan condo, Taylor's printer belched, sending white tongues of sheets on to the carpeted floor. Papers referencing the ritual murder of his kind barfed onto a colorful area rug resembling a Jackson Pollock painting. Such an absurd juxtaposition of everyday and horrific.

To the sound of mechanical buzzing, he gathered his thoughts. According to what he'd found, Taylor's father and his cronies were involved in a project to kidnap shifters, store them in some top-secret base, and traffic them to fight in wars. Espionage missions awaited those ill-equipped for battlefield combat. Why would corrupt leaders think twice about blabbing sensitive information just because an animal happened to be in the room?

Same as the conspiracy paper had claimed, more or less, except now, the awful additions of torture and sport killing that her brother had mentioned brewed in the poisoned pot.

Julian scrolled through his phone, pulling up a photo of minutes from some meeting. According to the blurry memo, this shadow organization made use of portal networks and otherworldly entities to aid in the capture of shifters. Apparently, they deployed fringe physics and even magic to conjure manmade wormholes and open doors in space and time, allowing beings from other dimensions to slip through.

This development aligned with the pale man's stalking him and the incident with Taylor in the hogan. Speaking of Taylor, how was she involved in the twisted project?

If he was wise, he'd be as worried about keeping himself safe from her and her family as much as he was preoccupied with protecting her from their adversaries.

But he had a way of becoming unwise where Taylor was concerned. She stirred up a maelstrom of tender yet fierce emotions in him, unwittingly casting him into the role of valiant knight.

A glimpse of movement twitched in the corner of his eye. Her pet snake pressed a pale, scaly underbelly against glass as the reptile explored a well-decorated aquarium. A shiver raced up his legs, and inside him, the wolf tensed and growled. Being alone in the living room with a reptilian predator wasn't his or the wolf's first choice, but he didn't want to bug Taylor again in case she was dealing with her monthly cycle or some such personal matter.

The snake writhed and flopped to the floor of its cage, and Julian squirmed in his seat.

The wolf bore his teeth as his black hair rose on end.

What was taking her so long? He jumped out of his chair. Her main window looked out over the twinkling lights of city buildings against their backdrop of night. In the distance, a skyscraper bearing a striking resemblance to an owl glowed with a beacon's majesty.

Some Native tribes believed owls to be messengers of death. The creeps crawled stubbornly across Julian's skin. Sure was a lot of death and dark energy orbiting around them.

He couldn't help but wonder if their poking around would backfire. If they were asking too many questions, the wrong questions, getting on the radars of those who would harm them.

His phone rang, rattling against the table. Itchy tributaries of adrenaline frayed his already taxed nerves. In his peripheral vision, the snake's tapered green tail slipped inside a hollow rock.

Julian sighed and went to his cell, grimacing when he looked at the glowing screen. According to a digit wrapped in parentheses beside the caller's number, this person had called four times today.

He swallowed a thick gulp and touched the circle to answer. "Hello?"

A young guy answered in a clipped tone, "Julian Nez, you are a hard man to reach. This is Alan Witt from the Witt Gallery. Please tell me you aren't pulling out of the exhibition on Friday, because I really need that paperwork. Need, as in needed yesterday."

Shit. He'd completely forgotten that the hip, up-and-coming gallery agreed to devote a special exhibit to his work over the upcoming weekend. Various big shot dealers and agents were sure to be in attendance. A boon to his career and a chance at visibility that local artists competed for, and the golden opportunity had completely escaped his mind.

"Of course not. I've had a lot going on this week, but I'll email you those signed documents tonight."

"Tonight works." Alan hung up.

Julian tossed the phone on the table. He couldn't blow it with the gallery and risk someone influential like Alan Witt blackballing him. The art community was connected, and even after he moved to Peru, he'd need to maintain his good name in order to hang on to his livelihood.

Insidious conspiracy or no, he still had to work, had to fund the trip to Peru and amass a war chest of starter money to pull from while he adjusted to South America. He ought to check in with Tim soon. Less than two weeks until the equinox, and he hadn't bought a plane ticket, let alone packed. Peru mattered to him, meaning he wouldn't allow the moving goal to fade. So he'd better not blow it with this exhibit.

"Can I use your computer for a minute?" he called out.

"Yeah. On my desk." She rattled off login credentials and the name of the Wi-Fi network.

Several clicks and an e-signature later, Julian emailed the art exhibit paperwork.

A clattering sound came from the bathroom.

Julian walked down the hallway and knocked on the door. "You need anything?"

When Taylor didn't reply, he knocked again.

"You alright?" He heard the fear in his voice, spiked and elevated, and his body responded with a new dump of stress chemicals.

"Come in and see this for yourself." She spoke in a flat tone, so matter-of-fact as to be chilling. Iced dread washed over him, his amorphous fear crystalizing into a problem with no name.

He opened the door and gasped. Taylor sat on the closed toilet lid. She held a razor blade in one bloody hand, and bright red streams flowed from an impact site on each arm. Her blood dripped scarlet, shocking white tile with obscene splatter stains.

His heart shattered. The trauma of the incident in the secret room hit her harder than he thought. What a clueless jerk he'd been, to miss the signs that she was suicidal. Julian pawed the toilet paper roll, tore off two wads, and held them to her wounds.

"I'm so sorry, Taylor." He knelt on the floor in front of her. "I had no idea."

At least she hadn't lost much blood, so they weren't facing an acute life or death crisis.

He'd have to proceed with care and caution, though, to get her the medical and mental help she needed without coming off as insensitive and risking alienating her.

"It's not what you think." She met him with steeled blue eyes and calm clarity of purpose. "This is a positive development. We're getting somewhere."

"What?" His stunned reply tumbled out. Confusion moved through his head in scrambled signals as he applied gentle pressure with his thumbs.

"I didn't self-harm. Not in the way you're thinking." She opened one hand. In her crimson-streaked palm lay two microchips, each about the size of a pinhead.

"You pulled those out of your body." Coming down from his initial horror, he noticed tweezers on the ground beside rubbing alcohol and cotton balls.

"I can't have them tracking me anymore. You saw that monitor in the hidden room. Heard what Donnie said. In addition to everything else with the symbols and programming, they're watching me. Following my movements. Or they were. And now they know I'm off the grid, and exactly where I was when I took myself offline."

"Meaning we can't stay here. God knows who'll show up at your door."

She gave a slow, solemn nod. Her lips pressed into a line. "I know someone who might be able to help us."

He kept the compress on her wounds. "You need a doctor."

She went to the medicine cabinet, spotty tissue sticking to her cuts as she set the blade and chips on top of the toilet. She winced and whimpered as she rummaged in a small plastic box. "I'm fine. The implants were close to the surface, so I didn't have to go deep. It looks worse than it is."

"It looks pretty bad." While he spoke the words, gravid with multiple meanings, his gaze slid from the bloodied chunks of metal on the toilet tank to where Taylor cleaned her arms with a wet wipe and dressed her injuries in gauze and medical tape.

She closed the cabinet door and made eye contact in the mirror. "I know."

He laid his hands on her shoulders and brushed his lips to the back of her head. Shoving doubt aside, he said, "Let's leave tonight. I have a contact in Peru from my research on the clans. They'll take us in. We can get as far away from this as possible, as fast as possible."

"No. It'll never work. We can't just run off. Besides, I don't have to tell you that there are trip logistics to plan for. Vaccines, papers, packing. I know you well enough to know that you have a plan worked out, and you don't want to show up down there disorganized and frazzled. It'll kill your credibility and ruin any rapport you've built. To say nothing of having a random stranger in tow."

The part where she said she knew him gave him a rush. Despite the blood and bleakness surrounding them, he fought a smile and lost. "You're no random stranger, Taylor."

"I'm aware." The tiniest glint of pleasure came to her eye. "But you take my point, to them, I would be. You won't be able to live with yourself if you botch this Peru thing and they ask you to leave. I can tell the possibility of finding a home there means a lot to you."

"You mean a lot to me, too." Those words came easily and naturally, but he struggled with the next ones. "Forget Peru. We'll go somewhere else. Back to Arizona, to the reservation."

He could handle that. Yeah. Julian loved his family, his people, all those scrappy rez dogs. He could re-adjust to the lean living he'd grown up with if he had to. Going home didn't have to mean going backwards. He could always sell his art and crafts to tourists passing through on their way to and from the Grand Canyon, which was how he'd started out. So what if he'd have to weave dreamcatchers all day long and answer ignorant questions? Taylor was worth it.

"Come on, Julian. I refuse to be the reason that you put your life on hold. If you let go of this Peru plan, you won't be able to live with yourself. You'll always be wondering what if."

Well, she had his number. "I'm pretty easy to read, huh?"

She leaned into him, her muscles loosening against his midsection. The slackening of her body into his gave him a fleeting glimpse of domestic happiness.

"You're open, which is a good quality. But more to the point, I can't run from this when I don't have any idea who is chasing me or why. We both know that."

He breathed in her sweet smell and swallowed his urge to pull up stakes. Peru would be there, and he'd figure out how to work Taylor into his plan and do so the right way.

As usual, she was right. Showing up in Peru unprepared and unannounced could come off erratic, and spooking the shifter clan with random behavior and an uninvited guest was the last thing he wanted to do. He was still gaining their trust, establishing himself as a trustworthy person, and antics reeking of desperation and trouble could backfire badly.

"Who do you know who can help us?" he rubbed the tops of her arms, giving warmth.

She left the bathroom, then walked back in with a chunky, outdated-looking cell phone resting against her ear. "My best friend is a robotics engineer. She has enough training in technology to look at these chips and at least be able to give a ballpark estimate of what they are and what they're doing."

Taylor paced, her bare heel smearing a streak of blood across the tile.

Julian took a moment to comprehend the sheer darkness of their situation. He didn't have to tell her how fucked up this all was, but he cared about her and would fight by her side regardless.

A muffled feminine voice came through the line.

Taylor said, "Ange? Can you meet me at your lab in thirty minutes? It's an emergency, but I'm okay for now. I'll explain in a minute. I'll have someone with me."

Ange must've said yes, because Taylor gave a curt nod.

She hung up and pressed the phone to her chest. "Ready?"

"Born that way." He slapped the outsides of his thighs, a wormy sensation crawling between his ribs. What would they find in this lab? Probably nothing good. But not good didn't equal useless, and they could both use facts.

The remains of a sarcastic laugh popped from her parted lips. "The disaster keeps getting crazier. Believe me, I get it. But I wanted to let you know that I appreciate you. I realize it's tough to play it cool right now, but you've been doing a stellar job."

She wet a washcloth, tossed it on the floor, and cleaned the blood by moving her foot around.

"We're in this together." He meant it, all the way.

If he wanted to get to Peru free and unencumbered, with or without Taylor, he'd better do what he could to get both of them out from under this plot. Once safe from harm, they could re-evaluate their personal situation.

As she stooped to gather her used home surgery supplies and toss them in a waste bin, Taylor sliced Julian a look so earnest her stare nearly knocked him flat. "Thank you. I mean that. But if at any point it gets to be too much, and you're freaked out and feel like you need to leave, don't hesitate to tap out. I can do this alone."

He caught one of her hands and pulled her to her feet. "I know. But I'm choosing to stay. Because you don't *have* to do this alone."

She pressed her belly to his and wrapped her arms around his back in a hug that unveiled many concepts. Care. Worry. Affection. Perhaps even the stirrings of deeper, albeit inconvenient, romantic emotions. Emotions that, regrettably, didn't factor into the equation.

"Thank you, Julian." Her sweet drawl trembled right below the surface toughness.

"You bet." He rubbed a hand up and down her spine, encouraging her to seek solace in his larger, stronger body. Maybe they'd get lucky someday and those deeper emotions could blossom. "Now let's roll."

She changed into a long-sleeved cotton shirt, packed quickly, and transferred her snake to a plastic travel case along with bedding and water.

"I'm going to ask Angie if it's okay to stay with her for a couple of days." Preoccupied by fumbling with pet accessories, Taylor didn't meet his gaze, though a gentleness smoothed the edges of her next words, "Would you want to spend the night, too, if she's cool with it?"

Julian took the animal crate by the handle as Taylor locked the door, figuring he could run home for a change of clothes in the morning and take her to his place and the upcoming art festival he'd signed up for. "Yes, I would."

He ought not to let her out of his sight. Tendering this intention without words, he laid his free hand on the small of her back while she locked the front door.

Her genuine smile, the way she leaned in to his protective, territorial touch, told him what he needed to know. She was strong and brave, but having him around permitted her to take a break from looking out for herself. That was his job—to be her rock if she needed one.

An uneventful car ride offered a tour of a few trendy Austin streets along the route to the university campus.

As they passed a famous local burger joint, Taylor's stomach growled.

She took one hand off the steering wheel and laid it over her navel area. "What an obnoxious noise."

Even in the dim lighting of her car, he caught sight of her cheeks pinking and felt empathy for her. Hunger was no joke. "You don't need to be embarrassed around me. When was the last time you ate?"

She chewed her lip, glancing at the fast-food spot while stopping at a red light. "I had my iced latte this morning and some orange juice. I've been forgetting meals."

"Understandable. I'm starving too. Pull on in."

She grinned and hung a sharp left, sliding in to the drive through. "I like when you tell me what to do."

"Do you now?" He affected a gruff rumble in his voice, remembering the fun they'd had in his bedroom. A glimmer of excitement bloomed below his belt. A repeat performance sure might help them forget their woes for an hour or two.

"I've been meaning to ask you about that." Her window slid down to face a menu board.

"Welcome to Stan's, I'll be with you in a moment." The voice of a young man came through the intercom along with gurgling static.

"Ask me about what?" Julian allowed himself a glimpse at Taylor's legs peeking out beneath polka dot shorts. Just because they were in trouble didn't mean he'd stopped being attracted to her. Didn't mean he'd stopped wanting her.

Before she responded, a musky-sweet aroma danced to his nose. His pulse quickened, and his chest swelled. She was sexually excited. Whatever thought was in her head had excited her. He loosened the part of his seatbelt stretched across his lap.

Her gaze was downright seductive as she turned to him, baring her throat with an upward tilt of her chin. Ambient yellow light from the outdoor security lamp guided his focus to her slender neck and down to a plane of peachy skin disappearing into the front of her tank top.

His hungry eyes roved back up to her gorgeous face, those eyes and ears and lips. Short hair looked amazing on Taylor, too, really complemented her pointed features and carved bone structure.

She licked her lips. "Does calling me your bitch and having me say it have some significance to you as a shifter, or does it just get you off?"

His breathing sped to a panting rhythm as thoughts of sex won the battle for his headspace. He welcomed their victory. "You got off on it too."

"For sure. But you *really* got off on the whole bitch in heat thing, didn't you?"

"Excuse me." Through the intercom, the teenage employee's voice cracked, and he blubbered a nervous laugh. "Are you, um, ready to order?"

Taylor covered her mouth, laughed, and whispered to Julian, "To be continued. You can order first. I'm still deciding."

"I sure hope there's a continuation." He leaned forward, taking the opportunity to stroke the velvet skin of Taylor's upper leg while he perused the menu. Best to pick something halfway sensible and not make a bad impression on her by coming across as a slob unconcerned with his health. "How about a grilled chicken sandwich with avocado and a bottle of water. What do you want, baby?"

He kissed her cheek. No harm in pretending they were out on a simple date, two people getting to know each other over flirting and food. Soon, he'd take her on a real date at an actual fancy restaurant. Someday, they'd be able to relax and be together. He hoped. The hope was all he had.

"I'll take the X-treme Bacon Blast Son of the Meat Monster Double Cheeseburger, large fry, and a large chocolate malt." She winked. "No shame in my game."

A chuckle possessed him, and he let it fill the car. He'd cherish their moment of stolen respite until the latest insidious development snatched it away. For now, though, he unwound.

"That'll be nineteen-ninety-six."

"I wasn't even born yet then." Taylor pulled forward, a look of sly mischief pulling at the corners of her lips and eyes.

"I plead the fifth," Julian said.

"Lucky for you I have bigger daddy issues than Luke Skywalker."

"Darth Vadar seems to be an apt comparison for your old man."

Though she said nothing, her entire energy field corroded as she grabbed two brown bags from a clean-cut guy in a visor. Hand shaking and jaw tight, she set the food on her lap and reached for her purse. "Ha. Yeah, totally."

Normally tempting aromas of French fry grease and grilled meat failed to entice him, though. No, his appetite fled and made room for an unpleasant and shameful realization. He'd come off like a complete asshole by speaking of a sore subject in a jesting manner.

He really needed to practice some tact and delicacy. Spending the last ten-plus years around people whose feelings he didn't care much about had atrophied his sensitivity muscle.

"Hey, I'm sorry. I didn't mean to make light of what you're going through with your family. My humor isn't always kind, and I apologize for hurting you."

"It's fine, it's me. My shit, my stuff. I started it." Her tone shook in time with her hand, and she fumbled in her handbag and took out her wallet.

A clear bubble floated to his surface, a mild epiphany of sorts. Money symbolized a helluva a lot to Taylor: love, loyalty, affection, gratitude. What she felt she couldn't express in words, she communicated via cash proxy.

He would honor her love language.

He caught her wrist with one hand and lifted her chin with two fingers with his opposite hand. "Allow me."

Once, while reading in the library, Julian had stumbled across a profound concept called an enthymeme. Coined by ancient Greek philosophers, the term was a fancy way of saying that the most important part of a sentence isn't always what's said, but what's left unspoken. And, if the other party gets the significance of meaning in the unspoken part, a strong bond forges between speaker and listener.

Allow me in. Allow me to take care of you. Allow me to support you. Allow me.

Her eyes moistened. "Thank you."

The raw sound of her whisper hit him right in the heart. He pulled his wallet from the back pocket of his pants, plucked out two tens, and paid the lanky kid hanging out of the window. "Any time."

Without a word, she vaulted over the center console and took him with a kiss powerful enough to erase his mind.

As her firm, wet tongue probed and stroked and his repaid in kind, grand emotions soared in Julian. Right then, he was done. Any remaining defenses inside him crumbled. Fault lines cracked, giving way for a bubbling eureka made of equal parts terror and euphoria.

Their fates were sealed. The kiss joined them in union, a communion as binding as any contract.

There was no going backwards anymore, only headlong into battle.

TEN

"Thanks, Ange." Taylor said with a swell of gratitude. She followed her best friend down the basement corridor of the lab, soles of her sandals and Angie's tennis shoes squeaking against linoleum.

"Sure." Angie's mane of black box braids swished near the back pockets of her jeans.

Julian's boot heels clicked their accompanying rhythm as the trio commenced a grim march to what she hoped would be clarity.

A cramp pinched Taylor's side while she trailed a few feet behind, and she paused to rub her hand in a circle over the pain. Not the best idea to eat a heavy Stan's meal while under extreme stress, but then again, the comfort food had been a relief at the time.

Indigestion was the price she'd paid for a few minutes of escape into sensory pleasure and a little relaxed enjoyment with Julian. It was worth it, and her digestive system would have to deal.

"You feeling okay?" Julian slowed his pace at her side and stroked her back.

She masked a wince as a new, denser discomfort coalesced near her waistband. Solid, like a hot rock in her lower belly.

What type of reaction would cause such a feeling? Bad meat? The onset of a dietary allergy? "Yeah. Just ate too much."

Taylor resumed her motions with careful steps, though the pain persisted.

She tried to distract herself by taking in her surroundings. A centralized cooling system emitted a low-grade electronic buzz as it circulated air tinged with lemony cleaning products and lab chemicals. The sterile, vaguely hospital-like atmosphere managed to make her feel worse, though. Like a patient.

One foot in front of the other, she kept going. From a room down the hall, Whitesnake's *Here I Go Again* wailed at midlevel while a male voice sang along out of key.

Laminated posters of white coat scientists brightened drab cinderblock walls, scientific legitimacy to outweigh the goofy hair metal and uninhibited karaoke. Overhead, halogen bulbs lit the space with the murky glow of an aquarium. Appropriately creepy given what they were about to do. Taylor gave up on redirecting her negative thoughts.

Angie unlocked a door. "You sure you're okay Tay? You look kinda tired and greenish." Angie's voice took on its worried, sisterly tone.

"Honestly, I don't know. I'm okay for now, I guess." Taylor wasn't even talking about the cramp, though the more she thought about it, the worse it throbbed.

Her heart sunk with the onset of a new, bad possibility. Food poisoning was the last thing she needed.

"Not a reassuring answer." Angie's dark brown eyes bounced between Taylor and Julian. "Who's this, by the way? You forgot to introduce us."

Angie's inquiry invited reflection on their relationship status, but now wasn't the time to ponder the "what are we" question. "This is Julian Nez. He has a stake in what's happening here. Julian, this is Angie. She and I were dorm roommates freshman year."

Angie hummed a sound full of nostalgia as she pushed open the thick metal door. "Remember the crap we threw together to fuel those late-night study sessions? We made the weirdest concoctions. Chocolate pudding with coffee grounds and candy mixed in. Pop Tart milkshakes, hot dog sandwiches smothered by canned cheese."

No doubt, Angie brought up their past in an attempt to cheer Taylor up. Ange was good at positivity, and her effort worked. Surprisingly, memories of gross food experiments didn't worsen Taylor's gastrointestinal issue.

"Oh yeah. Then there was the time you put Gummy Bears in the blender with lemonade and cola." Taylor forced the smile her best friend was striving to pull from her.

Angie's eyes narrowed in play-disdain. "That was you, Tay. And nice to meet you, Mr. Tall, Dark, and Handsome."

"Nice to meet you." Julian offered his hand, and Angie shook.

Her red lips quirking, Angie turned around and held the door open by pressing her back into it. "Look at you with your firm handshake and polite greeting. Got any single friends?"

"Nobody good enough to date. Hit me up after I move. I'll know a bunch of cool people then."

The Peru reference kindled a pain in Taylor's chest. Time to change the subject before unwelcome emotions messed with her mind. "I'm going to cut right to the chase. My dad is involved in some batshit project, and he's drawn me into it in the most outlandish way imaginable."

Angie scowled. "Oh dear God. What kind of crazy is your family up in now?"

Save for Chloe and of course Taylor, Angie had never liked the McClures. She'd come over for dinner once and said being there caused a strange disturbance in her force that she couldn't pinpoint. The whole house felt steeped in unease and malaise, Angie had explained, like a murder or other atrocity happened there and corpses decayed beneath the floorboards. And Angie was a scientist to her core, not a superstitious person whatsoever.

Perhaps her intuition wasn't far off. Who knew anymore?

"Microchips. I had microchip implants put in my arms without my knowledge. They were making me hallucinate and causing all of these odd pains, but they're out now."

Hallucinations no longer worked as an explanation in light of the office discovery, but Taylor ought to parcel out facts in increments. Asking Angie to accept a big info dump of wild paranormal things could backfire. Her well-meaning friend could run to the nearest mental health professional in a misguided effort to help.

Once her friend made a diagnosis of those chips, Taylor could proceed with caution and add more details on a need-to-know basis.

As she tucked a ring of keys in her back pocket, Angie clucked her tongue. "Let's take a look."

No second guessing, no emotional reactions, just goal-oriented efficiency. Taylor loved Angie for her straightforward approach to problem solving. Ange would make a great leader one day.

"Perfect." The first glimpse of a microscope caused jitters of nervous anticipation to take flight in Taylor's system. Answers were coming.

Julian beside her, Taylor followed Angie into a laboratory where hulking devices and dissected electronic equipment covered metal tables in an explosion of steel parts and tangled wires.

Angie led them to her work station, a corner table decorated with a picture from her cousin's wedding, a cluster of travel mugs, and flier advertising a conference for Black engineers.

While Angie sat on a stool and turned a dial on a microscope, Taylor's cramp morphed into a scarier, far more foreign sensation. Like some internal organ moved up and over, and another one slipped low to accommodate the repositioning. Her breath froze. Her blood chilled.

Fear sprinted through her in streaks, collapsing her focus to her body. She visualized her liver, her intestines, the rest of the parts filling her abdominal cavity. Was she suffering from a hernia? Or did organs ever detach from their placements and float unmoored? Was that a thing? Because it sure felt like it.

It felt like the sensation that had rushed in before she'd had her second attack of words and symbols that happened right after jumping out of Julian's bed.

Despite the tumult in her midsection, she lacked illness symptoms. No fever or dizziness, no fatigue or headache to corroborate a ho-hum explanation.

"Hand them over." Angie slid a glass square under a lens.

The inner movement stilled, but when the unseen agitation ceased, restlessness in Taylor's skull took over as if her brain squirmed. Shock and curiosity competed with fear. She smelled her own musky sweat under powdery deodorant and settled into dismal acceptance.

Whatever was happening to her wasn't normal or routine. This simple concept was devastating in its alien, unfathomable ambiguity. "Hand what over?"

"Um. The chips." Angie's eyes widened. "Hey Tay, do you need a pain pill? Cause you look kind of chewed up and spit out."

Julian took one of Taylor's hands in his larger, warm one and stared into her eyes with the mellow composure of a doctor performing an examination. "She's right. You might be going into shock from the cutting or blood loss. Let's drop the implants off and get you to Urgent Care."

"Wait, cutting? As in you pulled the chips out of your body yourself?" Angie drew back. Her jaw fell.

"Yes, but I'm fine. Not in shock. It's heartburn. And I'm staying to see this."

Yet now her arms and legs ached, a dull pulse thrumming deep in her bones. She forced herself to run down the possibilities with as much clinical detachment as she could muster. Not a heart attack, stroke, or seizure. Her symptoms fit no profile.

She'd ruled out organ failure when her mind halted the process of mundane medical elimination in a disturbing epiphany.

Angie puffed up her cheeks and blew out air, sliding Julian a distraught look.

Taylor looked at her friend, then her lover, as a silent realization spread between the three. Time crawled to a creep. A new rock song traveled through the walls; the faint grind of electric guitars incongruous in its upbeat cheesiness.

"Your body has to be reacting to the chips being out," Julian said. He cupped her face in both hands and studied her once again, his timbre a controlled inferno of mitigated dread. "Changing or adapting in response to whatever they were doing to you. Try not to panic. For all we know, an elevated heart rate or other heightened physical response could worsen the reaction."

The painful tugging sensation returned to her ears, pulling and pulling. Her blood heated, alternating swells of hot and cold flowing and ebbing like tides.

She chanced a glimpse at herself in a shiny piece of lab equipment and rode a wave of fright mingled with fascination.

Her features looked different, not the same. More tapered. Longer. Eyes wider apart.

Before her own amazed eyes, she changed into an uncanny facsimile of herself.

Taylor thrust a hand in her purse, pinched the envelope, and shook the two ominous bits of blood-flecked metal into her friend's palm. "Ange, please get these under your lens STAT."

A silent, collective non-sound of three people holding their breaths threaded the trio together into one tense collective. They were horror movie spectators united in despair.

Angie placed the chips on the glass plate and pushed them into position. She circled a grip above Taylor's elbow while Julian squeezed her hand.

"We've got you, Taylor. I promise to tell you everything I know based on what I see. Keep in mind I'm not a nanotech specialist, but with any luck, my training will suffice to provide an accurate assessment. Can you do your best to remain calm for me?" Angie said.

Taylor nodded, her heart hammering in her ears.

Julian adjusted his fingers, threading their hold into an interlaced, intimate grip. "You'll get through this. We'll get through this."

All she could do was nod again while Angie bent down and looked into her eyepiece.

Taylor's mouth dried. Her breath sped. She wasn't so anxious that she didn't notice the symptoms anymore, but they took a blessed leave into the background of her perception.

Silence mummified time. Taylor fixed a hard gaze on the back of her friend's head and clutched Julian's hand with an increasingly sweaty palm. At least she wasn't going through her ordeal alone. He was right about that, and she was blessed to have them both in her life.

"One chip is familiar to me right off the bat," Angie finally said, her somber cadence fit for delivering bad news. "I learned about it at a conference last summer. It's a tracking chip outfitted with a retinal or iris scanner in addition to your more basic RFID and GPS technology. In layman's terms, there's a tiny mechanical eye in this chip, and when light hits it, it communicates the signal to your real eye. Turning those outfitted with it into a living camcorder and capturing their point of view in real time."

Tendrils of horror slithered over Taylor. "To what end?"

"Last I heard, it was in the beta testing phase, with designs to market it to farmers. So they could track and recover expensive livestock if the animals got loose. If they use this product, all the farmers have to do is synch the tracking device with apps on their phones or computer software and see at a glance the precise location where the cow or horse ran off to. Or the land of the person who stole the cow or horse. All accomplished through a wireless transmitter. Stands to reason that it would have a military application such as spycraft, but if so, such a usage is still classified. I'd think because turning people into video recorders would amount to a clusterfuck of human rights violations."

The bitter hurt of betrayal overrode Taylor's physical symptoms. "So I rank with livestock, eh? Lovely. Screw my human rights, I guess. Do you remember the name of the company promoting it at the conference?"

"I remember their logo. Hold up." Angie rooted in a drawer, pulled out a magazine, and flipped to a classified page near the end. She pointed to a small advertisement. The name Scarab Inc., an email, and a graphic of a black beetle whose shell gleamed with an iridescent green sheen filled the square.

Julian snapped a picture with his phone. "Looks like an Egyptian scarab beetle. They symbolize transformation, change, death, and rebirth."

Taylor swallowed. Her pulse dropped to a natural resting state. Her father and brother had mentioned that name while fighting in the study. The connection between her father and what was happening to her was clearer than ever. Shining a light on actual details relieved the worst of her distress. She had to scramble for optimism wherever possible, guard her sanity, but at least they were no longer imprisoned in a black cube of unknown scariness. "Scarab Inc. Okay. Do they manufacture any products besides surveillance technology?"

Angie went online through her phone. "Yep. They're a freaking octopus with ties to private prisons, staffing solutions and personnel management, and defensive battlefield equipment like bulletproof vests.

Get this. They even own a company that makes nutritional supplements. How random is that?"

Near the front of her mind, pieces snapped into place. She turned to Julian, chewing her bottom lip. "When I went over to my parents' house to confront my dad about the things I was seeing, he tried to foist this ionized water on me. I didn't think much of it at the time, but then my mom took supplements and went all mind wiped. I think some ingredient in the water was supposed to erase my memory."

"Yeah, she was for sure not all there at the party," Julian said. "So the water or supplements could be designed to complement the technology. Re-up the programming."

"Holy shit," Angie added in a hushed drawl replete with disbelief. "The other chip, you guys. I can't believe I'm seeing one up close."

Taylor's knees wobbled. The abrupt bodily response rerouted her attention back to the storm inside, where an organ near her pelvis knotted and twisted.

Her center of gravity dropped in a disorienting plummet. A cracking sound ricocheted through her, followed by a painless click. Another followed it, a joint adjusting in an airy snap. She shuddered and heard herself vocalize a soft grunt.

"It's going to be okay." Julian spoke with a soothing, calm cadence.

Sounded like he knew something she didn't, which was more than a little unnerving.

"I've got you. Look at me and hold on to me, and if I give you directions, do your best to follow them." He petted her hair.

She jerked her head and looked up into his caring brown eyes. Her mind spun. Directions for what? "Do you know what's happening to me?"

His Adam's apple bobbed. "I think so. Let's hear what Angie has to say. I don't want to jump to any conclusions."

Cued, Angie resumed speaking. "Chip two is still in the experimental and design phase. Or so I thought. This type of implant acts upon the body on a biological, molecular level. It tricks the body and mind into behaving differently. The little pouches in there contain synthetic biomimicry agents that communicate chemically with the host body and learn of its unique makeup. It's thought to be the world's first intelligent, self-aware microchip. A microscopic artificial intelligence. Once it apprehends information on your DNA, it modifies and re-releases the altered data back into the host cells."

"M...modifies DNA how?" After Taylor pushed out the breathless question, her jaw wouldn't go back up. Her perception contracted. Dismay bombarded her veins in inky spurts.

She tried to set the lower half of her mouth back into place, but it wiggled like flab. Dislocated. And the joint kept stretching on its own volition. Wider, wider, tendons strained and fiery. Her stomach soured.

Julian wrapped Taylor in a bear hug and rocked her. "Breathe and ride the wave. Don't fight it, and don't panic."

"Fight what?" Her speech, compromised by the loose hinge, came out garbled. Her heart lurched, and two warm streams slid down her cheeks.

"It's okay." He rocked and rocked. "I'll help you control and manage the changes."

Angie turned around and gasped. Her face paled to an ashy hue, and her mouth and eyes stretched to Os.

"Angie, stay calm," Julian said with even, booming authority. "She's shifting her shape, and it must relate to how the second chip altered her DNA. Can you tell us any more?"

Angie slapped a hand over her gaping mouth and returned to the machine. Now, her voice trembled. "From my understanding, the specific modification depends on the program used, and its desired outcome. The first place they want to try it out is in the military. The idea is to make super soldiers. Guys who can run a hundred miles an hour, rip enemy bodies apart with their bare hands, take a magazine full of bullets and keep fighting. Go invisible, teleport even. Mind control and brainwashing designs are in the mix, too, along with more benign stuff. Treating cancer and degenerative diseases. Early models such as this can perform one, maybe two mental or physical modification functions. I can't tell how this one has been used because it's sustained corrosion from prolonged activity." Angie started to speak again and trailed off.

"You look like you have more to say," Julian said.

In a hushed tone, Angie said, "There are ingredients in here that I can't identify. A phosphorescent sheen covering the entire chip like smoke, or a cloud. And some kind of symbol glowing under the smoke. A red hand in an upside-down triangle. I have no idea how anyone was able to program something like that into a microchip."

That's the magic. The bad magic. Taylor failed to turn her thoughts into words as a blanket of hot air smothered her nose and mouth. A vise gripped her lungs. Her ears rang. Vision blurred, graying. Tears wet her lips with salty rivulets. Her essence became a world of pain and fear.

Once she could endure no more, she screamed, a primordial wail begging for relief that tore a ragged path up her throat.

Snaps and cracks, pops of bone and joint and muscle made for a ghastly gunfire chorus.

Her balance failed. She hung on to Julian's solid warmth, his strength and personal scent, as he tumbled to the ground right along with her, acting as an anchor of support.

A second high-pitched scream joined her own, a short squeak of terror.

Julian's breath peppered the shell of her ear with warm tickles. "Focus on drawing the wolf inward and putting her into a compartment for now. Do this with as much concentration as you can muster. Pull her in, back and up, like you're sucking in the biggest breath you've ever taken."

She obeyed, slurping air in three erratic sucks. Her ability to see returned in a scramble of bleeding colors, and she focused on Julian's eyes until the twin brown orbs brought stability.

"Hold her there. Right where you have her. Now visualize her as a ball of light, and your subconscious as a bunch of rooms. Put her in one of those rooms and tell her in an assertive tone to *stay*. So just like a pet dog, she knows who's in charge and to stay in her kennel until you're ready to let her out. You are the alpha of the two."

Taylor pictured a floating, fuzzy sphere, an incandescent glowing snowball. She concentrated and marshalled every ounce of her energy to move the wad of light down, down, down deeper until it hovered near the floor of a compartment.

Stay.

The sentient glow gave off a passive, submissive vibration and stayed put.

Taylor's symptoms left in a rush of ecstasy; the frenzy of tension undone.

She struggled to regulate her breathing and reacquainted herself with the normal lab surroundings. A miniature basketball hoop hung from the front door. Someone had written the words "now entering the nerd zone" in white chalk on a green chalkboard. Cold sweat glued Taylor's clothes to her shaking body.

Angie gawked, both hands plastered to her nose and lips.

Once she could form words without hyperventilating, Taylor spoke. "What happened to me?"

"You turned into a wolf," Angie said in a tinny squawk through the gaps in her fingers.

Bitter bile surged in her throat. Her own father had put transmitters in her body. Scarab sorcerers cast a dark magic spell on them, and they'd mutated her into an animal and filled her head with witchcraft symbolism.

Why? Was she nothing more than a toy, an experiment for her dad and his buddies to test their cool new tech toys on? No. There had to be more. This was connected to Julian, to what he claimed he could do.

His lips brushing against her temple, Julian spoke, "A gorgeous white wolf with eyes like sapphires. She was regal. So are you. We'll figure this out together."

"Okay." But the word she spoke was the last thing Taylor felt. This madness with those chips was the farthest possible thing from okay.

For the moment, though, she melted into his hug, the comfort of his big arms and muscled chest, allowing him to take care of her. For now, she'd accept the pleasure of his touch and the reassuring promises flowing from his kind voice.

She'd sit crumpled on the lab floor until she was strong enough to get back up and fight.

But soon she'd get back on her feet. Once there, she'd fight for the truth. And she wouldn't stop until she made whoever did this to her pay.

ELEVEN

JULIAN TOSSED THE DUFFEL BAG FULL OF TAYLOR'S CLOTHES ON HIS BED and made his way to the dining room.

She sat at his kitchen table and read off a laptop screen. Her pet lounged in his travel case.

He pulled up a chair beside her, the scrape of metal against tile piercing pregnant silence.

As much as he liked having Taylor around, and that she'd asked to stay with him instead of Angie, they had to figure out a sustainable long-term arrangement. They had to figure out a lot of things pertaining to their new reality.

First and foremost, they had to figure out whether they had a future together. If so, she'd have to face some major life changes alongside him.

But since he'd seen her shift before his eyes, figured out firsthand that she was one of his kind? He wouldn't let her out of his life without fighting for their budding bond. He'd known since he'd first seen her, on some primal level residing in the most ancient parts of him, that she was one of his kind.

Though he'd nursed an inkling since their first encounter, now that he'd seen her transformation, seen the sapphire eyes of her wolf staring back at him with their plea for guidance, support? The pull was electric, undeniable, as fierce as her beast's potential. He wanted to hold her in his arms and never let go. Never let one single thing stop him from loving his mate in a protective embrace until he exhaled for the final time.

A glimpse at his wall calendar made him jerk when he spotted the words "call Tim" written in red ink over the day's date. Speaking of long-term arrangements, he'd better put in some work soon to prevent the Peru operation from fading. They weren't going to beg him to come, meaning he needed to stay motivated and proactive.

For now, though, he turned his attention to Taylor and took her hand. "Any leads?"

She lowered the laptop lid a few inches and offered him a weak smile. "Sure, but they all take me down the conspiracy tunnel. Hard to tell real from false when you're in there."

"Well, we know one thing that's true. You shifted right in front of me and Angie. Two witnesses. And you felt it in your body. And your alteration must connect to those chips coming out. Can't be coincidental."

She looked off into space, the shards of afternoon light streaming in through the windows highlighting her tired expression, the bags under her eyes. "I was a camera, taking footage of presumably you so I could capture you. But also, I was being genetically modified by the other chip. Made into a wolf, or while it was in there, it stopped me from shifting. And then there was the symbol and the words and screams. Why? To what end? I have a lot of pieces of evidence, but I lack reasons."

Seeing her spinning in circles like this, grasping for answers and ending up with even more questions, knotted him in sympathy. Taylor needed a break, some rest, a chance to relax. But odds were, respite wasn't coming any time soon. He'd do his best to ease the strain on her, even if he couldn't offer much more than encouragement.

"I'm not sure it all matters anymore. The chips are out, so that's done. We saw how your body reacted, and I can help you weather the changes. Our primary concern right now is your safety."

He swallowed, preparing his next words. If he pressured her too hard to accompany him to Peru, she might spook. But the more he weighed their options, the fewer tenable choices remained in play, and he wasn't about to leave her well-being to chance. "Whoever was watching you knows where I live."

She sighed and drummed her fingers on the table. "Yeah. So why haven't they just come by and kidnapped you? It's like my function was to open some doorway in the backyard and pull down that creepy spirit. So are we safe as long as we don't go back into your hogan, or are we safe now that I'm deactivated? Alternatively, we could be completely unsafe from the next attack. It might be lying in wait. Too many loose ends."

"I'm gonna get in touch with my Peru contact." Julian walked to his desk and slid his own laptop off the spot by the printer table. He opened up the machine and logged on to video chat. "Maybe he can explain some of this madness if he has a frame of reference."

"You sure it's safe to talk about the details over the Internet?"

"Nope, I'm not sure." A brand icon in the middle of the screen jiggled while a ring came through. "But right now, all I can think of is to turn to someone else for help. Because from where I'm standing, it seems as if we're in short supply of allies, clarity, or facts we can use to protect ourselves."

"Fair enough." She rested her head on his shoulder, a gesture of affection that made him sigh with pleasure. He and Taylor's bodies fit together, gravitated to each other, in the most natural way imaginable.

He draped his arm around her back, both for their mutual comfort and to ensure Tim got the correct impression of him and Taylor as a strong, united front.

The screen flickered from black to color, a pixelated but decent quality feed showing a man's bare feet at the end of a swaying hammock. In the background, leafy vegetation draped the frame in verdant sheets.

"Jules my man," Tim said with his trademark high spirits. "How's it going, and who's the lovely lady?"

"Pretty good, man, pretty alright. This is Taylor. She's one of us."

A flurry of motion blurred the image, and when the action halted, Julian was face-to-face with Tim. The shifter in Peru wore a ball cap and a wide-eyed expression of surprise on his smooth brown face. From the looks of his reaction, Tim got the gist. Good. If Tim knew that Julian knew that the Peruvians were shifters, then all concerned could proceed with a new level of openness and honesty. No more holding back or secrets, forget all subterfuge or tiptoeing.

"For real?" Tim brought his phone close to his face.

Taylor nodded. "For real."

"You can vouch for this woman, Julian?"

"Absolutely. And I take it we're all on the same page as to what we're discussing."

"Yeah. We like to keep things discreet for as long as possible. Mostly to weed out the fakes and furries, not to mention zoophiles and other assorted perverts looking to creep on the women. You'd be surprised at the motley crew of undesirables and nutcases who've tried to ingratiate themselves into our community before we got stringent about vetting."

"I take it I've been given the green light."

Tim's smile combined friendliness with a leader's power play. "Someone contacted one of your tribal elders last week and had a long conversation. I'm of Ute ancestry myself, from Utah, so I'm on the level with indigenous shifters. What's your story, Taylor?"

"I...I'm not sure. I just found out today."

Tim narrowed his eyes and cocked his head. "You're what, twenty?"

"Twenty-two."

"And you had no indications of an animal aspect up until now? That's odd."

"I was the product of some kind of experiment. Either modified with technology to give me the ability to shift, or the programming that was used on me forced my capabilities into a dormant state. There's more involved, too, power that exceeds the bounds of science."

"I'm not sure I follow." Tim grimaced and sent Julian a long, concerned look.

"I know this sounds outlandish," Julian said to Tim, though his hope for a seamless introduction wavered. They weren't exactly selling Tim on Taylor, and Julian didn't blame the guy for his reservations. Her story wasn't commonplace. But neither was animal shifting, and Julian wasn't one to give up on people he cared about. Least of all Taylor. Tim would have to get on board. "I've seen what she can do, though, man. It's the real deal."

Tim leaned in and stared, riding a dramatic pause. "Swear to me. Give me your word that we can trust her and there's no bullshit going on."

Julian touched his forehead, chest, and shoulders, making the sign of the crucifix. His grandmother, his dear *amá sání*, had picked up this habit in boarding school, and Julian had always liked the dramatic impact made by the ritual nature of the gesture. And God, the Great Spirit, and any other deity who might be listening was welcome to pitch in with a blessing. "I swear on the graves of my ancestors, man."

Tim's cheeks puffed. He released a slow breath and took off his hat to reveal black hair boasting the crispness of a recent trim. "Alright, Taylor. If Jules says you're good, you're good."

She burrowed deeper into his hold, and he held her tight and kissed her cheek.

"I didn't actually call to try to get you to accept a new person, though." Awkward segue, but they needed to keep things moving.

A chuff from Tim. "So what's up?"

Julian adjusted his weight in the seat. The last thing he wanted was to freak Tim out, but he couldn't in good conscience move to Peru without getting closure on the matter of the tall man.

Taylor was right—just because the spirit hadn't shown up since the hogan incident didn't mean he was gone for good. If Tim had any insights to offer, useful input would mean more ammunition to fight the forces aligned against them.

"Some kind of ghastly being bothered me for a while. Taylor as well."

Tim's jaw clenched. "Can you describe what it looked like?"

Taylor sketched the profile, "Unnaturally tall, gaunt as a skeleton dipped in wax, bald and pale. I've had visions of this entity pacing some sort of underground chamber or dungeon. The other week, it came out of the sky, like literally floated down from above, and tried to drag Julian away."

"Fuck," Tim hissed. He screwed up his face and pinched the bridge of his nose.

Julian splayed both hands on the table and leaned close to the computer screen. The snake twitched as if infected by the tense energy. "Sounds like you're familiar with what she's talking about."

"We've been seeing them here recently, as in the last few months.

Meaning someone opened a portal. I didn't want to tell you about it, Jules, because I didn't want to turn you off us. But now I realize that I owed you full disclosure, and I apologize for my lack of transparency."

"I understand. I wasn't completely forthcoming myself, for similar reasons. But we're all on the same page now."

Taylor scooted to the edge of her seat, joining Julian in a posture of rapt attention. "A portal to where?"

Tim said, "Another dimension or galaxy. These scrawny and pale motherfuckers are called Other Ones. Mortal enemies of shifters. The legend is that our kind traveled to Earth thousands of years ago through a wormhole or other celestial portal, fleeing their persecution. It's said that one of our shifter kin had water magic, which she used to close the doorway in space time, trapping the Other Ones in their world. But now it appears the portal has been opened again, unfortunately. There's an evil spirit behind all this mayhem. Some kind of pre-Christian deity who wants to let these things into our reality to enhance her own power. We're supposed to avoid saying her name out loud, but it starts with an 'F' and rhymes with Molly."

Folly. She'd spoken to him telepathically. "Yep. That name came up in the hogan when the Other One appeared."

Taylor dropped her gaze and wrung her hands. "I might have some leads. If we can figure out how this deity opened the portal, we might be able to close the gap before another one of these Other Ones slips through."

"Does this circle back to the people who experimented on you?" Tim's brusque question belied a stern quality beneath the surface of his cool persona.

"Yeah." She glanced at Julian, then Tim. "And there's more."

Julian rubbed her arm in support.

"Shit," Tim said. "Of course there is."

Taylor spoke. "There's an underground bunker on an island where shifters are being imprisoned, tortured, and murdered. The people who put chips in me are behind these crimes. They have one of these Other Ones penned up in there too."

Tim gaped. "Do you know where this place is, have a way to get there? Christ. We have to save those shifters and get them here."

"Agreed," Taylor said. "I might have some ideas, but I need to go there myself first and survey the scene. I have a pretty good idea of who all is involved, meaning I stand a good chance of being able to trick them into taking me there. I don't have an approach worked out quite yet but give me some time."

Julian lobbed her a quizzical glance. Apprehension washed over him. This was the first he'd heard of her hatching a plot to infiltrate the island, and he didn't like the sounds of her plan. Too dangerous. "We haven't decided on a strategy."

She hit back with a dire look and a pointed comment, "Though you agree we need one before any more lives are lost."

"Of course, but I won't stand by and watch you march off headfirst and unarmed into a war zone."

"He's right," Tim said. "We need to work through this in steps. Assemble a team, assess the terrain, identify points of entry and exit."

"There isn't time," Taylor said. "It was nice to meet you, Tim, but I need to talk to Julian alone now. Hopefully updates will come soon."

"Yeah, okay. I'll see if I can find anything out on my end. Call me any time. That goes for both of you."

"Will do. Take care," Julian said to the screen.

Tim lifted his chin in closing, and the screen froze and blacked.

Julian shut the computer, intent on staying positive. Even given Taylor's alarming proposition, they'd made gains with Tim and strengthened a tie to South America.

Honesty paid dividends, and, speaking of which, an honest conversation with Taylor was in order. He swiveled to face her. "Your idea makes me uncomfortable. If you go, I'm going with you."

"No. You're on their radar, and they'll try to capture you. I'll bank on that right now. I should go because I'm uniquely positioned to penetrate the operation. I'll confront my dad about the chips and come up with an argument about why I should travel to the island. Maybe I can persuade him to accompany me so my trip there looks more plausible. It'll be like going undercover."

He weighed her proposition. If anyone could pull off such a feat, Taylor could. Still, though, he hated the idea of someone he cared about, a fellow shifter, venturing to such a grisly place. "What would be the pretense?"

Her eyes darted from side to side as if they moved in tandem with turning gears in her brain. "It depends on what I can suss out from him. One option is to go to him like I'm apologizing for disarming the chips and pretend I've turned on you or was working all along to gain your trust for capture purposes and collaborating with the Other One. I can bring up the Wall Street job and make the case that I need to go to the island to network. Riff on what Donnie said in the basement and come at the trip from the perspective of wanting to meet big shots."

She made a solid case, and her argument supported Tim's good points. They needed an action plan, and Taylor's connections were conducive to her executing a successful recognizance mission. "Have you thought through every angle? What if your dad tries to trap you there, or the plan all along was to lure you into a vulnerable position? Don't underestimate him."

"I just don't see it. I have a hunch that he had this done to me because he was backed into a corner somehow. You should have seen him in his home office the other day. He tried to hide his fear, but I saw through his defenses. He was scared. Not empowered."

"So one working theory is that you were chipped to keep you safe."

"Safe or dealt with. If what Donnie said is true, my modification appeases someone higher than my dad. I think his hands are tied, or at least he thinks they are. When I met with him at the house, he almost seemed helpless."

"Goddamn." Julian leaned back in his chair and stared at the ceiling. "I see where you're coming from, but I do not feel good about this."

"Me neither, but I think it's the only choice we have to move forward. You heard Tim, one or more of these Other Ones are making a menace down in Peru. So we can't run there and expect to remain safe."

"True." His mind itched with an important memory, and he peeked again at the wall calendar. Right. A popular, annual art fair started bright and early in the morning, and he needed to abide by his agreement to attend. With his relationship with Witt on thin ice, he couldn't afford to flake on any upcoming jobs. "Hey, I know the timing of this is bad, but I have that art fair starting tomorrow morning. I shouldn't cancel. Can we put the island excursion possibility on the back burner for now and revisit it soon?"

"Of course. I don't want you to cancel. In fact, a break sounds good. Is it okay if I come? I'll bring homework so you don't have to worry about entertaining me."

A rare, sunny glow filled his chest. "I'd love that. We should stick together."

"Plus I finally get to see your work. Can we check out your home studio?"

"What makes you so sure I have one?"

She bobbed one shoulder in a coy half-shrug. "You strike me as a dedicated person. I'd think you'd want to be able to work whenever and wherever inspiration happened to strike."

"Yep. You've got my number alright."

Julian led Taylor to the bedroom he'd converted into a workspace. Canvases in various stages of completion and the wooden frames he carved out of lumber and polished to shine rested against the walls. A few of his uncompleted works occupied easels. Finished products hung displayed, awaiting delivery to fairs and the gallery event.

The poker table where he wove a bestselling Native craft, the dreamcatcher, was cluttered with wire, leather, yarn, and feathers. He felt a little guilty creating a talisman that he didn't share a tribal connection to, but the things sold like mad, and he needed to eat.

Taylor walked to the corner where he kept his supply cleaning station. Brushes in all shapes and sizes covered the paint-splattered wooden table along with a bowl of murky water and a stained palette.

He didn't burn from neck to scalp until he realized what drew her to that particular part of the room. Christ, in all the recent chaos, he'd forgotten to hide the work in progress that was becoming his favorite piece.

She took a step back, tilting her head, the outline of her body bracketed by the carved mahogany frame holding the biggest acrylic on canvas piece he'd ever painted. No throwing a towel over the experiment now. If she hated the fairy tale reimagining, he'd cope.

Julian walked up behind her and contemplated the painting that had poured right out of his pounding heart in a few hours of feverish, inspired flow.

A woman stood on a tree-lined forest path at gunmetal dusk, sapphire waves cascading down her back. She faced a black wolf and offered him her hand to lick. The shade of his tongue matched her red t-shirt, and it was clear from her facial features in profile who inspired the female subject.

Little Red Riding Hood had some spunk and sass now, though, this woman was no victim passively skipping to a gruesome fate. She wore athletic shorts and tennis shoes in case she needed to run.

But the Big Bad Wolf wouldn't chase her down and eat her. He'd rather cuddle.

Because sometimes the ones we thought were monsters turn out to be decent, and the real monsters are the powerful ones who we don't even see.

He scratched the back of his neck. Too bad Taylor had to look at the work before he'd had a chance to decide if it was worth showing her. "I started this the day we met. I wanted to paint what you'd look like with long hair the color of your eyes. But if you don't like it, I can throw it out."

Yet when she turned to face him, her expression laid him bare.

Her eyes radiated the natural beauty of big blue flowers, open for him and moist with a spring dawn's dew.

In the background, one strand of the painted rendition's mane approximated her real irises' bluebonnet shade, though not perfectly. For the essence of Taylor, a wild thing eager to give and receive love, a predator and gentle woodland doe merged into one complex being, could never be replicated. Her glorious harmony of contrasts, so genuine and a touch frightening in their lightning strike of unapologetic intensity, resisted all capture or copy.

"Nobody's ever been inspired by me before." She took both of his hands and backed them to the edge of the rustic table with its messy spread of paintbrushes and cups.

"I highly doubt that." He moved with her, their bodies waltzing in synch, already one though their flesh had yet to join.

"It's like you see *into* me." Her voice shook as she swallowed and blinked a rapid flurry. Droplets serrated her lashes like blades of grass. "This goodness and purity that isn't even there. But now that you've seen it, I see it. And I can't un-see it. And it's beautiful."

He looped an arm around her back, pulling her body to his, and brushed his cheek into her smoother one. "Your goodness is there. Of course I see that light, Taylor. You're brave and strong and ferocious, loyal and loving. Not to mention the most beautiful woman ever to cross my tired eyes. You're all I want in another person and so much more."

"I've never met anyone like you." She whispered the words, her breath dancing tingles over his temple. "And I want to be all those things you tell me I am."

Julian planted both of his hands on Taylor's waist, hoisting her upward and sitting her bottom on the edge of the table. A couple of plastic brushes hit the ground in a series of skitters, but he didn't care. She was letting him in, and he would show her how much the gesture meant. Show her with his body and soul how deeply he cherished her invitation.

A dance with no music commenced, bodies giving and taking with wordless, synchronized fluidity.

He traced the tips of his fingers over her thighs and hips—such velveteen skin—and lifted her skirt, sliding her white cotton panties over her ankles as he lowered to his knees and tossed the scrap of fabric to the floor.

An area rug cushioned his joints, though he would've knelt on broken glass to please her.

A soft moan left Taylor's lips as she widened her legs, his palms on her knees easing her apart. Her intimate, excited scent of musk and sweetness ignited him like a lit match and hardened his cock. He pressed a kiss to the strip of hay-colored hair between her legs, breathing her in, getting high on her, memorizing every note of her natural perfume like inhaling the sacred female smell would merge her body chemistry with his.

Her hips punched up in invitation, the soles of her sandals pressing into his back as she urged him closer, communicating physically what she wanted.

In thrall, obedient, Julian gave her what she craved. No nonsense, no teasing or torture, just firm pressure, and a medium pace up and down on the hard button lodged an inch above the entrance to her body. Using steady ministrations, he worked her.

In under a minute, she tensed up and let out the low, telltale wail letting him know he was delivering the payoff. Her clit throbbed under his tongue, and wetness flowed from her, a treat he swallowed. After he'd wrung every drop of the climax from her and she flopped limp on the table, he rose to his feet.

"Amazing," Taylor whispered, an awestruck quality to her delivery letting him know that she meant more than the orgasm.

"We are pretty amazing together, yeah?" He moved between her legs and opened his belt, undoing fasteners and shoving his jeans past his ass.

This wasn't a moment for slow and gentle. He had to have her, had to claim her, and from the signals pulsing from her eyes and body, he could tell she wasn't interested in softness, either.

Tendering wordless acknowledgement, she pulled him down by the arms and slid her backside off the edge a few feet, bringing their bodies into alignment as she hung on with her legs wrapped around his waist. "All of me wants all of you."

In the wake of her devastating, heartfelt words, she sat up some, circled her fingers around the middle of his stiff poker, and guided him inside her.

He groaned, the bliss of her wet-hot tunnel molded around his dick.

The union of their bodies was primordial, mystical, affirming a bond he'd long ago relegated to the stuff of myths and fairy tales.

But as he slid into her and they moved in the ancient dance, breath speeding in comingled gasps of pleasure, he changed his mind.

She was his, and he was hers. They'd met through synchronicity and fate. He'd known, deep down, that she was his kind from that first encounter at the library. It was a primal thing, legendary, fecund with meanings transcending the sum of their mating parts. As he entertained the spiritual musing, a sliver of light winked in the window glass, catching her eye, and sparking a twinkle.

She squeezed his biceps, matching him thrust for thrust.

That was his woman, taking or giving, dominating or submitting, but always on her own terms. Never meek or unsure, never lagging behind.

His stare locked on hers, he pushed in and out, root to tip and repeat in vigorous thrusts.

"Oh, yeah, fuck me nice and hard like that." Her dirty words spurred him on, and he surrendered all control to the instincts of his flesh.

He took her hard. Heat gathered tense and tight deep in his belly and his moans grew tight, clipped. Pleasure ratcheted to frenzied ecstasy, then to base and unbearable need.

"Oh, fuck." She screamed, shameless, for no inhibitions stood in the way of their coupling as it roared to a glorious apex. "I'm close. Harder. Don't stop."

Her inner muscles clenched around his driving sex, pulling him deeper. Wet skin slapped. The table thumped dully into the wall. Another item fell and landed with a clunk.

He didn't stop, no way in hell, not as she dug her short nails into his arms and shouted his name in a series of reverent pleas.

Taylor threw her head back and cried out, baring the pale column of her throat, a flute of gorgeous skin straining with tendons and begging for a taste.

He leaned forward, his plunges speeding to a desperate and uncoordinated rhythm, and slid his tongue from her collarbone to her ear. He moved his insatiable mouth to hers and kissed her until their play of tongues and lips stole his mind.

As her heart pulsed against his chest and her groans filled his mouth, he devoured her joy. Consumed her essence, claimed her breath and gave her his. Her inner walls hugged him, clenching in timed contractions of carnal intimacy.

Taylor's climax egged on his own, the vicarious thrill of her excitement making his balls pull tight. His cock swelled more than he'd ever thought possible. He broke their kiss and pulled back enough to stare at the image of her face cast in frenzied exaltation. Spellbound, Julian barreled into her while gazing into her dazed eyes.

He thrust away, harder than he'd ever been in his life, but his total rapture amounted to more than physical arousal. He fell into Taylor, faded into her, flopped backward into a magical world where the powerful aura flowing between their bodies and souls was alpha and omega.

Emotions so strong he couldn't bear them, let alone name them, ran amok.

And as Julian ravished the woman who'd stolen his heart, he apprehended her wolf essence as an ethereal glimmer of light. In the lab, her change had come in bodily form, but this time, she shifted in a purely transcendental manner.

The luminous, ephemeral visit materialized as a translucent wisp of a mask hovering in the air above her face. The regal, alpha she-wolf merged with Taylor's own features in an arresting portrait of transformation, dissipating as it arrived, glitter dust dissolving in the ether.

His heart burst and reformed. His lips parted, and tears slid from his eyes and down his chin.

Of course Taylor was his fated mate. Who else?

Of course he could name his emotion. He loved her.

A simple concept, yet the most profound of sentiments.

She held his body close while she tapered into spasmodic twitches of aftershocks, glowing with sweat and smelling of sex and vanilla. "Julian, oh my God. Oh my God."

He came at last in a surge of splintering relief and hot, wet bursts, burying himself in her. White stars danced in his eyes. His own loose locks stuck to his face like black tape, messy with perspiration, the disarray of his ponytail apropos of his coming undone.

As if on a wavelength with him, she threaded a handful of his hair through her fingers and massaged his scalp.

He sighed, lost to a barrage of pleasure as she caressed, bringing stimulation to the under stimulated areas and a gentler touch to those spots fatigued from the hairbrush's pull.

Finally, he collapsed spent on her, holding and stroking, the contours of her figure perfect in his arms.

Any remaining maybes and uncertainties, all apprehension, trickled off as he held her and allowed her to hold him.

Their satisfied bodies and slowing breaths melted together until all aspects of them tangled as one, twinned in tandem the same as caduceus strands of DNA twisting serpentine under the skin, infinity loops encoded with ancient tapestries of blood bonds.

In a cruel resurgence of reality, he remembered a terrible thing. She planned to go to the island, and he had to let her go.

TWELVE

WHILE JULIAN MANEUVERED HIS TRUCK BETWEEN TWO CARS PARKED on the patch of grass converted to a makeshift lot, Taylor took another big bite of the wrap he'd thrown together the night before the art fair.

Her taste buds exploded with a party of seasoned ground beef, tangy sour cream, and the tartness of fresh tomato chunks. A crispy shell wrapped the delicious filling and rounded out the culinary delight with a satisfying, salty crunch. Sustenance would keep her mind and body healthy while providing a simple, sensory pleasure. She deserved a taste of happiness.

"Best taco ever," she said through a mouthful of food. She swallowed and shielded her mouth with one hand. "I'm glad we decided to designate today as an official day off."

And what a perfect day it was to relax and enjoy each other's company while Julian sold his wares. A blue sky domed the park, bringing good tidings in sunny weather.

Car doors slammed nearby, people chatting and laughing as they meandered to the village of white tents offset by a few small carnival rides.

He shoved the gear shift up and over, stilling the pickup in a single smooth motion. "Glad you like it. Traditional recipe."

Taylor allowed her eyes to linger on his big hand wrapped around the shift. Julian owned the vehicle like a man in control of his element. "It's hot that you know how to drive a stick."

He took his own foil-wrapped taco from the paper bag lodged between the seats and chowed down in a few hungry bites. "I could teach you how to drive a stick. I'm sure you'd catch on right away."

A tingle teased her sensitive parts. His proposition sounded hella sexy, even though he hadn't intended the practical offer as an innuendo. The hot sex they'd been having had apparently dirtied her mind. Or maybe Julian was just sexy in any context, without even trying.

Endorphins treated her to fuzzy feelings of contentment while she finished her food and Julian finished his. Though he didn't have the most expressive face, the relative evenness of his expression made it all that more fun to study him for reactions and responses. A privilege to catch a change in the tilt of his head or a quirk of the lips. Seeing secrets withheld from all but an elite few.

Yep. Sexy without even trying in that understated way of his.

But there was one big side of him she hadn't seen. Taylor downed her last mouthful, wadded the wrapping, and stuffed it in the bag. "Can you shift into a wolf whenever? Do you have total control over it?"

As if unfazed by her abrupt change of subject, he tucked away his trash before replying. "I do now, yes. Wasn't always the case, but I trained the wolf using the same methods I showed you in the lab. There used to be a lot of chaos in the beginning, and even though the wolf is prone to make demands of me and protest, he's at my will now."

"How long have you been able to do it?" Her muscles loosened as she sunk in to his story, intrigued to know more about this weird thing they apparently had in common.

"As far back as I can remember." One corner of his mouth lifted in a small, knowing smile. "You want to see, don't you?"

"Yeah. I do. Unless changing hurts you or causes discomfort like it did to me. I wouldn't wish that on anyone, let alone you."

An adamant shake of his head. "I hardly notice the sensation anymore. The more you train your wolf, the faster you'll be able to let her out and then put her away."

Taylor's gaze drifted to a filmy white cloud beyond the pickup window as she indulged a wistful, contemplative sentiment. She could construe this wolf thing as either a blessing or a curse, but it was hers now. In her and with her. "Why do you think some people are able to do this? Have this ability inside of us?"

He shrugged. "I used to think it was just how some are made. I wonder if, well, even if you were modified in some way, the fact that you manifested a wolf expression meant it was latent in you all along. Like destiny saw to it that your wolf found a way out. Fate."

Toasty sunshine filled the cabin, cocooning her. His assessment made a lot of sense. "That's a thoughtful way of putting it."

A wailing chord from an electric guitar threaded through the air, followed by muffled applause and the static whine of a microphone. Julian craned his neck and made a visor out of his hand before saying, "Do you want to see? Because I need to get to the tent. The band is setting up, so I'd better be open for business in twenty minutes."

A handful of jumpy grasshoppers joined the meal she'd eaten, anticipation sharpening into acuteness. "Yes. Absolutely."

He closed his eyes and drew in a long breath, and as he let it out, his skin darkened. Fur sprouted across the entire surface of his body as he contracted into a more compact center mass.

The morph happened without any visible effort or struggle. Before she could even blink, a massive black wolf, ebony hair shining with a healthy gloss, sat behind the wheel of Julian's pickup. Only those milk chocolate eyes, loving and sentient, betrayed his identity.

Well, his mesmerizing eyes as well as his clothes, garments that now fit his body in a comical manner. His boots hit the floor panel with two thumps, and she stifled an affectionate giggle.

Taylor leaned forward and wrapped her arms around Julian, coarse hairs tickling her neck as she petted lean canine muscle and sturdy bones. His scent, woodsy and feral, ensconced her in a fort of strange novelty and uncanny difference. Taylor nuzzled the side of her face against his furry one. "You make it look so fucking easy."

A yap which could have been either a chuckle or a general happy noise sprang from Wolf Julian.

She laughed in return and petted the fur covering his side, lost to the weird and unique happiness reserved for their bond, their bodies.

Lost to the moment, she barely noticed as he turned into a man once again.

He brushed a kiss to her cheek and slipped on his boots. "You'll get there, babe."

His term of endearment for her coaxed a wiggle from her shoulders. "Let's go sell the shit out of some art."

"Glad I have the businesswoman with me." He squeezed her leg and got out of the truck, walking around to where they'd loaded the bed full of paintings and crafts.

Taylor exited and joined Julian at the back of the vehicle. He loaded a large, wheeled box up with canvases.

Smoky smells of grilling meat complemented the mild weather and grind and wail of the classic rock band. A great day to spend outside, and so far, a great day in general.

He laid plastic sheeting atop the stack of canvases and set a batch of dreamcatchers and accessories over the layering. "I should have brought two." He patted the side of the box.

She leaned over the edge of the truck and picked up three wrapped paintings. "I can help you carry stuff."

"I'll come back for a second trip. I don't want to be the asshole who makes my girlfriend haul in and out for me."

Taylor hugged the canvases to her chest. "Girlfriend, eh? I like how you casually slipped that in."

He took a big step toward her, the loose strands that escaped his black ponytail animated by a warm, gentle breeze. "Seemed to fit. Unless you don't want to be. Or if you don't want to label us, that's cool too."

She was sure that the grin on her face was so stupid, all gums and teeth. "I do. Want to be yours, that is. Whatever we want to call it."

"Good." He leaned down and brushed his mouth over hers. No tongue, no urgency or insistence, just the unhurried sweetness of an innocent kiss on a beautiful day.

Taylor closed her eyes and vanished into the kiss, a few slow, exploratory nibbles imbued with the power to erase their woes if only for a moment.

The breath of his sigh, minty on her tongue, ended their play in a gentle transition. He pulled back, rubbing their noses together. "How about a real date after this? Dinner and a movie. Better yet, dinner and a dip in Barton Springs. So I can shamelessly ogle you in a bikini."

"I don't own a bikini." She lifted a brow in invitation to banter.

"I'll buy you one. Skimpy, with all sorts of strings for me to pull."

A fantasy of cool water and hot skin, Julian undressing her and kissing the pale swatches of her skin untouched by the sun, wetted her sex. "You pig."

His nostrils flared like he'd caught the scent of something delectable. "You mean dog."

Well damn, that comment made her think of more doggy-style sex. "True. And I'm your bitch."

His eyes blazed with desire hotter than the midday sun, and she drank it in.

He sucked in a sharp breath as his eyelids fell to half-mast. "Enough. Truce. I need the brain in my blood. I mean blood in my brain."

Taylor laughed and started moving in the direction of the festival. "To be continued."

"Hell yes."

He walked by her side, cart in tow, and after a short hike over a grassy knoll, they arrived at his tent.

While Julian laid out dreamcatchers on a table and displayed others on jewelry organizers, Taylor hung paintings from hooks on the display walls inside the tent, taking a moment to admire the colorful versatility of Julian's style. "How long have you painted?"

"Since I was a kid, around six or seven." He aided her in filling the fabric-lined walls with portraits of people, panoramic landscapes, and dreamy imaginings in the vein of the Red Riding Hood piece. "I was down at the convenience store, and I saw this package of watercolors. I was in awe of the little circles, like frozen rainbow puddles. Saved my allowance for another two weeks to buy them, and they were so pristine I almost didn't want to spoil them. But I did, and I painted a picture of a little Navajo girl riding a horse, sold it at the trading post to an elderly white couple for two hundred bucks. That was the day I found my main niche."

She affixed a framed piece to a wall, taking a step back to admire it. The sheer magnitude of the beauty washed over her. In the painting, a herd of sheep charged over a desert hill, kicking up clouds of red dust as a sunset of bleeding purple and liquid gold bathed their bodies in surreal, fantastical tones. The rendition was so accurate, so precise while maintaining its imaginative quality, that she could apprehend movement in the stillness.

Her chest swelled with the impact of sublime witnessing, and the inside of her nose stung. "God, you're talented."

His strong arms wrapped around her as the front of his body pressed into the back of hers. "Careful, I'm going to get an ego. But really, that one painted itself. Sheep are meaningful to my tribe, so I had all these positive associations with them that kind of poured out on their own."

"I feel like you should be famous. Exhibiting in New York. Why did you settle here?"

He sighed, swaying back and forth in a gentle rhythm while holding her close. "I found some mechanical work here in Austin, a steady job fixing cars. So I paused my travels to build up a decent supply of money. That's how I met the man who owned the house where I live now. We got to be good friends. Toward the end of his life, I was the only one of his friends or family who came around to check up on him. He willed the house to me when he died. So long story short, Austin was meant to be."

The visual portrait before her eyes completed the self-portrait Julian painted with his story, and she melted into him. As the band led into a cover of a popular eighties rock ballad, all entropy in the cosmos clicked into harmony.

"Excuse me, sir." A woman's Southern accent dissolved the sentimental haze. "Are you open for business?"

Taylor turned to see a trio of well-dressed, middle-aged women with wallets out and eager looks on their faces.

Julian nuzzled her temple. "To be continued, babe." He broke away, affixed a white cube to the top of his phone, and turned his attention to the steady stream of customers drifting into his tent.

Taylor got as comfortable as the extra folding chair at her disposal would allow and cracked a finance textbook. An hour later, half of his paintings were sold and none of the dreamcatchers remained. Her stomach rumbled and ached with hollow pain. "Jeez. I just ate."

Julian handed a bagged print to a member of a gay couple, and once they walked out of earshot said, "We need more calories than most people. You're probably still running a deficit from the lab."

A rich, sweet aroma of roasted nuts mingled with the perfume from a charcoal grill. Wheat and acid notes of beer drifted downwind to finish off the scrumptious buffet of scents.

The culinary temptations of summertime Americana had Taylor rising from her seat in acquiescence. "Sounds legit. You want a turkey leg?"

Julian's eyes widened into a charming, boyish mask of delight. "Now that you mention it, yes, yes I do."

"Be right back."

She wove through a cluster of people coming in to pick over the last of his artwork and exited the shade of his tent to a crowded sidewalk. Music and voices swirled together in a cacophony of sounds. A moving tide of bodies made for human obstacles for her to weave through on her way to the food trucks.

A guy texting and walking bumped into her, and she stumbled.

"Sorry, sorry," he said, face bent down as he kept moving.

She turned around to respond, catching sight of two men in black suits and dark sunglasses. Curlicue cords were looped around their ears, and they marched in tandem at a brisk pace.

Though a frying current dashed over her chest, she returned her eyes forward and resumed her trek, hanging a few turns around art booths and other obstacles.

Decorated with brand names and painted funky colors, the food trucks were about twenty feet away. Her heart beat faster, and the feeling of eyes watching her bored into the back of her skull.

With as much discretion as she could muster, Taylor glimpsed over her shoulder.

They were still there, closer now. Definitely following her.

She clenched her teeth, ducked around an old tree gigantic enough to serve as cover, and stopped. Her pulse slammed, but she planted her hands on her hips in a pose of confident authority and waited. Screw fleeing. Taylor wasn't prey. If the two goons had something to say to her, they could say it to her face.

Sure enough, the twin sentinels emerged, staring her down as they stood in front of her.

One pulled his earpiece to his mouth and muttered something indecipherable.

She raised her voice loud enough to defeat both the festive din and the shake in her tone. "What the hell do you want?"

"You disabled your chips." One towering oaf, a bald pinhead with a crooked nose, spoke in monotone.

"No shit." Her knees shook, but she lifted her chin and widened her stance. Whoever these spooks were had taken her dignity, her integrity, her privacy. They didn't get any more of her fear. "And I ought to sue the fuck out of your company for having them put in me."

The second brute muttered into his transmitter, "We located her."

Taylor's heart sunk. She glanced side-to-side, seeing throngs of people from all walks of life. No way would these two thugs attempt a kidnapping in such crowded circumstances. Though the chaos could provide cover. She balled two fists, each thumb on the outside. If one of them grabbed her, she'd knee him in the balls and start screaming, then repeat with the other one.

But before she could spend another second going over her getaway plan, Taylor's father joined her and the men in black behind the tree. Sunglasses and a cowboy hat concealed his identity but not the laser blast rage shooting from him.

"You stirred up quite the shitstorm, Taylor Bree." Yet beneath the quake of fury, frustration kicked his drawl up an octave.

"What do you mean *I* stirred up a shitstorm? Who are these two, and what did you do to me?"

"I was acting in your best interests, you little fool." Jeff bit out the words through clenched teeth, an undercurrent of fear shaking below his anger. "Of course you couldn't leave things be. Typical behavior from you, always talking back and challenging and arguing with every single goddamn thing I ever did for you. And now we're both fucked."

A swift and sudden fall from her pedestal, yet she welcomed the tumble from her father's corrupt perch and the clarity of mind that vacating her station entailed. "I don't care how mad at me you are. I did the right thing. Whatever you cooked up with those chips was unethical. It was wrong, and you know it."

"You think," he hissed, his shoulders hunched to his ears. "You think it's over? You think what, that you're gonna ride off into the sunset with your wolfman lover and live happily ever after? Jesus, Taylor, I figured you were smarter than that."

She scoffed. "Smart enough to what, be your mindless little capture drone without my knowledge or consent? Yeah, hard pass. And from here on out, what I do with Julian is none of your damn business. Is that how you knew I'd be here? Through surveillance?"

"Give me a break. You brought him to my party. All I had to do was ask a couple of questions about your date and run a few Google searches. More to the point, if you think what you have with him counts, you really are naïve and stupid."

Righteous indignation tore a blazing path, and she stood up straighter. "You spied on us through that camera microchip. You saw how much it counted."

Jeff stepped back a couple of feet, taking off his sunglasses and rubbing his eyes. They were red and puffy, evidence of tiredness or even crying, and the sight filled her with an undesirable combination of sympathy and unholy terror. She'd never, *ever* seen her father distressed. Certainly never seen him cry.

"I want you to know now, today, in case I don't get another chance to say it, that I did not steal your most private moments. The second that feed took an intimate turn, I shut it off. Am I angry at you for meddling? Yes. I'm on the ropes here in more ways than you know. But I'm not a creep. I've crossed a lot of lines, so many that I've forgotten that there were once lines there in the first place, but there's enough of me left to know where the clearest ones are drawn."

His weary confession poured out with regret and shame. Her head spun. She swallowed an excess of sour saliva, regaining her wits. She didn't trust him, but he was vulnerable. Too vulnerable to curate and maintain lies at the moment. Jeff was beside himself, and this was her best chance to make some headway toward getting answers. "Tell me the entire story. I deserve to know everything if I want to even begin to entertain the possibility of ever trusting you again."

His blue eyes hardened, and he slid them right to left, as if directing her attention to each of the big men.

She got the gesture. They might have been his bodyguards, but they were also his spies. Free and unfettered speech wouldn't happen in their presence.

Beneath his polo shirt, Jeff's trim belly rose and fell with a mega breath. "If you want Julian to stay alive, listen carefully to every single word that I say."

Not like she trusted him, at least not completely, but she'd be remiss to squander an opportunity to keep him talking. "Okay."

Jeff flinched. A muscle in his neck feathered. "No, Taylor, it's not okay. It's the farthest fucking possible thing from okay."

At the very least, she had a part to play now. An angle. "So tell me what I can do." A bead of sweat slipped down her spine and into her butt crack. Both she and her father were sweating, literally and figuratively. A pair of strained family members bound by the same ropes. An unhealthy bond, but a tie that bound them nonetheless.

"I need you to go to the island and be on your best networking behavior. Act like you still want the Bull Gordon job, because I'm going to assume that you do even though you sure aren't acting like it."

"Oh, so taking the covert genetic modification chips out of my body proves my disloyalty to the company? Then yeah, maybe I don't want the job anymore."

Taylor crossed her arms over her chest. Uncertainty jangled her thoughts. Did she still want the Bull Gordon job? Not like she had a backup plan in place, though she hadn't thought about Wall Street in quite some time.

"Cut the attitude. I can assure you that it's not helping. You will go to Scarab Island from the position of damage control. Of making amends."

She flashed another defiant jut of her chin, standing her ground though terror had begun to worm into her. If her visions of the island reflected reality, she might end up witnessing a true horror show. Still, though, her father was handing her quite the gift in the form of a golden excuse to get to Scarab. "How do I know this isn't a trap?"

Jeff ground his teeth. "You don't, but you'll have to trust me. Because some very powerful people are enraged. I can't protect you indefinitely, but I can prime them to accept your apology. *Once.* If we're lucky, they'll give you one pass. After that you've got a bull's eye on your forehead and a sniper on your tail. Ever heard of those high-frequency sound wave guns that can induce heart attacks? Yeah. One blast from twenty feet of distance could drop you dead without any trace of foul play."

The threat sent a flash freeze through her system. Stood to reason, that her removal of the chips screwed up some big operation and placed her squarely on the bad side of unseen big wigs.

Though she rarely, if ever, found herself at a loss for words, Taylor ejected a mere squeak from her lips.

"I'll take it from the deer-in-headlights look on your face that you're seeing things my way. The next flight leaves today. If you want to live and keep your boyfriend alive, show up at the small private airport on the edge of town at five, look for a black executive jet, and get your ass on that plane. I'll alert them to look out for you so you don't hit any snags."

Taylor mustered the most self-assured expression possible. "Message received. I'll be there."

"Good." Jeff patted her shoulder, and his touch made her flinch. "We can still fix this."

The moment Jeff and his goons merged into the crowd, Taylor hung her head and braced herself against the tree, fingers clenching rough bark. Nausea clamped her insides, and bile shot up her throat. This was a good development, though, a positive.

As horrified as she was at the prospect of travelling to Scarab, the visit would be a prime opportunity to figure out what these creeps were doing while gathering information on saving any captives.

All she had to do was channel her inner double agent. Go undercover, which was her idea. Doable. Totally doable.

Taylor took three big breaths, the sickness in her shrinking in the wake of relief. Time to head to Scarab Island with a cool head and a clear mission. Plus, she'd have a chance to assemble the tools needed to extract revenge on her enemies. Serve that fucking dish as cold as Salazar's blood.

She straightened her spine and turned around, coming face to face with the lug who'd radioed her father. Adrenaline hit her with an attack urge. "What do you want now?"

"Did the wolfman inseminate you?"

"Excuse me?"

He took a smart device out of his pocket and typed while saying, "We need to know if his semen entered any of your body cavities either immediately before or after the chips came out. Vaginally, orally, anally. Or even through your eyes, ears, or nostrils via splatter."

Taylor shoved past the brute, nearly toppling as she bumped into an immobile wall of muscle. "Fuck off, pervert."

He grabbed her upper arm, his grip hard and mean. "Tell the truth. It's vital we know this before you travel to the island."

She wrenched against pain and made the firm decision not to give this sketchy cretin a single fact that could be used against her and Julian. "No."

"No you won't tell me, or no his semen didn't come in contact with any entrances to your body?"

She lifted her foot and smashed her heel into his instep. He yelped and let her go.

"Leave me alone." Taylor ran back to Julian's tent. If they needed to know for her own good, Jeff would have asked. These assholes didn't get to take every single thing they wanted from her, not when they'd already taken so much.

Worry chased her heels as she closed in on her destination. Did it matter that his semen had entered her, would it make a difference during her stay on the island? No point in driving herself crazy now. She'd find out soon enough.

THIRTEEN

TAYLOR STRUGGLED TO REGULATE HER ELEVATED BREATHING, BUT SHE made it back to Julian unbothered by any more incidents. She halted her steps near the entrance and gathered her bearings by grounding herself in the familiar setting.

Save for a couple of watercolors, the walls were bare slates of gray felt. A short stack of prints rested against the side of the basket containing them, and a pair of punky teen girls picked through the leftovers. Julian stood with his back to Taylor, chatting up a family dripping with shopping bags, and handed a young boy a free charm from the craft table.

She squeezed her eyes shut and slowed her heart rate with breathing exercises. It sickened her to ruin her man's good day with her bad news, but she had no choice but to tell him, as the afternoon was wearing on and she had to get moving. Lying wasn't an option. She refused to build a new relationship on a foundation of deceit.

He must've smelled her or heard her sigh because he turned around while saying, "Hey, babe. How about we save the turkey legs for a snack, because I was thinking I'd take you to that new restaurant with the revolving tower overlooking downtown." Upon taking a closer look at her, he reeled like he'd been slapped. "Jesus. What happened?"

The family and teens left, concerned looks on their sun-pinked faces.

Julian ushered Taylor inside and brought the entryway flaps down with a pull on a cord. He rubbed her arms, his eyes flashing with anger. "Did someone hurt you?"

"No. I'm fine. My father and a couple of his henchmen tracked me down. Whoever they work for is pissed about the chips, but it's ultimately a good thing. An opportunity."

The darkness in his stare broke, giving way to a furrowed brow. "What are you talking about, an opportunity?"

She arranged her response. "He ordered me to go to the island to make amends. Get back on the good side of the higher ups and apologize. So basically a chance to poke around landed right in my lap. Look, I have to go. I'm going to play it cool, undercover agent style, and I'll report back what I find."

"You can't go alone. Way too dangerous. I'm coming."

"Julian. Think about that for a second. It will never work. There's no pretense or cover for you whatsoever."

"Wrong. Pretend you've captured me."

"We both know how their capture protocol works, and some bounty hunter routine isn't it. They'll see right through us."

He let go of her and paced. "I can't, I won't watch you deliver yourself right to them. Screw it. Let's go to Peru tonight. Once we're there, we can fall off the grid for as long as we need. Tim will vouch for you to the rest of the community."

She grabbed his elbow, and when his eyes met hers, the sight of the deep worry in them broke her heart. One way or another, she would end this nightmare. Julian deserved peace and quiet, not an endless barrage of emotional distress.

"Too many loose ends," she said. "What if they have operatives in South America, or the manpower and technology to tail us there? I refuse to put you at risk. I refuse to lead them right to the other shifters. And speaking of shifters, there might be a whole bunch of them imprisoned and suffering on that island. If we pull up the stakes and run away, we're giving up on them."

He raked two sets of fingers through his hair. "So that's it? I'm just supposed to sit back and watch you go? I can't, Taylor. I can't live with myself."

She looked up at him with a determined stare. "You have to try. Don't you have the Witt Gallery opening tomorrow?"

He scoffed. "That's the farthest thing from my mind right now."

"It shouldn't be. Go to your exhibit and do your thing. Try to take your mind off this for one day and trust that I'll be alright. I'll be in touch as soon as I'm back in Texas."

His chin trembled. He took her face in his hands and pressed their foreheads together, bringing them into a pose gravid with the tragic intimacy of forever goodbyes breaking sacred circles. "I have an awful feeling."

Her throat swelled, and she reminded herself over and over and over again that she'd be fine. More than fine. After this island visit, they'd be empowered with actionable facts and a clear plan. No more spinning wheels and endless psycho circuses rampaging through her mind.

"I'm not going off to war." Though the second she whispered the shaky words, she feared she'd never see him again. But such a fear was irrational. Jeff laid out the situation. Nobody wanted to kill her. Yet. "But right now, as it stands, this is the only choice we have. I promise I'll come back to you."

"Taylor." Her name on his lips was a tortured plea, a failed prayer, an abyss of devastation.

She grabbed both of his hands, and he gripped with a hard squeeze. "This is for us. I have to go now."

Julian pulled Taylor into an enveloping hold, and she cherished his touch. A terrible sense of finality swung above their heads like an axe hanging from a frayed rope as the blade dropped, dropped, dropped.

At last, she broke the desperate, terrible hug and left the tent in a state of numbness. Because if she felt all the feelings she struggled to repress, or even looked at Julian again, she'd change her mind. Right now was the time to be brave. Strong.

So Taylor undertook a variety of point a to point b preparation in a series of robotic steps. A bright sun beat down on her and the wobbling, in and out suck of vertigo effect threatened to make her vomit as physiological suffering substituted for mental.

Nevertheless, she persisted, ordering herself through a protocol of steps. Take out phone. Summon ride share car. Sit in aggressively scented backseat deflecting chatty driver's attempts to converse.

The driver, a heavyset white man with wisps of brown hair at his temples and taped-up plastic glasses, soon got the hint and gave up on small talk.

Drop off at Julian's, tell car to wait. Spare key opens door. Assemble overnight bag. Do not lose mind.

She breathed into the ache in her heart, scooping up her purse and checking her reflection in the mirror above his dresser. She looked haggard but not weak. She had to do this.

Taylor left the house, locking his front door and sliding the key back under the mat.

The ride to the airport was uneventful, a cruise through painless traffic. Sunshine cheer contradicting her dark mood filled the sedan.

The chauffeur pulled into a wide driveway guarded by a black gate and a call box. "I hope your day gets better," he said while she opened the car door in a big shove.

"Yeah. Me too." She marched to the call box and pushed a large button.

"Name," a man said in a bored voice.

"Taylor McClure." She gnawed her cheek until iron snapped on her taste buds, repeating the mantra "strong" in her mind.

Bars parted, and a security guard walked over and led Taylor into a dreary building dressed in outdated furnishings and emitting a strong stench of mold. He patted her down and waved a plastic wand over her body, threw her bag on a table, and rifled through clothes, and sent her in the direction of the airport's lone gate.

A second man greeted her on the tarmac, a black suit and shades type like the guys from the festival. He escorted her to a gleaming obsidian jet with an extended ladder.

Taylor ascended the steps, her upward movement ironic, because she felt like she was commencing a descent into the pit of Hades.

The interior was as predicted, leather seating and polished tables in a color scheme of steel, ebony, and ivory. Six men populated the plane, all graying and dressed in casual clothes.

Corruption smelled like the ink and smoke notes of bourbon, rank cigar smoke, and a touch of opium perfume.

All six halted their talk as soon as Taylor appeared and stared at her with an unsettling blend of amusement and suspicion, as if taking pleasure in designating her as the outsider.

Recognizing Jay Stearns by his bulky jawline and styled crown of silver hair, she forced a tight smile and sat alone on a padded bench.

But before she could pretend to relax, Stearns stood and walked over, sliding into the booth, too close so she had to smell his sandalwood aftershave.

Sweat glued her skirt to the backs of her legs and adhered the leather to her body in a kinky way that shook her with an odd, humiliation-adjacent shame. For the first time in maybe ever, she resonated with an acute existential distress of being the only woman in the room.

Once upon a time, she'd considered such a thing as status, distinction. Now, though, the "not like other girls" bullshit sickened her, and she wanted Chloe or Angie.

She fixed a hard gaze on Stearns's groomed gray brows to avoid eye contact and extended a hand, marshalling false enthusiasm. At the very least, she could ingratiate herself to him by appealing to his zest for vulture capitalism.

Maybe he'd see the version of her who once shared his taste and see past the fakery. "Taylor McClure. It's an honor to finally meet you in person. I read about the merger with Simmons, Beech, and Paul in the *Times*. Well played."

Stearns looked at her palm like she held a dog turd, then slid his gaze up to hers and curled his lip. His light green eyes floated in a field of brown freckles, and he would have been attractive if not for the contempt souring his expression.

He braced a hand on the top of the booth, his palm tacked above her shoulder, caging her with the aggressive posture. "Cut the false flattery, you're starting to remind me of a cut-rate hooker trying to charm her way out of doing anal. Now. This is me leveling with you. Your daddy saved my ass from racketeering charges last year, which is why you're still sucking oxygen through that smartass mouth of yours. You should still be able to do your work without the chips, as long as your device released enough of the active agent into your bloodstream. We'll get you to the labs and run some tests, but I'm optimistic."

As long as she was of use, they'd keep her alive. Dehumanizing, but at least she clenched a modicum of leverage. "Why me? Why was I chosen to do portal work?"

"We ask the questions here, sweetheart."

A flight attendant, her tight uniform hugging her breasts and hips, sashayed down the aisle, her made-up face expressionless.

Stearns snapped his fingers twice. "Candy, get the lady a drink. Then head into the back bedroom and join Burt, Steve, and Spencer, where you'll access your kitten programming."

"My pleasure," Candy said in monotone.

Taylor didn't ask about the nature of kitten programming. It was obvious. "I'll take a diet cola."

Candy ducked into a cubby near the cockpit and reappeared in short order with a can of soda and a glass full of ice. As she set the items on Taylor's tray, the door of the plane closed with an airy hum. The engine buzzed awake.

After Candy walked away, Taylor pressed her temple to the plastic square of window, sipping her sweet, fizzy soda and thankful for the sound of classical violins streaming through the cabin. At least she didn't have to hear the kitten programming activities going on in the back.

Poor Candy. Would she remember through bursts of recollection from her subconscious, like Taylor had begun to recall the lab experiments in Switzerland? For all Taylor knew, however, Candy was into it. She didn't want to assume that the woman was a victim and not a kinky, willing participant. It was impossible to tell in this upside-down world she'd entered.

A smooth takeoff devoid of turbulence buoyed her with the familiar roller coaster sensation of ascent into flight, but inside, dread dragged her low. Time passed in a dull haze.

Beyond the confines of the aircraft, open water broken by the occasional crest of white wave gave way to a smattering of brown islands. Elevation dropped, movement jostling her as a surge of soda splashed over the plastic rim of her cup.

The sounds of male laughter and Candy's giggles broke the silence. A door shut with a click.

"Are there games tonight?" a man asked in a jovial tone.

Taylor sat up straighter. The eager way he asked about games might produce a clue.

"A definite possibility." This from Stearns. "The beasties have been punchy and lethargic these last few days, though, I'm sad to say. Less fun for a hunt. I think they're already feeling the pull of the equinox. We might have to wait until the Harvest Moon celebration."

"As in run a hunt the night of the sacrifice?" The first man clarified.

Taylor's guts bunched. She bit down on her tongue. Whatever these creeps had planned for the equinox was not good, but at least she could provide Julian a specific date along with her warning of the planned atrocity.

Cabin pressure plummeted, and her ears popped. She plugged her nose and pulled in air. The splash of brown drops enlarged to rocks, grass, and a smattering of palm trees as the plane lowered onto a runway.

"I don't see why not. You okay over there, Taylor?" A haughty, liquid metal quality to Stearns's inflection let Taylor know that he knew she'd heard the entire conversation about sacrifice and hunts and didn't care. Power play. They didn't have to be discreet around her.

"Fine."

The plane halted, and the door whooshed open. Taylor dabbed her thighs with a paper napkin.

Stearns glanced down as he stopped in the aisle, pausing right beside her seat. "Watch the spillage. You don't want to inspire fantasies of someone relieving you of your blood."

Following the cryptic, heart-shriveling comment, he flashed a smarmy wink, then burst into a robust belly laugh. "Calm down, I'm just fucking with you. Look at your face. Come on, kid, I'm just giving you a hard time for being naughty. Stick with me, and you'll be fine."

He extended a hand, and Taylor grasped his dry, firm flesh in a show of confidence. She rose, and he let her go and led the procession of guests out of the plane and into a balmy night animated with warm breezes, the elemental smell of saltwater rich in the air. Water surrounded them in all directions, a liquid expanse bereft of neighbors save for a single lighthouse starburst twinkling far in the distance.

Palm trees galore decorated the bumpy terrain along with a network of dirt roads. A sprawling, tropical-style mansion with elegant marble columns lining the front sat fifty or so feet in the distance, and a few huts styled in the estate's aesthetic ringed the large structure.

Recognition crawled in a loathsome creep, a slow-moving a-ha, but she didn't have to swallow a bolt of terror until she turned her head to the right and saw the temple.

Gold dome, blue and white stripes, rounded double door with a bar lock on the outside.

She'd known, more or less, but now she *knew* where she was. Where the unthinkable screamed in agony beneath a polished veneer of wealth.

Stearns laughed again, the others filing out of the plane. A dark SUV crawled along the path, stopping near the group. "You look like a scared mouse, Taylor. Is it truly the case that Jeff McClure's daughter has never been to a private island?"

She schooled her face into a smile. "Nope. It's stunning. Is all this yours?"

"Absolutely." He opened the car door and motioned for her to get in. "Let's get you squared away, and then I'll show you around. Lots of fun to be had here. Are you okay spending the night in one of the guest houses? We'll fly out in the morning."

She wasn't sure what sounded worse, the ominous reference to fun or whatever her getting squared away entailed. But she had privileged access she dared not squander. "Yes. That's fine."

Everyone piled in. "Drop Ms. McClure and I at the tunnels, then take everyone else back to the main house," Stearns told the driver.

The car curved a downward path around a hill and stopped at a metal door built into the side of a bluff. To her right, waves slicked jagged rocks and glossed them in the glow of the emerging moon. She fought an urge to bounce her knee. Time to drive underground.

One of the other guys from the plane hopped out of the backseat, opened a padlock on the doors, and climbed back into the car. A void gaped back at her; the maw of darkness punctuated by dual rows of lamps lining stone walls.

"It really is a great program you're working for." Stearns leaned around his front passenger seat and addressed Taylor. "We've got good deals with armies and intelligence agencies all over the world, everywhere from Israel to Columbia. Beasties play *extremely* well in global markets. A top-tier investment."

The driver moved through the tunnel at a slow pace, with the front of the vehicle angled down.

"How many do you hold here?" Taylor asked, careful not to sound too interested.

Stearns flashed a straight line of gleaming teeth. "At any given time, thousands. I pioneered this operation myself. When I became CEO of Scarab Enterprises, I turned the company around from some bullshit human trafficking nonsense fronted by a travel company and made it the innovative, cutting-edge war logistics and elite entertainment emporium it is today. Let me tell you, this operation is extensive." Breathing heavily, he watched her.

Ah, so he enjoyed bragging about his creation and would sing like a bird about the greatness of Scarab at the slightest provocation. Good to know.

"I'm listening." Taylor stretched her eyes to saucers.

The car pulled up alongside a metal door with a crank handle in the middle. The driver got out and yanked the lever in a half-circle.

"Perfect timing," Stearns said in a theatrical boom. "We're on foot from here on out. Taylor, I'll give you the tour. We'll take the long route to the lab and do a little sightseeing before getting you all patched up. Once we're on the other side of the chambers, I'll call us a tram, and we'll leave these caverns and head to the party."

Taylor exited, and goosebumps pricked at the first brush of chilly, humid air. Dank smells of dirt and wetness suited the underground bunker.

As she trudged with her minder through a walking tunnel, a more sinister miasma loomed. The acrid stench of death doused in fear and finished in despair hung from the ceiling like cobwebs.

The car started and drove off, snuffing the light of escape as red taillights vanished. Just her and Stearns in the dungeon. She killed an urge to scream and run after the car.

A muffled bestial roar traveled through subterranean layers. Taylor shuddered, grim with anticipation of what she might see.

"Ah, yes." Stearns said with great smugness. "We got a fresh batch in yesterday. A few really strong runners with excellent jaw pressure capabilities and a trio of healthy breeder sisters."

"Batch? So some are brought here by other means than portal capture? Or are some scouts rounding up multiple shifters—*beasties* at a time?"

Stearns turned right at the fork, dipping out of sight. A metallic creak accompanied by a groan signaled his nearby whereabouts. "We have multiple methods. Our top scouts have been able to infiltrate entire communities, and once we get a read on the location through their eye programming, we can show up with tranquilizers and round up hundreds. My people ambushed a massive nest of them in Eastern Europe this way. Then we move them here via water travel. There's a submarine bay up top. Portals are good for one-at-a-time loner snatches and small jobs, such as your assignment to procure Texas wolfie with the nice hair. They all know each other or know *of* each other, which is why we nab every single one we can. Your boy's gonna give up a big batch from South America after we hit him with some enhanced interrogation techniques. You helped us contact trace that Julian guy to the jungle crew, so thank you for your service. We had a hunch that there was a beastie roaming around in Central Texas. Glad the pursuit of that lead paid off."

So the goal with Julian was to torture him into giving up the Peruvian clan. A hateful, righteous urge spiked in Taylor. She ought to kill this fucker on the spot. But then she'd be trapped. She had to maintain patience and wait for her moment, so she followed Stearns to where a rusty slab hung open.

With both hands, he turned a wheel on an inner door, grunting and pulling. "You gotta see this to believe it."

The sounds hit her first. Screams, cries, and sobs joined with snarls and roars, making for a hideous concert of suffering and anguish.

With a rhythmic drumbeat of empathy and disgust encompassing her emotional range, she followed Stearns into the worst place she'd ever seen.

Stacked cells made of clear plastic lined three stories of walls and rendered a room about the size of a soccer field into a panoptic prison. Some cells held people of all ages and backgrounds, while others contained bears, wolves, or mountain lions. No toilets or sinks had been provided, leading to pitiful pools of filth.

Blood drained from her at the sight of shifters penned up like animals in a sketchy zoo and left to wallow in their own excrement.

Humans pounded fists against their confines with muted thumps, while the animals charged and rammed their sides against walls. Raptors flashed massive wingspans. A majestic rope of a cobra flared an olive hood.

In one cage, a group of human children huddled together in the middle of their barren room, crying and hugging.

"Help," a chorus screamed, seeming to recognize her. "Help, help, help."

The voices didn't sound off in her head anymore, but they didn't need to for her to make the connection. She locked eye contact with a woman holding a baby. They'd found a way to call out to her, align their voices with her brain waves. The chips must've opened up her consciousness, made her prone to hacking and hijacking like one might take over a radio signal.

One day, perhaps, she'd dig to the root of how the shifters managed to reach out to her. But right now, the past didn't matter. Only the future did, and soon she'd return to save them.

For now, she tracked Stearns across the jail floor and out the other side, taking note of nests of security cameras peering at them from their mounted perches in each of the room's four corners.

Whistling some infantile melody, he opened a second soundproof door. Whistling. This was just another day at the office for Stearns the sociopath. Taylor boiled inside but held her calm, poised demeanor. Sounding off or losing her temper wouldn't help.

A new network of tunnels enjoyed better lighting along with cement flooring. As they hiked upward, an idea sparked in Taylor's mind. If she could get to a portal, she could escape. Plug in the geographic coordinates to Julian's hogan and transport back to Texas. Maybe. Not a perfect plan, but a start.

First, she'd better draw some more good stuff out of her captor. At least she had the drop on him. Having ascertained his favored sin, she could leverage his bloated sense of pride against him.

"I'm absolutely fascinated by portals." Taylor spoke in the breathy, ingénue's timbre of Marilyn Monroe for good measure. "God, Jay, when my dad used to work in theoretical physics, I was rapt by the possibilities for using science to transcend the limits of time and space. It seemed almost like magic, or maybe even actually magical. Is there a manmade portal here that you designed?"

Stearns glanced over his shoulder and tossed her a sleazy smirk, clearly too horny and drunk on his own ego to see through her act. "Maaaaybe. I loved the way you said my name along with God's. Can I make a confession?"

"Of course," she gritted out in her fake-ditz tone.

"Taylor, I feel as if I've been tasked with doing a divine sort of work. After all, conjuring something out of nothing is the essence of omnipotence. And what else is construction of a portal but manufacturing dimensional doors out of thin air? So I am, in quite factual terms, godlike. I'm not bragging. I'm really not. It's an enormous burden to bear. Exhilarating, yet daunting."

Good grief, this was the worst case of malignant narcissism she'd ever seen, which was saying a lot given her history of moving in finance and political circles. She struck a coquettish pose of batted eyelashes paired with a fig leaf hand clasp and shifted her weight to one foot. "Could I see? Pretty please?"

He raked a glittery gaze up and down her figure. "Shit, if you weren't McClure's daughter, I'd be all over you. I'd dress you in diamond-encrusted Chanel and show you the world in my private yacht. Pour fine champagne all over that fine little hardbody of yours and fuck you on the shores of the Cayman Islands."

Her stomach soured at an image of this asshole pawing at her, but she stayed in character and barfed out a cutie-pie giggle. "Maybe next lifetime. Speaking of your godlike prowess, are the rumors true?"

The corridor they now walked, a further aesthetic improvement with crisp white walls and a checkerboard-style floor tile, contained a plethora of black doors. An antiseptic smell imbued the space with a clinical feel, albeit one juiced with a frightening occult charge.

"Oh, no, what are the gossips saying now? I'm so tired of the chatter." Stearns's false humility didn't land. He salivated for what she'd say next.

Taylor bent into an absurd conspiratorial lean that she considered a master stroke of playing dumb. Like she was naïve enough to think that her actions could defeat any surveillance they used. "Is it true that you summoned a creature from another dimension?"

"Demon, fallen angel, alien, creature from another dimension. Potato, po-*tah*-to. But yeah. We got a freak on retainer alright, and my expertise brought him on board."

"Freak is right. He looks like a skeleton on stilts. I about had a heart attack when I saw him."

Stearns licked his lips and paused in front of a door. "Right, you've met the Other One."

Bingo. Keep yakking, asshole. "Yeah. I was scared at first, but now I'm *fascinated*. What's that all about?"

"It's a long story." His breathing rate approached a pant. Sweat slicked his brow.

"I've got all the time in the world for your story, Jay."

His nostrils flared. "You better not tell a goddamn soul a word about what I'm about to say."

"My lips are sealed." She pouted for suggestive effect. "Promise."

"Good girl."

Girding herself against impending revulsion, Taylor leaned in close enough to smell Stearns's crisp, expensive cologne. "I can be a *very* good girl. And I wouldn't even tell my dad."

"For real?" He licked his lips. Now that he was officially thinking with his dick, she had the perfect opportunity to strike and get him yapping.

"I can be very discreet. And this kind of stuff turns me on. Gets me so damn hot." Taylor stuck the tip of her finger into her mouth, diving all in with her act. The routine was working. Stearns was loosening up fast.

He pulled on his tie, staring at her chest while he spoke his next words. "When we were in the thick of our portal work and research, we found out that science might not be enough. There are natural portals everywhere, positioned under certain stars, but putting together a manmade equivalent requires a bit of finesse. So we turned to otherworldly sources for some help in opening our own. We got into séances, Ouija, ritual magick—any tool we could find to help us conjure entities who could lend their powers to the manipulation of doorways. We made contact with some kind of deity with the power to send us these Other Ones. Turns out that negative energy helps keep portal doors open, and this thing's good at drumming it up."

Messing with the supernatural. What could go wrong, dumbass? "Wow, just wow."

"You want to see?"

"Um, duh. Of course."

Stearns walked three doors down.

She watched closely as he bent forward. His motion triggered a beep, and a grid of red lights scanned his face. A lock clicked. Okay, a retina scanner. No key ring for her to grab, no way for her to rush in and lock him out. Bummer.

He turned a knob, leading them into a shiny laboratory stocked with lots of chrome equipment. Electric blue light so bright she had to squint drew her eyes to the middle of the room. There, a column of incandescent energy, its hue so deep it surpassed sapphire, vibrated between two floor-to-ceiling metal pillars.

"This here is Grand Central Station. Ninety percent of the portal snatches we run deposit the product in the master chamber here." He pointed to a clear plastic booth like the one she'd seen in her father's study but large enough to hold several adults. A hushed, reverent tone stretched out the two syllables of Stearns's next words as he lifted his face to the ceiling. "Look up."

And when she did, what she saw stabbed shock into her heart. Fried head to toe from the adrenaline charging through her in spurts, she jerked at the sight of pale flesh and jutting bones, those hellfire eyes leveling a vacant stare.

The Other One floated, unaware, a line of the stark blue light running from his navel and joining the tube between the pillars.

"So you drain his essence to keep the portals working?" She stole a fast peek at the door. Run? But to where?

"Well yeah, but we have a deal with him. There's a code to release him, these magic symbols, and we send him along on portal snatches now and then. All he wants is to kill and eat shifters. That's how he retains whatever magic he supposedly has. So in exchange for being our battery, he gets his very own kill room and the chance to portal hop and take one out of every ten shifters for himself. We're gonna let him have your Texas wolfie after he gives up the jungle batch."

Blood roared in her ears. "Can Grand Central Station teleport out as well?"

"Oh yeah. All portals are two-way." He turned his back to her and strutted over to the plastic box. "The possibilities really are endless. We can ship a batch of beasties across the globe in minutes, but there's fun stuff too. We could hop in this thing and be sipping wine in Paris two seconds later, shopping in Milan in the blink of an eye after that. I think you'll find our technology a tremendous asset as you move into your finance career. Or into service as my favorite escort." He flashed her a sneering wink. "Your choice, but I know which pays better."

Before she could overthink, Taylor rushed Stearns and jammed her knee between his ass cheeks. Flesh met bone with a heinous crunch, and a piece inside of him caved on impact. He howled and sunk to his knees, doubling over into the fetal position.

"You fucking cunt," he wheezed, face twisted in agony as he clutched his midsection.

"Not gonna argue." She dragged him ten feet away from the box and kicked him in the stomach. "Next time you see me, I won't be alone. We're going to free every one of those captive shifters and burn this godforsaken place to the ground."

In lieu of waiting for the grimacing monster in tailored slacks to answer, Taylor dashed into the booth, hope flooring her at the sight of a small QWERTY keyboard built into the floor. She squatted and mouthed the coordinates to the hogan that she'd deciphered from her download, begging no particular god that her memory would serve her as she typed with trembling hands.

"Stop." Stearns's voice was pained but lucid.

She jerked her neck up to see him lurching, hunched zombielike, toward her.

Her pulse sped; her breath came out in choppy gasps. She keyed in more data, and a glowing web of blue veins raced across the ceiling and poured light into the center tube.

"Stop right now." Stearns rattled at the door handle. "You have no idea who you're messing with."

As she finished plugging in the coordinates, arresting blue plumes spewed like a geyser, ensconcing the square pen in a phosphorescent prism of hues ranging from navy to cerulean.

"No, you have it backwards." Taylor pressed the four key the moment Stearns got the door handle down, and a deafening whir filled her ears. "Don't mess with Texas."

The noise was intensifying, and she reeled against a thud, then hurdled headfirst down a vortex of spinning kaleidoscope lights. She landed face-down on dirt, her cheek throbbing from the impact.

Taylor scrambled onto her palms and knees, looking around in an effort to quell frantic disorientation. Circular walls, opening at the top. She spit out a clump of dirt and grass and smiled despite the pain radiating through her body. No mistaking Julian's hogan.

FOURTEEN

Orbiting the perimeter of a space devoted to presenting the labors of his soul, Julian should have been elated. Everywhere he looked, he saw the stunning evidence of his success.

Yet as he cycled through the three urban-chic rooms of the Witt Gallery, exposed pipes and redbrick accent walls testifying to a hip and gritty authenticity suited to his style, he couldn't appreciate the sights of his paintings and the patrons admiring them.

The pleasant chatter of a well-attended event blended with a soft background of modern folk music, but the spoils of his lifelong efforts retreated into the backdrop of his mind. The sights and sounds of a dream come true failed to stir him.

That he couldn't feel gratitude for any of the day's blessings bathed him in guilt. But worry and distress on Taylor's behalf dominated his thoughts.

She wasn't with him. Bad enough.

Worse, she wasn't safe. His heart kicked into his throat, and a fresh spray of jitters took flight as he acknowledged a visitor with a friendly hello. He stopped by a blank wall near the emergency exit, an unpopulated area at the back of the gallery, and checked his phone again. No calls or texts. He sighed.

"You okay, man?" This from Witt, who sidled up to Julian wearing a seersucker suit, glasses with cherry-red frames, and a stern aura. "You seem a little distracted."

He'd been all over Witt's radar since the paperwork incident, and he'd better keep his messiness in check so as not to burn a bridge. "I'm fine. Just checking to see if someone I'm expecting is coming."

Witt adjusted his frames. "Ah. If you have a second, there's someone here I'd like to introduce you to." A tart note of professionalism crisped the syllables of Witt's naturally brusque voice, letting Julian know that the gallery owner put stock in this introduction.

Wouldn't do him any good to waste his energy pacing the floor, wound up tight and obsessing about Taylor. She said she'd return in the morning and be in touch then, and agonizing about hypothetical, worst-case scenarios didn't do a thing for either of them. "Sounds great. Thanks."

Witt led Julian into the master room, a tidy white cube decorated by the rich, saturated hues of Julian's bleeding sunsets, experiments in surrealism rendered in chewy purples and sweet oranges, and the portraits of his people occupied with slice of life activities.

Spectators sipped red wine from stemless glasses, women's heels clattering softly against hardwood. A crimson decal in a no-nonsense font stamped one wall with the words Blood Red/Red Blood, announcing the exhibit's title.

Killer setup, his pieces and the space working together in profound and cerebral congruity designed to encourage thoughtful contemplation. Despite other areas of his life going off the rails, at least he had his talent, his livelihood.

Forcing himself to a grounded headspace, Julian followed Witt to where a severe-looking man with a Q-Tip puff of white hair, beef jerky skin, and a crooked bowtie rubbed his chin while studying one of Julian's more experimental pieces.

"Albert Font, this is Julian Nez." Witt laid a hand in the middle of the older man's back. "Albert, thank you for coming tonight. Doesn't our feature artist have the most exquisite style? A uniquely talented eye for apprehending the unusual and fantastic lying beneath the surface of the mundane. Julian, Albert patronizes several local artists in a variety of mediums. He's been on the lookout for a top painter with a compelling take on humanity."

Julian molded his features into a smile and tipped a nod of thanks at Witt. Possessing the ability to shift his shape into a wolf had blessed him with a philosophical curiosity of the sort Witt identified. Funny how others' impressions could skate the edges of reality while lacking awareness of the most essential details. It proved how subjective and mysterious art was, a true window to the soul.

"Breathtaking," Font said in a quiet, powerful tone lilted with the remnants of an English accent. "What inspires you, Julian?"

Maybe someday he could talk openly. Share his reflections on who he was with people who could accept him, wolf and all. "I suppose I'm fascinated by the notion that identity has many layers. How our core values and personality might stay the same, yet we change our roles depending on context."

"Like Erving Goffman's role theory in sociology," Witt offered in a supportive cadence.

Jesus, he ought to get his head in the game, because Witt was doing him a solid favor he probably didn't deserve, and impressing Albert Font might catapult his career to exciting new heights. If he could sell a major piece and secure payment before leaving for Peru, he'd be able to leave the United States unburdened by financial stress and support both himself and Taylor in the medium-term. But he didn't want to get ahead of himself or start fixating on idealized outcomes.

Albert hummed an appreciative noise and nodded, his attention still stuck on the painting. "There is no such thing as a completely pristine, whitewashed surface."

Julian slid his gaze from Albert's profile to the art, catching sight of how a small crowd had formed a circle around the three men.

The painting in question consisted of mostly unused canvas, an alabaster square the size of car windshield glossed to a sparkling shine. A cardboard cube like a ring box raised a bump in the lower-left hand corner of the colorless slate. If the spectator leaned down and peered closely at the small square, they would see a viewing hole. And through that pinprick window they'd discover a chunk of magnifying glass enlarging half of Julian's thumbprint, the color of the smudge making a stain the color of arterial blood.

No point in sugarcoating. Since Albert had focused on one of Julian's more explicitly political pieces, the guy could handle the heavy rundown. "Exactly. Even when there's an attempt to whitewash history, a trace of the other persists. Same with the original sins of America. It's there, always, under the surface. We may not choose to see it, but the stain remains. Once we look deeper and see, though, our gaze bears witness to the spilled blood of others."

"And in the process of seeing, we've incurred a responsibility to confront the blood on our own hands." Still rapt, Albert removed his glasses, polished the lenses, and put them back on. "As we witness atrocities of the past, we see ourselves in the box of mirrors."

The group of a dozen or so onlookers supplied a chorus of murmurs and whispers, tasteful sounds of affirmation.

At last, Albert broke his reverie and sliced Julian a shark-like teal stare. "As it stands right now, do you enjoy quality patronage?"

Fuck. He was hitting a home run. If not for the situation with Taylor eating him alive, he'd be soaring to the stars from elation. If she stood by his side, he'd soar even higher. He summoned every iota of his willpower to arm himself with wit and cleverness. "Not unless you count lean living and a frugal budget."

"Scarcity will never produce abundance, so start thinking about money flowing to you. We'll chat more at the end of the night," Albert said in a businessman's tone. "Phenomenal stuff here, Nez. You've captured the essence of what the rest of us can't see but wish we could articulate."

"Excuse me, Mr. Nez can I bend your ear for a minute?" This from a tall Indigenous woman with a pair of ebony braids and eyes the color of sand. She touched the shoulder of an older lady, whose sweet smile and cropped black hair made Julian's heart hurt from missing his dear mama. "My auntie and I were wondering if we could interview you for a story we're writing for the Austin Beat. It'll run on Indigenous People's Day."

Great magazine, attuned to the cutting edge of the local cultural scene. Julian allowed a smidgeon of tension to leak out of him. "Sure. Ask whatever you want."

Wind chimes played in a whimsical tinkle as the front door opened and shut. A man amidst the circle of spectators scrunched his face in a puzzled look and coughed awkwardly.

"Julian." Taylor's voice, strung tense and pitched high with urgency. "Thank God. Thank God. We have to leave tonight. He's after us. They're after us."

Fear, relief, and confusion walloped him in a big crack that sent his thoughts sprawling. He snapped his stare to where she ran through the main room, clothes disheveled and streaked with dirt. His awareness shrunk to a beam leading to her as his pulse spiked to a staccato that drowned out the bemused chatter of everyone else. A fresh bruise with an oozing cut in the middle stained her pale cheek red and blue, and grass stuck to the side of her head.

Witt stepped in front of Julian and laid his hands on Taylor's shoulders. "Excuse me, miss, excuse me. This is a private event. Do you need the address of a women's shelter?"

She pushed Witt aside and grabbed Julian's wrist. "It's worse than we thought. They've got an underground dungeon where they've trapped hundreds of them—of *us*. There's a teleportation machine down there too, powered by this Other One. They run kidnapping operations all over the globe and bring them back there...I escaped...I'm sure they're after me." She shook all over and fell into Julian's arms, gasping and gurgling wet sounds.

"What the fuck is happening?" Breath hot against Julian's ear, Witt spoke in a slow whisper through clenched teeth. "Do you know this woman? Is she having some kind of mental breakdown episode?"

He had to think fast and play off this twist somehow. Julian pointed at the fingerprint painting with his free hand, rubbing Taylor's back with the other. "Atrocities. She's right. Atrocities are happening every day, perpetrated by the people we don't see."

Witt's eyes lit up. Julian could practically see the gears in his head turning as he worked to spin the situation on the fly. "Absolutely. Under your skin, under our collective skin, is where evil teems. Beneath the register of our sight, ladies and gentlemen, the blood of murdered others flows. And blood has been spilled, literally and figuratively, tonight. This woman is the scandal personified, the witness, a town crier forcing to the surface that which we cannot or will not see." Head high and shoulders back as he boomed his proclamations in a theatrical timbre fit for a Broadway stage, Witt migrated to the middle of the circle. All eyes turned to the gallery owner.

Julian mouthed the flamboyant curator a silent "thanks" for saving his ass.

Taylor broke the embrace, bore her stare into Julian's, and said, "Now."

The shrewd curator continued his speech, framing Taylor's panicked intrusion as a deliberate act of performance art. His impressionable audience gaped and nodded before breaking into a round of applause.

Julian couldn't pinpoint whether Witt was authentically invested in his slant or using the act to give Julian an out, but either way, the routine served as his sole escape hatch. He snatched Taylor's hand and ran with her to the front door.

They burst out into a balmy night animated with the usual Friday night flair of honking horns and laughing pedestrians strolling between bars or events.

"Tell me what happened to you." He looked in her eyes, gingerly grazing the injury on her face with the back of his hand. "Were you attacked?"

"No. One of the ringleaders wanted to get me into a lab and re-up my programming somehow, but I tricked him into leading me to the master portal. On the way there, I passed through where they're being held captive. The shifters. So many. In an underground tunnel network."

"I agree with you. We need to get to Peru and link up with Tim and the others, get their help and their takes on how to go forward." A quick glimpse inside the gallery resulted in a jerk of stress. "I was hoping to tie up a couple more loose ends on the life front before we left, but here we are."

"Yep. Here we are. We need to talk to Tim about portals. Tell him what we know and see if he can find one down there. I think if I get in your hogan, I can portal direct us to Peru. Provided there's a port somewhere near enough to them."

"I'm just glad you're safe." Clasping her hand in his larger one in a gesture of protection, he walked them around the back of the building and through the small, full parking lot. He unlocked his truck, and an instant after they belted up he started driving. "I think we ought to sit down and review every piece of data we have before we contact Tim. Make a chart or graph of the facts so we have the best possible sense of how all these pieces—everything we found in your dad's office, what you saw tonight, and what I've read—lines up."

"Agreed." She covered her face and barked a bitter laugh.

Julian sailed onto the exit ramp and pushed down on the gas pedal, his speedometer twitching just above the speed limit as the truck cruised southbound on the Interstate. He offered a quizzical laugh in reply to her harsh one. "What's funny?"

"When we first met at the library, I completely recoiled at the idea that there could be weird happenings lining up. Goes to show how wrong I was."

"We're inherently rational beings. Takes a lot to override that skepticism."

"And now I have no idea who or what I am anymore."

"Well, I have an idea. You're strong and brave and uncompromising. You're someone with staunch principles who isn't afraid to fight for their beliefs. For what's right."

She turned to him and ticked a corner of her mouth, as if the potential for happiness fought for release from all the pain. "Thank you for always seeing the best in me. It means so much."

It would mean more, though, if he could free them from the nightmare that had swallowed their lives. Take away the pain and suffering and replace it with movies and lazy Sundays with crossword puzzles and flirtations over dinner. Wouldn't be easy, but Taylor was worth the fight. "I don't have to look too hard."

Without a word, she leaned her head against his arm, and the drive continued in comfortable silence, a stolen moment teasing him with a glimpse into what a content, happy relationship might look like. They could go on a road trip to Arizona. Meet his folks. A lump lodged in his throat. No time for fantasies, not yet.

When he pulled into the driveway, Julian steered his mentality back on track. "When you say you escaped, am I guessing correctly that you got yourself into a teleportation machine and used coordinates to make it back to the hogan?"

"Bingo." She followed him to the front door.

He unlocked, flipped on several lights, and went right to his laptop. "So we've got a good idea of what they're doing and why. But what I can't figure out is why you. Why were you programmed to capture, and how does that relate to your ability to shift?" The chips might have precipitated her ability to transform or halted it. Lots of unknowns were in play.

She joined him at the kitchen table. "They had a lead on a shifter in Texas, so part of the "why me" question relates to sheer proximity. I don't know about the rest. I asked, but Stearns wouldn't tell me. We know it has to do with my father and whatever sense in which he's indebted or in over his head, but I didn't come back from that island with any more details."

The dim light of the kitchen drew his attention to her wounded face. "Hold up." He jogged to the bathroom, returning with rubbing alcohol and swabs, antibacterial ointment, and a bandage.

"A minor infection is the least of our worries."

"Not when we're about to go to the jungle." And besides, he liked having an opportunity to take care of Taylor.

"Fair. We don't have a natural immunity to whatever bacteria we'd encounter there." A pragmatic and sensible reply, though the way she closed her eyes and sighed while he applied the medicine let him know that she needed his tenderness, his comfort. Even though she didn't always articulate her longing for care, Julian would do his best to anticipate and provide the gentle things she needed.

"No flesh-eating bacteria for you." He unpeeled the sticky bandage from its backing and smoothed it over her buttery cheek.

She laughed with a touch of mirth. "Nothing but a pretty face, huh? Are you saying you wouldn't be with me anymore if I was missing half of my head?"

Of course he would, because there was no deformity on the planet capable of ruining Taylor's spirit or personality. Though he'd be remiss to squander an opportunity for banter. "Now there's a wicked double bind for me. No comment." Julian flipped open his laptop and pulled up the video chat program.

She bit a nail and dropped her stare to the floor. "Shit, I just thought of something."

He paused before dialing Tim. "What?"

"Stearns talked about using scouts to pass through portals and infiltrate entire shifter communities. I don't want to go if it means putting anyone at risk. Maybe you should go alone."

"Good thought, but let's see what he says first. I won't leave you behind. We're in this together."

Her shoulders relaxed from a stressed hunch. "Yes."

With the press of a key, he resumed the call. Julian's heartbeat quickened in time with the vibrating phone icon in the middle of the screen.

"Hey guys. Good to see you again." Log cabin walls and a hanging rack of pots and pans made up the background behind Tim's face. "What's new?"

He hated to act as the harbinger of gloom and doom, but lying or hiding things made him feel worse. "I'm gonna level with you. We're in trouble. Looks like in addition to an Other One, we've got some kind of clandestine black ops capture operation after us."

"Yeah. We're up to speed on those now. I did some research after our last chat. They're going on all over the world. Teleportation capture in some cases, in others, they just ambush costal and port cities and drag off women and children. Put them in a fucking submarine or yacht."

"Have you experienced any invasion attempts?"

"No. A former community member, a magic user, cast a protection spell on our star portal. Nobody knows if shifters are drawn to areas with portals or if the presence of a shifter causes a natural portal to form, but the point is there's one near us. We've got about a million layers of security protecting against hacking and surveillance. Akin to a massive firewall on your computer. So don't worry about us. But the others, man. Gotta get them out."

"I know where they are, roughly. I just need to pull the coordinates out of the algorithm the captives sent me, and I can get us there," Taylor said.

Tim nodded. "Get here as soon as you can. Once we're all together, we'll strategize."

"How do we direct portal travel without a machine to plug in the latitude and longitude?" Taylor asked.

"I don't know anyone who's done it," Tim admitted. "But from what I've heard, if you can find a portal location to launch from, the process involves locking in on the Sirius star and meditating on exactly where you want to go."

"Where's yours?" Julian asked.

"About fifty feet deep in the jungle in the middle of a clearing near a creek and an outhouse. I don't have the exact coordinates, but if you send the intention to get to Iquitos, you should end up where you need to be. We'll have a team out there to greet you, so let me know when you plan to come."

"Tonight," Taylor said.

"Yeah." Julian nodded.

"Alright." Tim tilted his head to one side. "But give yourselves time to prepare. Spray yourself with bug repellant and bring any weapons you can carry as well as flashlights. I don't mean to scare you, but the jungle is gnarly. We've got big cats and venomous snakes, and mosquitos can carry malaria. Don't take this lightly."

"Not a chance," Julian said.

"Will we need tents? Sleeping bags, bedding, anything like that?" Taylor fished a day planner and pen from her purse and scribbled notes.

"No, we're more developed than you might think. I've got an empty guest cabin that's perfect for you two. Any pets I should be aware of? Somebody once showed up with two surprise horses in tow, and getting them situated without notice caused a headache. So I like to know in advance what animal accommodations I'll need to make."

"Ball python," Taylor said with a hint of concern. "He's very tame and quite low maintenance."

Tim chuckled. "Didn't see that coming. No problem, caged critters are easy. See you guys soon."

"Thank you," Julian said.

"You bet." The screen blinked black.

As Julian closed the laptop lid, a silent understanding passed between him and Taylor. They were in this together, comrades and companions in multiple and complex senses of the word. Ready to act as a team. Ready to fight. They jumped up in unison, a flash of synchronicity that reassured Julian with promises of good outcomes.

Wordless, methodical preparation commenced in a fast sweep of Julian's home. Upon completion, his kitchen table was covered with four soft gun cases containing rifles, shotguns, and ammunition, a massive Maglite fit to bludgeon, and the heaviest boots and thickest socks each of them owned.

He scrounged up a few varieties of bug spray, a camping pack and two portable water bottles, and a tube of sunscreen. Various and sundry other items deemed of possible use—energy bars, ibuprofen, batteries, a compass—rounded out the spread. They each loaded a backpack, changed shoes, and slung two gun cases apiece over their shoulders.

Aerosol hisses filled the room as they sprayed repellant, turning his kitchen into a foggy cloud of citronella stickiness.

In his travel case, Salazar peeked out from his hollow hiding rock, unaware of the adventure ahead.

"Our first vacation," Taylor said dryly, sliding a textbook into a backpack full of clothes and supplies.

Sadness threaded needles through him. She deserved so much better than all this. "I promise to take you somewhere as soon as possible. Good for you for bringing the book. Nobody's had an issue with you missing class?"

"No. I told them I needed to finish the semester online for personal reasons, and they took me at my word. Totally cool with it, and I'm still on track to graduate in December."

"Good. I'd hate to see you give up on your dreams."

"My dreams have changed, but I'm not abandoning school—"

She quit speaking when a flash of white light flickered in his living room window and skittered over the sofa.

He glimpsed out the big window overlooking the driveway, and his blood went to poison and electric chemical rushes. Two men in suits exited a black sedan. "Get down and run to the hogan."

Taylor snatched up the plastic aquarium, dropped to a crouch, and scurried out the back. She must've propped the door—smart woman—because it didn't slam.

Julian ducked and followed. Fists thudded the front door the instant he made it out of the mudroom and into the yard.

FIFTEEN

IT WAS TOUGH TO CONCENTRATE, LET ALONE MEDITATE, WITH ICY flashlight beams flickering over the house's interior windows as the intruders commenced their search. At least the uninvited guests hadn't moved out to the yard, so Taylor hadn't given up yet.

"They know about the hogan." She clutched the plastic sides of her pet's on-the-go tank. "They'll put two and two together any second."

A zipper zinged, followed by the distinctive click-click of a shotgun cocking. With a hollow tap, a shell hit the dirt ground. "Let them. We aren't helpless here, babe." Crouching, Julian pointed the business end of his firearm at the entryway.

She better hustle unless she wanted this to escalate. Which she did not. A dead thug or two could worsen their predicament in many ways. Speaking of thugs in black suits, what was up with that comment about insemination? Now, though, wasn't the time to worry about loose ends.

"Looks like they're coming out of the bedrooms and back into the kitchen. Finishing their sweep," Julian said evenly, his gaze set in a line down the barrel of his weapon.

Meaning they'd be in the yard any second. Taylor tipped her head to the ceiling opening, where Sirius ruled the heavens with celestial, diamond majesty. The longer she stared, the weirder and dreamier her head became. So she kept on staring, chasing the lead.

Taylor slipped and slid into oddness, her lucidity falling away scrap by scrap. She allowed her perception to melt into the star's five icicle needles, a radiant ball of glowing spears at the end of Orion's belt, until she lost track of where she ended, and the star began.

A familiar hum filled her mind, like the buzzing she'd heard in the library but not as frightening. On some primal level, the symptom made a shred more sense now. Due to whatever mutation afflicted her cells and enabled her to shift, she could connect with forces and energies in different parts of space and time. The other shifters could very well have reached out to her using a similar meditation technique.

As if tendering confirmation, her whole body heated in a series of rhythmic, vaguely sensual pulses.

"Hang on, Julian. Bear with me." She pictured the Amazon, lush and vivid, a vibrant world of green canopies. Yellow-eyed jaguars prowled obsidian nights, and serpents ten times the size of Salazar coiled up ancient tree trunks to make caduceus after caduceus.

"Two men in the mudroom," Julian said in a harsh whisper.

Taylor slipped beside herself, her perception surreal and strange, removed. A whirling sound from her snake's tank directed her attention, and she glanced at his water bowl. The liquid in there swirled in a tiny tempest in motions, mirroring the infinite loops of DNA coils.

"I think I'm linking in," she whispered through a hypnotic stupor, mouth full of molasses.

"Opening the door to the yard." Julian's tense declaration could have been a hundred miles away and underwater, given how garbled his statement sounded to her. "Once they approach the hogan's doorway, I'm going to give them one warning before I shoot to kill."

A rush of energy surged from her chest, invisible yet tangible enough to bend the air in front of her with wobbles like heat waves. The force blasted upward, through the roof hole, and kept on going. As the controlled liquid whirlpool maintained a frantic tempo, Taylor saw flickering impressions of her DNA swirls blinking before her eyes.

Sirius copied her, the shape of outer space changing to mirror her inner dimensions. Five points of brightness looped, merged, melded until an infinity loop formed, matching the twenty-three pairs of chromosomes that spun in her. Synthesis. Next, transport.

"Drop your weapon or I shoot!" This from Julian in a commanding, scary cadence she'd never heard.

Light filled the hogan, forcing her to squint and blink. A few drops of water splashed her face in tepid pats.

"Now." She forced the word to come in a shout, the utterance blasting her out of her trance. "Now, Julian, grab on to me."

A crack and boom made her ears ring. Less than a second later, Julian rolled into her body and wrapped his arms around her middle. Her particles ripped apart in sharp, intermittent stabs of pain.

She flipped upside down with a clamp of nausea, and a second later, her belly slammed down on hard ground. The impact knocked out her wind, and she wheezed for inadequate slurps of air, head throbbing. "Julian?" she gasped, blurry eyes adjusting to darkness.

"I'm here, babe, I'm here." He coughed and spit. "Jesus. Are you okay? Was your first landing this rough?"

"Oh yeah, it was gnarly. And I'm fine. Are you alright?"

"I think so."

White stars danced in her vision as the surroundings coalesced into hazy focus. They lay in nature, at night. Fecund smells of wet soil steeped in bacteria permeated dank, humid air. An ensemble of chirps, croaks, and hoots serenaded her and Julian's arrival.

A burly, bearded man wearing a band t-shirt and leather jacket with the sleeves sawed off stood over them, the tip of his rifle shoved in Taylor's face. "State your names and the nature of your visit." His gruff tone fit his aggressive stance and style.

"It's me, Julian, and this is Taylor. We spoke with Tim."

"This is them, Chaz. We're cool." The assurance came in a smoother, more youthful male voice.

Taylor could see well enough now to make out three people ringing her, Julian, and a caged Salazar. In addition to the big dude Chaz, a gangly twenty-something in jeans and an old hippie with a long gray braid and a musty, patchouli odor lowered drawn guns.

Chaz extended a meaty hand, and Taylor grabbed on and used his leverage to spring to her feet. Julian rose unaided, bringing all five people eye-to-eye.

"Sorry to alarm you." Chaz pulled a strap, sliding his rifle to rest against his back. "But we've had people try to pull all kinds of shit on us in the past."

"I get it." Julian donned his supplies and picked up Salazar's cage by the handle. "I wish we had time for pleasantries, but we've got a situation here. A bad situation that's deteriorating."

"Tim more or less gave us the gist," the oldest man said as he took off walking. "You have a detail on your tail, yeah? Fake government agent types?"

Taylor adjusted the hiking pack and gun case slung over her shoulders and started moving, twigs snapping underfoot as the quintet trod a worn path. She pressed a button on her flashlight, and a fluorescent cone lit a swath of thick darkness before her. Leaves and tree trunks popped into sharp, ominous relief. "Yeah. I was implanted with microchips and programmed to capture Julian. But my programming started breaking down, because I managed to resist whatever brainwashing component would have me complete the job. The next thing I know, I'm shifting into a wolf, same as Julian."

In a silent gesture of support, Julian caught her hand, interlaced their fingers, and squeezed.

In the midst of so much madness and disorder, her belly fluttered with gratitude. No action from another person had ever meant so much to her, had ever carried with it such a powerful symbolism of trust and hope and loyalty. She looked up at him and smiled.

Chaz looked back at her, the beam from his own flashlight highlighting suspicion in his slitted eyes. "You keep speaking in the passive voice. Do you really have no idea who did this to you or why?"

"I do." She smashed her palm into Julian's, her other hand clutching a death grip on the Maglite. "My father did it, or ordered it done. No idea why, other than proximity to Julian. He picked me to serve as a capture scout for this program he's mixed up in. I can't say for certain why he's involved, but from the way he's been acting, I think he was blackmailed or coerced. My theory is that someone with power over him put his back against the wall."

"Bro, are you sure about her?" the skinny guy asked Julian. "This sounds sketchy as hell. Her own family is tied up in this kidnapping program, and she's hella implicated."

Taylor trapped her tongue between her teeth before she fired back with a sharp comment. She hated being talked about like she wasn't there, loathed feeling erased by bro solidarity, but at the moment, her ego needed to take a backseat to the concerns of the group. Life wasn't all about her personal empowerment anymore. Perhaps it never should have been.

"I'm sure about her." Julian said with steady, resolute kindness. "And that subject is now closed. You feel me?"

The thin man grunted, kicking debris out of his way as he took large steps. "If you say so. I don't follow is all. Do you have any theories, Taylor? Any insights into why you got sucked into this? There are big pieces of this story missing. The most important ones."

"I'm not sure the origin matters at this point." Fifty feet ahead, the trail opened into another clearing occupied by a smattering of cabins. It was a relief to exit rough wilderness and stumble upon familiarity in the form of shelter, at least. "I'll keep you informed as soon as I know more, but right now what I want to do is help. And since Julian and I know where the others are imprisoned, I'm in a position to assist."

"What's in this for you?" the aging burnout type asked. "Why do you care if shifters live or die?"

"Give it a rest," Julian said with authority. "I told you, she's one of us."

The hippie bunched his shoulders. "Sorry—"

"It's okay. I appreciate it, but he's right. I ought to explain myself." Taylor nodded a silent thanks to Julian. "I totally see how I can come off as a sketchy character, or at least an unknown. I suppose I never knew injustice until I found out that I'd been tampered with against my will, until my body stopped being mine to predict or control. The loss of autonomy terrified me. There I was, sitting in a lecture hall daydreaming about going off to Wall Street and getting richer and more powerful. That's been my whole life basically, money and power and privilege. So I guess when my agency was stripped away, when I started mutating and hearing voices, seeing things, I became indignant and outraged. But those feelings can't just be for me anymore because I allowed myself to become blind to the atrocities that happen everyday. I'm tired of being selfish, and somewhere along the way, I opened my eyes to how self-absorbed I'd been. I want to change. If that doesn't make any sense, I apologize."

Julian brushed his lips against her temple. "It makes perfect sense. I'm proud of you."

"I want to be better, and I'm trying. Maybe I'm glad all this crazy shit started happening to me. It forced me to take stock, to see things in a new way, things I was able to ignore before."

"Sounds like you got a kick in the ass for sure," the young man offered, and at last everyone laughed a good-natured round of chuckles grounded in camaraderie.

In the front of the group, Chaz forged ahead and stopped at the threshold of one of the cabins. He rummaged in a jacket pocket, and keys jingled. "Pretty bare bones accommodations, but you've got a gas stove, a cold shower, and a pump toilet. Don't put anything besides bodily waste in the septic system. Linens and towels are in the side closet. I'll give you an hour to get situated, and then I'll send Tim over. Sound good?"

"Yes. We really appreciate this," Julian said.

"Absolutely." Still holding her man's hand, Taylor stepped to the front door of the single-story log building.

"Glamping at its finest." Chaz winked. "See you in the morning. We all pitch in to make breakfast at six thirty and eat at eight. Listen for a horn at sunrise."

Flanked by the other two men, Chaz walked off.

The bearded escort hadn't handed over the keys. A low-tech surveillance that communicated his lingering vestiges of doubt by denying Julian and Taylor the ability to lock themselves and their belongings away from the eyes of the rest of the group. Fair enough. The shifter clan had their reasons, legitimate ones, for exercising extreme caution about newcomers.

Julian walked in first and flipped a light switch. A simple living room held a couch and two recliners, one lamp, and a coffee table with some boxed board games stacked underneath. To the right was the kitchen, basic with a fridge, range, and minimalist table for two. The bedroom consisted of a double bed behind a changing screen. A single door beside the sleeping quarters must've led to the bathroom. Julian strode over and opened the door in question.

Once he'd checked out the space, he signaled with a sweep of his hand for Taylor to enter. He set Salazar's cage on the coffee table and sloughed off his pack and gun.

"Thanks for looking out for us." Nerves skittered through Taylor as she took a seat on the couch, springs creaking beneath her bottom. The cabin's scent of cedar offered a pleasurable taste of rustic novelty, though not enough to put her at ease. "I need to tell you about something that happened. In the interest of full disclosure."

"Yeah. Of course." He sat close to her and laid a hand on her knee, concern thick in his brown eyes.

"At the art fair, one of the goons interrogated me about whether your semen entered my body. He got explicit about all possible ways, so he wasn't just talking about pregnancy. He seemed really invested in knowing and said it was important that I tell him before I went to the island. Does that mean anything to you? From a shifter standpoint?"

Julian moved his head back and forth. "The entirety of what I know comes from research, since as you know, this is my first experience meeting others like me."

"So what's your sense of it?" She picked a nail.

"Like I said, the information I'm able to provide all comes from lore and myth, so best taken with a grain of salt. That being said, there's a theory that once fated shifters mate, their bond can't be broken." He brushed his knuckles against hers.

She nudged the side of his foot with her toe. "Luckily I don't have a fear of commitment, because that's intense."

He draped an arm around her shoulders and pulled her close. "Indeed. But it seems too benign of an explanation to account for whatever this jerk was talking about."

"Yeah." Taylor relaxed against Julian's form. "Unless he felt he needed to know whether it was plausible to try and tear us apart. I suppose if there was no way I'd turn on you, this would diminish their return on investment for continuing the project."

"Good point, but the fact that he was so obsessed with getting that question answered before you went to the island makes me think they've got an agenda."

"Their plan could involve my programming, but who knows. The chips and protocol and mutations, why I turned into a wolf...so much of it is a black box at this point. Though I wonder if it ties in with whatever they were going to do to reprogram me. Like they needed to figure out other effects that took place in my body before going forward."

"I'm just glad that you escaped."

"Same, but I also didn't get as much out of the visit as I hoped I would."

"Well, we can't have you being a mad scientist experimenting on yourself. That's a bridge too far if you ask me."

She laughed and nuzzled his shoulder. "Thanks for being the brake, Julian."

"What can I say? I'm a sensible guy." His stare took on an intense sheen of desire, and he traced light fingertips down her ear and jaw. "Tim won't be here for another thirty minutes." He spoke with a gruff, randy murmur.

"Sensible, but with a definite wild side." Taylor angled her hip and started to swing her leg over his lap when a series of knocks struck the door. She groaned and rolled her eyes. "We summoned him, huh?"

Julian set a throw pillow on his lap. "Come in."

Tim breezed into the condo, all long legs and lean muscle clad in cargo pants and an athletic tee. He carried a plastic water bottle covered in stickers and a rolled tube of paper, the confidence in his motions and posture giving off an aura of leadership. "Hey, guys, glad you made it. Mind if we get right down to business?"

Taylor scooted to the edge of her seat and switched into serious mode. "The reason we're here."

"Okay, here's what I was able to reconstruct from my Internet deep dive." Tim sat in one of the recliners, unfurled his tube, and weighed down one corner with his bottle and the other using his hand. A printed blueprint of a structure covered the sheet. "The teleportation chamber is here." He tapped an area in the middle of the map. "And here is the containment cell. What Taylor saw." He slid his finger a few inches over. "Once we get in, we'll need lock breaking capabilities. I say we prepare for multiple methods. Brute force, lock picking, and code breaking. Sound doable?"

"Yeah." Movement in her peripheral vision snagged her awareness, and she glimpsed at Tim's water bottle. Her heartbeat skittered. The liquid swirled in a whirlpool, same as the stuff in Salazar's drinking dish. She blinked. Someone could have bumped the container. "The locks I saw there were facial recognition, though. Retinal scanners. To get through those, we might need to capture someone who works there. Use an employee to open the high-tech doors."

The funnel spun, faster and faster, unravelling her brain and sucking long strands of gray matter into a mighty orbital pull. Her eyelids drooped. Had she crossed an event horizon, come face-to-face with a small, contained portal inside Tim's sporty Nalgene bottle peppered with decals advertising bands and camping gear?

Tim said, "On Reddit, I found what looks to be leaked security footage. From what I could surmise, the big shots only go down there intermittently. But they're more securitized at night, have a predictable guard patrol of around five people. So one of them could serve as an asset for opening doors and cages. Once we teleport, we can stake out a guard and kidnap him. Subdue the rest."

"Then we lead the shifters to the portal and send them here in batches," Julian said.

"If all goes according to plan." Tim trailed off. "You okay, Taylor?"

"Your water," she managed to slur, muzzy and overheated. Symbols appeared in the water. The same one, the handprint inside the upside-down triangle.

Tim's eyes bugged, and he picked up the clear bottle. "No way." He drew out the words, turning the container upside down as the vortex spun.

Julian looked between Taylor and Tim. "No way what?"

"Latent magic. You have latent magic. Water magic. Portal travel can cause magical abilities to manifest in shifters. There was a woman who lived with us until last year, the one I told you about who cast a protection spell on our portal, who came in to her air magic the day after she portal jumped. Some feature of the energy changes the alignment of our particles and brings buried magic to the surface. Have you seen a symbol of what looks like a handprint with broken fingers popping up? Supposedly that's the prophetic key that ties six magic users to the system that they pull from. She saw it. A handprint inside of the elemental symbol for air."

"I did see that key, that symbol. Yes. And what is probably the elemental sign for water too." A bolt of clarity struck Taylor. She looked at Julian. "That has to be it. Why the goon from the fair cared so much about whether your fluids entered me. Mating must link in with the unlocking, facilitate it, and/or affect the other features of my changing and mutation that are relevant to my being on the island. Goddamn. They know so much that we don't. We need more. We have to get there. There could be stashes of documents, computer hard drives."

A layer of frosty detachment dusted Tim's dark-eyed stare. "Okay, we can leave as early as tomorrow, after we have some prep time. But I need to know that you're in this for the right reasons—to rescue those shifters and bring them to the sanctuary here. If this is purely personal to you, a revenge vendetta, or a quest for answers, I'm less comfortable bringing you on board with the team."

Julian pointed at Tim. "She stood on the trail and told Chaz and the others why she wants a part of this. Her investment is for all the right reasons. Moral, ethical ones. Justice. Come on, man. Don't assume the worst just because you've been burned by outsiders in the past."

"Don't you assume my motives," Tim shot back. "I like you, Jules, seriously, but I'm starting to worry that your obvious romantic feelings are taking up space where healthy skepticism ought to be."

"Oh, Christ, that's not patronizing at all. I'm not some teenage boy in puppy love."

Taylor slapped the table with a smack that cut off the argument. "Of course this is personal. How could it not be personal to me, being genetically modified against my will? But I assure you, I promise you, that I have the same vision that you have. Save the others. So yes, I'm not going to lie. I want closure, I want answers, and I want them bad. And there is a teeny part of me that wants to bury the assholes who did this to me. But I think I have grounds for being pissed. And, more importantly, whatever feelings and personal motives I might have will in no way compromise me. I give you my word."

Tim looked at Taylor, paused, and glanced at Julian.

"I stand with her." Julian said.

Tim slid a cautious eye back to Taylor and rolled up his blueprint. With a bemused look at the still-raging baby storm contained in plastic, he collected his bottle. "We'll assemble by the campfire circle after breakfast and make a plan."

"Then ship out at nightfall to catch those security guards at the beginning of their shift," Julian added.

"Who retired and made you alpha?" Tim delivered the dry rhetorical question as a playful yet pointed quip. "Because it wasn't me."

Julian shrugged with a certain teasing nonchalance that made Taylor look at him differently, catch a glimpse at an intriguing, hidden side of him. Julian didn't vie for leadership opportunities in the aggressive way she did, but he didn't shrink in the face of challenges either.

He knew when to stand up for himself and others and held his ground with an understated, cool breeze cockiness suited to his Texas swagger and somewhat aloof personality.

Until now, she'd never bothered to get to know anyone other than her sister as well as she cared to know Julian. The change in outlook greeted her as a welcome trespass into her psyche, a fun burst of intellectual and interpersonal curiosity.

"Julian's right," she said smoothly. "Also, please make more copies of that blueprint for everyone who goes. We should also have radios to communicate."

"Glad to see you two are a united front." One corner of Tim's mouth ticked up in a near-smile. "See you in the morning. Be in the dining hall five minutes after the first horn blows. Get some rest because the alarm goes off before sunrise." Off he went.

An additional tidbit of possible value shone in Taylor's mind. "What happens on the autumnal equinox, by the way? The harvest moon?"

Hand on the knob, Tim furrowed his brow. "How did you know about that?"

"I don't. Not really. When I rode the plane to Scarab, I overhead some guy mentioning a ritual planned for that day. A hunt in the woods. It sounded violent. Bad."

"Good thing we'll be getting there in time to free everyone before it happens." Tim's smile was as tight as his reply.

Taylor's mind stewed in a murky soup of unknowns as she peered at Tim through an emerging lens of apprehension and even suspicion. All kinds of crazy shit could go down in this isolated, vast jungle, acres and acres of wilderness hidden from Google maps and off the radar of civilization. She shivered in the warm air. "Are we talking about the same thing?"

"Unclear. See you bright and early tomorrow." Tim left.

Julian turned to her. "You get a weird vibe about this equinox thing too, eh?"

She pulled on her earlobe and bobbed a knee, overcome by an anxious pique that left her vexed. "Yeah, but I can't tell if it's founded or just me being aggravated in the face of ignorance." She stared angrily at the door, where a trace of Tim and his irritating, cagey behavior remained. "Didn't help that he played hide the ball just now when everything should be out in the open."

Julian hummed in agreement. "True, but I'm sure they have their reasons. I agree he acted weird, but right now, this crew is our best bet for getting out from under our predicament and helping the others."

"I know. I guess the secrecy doesn't sit well with me though. In the wake of all the other stuff, the side eye and tight lips and aggressive questioning puts me on the defensive."

"You think you're up for this trip tomorrow? For planning and executing this mission with them?" Julian asked, straightforward.

"I know I am. I have to be. It's the right choice."

Though the moment the final word left her lips, doubt nagged at the back of her mind.

She wasn't afraid, nor reluctant, nor conflicted. No, the worrying sensation was akin to the feeling of an open cabinet door in her mind, a loose and unguarded flank. The Peruvian clan was confusing and private, a pack of tenuous allies, but they were all she and Julian had.

Worse, Scarab had the drop on her, leverage, an edge. If she wanted to protect Julian and the others, she'd better head to that island with the intention of reclaiming some of her lost power.

SIXTEEN

JULIAN OPENED HEAVY EYELIDS TO DARKNESS, HIS BODY STILL BUZZING from sleep as the watery remnants of dream narratives flittered out of his mind. He stretched, running a hand up and down the warm length of Taylor's back, enjoying the pillow softness of her breasts against his ribs.

She lay nude against him, her silken skin a tantalizing contrast against their itchy sheets and stiff blanket. In the pre-dawn silence of the cabin, he took a moment to appreciate the intimacy he shared with this fierce woman, the simple pleasure of her lying beside him in bed.

As his eyes adjusted and shadows faded, he allowed his stare to roam to the dresser carved from raw lumber, the simple furniture and lack of decorative flair. The walls could use a whole lot of color, but overall the cabin wasn't half-bad. In fact, its barren state represented potential.

Even the little reptile in the plastic cage on top of the bureau made him smile. If his deepening desire to make a home with Taylor came true, he'd better get used to her wiggly pet.

He sighed with pleasure and kissed the crown of her head, inhaling the sweet fragrance of her hair and urging her slumbering form closer to him. For a precious moment, Julian could escape his thoughts, his mind, the crush of their problems. If not a millimeter of space remained between the two of them, if they could fuse into one, no wedge could drive a crevice between their souls. Hard to say if he'd fit in with the Peru pack after all, but he sure as hell made sense with Taylor.

She groaned softly as she stirred. Her fingertips slid through the loose cascade of his hair and moved to caress his wolf tattoo. "It's pitch black still."

"Yeah. Not time to get up yet. I just woke up from a dream."

She glanced up at him, her eyes mysterious and bewitching in the heavy cast of ebony. Far in the distance, a bird hooted, enhancing the pull of night magic. "Do you remember what you dreamt?"

He didn't, not in terms of distinct images at least, though he'd carried emotions and concepts back with him to his waking state. Julian almost never remembered his dreams as pictures or coherent stories. Every now and then this made him sad, heavy with lack and loss, but he tried to compensate by hanging on to the energetic impressions generated by the change in brain waves that accompanied his sleep. "Today is a good day to die."

She stared at him.

Sensing her mild though evident duress, he stroked an assuring touch down the buttery length of her bare arm. "The saying sounds disturbing out loud without context, but what it means is that there are moments so perfect, so aligned in wonder and serendipity, that if you died right then, you'd have passed away utterly fulfilled. In a state of divine joy almost. Witnessing the sublime in that fleeting instant before it vanishes out of the corner of an eye. And when I woke up with you sleeping beside me, I felt it."

Her breath came out in a hot sigh against his neck as she sidled up higher, melting into him. When she spoke next, her lips grazed his throat and delivered soft but sensual kisses that hardened his cock into an obedient rod tenting his covers.

"That's beautiful, Julian. Did you think it all up yourself?"

He chuckled with good humor and tilted his head to one side, giving her wandering mouth more unfettered access. If he were a douche, he'd lie and say yes, all but guaranteeing a blow job. "Sadly, no. The saying's attributed to this old-time Lakota leader. Most people interpret the meaning as stereotypical 'badass Indian on the warpath stuff,' but that's not right. The expression's about finding contentment.

Finding the ability to live without regrets. Never to leave tasks undone."

"You listed three different possible interpretations in your analysis just there." Following her gentle taunt, Taylor sloughed off their patchwork quilt and slung her leg over his body.

With the trademark assertiveness he'd grown to expect and cherish, she circled a hand around his stiff cock and guided him into the depths of her tight, hot wetness.

And before he could process, she was riding him, bouncing and grinding in a way that made her perky breasts and pointed nipples bob. The smooth planes of her pale skin reflected what little light entered the room. She kept moving, faster and faster, gaze rapt on his face though she made not a sound.

He grabbed her hips as tight pressure ratcheted in his lower belly, his balls, base urgency tense and insistent on popping.

She humped up and down faster, impaling herself on his length again and again.

Again. And again, again, again, in glorious bolt upright plunges.

Wet suction slurps filled his ears. He groaned, his pleasure mounting as he stared at the visual feast of womanly flesh on top of him. So much goodness. Slender neck fit for a doe, shallow dip of a belly button piercing her flat stomach. The curve of her hip, trim thighs. Ripe bottom lip, parted and glistening, tits and ass jiggling.

Every one of her sexy body parts tantalized his horny, banal gaze. His prick swelled inside her juicy pussy as he returned a lustful stare to her breasts.

Yes, he was objectifying Taylor. But since he knew how much he loved and respected her mind and heart and spirit the cruder feelings didn't bother him. In fact, they completed a circle of sorts. He appreciated her wholly, inside and out. In manners both sacred and profane, elevated and filthy, he adored her. "Better slow down, babe, or I won't last long enough to satisfy you."

"So come for me, then. Use me." Her tone was raspy and aggressive, shameless in the way he loved.

He licked the pad of his thumb and slicked it over her clit, finding the nub bulging and ready to blow. "You first."

"That feels so good." Back and forth, her hips gyrated, motions changing as she lost control and sought her own release.

He smirked and rubbed his thumb in a circle, slowing his rate as she got closer. It was too much fun, not to cede all control to her and lie on his back like a dumb lump of a lust-crazed male while she worked him over as top dog.

Though they both knew who the true alpha was, Julian wasn't about to hand over the power too easily. He backed off on some pressure and slowed his strokes to a torturous crawl.

She compensated by grinding harder and angling her pelvis forward, trying to press her clit against his flesh. "Don't stop. Harder. Faster."

"Your orgasm will be better if you aren't in control of it." He moved his touch away from the hard bulge of her arousal and to her inner lips, less sensitive places. Though his dick and balls throbbed, the spectacle of her ruin would taste far more delectable than any quick climax.

"Fuck off, make me come."

"Fuck off? Ouch, not rewarding that." He dragged out his reply in a lazy taunt and removed his hand.

"Oh, come on," she whined, delivering a not altogether gentle slug to his upper arm.

"Come on what?" He skated the touch she craved over her outer lips, the soft hairs of her mound.

"I'm not saying please," she bit back, riding him hard. "Unless you spank me."

He lifted a hand high in the air, a power thrill running through his veins at the sight of her eyes widening. He brought his open palm down on her ass with a sharp crack.

She yowled, and upon regaining her composure, said, "I'm not saying please."

Smack.

"Bite me."

"Tempting." Smack. Followed by two strokes where she wanted it.

"Ah, fuck. Please, Julian, please please get me off or I'll cry." When she moaned, her mouth stretched wide, and gleaming tips of sharp incisors poked from her gums. Her ears elongated into those points he adored as her jaw squared and her eyes took on a wide set to accommodate her growing brow. Her short shock of hair grew thicker, more plush.

"Good girl." He went back to massaging her clit, quickly and efficiently, and she came with a scream, her inner wall clenching around his cock. The glow of her wolf essence burst from her pores in a blinding voltage. His focus zeroed on her feral blue eyes.

Damn, this bitch looked ready to eat him alive. The sight of his goddamn life, better than laying eyes on the golden gates to heaven.

He let go of all control, too, as his own finish rushed from the root of his shaft to the tip, electric and wet. His partial wolf essence—not a full shift, just the energetic aspect to mirror hers—erupted as a profound sense of primal abandon.

A piston on top of him, Taylor threw her head back and howled like a full moon hung in the sky.

Julian joined her until their calls merged as one, indistinguishable yells that seemed to blow the walls of the cabin down and blend with the multitude of jungle sounds beyond. Two wild hearts united in unspeakable frenzy.

He climaxed forever, screaming and splintering out of himself, and when he finally lowered, moisture streamed down his cheeks and flowed salty between his parted lips. They were here. They were home. They were mated and pair-bonded, forever.

"I love you, Taylor. Love you so much." And following the declaration he sobbed, and let go, releasing years of loneliness and isolation and despair.

Panting, she collapsed beside him and stroked his hair. Wiped away his tears, kissed his nose and lips. Her regular person form took over, though a barely perceptible shimmer of the wolf spirit sparkled near her forehead, her sex, and her heart. "I love you too, Julian. You're everything I could ever want and so much more than I deserve."

He threw his arms around her smaller body and wrapped her in the biggest, heartiest hug he could, relishing the pounding of her heartbeat, a drum of celebration thundering between the damp expanses of their sweaty bodies. While they embraced, the gulf dividing them bridged. "You deserve the stars and moon. And once we're out from under this ordeal, I'll give you the world."

"I controlled her," Taylor said with reverence and awe, pulling back enough to gaze into his eyes. "With no pain. Up and in, sit and stay."

He knew precisely what she meant. "Great work."

They cuddled in silence for a bit, and when she'd had enough, Taylor flopped to her back and turned her head to lob him a sly look. "I think I get what Crazy Horse was talking about now."

Julian laughed in appreciation of her cleverness, rubbing his stomach as the content spell of afterglow faded and a return to humanity eclipsed the intensity of sharing sexual disbelief with another person.

A conch horn blared outside, the sound verging on baleful with its low, ritualistic bleat. Only then did he notice the gray-blue seep of dawn breaking outside the bedroom window.

Seconds later, the alarm bellowed again. The unusual and anachronistic noise served as a swift reminder that they'd left the familiar behind, traded mundane daily life for an entirely different, strange existence. No need to put a damper on the mood, though. "Good thing we worked up an appetite."

"For real, I could nosh on an entire cow." She rolled out of bed, squatted by her hiking pack, and unzipped. "Fucking seriously?" Indignation pitched her tone tight and high as she pulled out clothes.

"What?" He sat on the edge of the mattress.

"Someone went through our stuff while we slept." With an aggravated sigh, she threw a shirt across the room and shimmied into a pair of panties. "So violating. And annoying. Full disclosure, I'm not sure I like these people. And it's tiresome how little they trust us."

He opened his own gear and saw the disturbance right away. The shirts and pants he'd folded were crumpled now, stuffed back in the bag in a state of disarray. Violating was the right word to describe the furtive, rough intrusion into their privacy. Plus, whoever did the rummaging hadn't bothered to cover up their effort. Total power play. "I hear you. But we need them. They've obviously had some bad things go down with guests, and I'm sure you being Jeff McClure's daughter doesn't help."

Julian swallowed a groan as he buttoned up a flannel shirt and dragged a comb through his long hair. He should not have said that.

"Please don't suggest that it's my fault they hate us." She yanked a hoodie over her head in an aggressive manner, as if the pullover had committed the gaffe.

He stepped into a pair of pants. "No, it isn't your fault, and I'm sorry my words came out like that. And no one hates us. We just need some time to warm up to each other."

She slid jeans up her legs. "I struggle with the idea that I need to warm up to hosts who won't allow me to lock my door at night and who root around in my personal effects like freaking serial killers. Worst Airbnb ever."

"Come on, babe, calling them serial killers is pretty melodramatic."

"You sure? What in the actual fuck is up with Tim and his top-secret equinox ritual?" Taylor threw him a crabby look while she hopped on one foot and pulled wool socks over her ankles.

His chest tightened. The last thing he wanted was a quarrel with his woman, but her bout of petulance was making peacekeeping difficult. He got it, though, she was under stress and lashing out in the face of an uncertain situation. Plus, the issues she'd identified were legitimate.

The horn went off again, deep and bestial brays delivered in three equally spaced intervals. A bit of extra fanfare to imply they needed to get a move on, another grab at the upper hand that bothered him. They weren't prisoners and ought to be able to come to breakfast at their leisure. What gave with the fixation on extreme punctuality, if not just to prove who was in charge?

Taylor pointed to the window, where the pale pink beginnings of sunrise beckoned beyond cheap curtains. "Exhibit B. Why can't they just use a bell like normal people or, better yet, come by and *knock*? I really hope it's just showmanship because I'm starting to get shady cult vibes off this place. What if they try to sacrifice us to some ancient horned jungle god?"

Taylor was lashing out because she was afraid, and his role now was to help her relax as much as possible. Keep the energy positive on their end. He went to her and took her hand. "Your feelings are completely valid. Is there anything I can do to help?"

She dropped her forehead to the middle of his chest. "Not be so damn perfect."

With a short laugh, he rubbed the back of her scalp. "It would make it easier to fight with me, huh?"

Taylor took a step to the side and eased into hiking boots. She stooped to lace them. "Fighting with you is the last thing I want. I guess I don't do well when I feel a loss of control and others have leverage over me. Gives me anxiety. And that's exactly where we are. In my anxious place. One down."

"Not completely." He sat and pulled on his lucky cowboy boots, designated as such because he'd had them on the day he met Taylor. "We need them, sure, but they also need us."

"How so?" She plucked a plastic baggie from her luggage and ducked into the bathroom. Water ran.

He moved to stand in the doorway, making eye contact with Taylor in the mirror while she brushed her teeth.

"Look." With a tip of his chin, he directed her focus to the stream trickling into the basin.

A line of water moved back and forth, back and forth, miming the motions of her hand as she guided the toothbrush.

"Holy crap." The plastic stick poking from her mouth impeded her speech in the cutest way, the look of toothpaste foam all over the lips he'd kissed and felt on his cock an amusing and intimate visual.

It was a barrier broken, but at least they weren't peeing in front of each other yet. He couldn't help but reach out and touch her lower back. In a weird, stolen way, he got to appreciate the joys of deepening a bond through humdrum domestic bliss. A long time without a serious relationship inspired him to find gratitude in the little things.

Taylor jerked her arm to the right, and a slash of water leapt from the faucet and flung itself on the shower curtain as a spray of beads. She spit, washed the mess down, and wiped her mouth. "I can control the water."

"So I'm saying talk it up, play it up. Remember how Tim mentioned that air mage, how they relied on her to protect their portal? You have a skill that's of potential value to them. Make sure they know it. There's your leverage." Kind of bummed him out that he didn't get a cool shifter superpower from their portal travel, but oh well.

More to the point, Julian could be shrewd when it counted. Earning a living in the fine arts had taught him the art of the hustle, how to sell himself in a buyer's market. Handy skill sets and quite transferable. He snagged his own toiletry bag and scrubbed his mouth. The cleansing bite of mint on his tongue cleared out lingering sleep scuzzies and put him in a focused headspace for dealing with Tim and his crew.

"Can I tell you a secret?" The tone of her question, abrupt though soft, carried the weight of a confession.

"Of course."

"I've never really felt that I've had value to offer others. I think that's why I've been so greedy and selfish for much of my life."

"Hey, now, whoa nelly. You aren't greedy or selfish." Assertive and confident, yes. Julian didn't ascribe a negative connotation to Taylor's self-assuredness. He admired her strength and how she went after what she wanted.

She shrugged, though her face drooped in a suggestion of wistful sadness. "I am, though, or I was. My number one goal for so long was to get rich as a financier and become a billionaire. In it for myself, all the way. Other people were barely even real to me. Total narcissist. Disgusting."

"Stop. I wish you'd be gentler with yourself and show yourself some compassion. It's clear you care about Angie and your sister, even your parents despite all they've done. Your loyalty is unmatched. And you care about me. Do I need to remind you that we're here because you were horrified by what you saw happening on that island and decided to stop it? You're more than caring or concerned, you're the bravest warrior I know. You're a hero."

She gazed up at him with such openness, as if she wished she could grab on to the version of herself reflected in his eyes. Perhaps one day, she would. Grab on and allow the version he saw to fill her heart until she was at peace with the inner beauty she denied she possessed.

"Maybe that's why I was so self-absorbed." She leaned against the bathroom wall.

"What do you mean?"

She touched the splash of wet beads slicking the thin plastic. "I didn't spend too much time thinking of others because I didn't feel like I owed anyone or that I had a right to feel entitled to appreciation or love. I couldn't give, and I couldn't accept. So other people became challenges.

Obstacles, nuisances, pests. It's like I've lived my whole life in an emotional deficit, knocking myself out just to break even. I'd fight to get in the black, and a setback would happen and clobber me into the red again. There I go with the money metaphors. Capital filled the void where love was supposed to be."

He looked in her eyes, finding her expression liquid and sorrowful. "You think about life in economic terms because you're gifted with numbers. You're a genius."

"I never deserved love. I always had to work for it, to earn it. So that's who I became, what I accepted as my identity. An earner. The microchips were the next logical step, really. From an earner of money to currency incarnate. Or a commodity. Poetic justice in a way, to be turned into an experiment, a soulless robot for my father and his rich buddies to test out their new toys on."

"What they did to you was unconscionable. Please don't think you had it coming. You deserve better."

Her lips wobbled out her next words, "I'm not sure. When I look into my heart, I see a cold place."

He pressed his palm over the area in question. "You don't have to be some stereotype of a nice lady to be loveable, Taylor. You just have to be you. And trust that what I see is there. Raw and true and perfect. Good."

A rueful twitch of a smile graced her mouth. "How is it even possible to love a stone-cold bitch like me?"

"There's no bitch I'd rather love."

She laughed. "I must have been a saint in a past life."

"Who cares about the past? Like I said, you're you. The one I want. The one I love."

Taylor rose to her tiptoes and kissed his lips. "Love you so much." Her breath was hot and spicy-sweet, teasing him with thoughts of round two. "Let's get to breakfast before they kick us out."

He led the way, and she closed the door behind them. About thirty feet in the distance, smoke billowed from a log cabin. He inhaled faint whiffs of bacon and coffee and set off for their destination with cautious optimism and more reluctance than he would have liked.

Might be time to surrender those old fantasies of a perfect transition into the shifter clan, his idealized hopes of ensconcing himself in the accepting bosom of found family. The name of the current game involved a mix of damage control, walking on eggshells, and impression management. A sad thought, but adult life demanded flexibility. The ability to adapt to changing goals defined a mature person.

He kissed Taylor's cheek as they marched across trodden ground en route to their destination. "It's going to go well. I can feel it."

He spoke the words for himself as much as her. Boisterous voices, laughter, and upbeat conversation, streamed through walls of lumber as Julian opened the front door.

Here goes.

SEVENTEEN

A SPURT OF CHEMICALS KICKED JULIAN INTO THE FIGHT REFLEX AS TIM looked up from a pot bubbling on a gas range, his dark eyes narrow with irritation. The guy spiked a potholder onto a long table in the middle of the room where a bunch of folks peeled potatoes, causing a pregnant woman with red hair to grimace and an older Latino man to put a hand over his mouth.

Julian sucked his teeth. It was tiresome, how harmless tardiness earned them a spot at the top of Tim's shit list. The visit was officially not going well.

Striking a stride of leadership, Tim cut through the crowd, a portrait of seriousness amidst chatter and camaraderie.

"Morning, Taylor," he said with an air of terse politeness. "Why don't you go pitch in mixing up the muffins?" Tim gestured to a corner, where several people leaned over a counter pouring liquid into bowls.

Taylor looked at Julian.

Though the prospect of deferring to Tim in front of her made the back of his neck prick with tight discomfort, provoking more conflict wouldn't help them save whatever remained salvageable. "I'll catch up to you in a minute," Julian said to her.

"Alright." She shrugged and walked to the baking station, casting him a backwards glance of concern.

Tim stood there mad mugging, hands on his hips, surly and condescending as a school principal ready to mete out detention. "You're really late, man."

"Had to sort a few things out. How can I help?"

Tim scoffed. "By not lying to me, for starters. From here on out, you tell the truth, or this won't work. In this case, the truth would sound like 'sorry, Tim, I woke up wanting to get laid, and so I chose to satisfy that urge instead of doing the thing that you asked me to do.'"

A rotten, macho instinct raced through Julian, and he puffed out his chest and stepped up to Tim. He didn't want to hit or fight the guy, but he would. If the options were to knock a couple of Tim's teeth out or kowtow with his tail between his legs, he'd choose the unsavory option that allowed him to hang on to some dignity and protect Taylor's.

He closed his hand into a hard knot, and he didn't bother lowering his voice for the benefit of the others. Let them witness a challenge to Tim's authority. Because if you asked Julian, the guy executed his leadership in some pretty ridiculous, arbitrary ways. "I don't know what your problem is with me all of a sudden, but you don't get to speak of Taylor in those crude terms. If we want to make love, we will, and I won't tolerate you cheapening her or what we have with bullshit talk. Got it?"

Tim's nostrils flared as he looked up a couple of notable inches at Julian. He jutted his own chest and knocked his mass into Julian in a symbolic bump. "You want to settle this outside or what?"

"No. Not really." Julian uncurled his fist and used his palm to push Tim back with a shove to the middle of his chest, hard enough so the impact sent a message of strength. "But I'm confused. I thought we were friends, but when Taylor and I showed up, you changed. Seems like you've undergone a personality transplant since our halcyon buddy days of video chats."

Tim took a big step to the side. "Join me for a second. Just to talk. I won't throw a punch if you don't." With a scoop of one hand, he beckoned Julian to the doorway.

More perplexed than ever, Julian joined the younger dude outside. A rising sun flung bright shards through peeps in leaves and spilled lemon light over the ground, a cheerful glow incongruous to the tension vibrating between the two men.

A pack of five scrappy chickens scurried past while Tim pulled a hand-rolled cigarette from his back jeans pocket and lit up. "All-natural tobacco, no chemicals or additives. Want one?"

"Okay. Sure." Save for the occasional shared marijuana joint, Julian almost never smoked, but perhaps a bit of shared indulgence would loosen up this encounter.

Tim slipped out another slender paper tube and sparked the tip with his own flaming cherry.

Julian pinched the rollup between thumb and forefinger and sucked down a drag of heady, woodsy smoke. Yeah, Tim could be attempting to drug him, but such a notion didn't make sense. Also, Julian liked to assume the best in everyone, starting from the premise that others were good-faith actors until they proved otherwise. The alpha struck him as straightforward and lacking a zest for manipulation or cunning. The kind of person who'd stab you in the heart, not the back.

Making his mouth into an O, Julian blew three smoke rings. They wobbled flimsy and gray in the air before dissolving. "Good stuff. I haven't had a rolled cigarette since I was a teenager. God knows what was mixed in with those."

Snorting, Tim hollowed his cheeks and pulled another hit into his lungs. "Yeah, I partook in a lot of ditch weed back then. Anything for a buzz."

Sensing movement into less confrontational territory, Julian sought friendly conversation. "How long have you lived here?"

"Since I was sixteen. You want the long story or the abridged version?" Smoke flowed out with Tim's question, and the look in his nut-brown eyes softened.

Looked like peace would come by way of small talk, and Julian could handle easy chit chat. His line of work required a baseline level of frequent socializing, so he'd honed the skill. "Whichever you prefer."

Using the tip of his sneaker, Tim drew a half-circle in the dirt. "Child Protective Services snagged me and put me into the system when I was twelve. The state had a hard-on for removing Native kids from their homes and placing them with white Christian foster parents. Which is exactly what happened. Totally dubious circumstances, man. We were poor, but I had a good home life. No abuse. But one day, I went to school without socks or shoes. I don't even remember why. Just forgot, I think, cause I was an absent-minded kid. Not my parents' fault at all, but some busybody teacher clutched her pearls and filed a report with CPS. Next thing I know, the gears are turning, and I'm going from home to home. I ended up getting adopted by these two missionaries. Religious fanatics, but otherwise decent people. They moved me down to Peru, and I got tired of the nonstop Bible thumping, so I ran away. Caught a bus and took up begging. One day while hitchhiking, I met a drifter on the side of the road. He led me here."

Though he and Tim might never be best buds like Julian had once hoped, he connected to the man's story of feeling alone and heeding the urge to run. Not to flee, but to seek. In Julian's case, the choice had been sorrowful and shot through with ambivalence, but he saw a common drive underlying their motivations. Yearning to fit in, abiding the call to find pack, sang to his core personality. A wolf thing, he bet.

So, he said, "I left home too. Bought a shitty motorcycle with all the money in my pocket and started driving down the highway. I hitched a post in Texas when a decent opportunity showed up, and I just sorta stayed."

Just sorta stayed. And wasn't that the truth? He hadn't found what he was looking for in Austin. He'd stopped looking and resigned himself to the low-grade dissatisfaction that came to constitute his emotional life. The dull, flat feeling that caused a wall of clear gel to form between him and the best parts of life.

Julian knew that if he could just push through that thick, gelatinous mass, joy would await, but he didn't know how to breach the barrier. Didn't know how to cultivate deep, rich friendships or true love with women, so he'd settled for bar buddies and short-term romantic affairs that petered out after a few months.

At least he had his art to escape to, or his lost soul would have fallen prey to depression, or worse, years ago.

Tim said, "It's not that we don't want you and Taylor here. I apologize for being such a dick. I'm just under so much stress, a ton of pressure. There's over two hundred people here who look to me for solutions, answers to keep them safe. Pregnant single mothers, children. I have to project nonstop how I'm a good leader, and I have to feel the energy myself so I don't come off as inauthentic and lose their faith. There's this strong, untapped alpha energy spilling out of you, out of *both* of you, and when I first sensed it in the flesh, I balked."

After catching his breath, Tim continued, "Don't get me wrong, I've dealt with alpha wolf dudes before, but they haven't had the brains or the thoughtfulness to match their bravado. Easy to outwit and think circles around, dominate intellectually. But not you, and especially not her. My instinct was to put both of you in your place, but I need to be better than my instincts. So, again, I'm sorry for how I've been mishandling our first couple of days together. Forgive me."

"Yeah, man, of course." Julian focused on his smoke, thinking for several beats before he spoke more. "There's no shame in asking for help. To share the responsibility."

The look in Tim's eyes grew fierce and territorial. Gray clouds coiled in the air around his head in a clear smoke signal. "We aren't there yet. I'm not abdicating or sharing power. Case closed."

Julian pulled in more of the burning plant. Some mysterious property to one of the herbs mellowed his nerves as the brew offered a pleasant, minor head rush. "That's fair. But we aren't here to make a power grab. We're here because we are, frankly, desperate. Under siege. And I have to tell you, sending people to go through our belongings wasn't the warm welcome we were hoping for."

"I know. Separate issue, though. Last group that came here were these idiot frat boys from California who claimed to be a sleuth of bear shifters hailing from the Sierra Nevadas. Complete horseshit. Turned out they were just a crew of jackasses cavorting around the world, using lies to ingratiate themselves into various communities. They smuggled in ten bottles of Rohypnol in their backpacks. Fortunately, we found out before any women were victimized."

Julian's heart sunk. Men could be such assholes. No wonder Tim had become hyper-vigilant about protecting his clan from harmful outsiders. "I got you. No apologies necessary."

Tim peered at Julian, a cautious and sidelong consideration, while pale haze the color of rock shrouded his sculpted features. Julian returned the careful stare, acutely aware of the fact that, though they'd worked through much friction, they hadn't stopped sizing each other up.

Julian dropped eye contact to his foot, lifted his sole, and crushed out his cigarette. A calculated gesture of deference that conveyed purpose. Upon completion of his task by sliding the burnt nub into his pocket, he aligned his gaze with Tim's once again. "I think it would help bolster our mutual goodwill if you were completely forthright with me."

Tim nodded and copied Julian's cigarette-snuffing procedure. Julian liked to think that the man's actions here represented a concession, a give and take. They had more important things to think about than the alpha role. Or they were both quietly reevaluating the alpha role, and the needs of the community, in light of various disruptions.

"Agree." Tim's speech was soft but firm. "It's no secret that I'm skittish because of who Taylor is and what she's been through. Her motives could become a bit of a wild card. I'm gonna level with you. This search and rescue mission has a lot of moving parts and all the vagaries that entails."

"Taylor is in this all the way," Julian interrupted, though he sensed there was more trepidation on Tim's thought horizon. The heavy silence of things held back hung around like a looming third party. "But we all need to be on the same page here. We have to act in full awareness of what's happening. No secrets."

"Fuck," Tim hissed, craning his neck enough to show the outline of his Adam's apple against stretched skin. "I didn't want to scare or alarm anyone."

The meaty organ in Julian's chest clenched as his pulse kicked, though he forced his face to stay stable in a mask of neutrality. "I'm a pretty cool customer." More accurately, he could channel stoicism when the situation demanded that he subdue his emotions.

Tim lowered his head, features grim. "I fell into a deep hole of research while investigating that screwed up place. How much do you know?"

Julian gave Tim the gist of what he'd learned from Taylor, their research, and the McClure estate eavesdropping session.

"Right. What would you say if I told you that canned hunts,

trafficking, and even the use of an Other One as a portal battery are only the beginning?"

Julian's mouth dried, residue from the cigarette bitter and stale on his taste buds. The green canopy dome above closed in as mild autumnal air grew stuffy and oppressive. "The beginning of what?"

"Ritual practice. Magic. A perverse inversion of what we do."

"Please elaborate." Julian swallowed as if clearing excess saliva would negate his absolute horror.

"On the equinox, the harvest moon, we hold a ceremony in the jungle. Food, drink, games, and general merriment ensue. Good times, wholesome family fun. When the moon reaches its apex, we offer everyone the opportunity to participate in communal mating play. Totally optional. The kids and any shifter who wishes to dip out are brought back to the camp, and the rest let loose. Legends say that the abandon is healthy for our animal aspects, that engaging in this sort of no-holds-barred bacchanal allows our beast side to actualize its truest potential."

As the point sunk in, Julian lifted his brows, both intrigued and wary. "An orgy."

Tim shrugged one shoulder. "What each shifter chooses to do and with whom is between the individual and their mated partner, if they have one. Solo sex and monogamous, hetero couplings with a spouse are a-OK. As are gay and lesbian experiments, threesomes, foursomes, moresomes. Anything goes."

"So what do your liberated adventures in free love have to do with our search and rescue mission?"

"Hey, guys," an unknown, female voice called from the dining hall. "Food's getting cold. And you're missing out on a very intense debate about werewolves versus dragons."

"One sec, Jenny." Tim pulled on Julian's arm and led him ten feet away, out of earshot. "They run a twisted flip of our practice and have been doing so for years on the same night. Rapes, sacrifice of innocents, drinking and bathing in our blood, cavorting around the island dressed in our skins. Shifters are tortured and murdered in dungeons—kill rooms. Allegedly. These sick freaks think that by bastardizing our erotic traditions and undertaking sinister rites, they'll absorb our powers and become like us. Or gain immortality."

The light flickering through leaves hurt Julian's eyes. Nausea roiled his insides, and dizziness threatened his stability. He stumbled before regaining balance. Outrage, and an intense desire to save the victims, overrode his physical revulsion. "That's the most heinous thing I've ever heard. Jesus, Tim. Screw breakfast. We have to get there now."

"The problem is," Tim barked a dark laugh devoid of mirth, "every single thing they do seems to do double or triple duty, so we've gotta be smart. I found a 4chan post by someone who claims to be an escaped Scarab captive. They peppered their account with too much detail for the story to be fake. This person claims that Scarab has some ancient, evil artifact stashed in the bowels of their tunnels. The skull of a demon, or a puzzle prism trapping an imprisoned demonic essence or multiple essences. Apparently, they use it for prognostications and money magic, even necromancy."

Bereft, Julian motioned for Tim to keep going, and the younger man heeded,

"The negative energy they churn up from their dark ritual feeds this malevolent fetish object, as does the blood of our kin when it seeps into the earth. This is how they called down the Other One and were able to open portals in the first place. So if this testimony is real, the assholes we're dealing with aren't just warmongers and flesh traffickers, or even basic sadists. They're sorcerers, and they know enough about us where they might be able to use who we are against us. At the risk of sounding paranoid, I'm afraid they *want* us there."

Julian's mind spun. The hairs on his arms stood alert. "So are you saying that if we go, we make ourselves vulnerable to spells? Black magic? Or are you intimating that the fact that we're already considering going means we could have been lured or bewitched?"

Tim swiped a hand over his jet-black hair, the strands now slick with a sheen of sweat. "Both sound theories, yes. I'm concerned. About all contingencies. And since Scarab's operation seems to feed on negative energy, disillusionment and discontent, it is paramount to me that everyone we bring there is in the proper state of mind, of *sound* mind, and in possession of a fucking braided steel rope of integrity impervious to compromise. You feel me?"

Stood to reason that Tim might have situated Taylor, Jeff McClure's daughter and former acolyte of Jay Stearns, in the eye of this mad storm. If not as a suspicious turncoat, as a party vulnerable to manipulation. "Yeah. But I swear on my mama's life you don't have a damn thing to worry about."

"You give me your word." Tim's command hissed through clenched teeth and came on a gust of smoky breath. A clamp on Julian's forearm squeezed hard. "That you can vouch for her with every ounce of intuition buried in the marrow of your bones. Every part of you that's ever felt connected to spirit, to God, to the road beyond, to those mysteries bigger than yourself must *know*."

Julian did the sign of the cross. "I swear."

Tim let Julian go, and as he broke the hold, it was like all the air left. "Alright. Let's go eat. We're gonna need our strength."

Scents of meat, bread, and sugar wafted from the structure, but the smell of food made Julian sick. How could he concentrate on the pleasures of daily life while in possession of these facts about Scarab? And though he trusted Taylor implicitly, would take a bullet for her, he now worried about the possibility of aftereffects of her programming. They still weren't clear what all had been done to her, the full extent of her mutations.

Hell, she'd changed more in the aftermath of portal travel. What could happen to her on Scarab island? In the context of total madness, did a boundary or limit exist? Or would more horrible surprises spring up from the fault crevices where a line in the sand used to be?

"You got quiet. You alright?" Tim opened the door, his pull ushering out enviable, easy noises of conversation and amusement from the community.

"Fine. Processing, but fine." He ought to shut off his monkey mind and at least attempt to enjoy food and socialization. Allowing dark thoughts to consume him wouldn't help. If he fell prey to ruminations on the sinister, such black hole obsessing could ruin his energy.

Tim slapped Julian's back and went to sit at the head of the long picnic-style table.

Taylor patted a bench seat next to her. "You have got to try this quiche. I thought I sucked at cooking, but Jenny here said something that blew my mind, and I had a breakthrough."

Julian forced a thin smile and went to Taylor, the burden of everything Tim told him settling heavy on his shoulders. But he refused to spoil the conviviality. He refused.

"I basically explained to her how cooking is a science," Jenny, stocky and brunette, continued while Julian sat by his girlfriend and tried to work up an appetite at the sight of steaming heaps of eggs, bacon, sausage, and muffins, all laid out on family-style platters. "Whereby obtaining the desired result is not only a matter of combining the right ingredients in the right quantities, but employing factors like temperature, chemical reaction, and time."

Taylor covered her chewing mouth and said, "Jenny's a chemist." She pushed a full plate at Julian. Metal scraped against wood, and he found himself staring at mounds of meat and baked goods.

A trickle of watery blood oozed from the dark middle of a halved, fat sausage. The miniature red river flowed across the plate and stained an expanse of bread as a fluffy muffin absorbed the fluid like a sponge.

"They run a twisted flip of our practice and have been doing so for years on the same night. Rapes, sacrifice of innocents, drinking and bathing in our blood, cavorting around the island dressed in our skins. Shifters are tortured and murdered in dungeons—kill rooms."

"Aren't you hungry, babe?" A twinge of hurt plucked Taylor's timbre as she speared a forkful of the quiche she'd cooked. "I promise I don't suck."

Fucking hell. On top of everything else, he couldn't be a jerk and reject the meal his partner had prepared for him. But the sight of food, and the smell of cooked flesh in particular, slid a queasy wave through him. "I'm famished." He sawed the meat, and the chunk bled puddles onto his plate.

Silverware scraped dishes, everyone talking at once. Voices, voices, so many voices blurred together in a cacophony of unintelligible gibberish. The babbling static was all Julian could focus on as he forced food into his mouth. Carbs and meat tasted like cardboard, the fault of his mental state and not Taylor's cooking.

His head overheated as he tried in vain to wake up his taste buds. Flecks of white danced in his vision, and his throat shrunk around a dry mass of egg. He was about to teleport to an island where those of his kind were systematically being exterminated. Slaughtered. Wiped out.

Could he go through with it? Could he set foot on the desecrated ground of genocide, the weeping soil soaked by life stolen? What would happen when he faced the horror head on? Would his spirit, his soul, survive the visceral spectacle of witnessing?

Annihilation. The word kept ringing. The meaning, snarling and hateful as an injection of pure contempt. Demonic.

A vise clamped his lungs. He forced the bite of whatever down, vision going black as the jumble of voices reached a fever pitch. All voices. So many voices.

Annihilation.

Annihilation.

Annihilation.

Pressure pushed into the sides of his skull. His heart raced.

"Julian?" Taylor's voice could have come from outer space. "What's wrong?"

He had to get out before his head exploded. Julian rose from his seat with as much composure as he could summon, pushed the door open, and planted both palms on rough wood.

As he breathed big yoga breaths, in and hold and release, Julian questioned for the first time in his life if he was strong enough to survive.

EIGHTEEN

"YOU'RE GOING TO BE FINE." TAYLOR STROKED JULIAN'S BACK IN BIG up and down motions, doing her best to offer him a soothing voice and assuring touch as he stood hunched, hand planted on the cabin wall with his head hung. "Keep breathing."

The old her would have laughed at the mere suggestion that she would have ever tried to nurture or comfort another person. The old Taylor McClure didn't possess one shred of a nurturing instinct. She hunted and predated, knocked off rivals on her way to the top. But Julian mattered to her, and he needed that kindness and love, so she pulled up every bit of tender care she had to offer.

"I'm a disaster." He peeled himself off the wall and turned around, the look on his face weary. But at least his breathing had returned to normal.

"No, you aren't. You're clearly upset, though. Did something bad happen with Tim?"

Julian pinched the inner corners of his eyes. "You could say that. I'll be okay. Sorry for scaring you."

"Well what happened out here with Tim? What did he say?"

Julian opened his mouth, but before he could speak, a person in overalls jogged up to them carrying a plastic bowl with holes poked into the lid. A plump brown mouse darted around inside.

"Hey, Taylor, did you still want this?" Speaking in an earnest, androgynous voice, Case, the bearer of the rodent, looked between Taylor and Julian with concern and puzzlement.

Crap. Over breakfast, Taylor had talked about Salazar with Case, a friendly nonbinary falcon shifter with floppy hair and a sweet, dimpled smile. They had offered to catch a meal for Salazar.

"Yes. Thank you." Taylor took the container from Case, who ducked into the cafeteria building as if to say: hint taken, I'm out. She returned her attention to Julian as the critter bounced up and down. "What's on your mind?"

He glimpsed at the jumpy meal-to-be, lips pulled into a contorted relative of a smile, and looked away. "A lot. I think I need a few moments to organize my head, take a short walk. I'm gonna hit that half-mile trail loop behind the outhouse. Why don't you go feed Salazar, and we'll reconnect in twenty minutes. That okay?" His smile warmed into one rich with authenticity, and he dropped a kiss to her forehead.

"Of course."

"Thanks for understanding." His reply came out in a ragged breath.

Though she itched for details, she had to give Julian his space. Healthy relationships necessitated respecting boundaries, an insight she'd picked up despite growing up in the McClure shitshow household. Luckily, she'd had nourishing friendships with Angie and a few others to prevent her from completely normalizing dysfunction. "You bet. You'll stay around in this area?"

He nodded. "I have no desire to get lost in the jungle today."

"Same." She gave his arm one final rub of assurance and walked the short stretch of distance back to their quarters.

The moment she pushed the door open, a terrible feeling of wrongness smothered her. Whether she saw the disturbance, sensed chaos, or predicted trouble, Taylor could not say. She just felt ill at ease in a deep place. Order was skewed. Upended.

Her gaze darted, assessing. Furniture normal, no broken dishes or shattered windows.

And then she saw. Salazar's cage was on the floor, on its side, laying open with the lid pried off.

"Shit." She ran over and picked it up, looked inside. No snake. Her thoughts darkening, she examined the lid. No cracks or damage to the plastic clasps. No way her skinny little noodle could have busted open the top of the cage. He wasn't nearly strong or large enough to break his enclosure and escape. Somebody had let him out. Or taken him.

Her theory didn't explain why the cage was on the floor, but perhaps the culprit tried to cover their tracks.

She put the mouse bowl on top of the dresser, dropped to her knees, and peered under the bed. Two dust bunnies stared back at her. Next, she looked under the couch. No Salazar. A check of the cabinets, corners, and the space under the sink all came up empty.

Taylor gave up on her fruitless search and stomped to the breakfast spot with her fists balled.

Seeing in tunnel vision as she trekked to the mealtime cabin, she staved off tears. Whoever had messed with her dear pet would pay. She stormed into the place where they'd eaten and made a beeline for Tim, who was in the process of ushering the last bits of his breakfast onto his fork.

"Who took Salazar out of his cage?"

Tim blinked in response to her demand. "Excuse me?"

"You heard me. Who messed with my snake? Did you do it yourself or give the order?"

The people flanking Tim quieted their conversations and stared.

Tim stood. "I have no idea what you're talking about."

The alpha looked genuinely bewildered, but she didn't buy his claim to total ignorance. Not given how much of a control freak he seemed to be.

"Well, someone does. Because his cage is on the floor, and there's no way he could have escaped on his own." She glared up at him.

Chaz from the armed welcome brigade pushed back his chair with a scrape of wood against wood and walked to her. "We'll put out a search for him. Pets have gotten loose before."

"He didn't get loose," Taylor said. "Physically impossible."

Tim touched her wrist. "I know that we haven't necessarily gotten off on the right foot, but you have to believe me when I tell you that no one here would harm your pet. I'll start by checking with all the parents to see if any kids got curious and decided to play with him without permission, and if we don't find him after that, we'll scour the jungle."

She jerked away as emotional pain lanced through her and fury-soaked grief set in. "If you would have let us lock our door, no curious kids would've gotten to him in the first place. He won't survive on his own for a day." A nest of old insecurities hatched. She was so selfish she couldn't even keep a low-maintenance pet alive. Her scaly baby would join the grim ranks of five dead houseplants no doubt withered by now. Poor Salazar, doomed to become lunch for a larger predator because of her.

"Snakes are wily," Chaz said. "Don't underestimate him. If he struck off on his own, the first thing he would have done was seek out a place to hide."

I hate it here. I want to go home. At least she managed not to blurt out the defeatist thoughts. Not like she had a home to go back to anymore, not really.

"Yeah. Okay. Thanks." Taylor turned on her heel and left the community kitchen before she popped off a rude remark or cried.

She exited to sunshine that warmed her face, making a mockery of her bleak thoughts. In front of the cabin, three children of various ages played a makeshift game of soccer in a small, dusty expanse between two big trees.

Seizing an investigative opportunity, she walked over and crouched. "Hey, can I ask you guys a question?"

"'Kay." This from a ropy girl of perhaps twelve with brown hair and dirty knees. She bounced the soccer ball between two long feet.

"Have you guys seen a snake crawling around? The kind you buy in the pet store, green with brown spots and about this big?" Taylor held her hands three feet apart, hoping that one or more of these kids had some awareness of the kind of snakes that people sold and bought as pets versus the wild variety.

An elementary-aged blond boy widened his eyes. "Yeah. But he was way bigger."

Taylor's stomach leapt with hope. Perhaps, given their smaller bodies, the little ones imagined Salazar as larger than he really was. "Where? When?"

Nodding vigorously, a Black girl in pink sweats grabbed a stick off the ground. She walked the equivalent length of a living room while dragging her tool through the dust, soon finishing the etching of a crude snake with a forked tongue. The child continued to work on her creation, sketching small wings on the middle of her serpent's back. The proportional size of T-Rex arms, they looked silly on her gigantic beast. "He kept trying to fly." She dropped her stick and flapped her arms.

The balloon of optimism lifting Taylor slowly deflated. Kids and their wild imaginations. If not for her sad mood, she would have found their story time flight of fancy amusing. She rose. "If you see the big flying snake again, ask him to keep an eye out for a little guy. He's scared and alone and could use a big brother right now."

"My mommy told me a story about my daddy." The blond boy said.

"What's that, hon?" Taylor sighed out her words and surveyed the green wilderness beyond the camp. No sign of a ball python slithering amidst the underbrush.

"Daddy was a snake shifter. His people descended from dragons. They still have the pee-n-ay of the old ones in their bodies and are waiting for a magic key to unlock it. Then the age of dragons will come again."

The girl who'd drawn in the dirt doubled over giggling. "It's called DNA. You said pee."

"I did not," he whined, kicking the ball at the girl.

Taylor's ovaries shrunk as her ambivalence toward children swayed to the negative end of the spectrum. "That's a really cool story. I'll let you get back to your game." She turned her back on the rugrats.

"The age of dragons will come again." A low smoothness in the blond boy's tone added an uncanny, eerie dimension of adult confidence to his prepubescent squeak.

She glanced over her shoulder at him. Beady eyes like emeralds peered at her from their lookout post atop his beak nose.

The longer she looked, the more she noticed a strangeness to his features. Face a bit too long, dominated by a pointy chin. An ashy quality to his fair skin suggested that he would be rough to the touch.

For a weird second, the light struck him just so, and the networks of tiny creases gridding his hands and neck resembled scales.

She squinted, suddenly spaced out. Must've been the sun in her eyes.

"See you guys around." Unsettled without a clear reason why, Taylor broke into a trot and caught up to Julian right as he was completing a circle around the trail.

"How are you feeling?" she asked as he popped out of the thicket right by the outhouse.

"Better." He came to her. "But now you look a little distracted."

She sat on a ratty hammock tied to two tree trunks, the netting going taut beneath her bottom. "Salazar's gone."

Julian joined her with empathy in his eyes. "Gone? As in..."

"No." She booted the depressing thought out of her mind. The worst-case scenario hadn't been confirmed. "At least not yet. He got out of his cage. Somehow. I don't buy that he escaped on his own. I shouldn't have jumped to conclusions, but I basically accused Tim of taking him or knowing who did."

He looked off into the distance, and she noticed the bags under his eyes and the way he rubbed his hands together. Usually so composed and cool, Julian looked disturbingly haggard. Only upon realizing how his decline bothered her did she understand how she'd come to count on him.

"It's not going so great here, is it?" His smile, halfhearted and worn, sunk her deeper into self-doubt and guilt. Was she to blame for the Peru excursion going sideways?

"No." The word came out of her mouth like a hot rock and left a burn. The next comment tasted like poison. "And I feel like that's because of me. Tim and Chaz and the others were wary because of who I am. That's why they searched our bags, why they don't trust us. And now Salazar. Guess what? Another problem traceable back to me. Me, me, me, the source of all problems."

"Babe. Stop. You're wrong." He clamped his larger hand over the top of her trembling one. "They searched our bags because they don't trust anyone at first. Tim told me. They had a bad experience with some scumbags who came down here with rape drugs."

"Ugh. Awful." What pieces of shit. Though terrible, the new

information relaxed her some. She could understand Tim's reasoning. But still. The issue with the scumbags didn't account for all woes. "I still wonder if I'm dragging you down, you know? McClure's daughter, a big red flag."

He frowned, grooving lines into his forehead. "Untrue. Finding you was the best thing that ever happened to me. Yes, we're running into some obstacles adjusting here, but it isn't your fault. They're just challenges to overcome. And we will persevere. But we have to stick together. And stay strong."

Shame impressed upon her body and mind. "There isn't a part of you, one tiny little piece, that wishes you were here by yourself? No complications, no baggage, just a fresh start?" She dropped her gaze to her swinging, sneakered feet. It wasn't a trick question or a trap. She would not blame Julian if he admitted, even in the gentlest way, that part of him longed for a life with less complication. A life without her.

The tips of his first two fingers landed under her chin, callused and firm, and lifted her face to meet his. "No. You are mine, and I am yours. We are one. As simple as that."

When she looked in his eyes right then, she saw yet again the best parts of herself reflected back to her. The woman worth loving. The woman who deserved love and was capable of giving it. The woman with a heart and a soul. Someone good.

And, more importantly, she saw the goodness of a man who had taken a chance on her. She could not fail him.

But the terrible, encroaching feeling that she would be his downfall remained unshakable and persistent.

Loving her would cost a terrible price. She detested the simplicity with which her hunch announced itself. "I'm a liability, Julian. I say this because I love you so damn much. But I've always been a danger to you. Right from the start, I was supposed to be some kind of honey trap. And we can't be sure that the threat has passed. The onslaught of bad omens down here is not boosting my confidence."

For all she knew, she was still deadly. And not knowing made her angst on Julian's behalf worse.

"I don't care what you were supposed to be. And I don't care if you're dangerous or risky, Taylor. You came to me, my wolf mate. Screw the circumstances. Forget the past. Here we are." He slipped his hand over her cheek, fingers massaging comfort into the side of her face.

Her heart grew heavy. Could she always protect Julian from herself, from the sorrows she brought, even unwittingly?

"I'm scared." Words she'd never uttered, a previously fearless seeker of challenges who smashed obstacles under her heel. But it felt good to admit weakness and depend on another person, a loved one, to provide the strength. A human admission and final, welcome surrender of her sociopath card.

"Don't be," he whispered, brushing a gentle kiss between her brows. "Just love and have faith."

Her throat ached, and she swallowed hard. "Have you always been so hopeful and optimistic?"

"Hell no." He spoke into her forehead. "I'm a lot less cynical now, though. Because I believe in fate. Destiny."

"I just want a sign, you know? Some encouragement that we're on the right path. That I'm doing what I'm supposed to be doing. Because I can't think straight anymore."

"I hear you, babe." He urged her into the crook under his arm, making himself into her haven.

She settled into the nook. His rich scent beckoned her closer. Taylor lost herself to a moment of reprieve, to the gentle sway of the hammock and a soft din of animal noises issuing from the leaves.

Closing her eyes, she cherished Julian's body, his physicality, and inhaled him. Before Julian, she'd never considered the power of pheromones, the important role of chemical magnetism in attraction. Guys either had decent hygiene or reeked, with unoffensive neutrality being the optimal olfactory state. But now, she got how scent was so powerful. An alluring personal fragrance lured, seduced with a desire to investigate.

She followed the steady, rhythmic thump of his heartbeat. "I hear you too."

He made a happy noise and simply held her.

Crunching underbrush, voices, and rustles punctured their sweet escape.

Taylor glanced to the left, searching for the origin of the noise. Tim,

Chaz, Case, the old hippie, and two others trudged out of the forest. Tim swung a machete and hacked through foliage.

Glistening with a fresh sweat, the leader emerged first. "Sorry, Taylor. We shifted and pooled our tracking abilities. Combed a ten-mile radius." Frustration tightened his voice. He pulled a handkerchief from his pocket and wiped it across his brow in a single angry swipe.

Chaz, his breath labored, added, "Looked under every rock we could find, every hill of old leaves. We climbed as many trees as possible and went inside holes in tree trunks too. Either he's the fastest snake ever hatched or he's already been eaten."

Tim glowered. "Sensitivity, please."

Taylor bit her lip and leaned into Julian. These guys were being genuine. No way were they Oscar-worthy actors, and besides the idea that they'd tamper with her snake's cage and then concoct an elaborate ruse to gaslight her made no sense. "Thanks anyway. He must've wanted to be free more than anything. Where there's a will, there's a way I guess."

The hippie opened his mouth and made a low sound.

"Yeah, could be," Tim interrupted in a terse manner. "Perhaps the urge to mate overcame him. As we all know, the animal instinct wants what it wants."

Taylor's muscles clenched. She grew suspicious once again and scanned for evidence of culpability on the others' faces. No nervous eyes, senseless fidgets, or other lie tells outed them, though.

Tim continued, "I don't want to be the insensitive asshole here, but we need to talk about our plan for Scarab. There's no time to waste, so we ought to get there today."

"Of course." Taylor did her best to redirect. Despite the mysterious disappearance of Salazar, they still had a big fucking problem on their hands.

"The team will consist of everyone here plus a few more of our strongest. There will be ten of us total, and we'll each go armed with a rifle and a handgun. That'll exhaust the arsenal available to us here. Both of you are proficient with those firearms you showed up with, right?"

Taylor raised her chin to Tim. All those times her father had taken her to the gun range and taught her how to shred paper targets were about to pay off. "I can aim like Annie Oakley and fire twice as fast." For good measure, she bored her eyes into his while she spoke, so her remark skirted the edges of threat territory. A little extra oomph for Salazar's sake.

Tim held her stare in silence for three seconds too long, entering an unspoken showdown of strong wills. "Cool. You too, Jules?"

"I hunt venison and wild pigs as a side gig. Sell the meat at the farmer's market. So yeah."

Taylor forgot about fucking with Tim and smiled at her man. So industrious.

"Great. We'll review the blueprint and go over our attack plan a few times. But the Cliff's Notes version is we stick together at all costs. That place is a damn labyrinth as far as I can tell, and an isolated shifter is a dead shifter."

Julian added, "First order of business is to capture a guard and use them to direct us to the prison, at which point we unlock the cells and guide everyone to the portal. If any other guards show up, shoot to kill."

Tim's eyes narrowed a sliver. "Right, I was about to say that. Thanks, Jules. If we can maintain control over our hostage, we should be able to get back to the portal room with the freed shifters."

A new, awful idea intruded into Taylor's mind. "What if our invasion triggers a lockdown protocol, and the security system traps us inside?" Likely, she'd pulled the reference from some thriller blockbuster, but her fear seemed logical.

An aggressive shrug served as Tim's acknowledgment of her point. "There are unknown variables and a lot of moving parts. From what I've been able to find in my research, their system doesn't have an override function like that, but you are correct that we can't rule out the possibility. Do either of you have a better idea?"

"No. This is a risk we all need to take," Julian said.

What if they ran out of options? Hypothetically speaking, if she brought her phone and called her father, could he save them from death? *Would* he save his traitorous daughter's life?

More importantly, why was she even worried about her father taking on an unexpected and vital role in the rescue mission? He hadn't been on her radar since the art fair, when he'd made his intention to discard her quite clear. Besides, she welcomed severing ties.

Though she'd given up on a stable, healthy relationship with her dad, a tiny part of her that would always be his little girl felt small and afraid and longed for the security of his assurance. His protection. That part of her that used to fear the dark still wanted her dad, the closest thing to unconditional love that she'd ever known.

"Taylor?" Julian squeezed her hand. "Did you have a point to add?"

"No." Her nostalgia was stupid and had no place. She and *Senator Jeff McClure* were done. Over. Yeah, blood was thicker than water and all, but blood also decomposed in rotten graves. The lives of her fellow shifters meant more to her than some vestigial remnant of filial loyalty. "Let's go review that blueprint and teleport."

NINETEEN

TAYLOR BLINKED UNTIL THE RINGING IN HER EARS SUBSIDED AND THE swirling loop of her fuzzy perception returned to normal. Bodies pressed into all sides of her, their smells of sweat and soap a grounding comfort. She grabbed Julian's wrist the instant she noted the keyboard and console on the ground and the plastic cylinder encasing the shifters.

Thanks to her mantra repetition of the coordinates, they'd pulled off the teleport. She counted heads, her shoulders slackening when she finished. All members of the team had arrived in the Scarab bunker.

Rifle pointed in front of him, Tim nodded and wrapped his fingers around the door handle. He opened the clear slab slowly, his lips parting as he craned his neck to the atrocity on the ceiling. "Good God. There it is."

Taylor pushed through the mass of flesh and squeezed out of the confined space, chancing a glance at the monster. Still in his stupor, he hadn't budged since the showdown with Stearns. His eyes sparkled with awareness, though, glittering rubies pushed deep in a corpse's face.

She shivered. "At least he's secured up there until they punch in the code to release him."

Which would amount to a separate, awful problem, though thankfully not a pressing one.

Julian took his place at Taylor's side, lip curling as he beheld the Other One. "Let's keep moving."

"Agreed," Chaz said, and the others murmured in consensus.

The gun made an assuring weight in Taylor's hands, cold steel tasked with protecting her. She brushed her fingertip over the half-moon curve of the trigger, squeezed the hard barrel.

Equally weaponized, Julian met her with a serious face. In the moment, he looked at her as a comrade-in-arms. She returned the stare as the group walked to the door, the quiet communion between her and Julian acknowledging the richness of their relationship, the multiple roles they played in their partnership. Today they would enter the battlefield as a team. Go to war together.

Julian moved first, his steps so delicate you'd swear they wouldn't leave footprints, as he advanced on the door with his gun drawn.

Her footfalls were just as deliberate and quiet. A low buzz made by the machine supplied the room's only sound.

Tim caught up, exited the room, and ducked back in. He signaled the team to follow with a big sweep of his hand.

Her breathing became a prayer of steady, controlled hums as she encroached upon the hallway she'd walked down with Stearns. Same clinical feel, linoleum sprayed with antiseptic. Above, halogen lighting flickered in a menacing pattern.

The group traipsed a length of hall and followed the plan until they came upon a door.

A plaque hung on the wall with the word "security" forged in raised black letters glued on a rectangle of fake wood.

If the operation worked out as hoped, one guard would be in the room. An exchange of nods tendered confirmation, for speech might signal their presence and ruin the advantage of surprise. At some point, Scarab would get wind of their trespass anyway, but there was no point in expediting the inevitable and knocking the team into a defensive position of weakness.

Tim reared back and slammed the sole of his boot into the doorknob.

Men shouted as the force of Tim's kick broke wood and metal with a monster crunch.

"Ahh!" A stranger's voice.

"Hey!" A second man.

Taylor's heart sunk. Two voices came from the room. Two people. Already, a miscalculation or curve ball dogged the shifter brigade.

Sure enough, her gaze landed on two dudes seated across from each other at a cheap card table. A mini fridge, a small waste basket, and a black and white monitor divided into sixteen squares of security footage constituted the drab room's décor. A cluster of dead horse flies in one corner added a macabre embellishment.

"Hey, what the fuck?" A short frog of a man with sloped shoulders and a paunch leapt to his feet, but Tim bum rushed him before he could draw his gun and shoved the muzzle of his own rifle into the guy's neck.

"Take off your equipment belts and hand them over." Julian gave the order with bone-chilling authority and pure composure as he trained his weapon on the second guard, a jaundiced and balding fellow who looked eligible for retirement.

She took solace in the fact that, though double the numbers they'd planned for, the adversaries were aged and small. Outmatched and outnumbered. The team's research confirmed a hunch that Scarab didn't need to invest in a huge, elite security force. The building itself offered substantial protection from interlopers. It was reinforced to the hilt and secreted away from the public eye.

The little guy worked his belt like he couldn't comply fast enough and surrendered the supplies. Tim slung the thick black strap over his shoulder.

"What do you want?" The old guy asked, keeping his cool as he unbuckled a low-slung holster chock full of all kinds of supplies. The guard handed the belt to Julian, who handed it to Taylor. "Money? Guns? Top-secret technology?"

She took a moment to admire the bounty of spoils before clicking a buckle into place below her navel, getting used to the bulk and weight. A handgun, mace, spools of plastic handcuffs, and a Taser adorned the belt like charms on a violent bracelet. The score buoyed her optimism.

"Nope." Julian used his gun to motion the aging man closer. "Turn around and put your hands up. You're going to lead us to the cages where you're holding shifters captive so we can free them."

The guard raised his arms, though his posture didn't sag in submission. Julian aimed the gun between his shoulder blades.

"You're going to let us go, right?" This from Tim's captive in a sniveling whimper. The little man began to shake. "Please don't hurt us. We just do as we're told. The big bosses up top give the orders, and we basement monkeys follow them is all. Coupla nobodies down here, I assure you."

Righteousness and power threaded with a trace of shame filled Taylor's veins in arresting currents. If fate had worked out differently, she might have ended up as wretched as these two. Hunched over a computer in some Manhattan high rise, cheating people out of their pensions because her criminal father and Jay Stearns told her to. But Taylor wasn't an obedient little monkey for The Man anymore. She was a wolf, leader of a new pack.

She commenced a slow stroll up to the trembling ogre and raked a contemptuous appraisal over him. He deserved a good lesson in the nature of his misdeeds. A healthy scare was long overdue. "Have you ever read Hannah Arendt?"

"Huh?" Flab under his chin wobbled, testimony to his cowardice. "I don't know anything. I only took this job because they offered a nice signing bonus and retirement package. I'm not a bad guy, but I'm hamstrung. The wife wants to retire in the Florida Keys, and I've got two college tuition bills and my daughter's wedding to pay for. You've gotta understand. Scarab started me at six figures."

"Shifters are being systematically exterminated, so I could give a single wet fart about your daughter's wedding. Anyway, listen up, chump. Arendt was a political philosopher who wrote about the banality of evil. It's the idea that everyone who is complicit in an oppressive, heinous system is guilty of the crimes said organization perpetrates."

Tim slid her a side eye that asked the "is this really necessary?" question, but nevertheless, she persisted.

Taylor stepped close enough to notice the greasy sheen on the guard's forehead and catch a whiff of the ammonia stench he emitted. "In other words, the guys who stamped the Nazi paperwork were evil too. Even though it's easier for our brains to only focus on the big baddies like Hitler, every single person who kept their head down when they should have stood up and fought is on the hook. This analogy applies perfectly to you. So the next time you beg for your life, fucking spare me this 'I was only following orders' bullshit. Are we clear?"

One corner of Tim's mouth kicked up, and for a split second, he looked to Taylor with respect.

The guard's bulbous eyes acted as windows into his various character flaws and weaknesses. "Y...yes ma'am."

"Good." She lowered her weapon. "Now take us to the prisoners."

As the march resumed, Tim and Julian in control of the guards, Taylor's spine straightened into a steel beam. She walked with big, long strides. Today she would fight on behalf of others for once, and do her best to liberate the powerless.

A top dog is only worth her claws if she's willing to battle for the underdog. Taylor threw her shoulders back and pointed her focus straight ahead. She felt ten feet tall.

His captive trudging in front of him, Julian caught up to Taylor. "That was powerful, what you said back there."

"This is going to sound really weird." A laugh snapped out of her.

Julian quirked a brow.

"I'm glad we're here."

Instead of a confused rebuttal or pushback, Julian offered a thoughtful tilt of the head. God, she loved this man. His inquisitive nature covered a deeper, admirable drive to give others the benefit of the doubt.

"Why?"

"This whole ordeal has showed me how I can be a better person. If not for this, I'd still be fixated on getting to Wall Street. Laying the groundwork for a lonely life at the apex of a mountain made of toxic waste."

The older captive lobbed Taylor a crusty, resentful look but kept marching.

Julian's dark eyes betrayed the depths of his good soul and the degree to which he *saw* her. "Hell yeah, babe. Now let's go save our people and bring them home."

With a little work and some patience, Peru could fit the definition of home. Many pairs of feet made a chorus of squeaks as the band of shifters and their hostages approached the prison chamber. They passed an elevator shaft with both up and down buttons, and the sheer size of this bunker, and how much of it remained unseen, hit Taylor with disturbing force.

"Where's the rest of security?" Julian asked his man, a knowing rumble to his tone. "There have to be more guards than the two of you roaming this place."

The old man shrugged. "There are floaters on every level, yeah. I feel like I see new guys and gals around here every day."

A quickening of adrenaline propelled her to the edge and sharpened her senses. Above, somewhere distant, movement produced a creak. If she concentrated hard enough, she could distinguish between different electronic sounds and even hear a faucet drip.

At last, they approached the hermetically sealed door, a slab of reinforced metal with a thick wheel fit for steering a boat. To the side, the dark screen of a wall-mounted rectangle blocked the unauthorized with high-tech identification.

"How many levels are there here?" she asked.

"Above ground, just the temple. Below, in the subterranean sections... at least thirteen." He had to think about it and didn't sound sure.

Julian gripped the guy by the back of his neck and pressed the man's forehead against glass. The machine woke up with a soft white glow, and a grid of red lights slid over the hostage's face and blinked to green. "You don't know?" Julian clarified.

The captured guard shook his head. A metallic snap, the click of a heavy lock disengaging, sounded in a nice juicy burst. Taylor, though, remained preoccupied by an earlier part of the man's comment. Must've been her inherent drive to learn that spurred the follow-up question, "What's the temple for?"

The guard sneered. "You really want to know?" He asked in a taunting manner, that gross singsong.

"Don't let him manipulate you, babe. You got him covered while I work the door?" Julian's countenance took on a certain sternness. He needed to know that she'd keep a cool head. Fair enough, and no problem on the cool customer front.

"Yeah." She pointed the business end of her rifle at the hostage's smirking face. Her right hand itched despite her desire to maintain the aforementioned cool customer front. How easy it would be to knock his block right off. Punch this fucking Nazi until his brittle skull caved in like a piñata. "Tell me."

Julian grunted, his legs braced wide while he yanked the steel circle to the left. Metal scraped against metal with a wail, the noises bigger and longer as the seal broke beneath his strength.

The captive appeared unfazed despite the gun aimed at his nose. He'd likely reached that empowered state of freedom one obtains when they feel as if they have nothing to lose.

While Julian worked, a look of pure, undiluted hate chased across the guard's face, and an uncanny element to his appearance made her shudder.

Sure, he had the whole glittery-eyed, curled lip thing going on, but it wasn't just his physical features that exposed the malevolence inside of him. His entire countenance became walled off, his inner state an oubliette that had long since trapped his humanity until it shriveled into a desiccated mummy.

For the first time in her life, Taylor was truly mortified. The entirety of her shrank to the evil spectacle in this low-level grunt's bottomless stare.

A traffic jam of yellowed teeth peeked beneath twisted lips as he talked in a low, scummy voice. "In the temple, we purify. After we're through having our fun with you filthy animals, we take what's left of you up there. The parts of you that are worth anything, your skins and blood, are given a blessing and cleansed of your inherent impurities. Only then can we coat our bodies red and don the hides for our annual run through the woods."

Garnet light flashed in Taylor's vision. Her "impure" blood roared. The entirety of a host of atrocities snowballed and clobbered her in a cumulative wallop. The microchips and forced mutation, how they constituted such a heinous violation of her bodily autonomy. Scarab's genocidal crimes, vast and unrepentant, went back God knew how long.

Her heart broke and raged for the ones they hadn't gotten to in time.

She clenched a fist, thumb on the outside, as aggressive chemical injections goaded her. "How dare you?"

A cacophony of torturous sobs, screams, pleas, and animal noises rushed the hall, followed by a slam of metal on metal. "Let's move," Julian shouted.

The guard snickered. "Oh, I'm so sorry. Is the special little snowflake here offended by our holiday celebration? Well guess what, miss Social Justice Warrior? Rules operate differently on the island. Swing your feminist battle axe all you like, but Human Resources isn't going to shut us down because our costumes are culturally insensitive."

A fresh, liquid surge sent lava through her veins, and before she could think too much, she reared back and slammed her knuckles into a spot right below his ear. A snakebite of pain screamed up her arm as bone shattered against bone with a sickening, unwholesome sound of flesh on hardness and hardness on flesh.

The rest happened in slow motion. His eyes stretched with shock, then the light fled them. Slack jaw hanging ruined at the hinge, he sagged and collapsed to the floor. Blood trickled out of one corner of his mouth. As his shoulder hit the ground, two objects fell from his lips and landed on the ground. Teeth.

"Taylor, Jesus Christ." This from Tim, an exasperated sound of shock.

She wasn't afforded seconds to think about what she'd done, because the next voice came from the other captive. "Intruder alert. Intruders on Pen Level. Hostages taken. Man down. Man down!"

Whipping her head in the direction of the girlish screech, Taylor cursed her bout of impulsivity and shook her hurting hand.

The diminutive guard must have seized advantage of the situation and grabbed his belt back from Tim, because he was holding the strap with one hand and yelling into his transmitter with the other.

Tim snatched the black band and radio out of the guard's hands and tossed the things to Chaz, but a crackly reply in a woman's voice meant the damage was done: "Roger. Alpha and medical teams dispatching to Pen Level immediately."

Julian sucked his teeth in a tense hiss. "Throw me the downed one's keys. We gotta move in fast."

Taylor nodded and lobbed the big metal ring to Julian, chancing a glance at the asshole she'd rightfully punched. His chest rose and fell, so at least she hadn't killed him, even though he'd deserved a snuff out. But the unconscious man's wellness was the least of their worries now because her actions had led to consequences.

She raced in behind Julian, Tim on her heels and the others bringing up the rear.

Fortunately, the remaining guard didn't put up a fight when ordered to identify the correct key, and the team went to work on locks.

Panicked, shrieking, and wailing people flooded the clearing in the middle of the panoptic cell arrangement, clinging to their rescuers and each other.

A low, repetitive alarm blared. Shit. She'd fucked up by KO-ing the hostage, but now wasn't the time to beat herself up for mistakes.

Taylor aimed her filched handgun at the nexus between a cell door and the jamb, motioning for a trio of teenaged males to huddle in the farthest corner.

She fired her weapon at the lock, the blast putting a deafening ring in her ears as the force knocked her back with a swift kick as she emptied her chamber. In a flash of victory amidst the chaos, metal and plastic rained down in splinters and the front of the clear confine wobbled in the impact's wake.

Following Taylor's lead, a succession of additional gunfire booms and shattering cracks competed with the drone of the siren. Gunshots took out the security cameras, not that it mattered anymore.

All three boys shifted seamlessly into mountain lions and charged. Taylor leapt aside as their bodies connected with the weakened door and broke free in a tornado of snarls, bared teeth fashioned to rend muscle, and paws the size of appetizer plates.

They went right for the runty Scarab security guard. A feline jaw locked the howling employee's ankle, and the big cat pulled the man out of Tim's hold. The employee flailed his arms, screeching as his belly slid along the floor.

Cats descended and made quick work, closing ranks in humps of tawny fur. Clouds of red mist flew as his cries grew unspeakable, then died. Once they'd dispatched their first target, the mountain lions sprinted to the breached entrance, presumably en route to the second jailer.

As more and more shifters ran on to the floor and pandemonium ratcheted, a sense of urgency propelled her brain into high gear. She blew the whistle around her neck, and a high-pitched shriek sliced through the air and shut most everyone up.

"We need to get them to the portal and deliver them in batches." Her stomach dropped when the alarm became audible again. The loudness of the last few minutes would've swallowed any signals that the guards and medics might be close.

Tim and Julian blew their own whistles in unison, killing the remaining few voices.

Julian shouted to the legion, "Follow the three of us out of here single file and do every single thing we say. We're here to help and get you to safety, but you need to trust and listen. Can you?"

Heads bobbed. People hugged and rocked crying children, gently shushing them.

"You and Tim take the front. I'll bring up the rear," Taylor called. Made sense, as she'd ended up at the end of the dungeon opposite Tim and Julian. She had the best placement to corral any stragglers or hesitant types and ensure that every last shifter got out.

Julian gave her a thumbs up, and she returned the confirmation.

The other two leaders assumed positions near the entrance, their backs turned to Taylor, and the legion of freed shifters coalesced into a single-file line. Tim and Julian vanished from view, and the cluster behind them began to shuffle out in a synchronized tide of movement.

Taylor swept a quick panoramic gaze through the cell block, noting how every door had been blown open. She nodded at the results of the Peruvian team's handiwork and released a mega exhale. Albeit with a few surprises and hiccups, they'd succeeded. Time to get everyone home.

"Mama?" a girl of perhaps four wailed. "Where's my mama? I want my mama."

Taylor dashed in the direction of the frightened voice, coming up on a child crumpled in a corner cage, rocking with her knees clutched to her chest.

She squatted by the whimpering preschooler. "It's okay. You're safe now. Follow the others, okay?"

Her big blue eyes went wide. "Is my mama there?"

God knew, but the sands of time ran low as the alarm banged on. "I hope so. There are people who love you and will take care of you. I promise. But you need to hurry and go with them."

The child sprinted on skinny legs, assumed a spot at the end of the shuffling line, and took the hand of an older girl with nurturing body language.

Taylor wiped her brow and stood. Good thing she'd taken her post near the back, or they might have overlooked the little girl.

A soft click of mechanical engagement routed her focus to the space behind her. Shock stole her voice as she saw an opening appear where none had existed before. A door had opened in the slice of wall dividing two cell blocks, its existence camouflaged to look like the surrounding paint pattern.

One man and one woman, gun holsters peeking out beneath unbuttoned lab coats, stood in the trapdoor's threshold. A dim tunnel behind them, they descended upon Taylor in a fast, choreographed motion.

A mean hand clamped over her nose and mouth before she could scream, and pain pierced her neck with a sharp bite. Cold fluid ran under her skin, acting fast to make her sleepy and sluggish. Her heels dragged the ground, the sight of her sneakers going blurry until her vision merged with the darkness.

TWENTY

Julian didn't have magical powers of intuition, but he damn well knew when things were flat wrong. For starters, the alarm kept on going, but there were no signs of any Scarab backup yet. Why the leisurely pace in responding to the guard's emergency call? At least a half-hour had passed since the now-dead man grabbed his radio from Tim. Surely, Scarab wanted to reclaim their stock and do away with the interlopers. But a bigger concern lurked in the foreground of his mind.

"Taylor," he called down the hall as the line commenced a march to the portal. "Let me know you're there."

"Where else would she be? There were two ways in, and we would have noticed anyone coming in through either of them." Tim approached their destination, then switched focus to address the refugees. "We're going to travel twelve at a time, and one of us will take some of you to the camp and stay there until another of us teleports to Peru for a switch. We'll run through this relay style until all of you are out of here. Case, take the first group back to the camp."

"You got it boss." The falcon shifter led the first twelve in line into the portal lab, and everyone crammed in to the tank.

Tim was correct insofar as logic ought to dictate Taylor's whereabouts. All bets were off in this place, though. For all Julian knew, a portal could have opened in the floor and swallowed her. "I don't know, but she should have answered me by now. You back there, babe?"

No reply, just the worried stares of frightened evacuees. Julian ran to the back of the line, wracked with anxious jitters as his heart calcified. She was not there.

Two young girls brought up the rear, standing a few feet in front of the shredded mound of gore that was once the old guard. Julian quelled the worst of his urge to get upset at Taylor, but fucking hell, this operation would have run through smooth as silk had she not socked that guy.

"What happened to the woman who was back here with you two?" he asked the older child, an Asian girl of around sixteen with faded purple highlights and a nose ring. "Petite and white with short blonde hair, armed, was shooting open the cells."

No way had the love of his life, his fated mate, vanished into nothing. Some misdeed was afoot, and with each passing second spent thinking about possible scenarios, he got sicker.

"She saved me," the little one said, pointing a stumpy finger at a spot behind her. "She was right here."

And now she was not. Every one of his organs dropped to his shoes. He ran into the holding pen and into the first vacated cell he saw in search of portal equipment or other means of exit.

Heavy, odious stenches of ammonia and shit sourness forced him to lay a forearm over his face and breathe through his mouth as he cased the emptied pens, stepping around yellow puddles and brown piles.

But they were all barren, bereft of escape options even in the form of toilets or sinks.

The narrowest pipes might facilitate the travels of those who changed into rats, snakes, beetles, etcetera. Hence the lack of plumbing. The humiliation of no sanitation was an added bonus for Scarab, he bet.

"Any luck?" Tim's voice echoed as the line shortened into the transport room.

"No." But Julian didn't give up. Surrender wasn't his thing. Without a stubborn will and indefatigable spirit, he wouldn't have survived all these years, so no way would he fold on his true love.

So he knelt and ran his hand along the floor. No handles or knobs.

While down on his knees, a marking on the wall made him gasp with dread. A barely perceptible seam traced an upright rectangle in the building material.

He ran to the suspicious development and touched the lines. Sure enough, there were gasps. Anger made him hot and shaky. These heinous people and their secret doors. Bunch of cowards, operating through the trickery of light and shadow. "I found something."

Footsteps clomped, and Tim appeared at Julian's side and said, "Oh, no."

"Yeah." Julian pushed the door to no avail, dug the tips of his fingers into the grooves. But the mechanism wasn't designed to be opened from this side of the room. "Whoever they sent came in this way, undetected. They ambushed her."

A sad expression chased across Tim's features. He glanced at the diminished line of shifters filing down the hall. "We've only got two more groups to transport. And look, man, I didn't want to say anything in front of the evacuees and scare anyone, but the Other One is gone. So as I'm sure you are aware now, Scarab has set a new phase of whatever this is into motion, and they seem adept at stealth. We need to save those shifters and get all of us out of here."

"I know what you're suggesting." Though tears stung Julian's eyes, and his breaking heart cried out for Taylor, he stood tall with conviction. "But I refuse to chalk her up to a battlefield loss. I cannot lose her. Not when I've just now found her."

Tim's lips thinned. His Adam's apple bobbed, and he tipped his chin in a single nod. "I lost someone special. A jaguar woman. We started off hating each other, cliché cats and dogs crap, but oh boy did our situation change."

"What happened?" Julian laid a hand of support on Tim's shoulder. From the man's tone, it was clear this story didn't include a happy ending.

The other man's eyes burned with sorrow and rage. "A poacher got her. This asshole and his stupid sons were in Peru on a big game hunt. He went to jail in the end, but not before my Mina's spots ended up as a trophy on the wall of that worthless fast-food CEO."

"I'm so sorry, man. So sorry." He swept Tim into a hug and felt the trembling of his body as he fought to keep it together.

"I can't break down. Not now. Not anymore. I have to help the ones I'm able to save. But the grief, the death, it just...sticks on you and stays." His voice kicked up an octave and shook.

Julian released Tim, and they looked at each other in silent communion.

Tim unclipped his equipment belt, unstrapped his rifle, and extended his arms with the weapons in them.

Julian accepted and suited up.

"I'll send Chaz and a couple of others to come with you as backup," Tim said.

"No. Get them to safety. I won't put anyone else at risk. Taylor is here because of me, and I'll get her out myself or die trying. Besides, if that guard was telling the truth, there aren't too many other security guards here."

"Plus a medical team." Tim sounded concerned.

"I can handle it." Julian spoke with all the confidence inside of him. This was his fight. If he lost, then fate had spoken. But he refused to draw others into the orbit of what could be a doomed endeavor, a suicide mission.

Tim reached into a side pocket on his cargo pants and produced a tube of paper. Right. The blueprint of the compound's layout, or what they knew of it at least.

Julian took the roll and stuck it down the side of his jeans, his waistband and hip pinning the map in place. "You any good at picking locks?"

Tim smirked for the first time since Julian had known him. He took a pouch from another pocket and unzipped it to reveal a collection of metal tools. Working fast, he slipped out two and jiggled them in a gap until his work led to a snick of disengagement. He confirmed his results with a gentle push, and voila, the door was ajar. "I knew my juvenile delinquent days would come in handy." He gave the kit to Julian.

"Let's go with rebel." Julian pocketed Tim's offering. "See you back at the camp."

"Yeah." The word came out slow and smooth with faith, the vote of confidence bolstering Julian's respect for the guy. Friends who believed in you, even when you weren't sure of yourself? Keep those people close. "See you back at the camp."

Once Tim left to attend to the rescue party, Julian entered the secret space and found himself in another tunnel. At least the layout lacked any creative design flair. He could use predictable terrain to his advantage. Positive thinking was his only chance to save Taylor.

Dim electric lamps dotted the walls, minimal beacons against a cloud of enveloping darkness. He squinted and blinked as the cloud of black submitted to his ocular adjustment.

The Sig Sauer aimed with assurance at potential targets in front of him, Julian slinked down the passage with his back pressed into the corridor.

"They've got her in Medical, I guess." A man spoke like he was recounting the most boring fact he'd heard all week, but Julian damn near leapt with hope. "Her" could mean Taylor, and Medical was where live people went. Slow and steady with the firearm leading, he kept moving.

"I still don't get it." This from a woman, followed by the plop of a soft object hitting a soft object. "What's so special about this girl?"

"I dunno, I heard she's a mutant. They can do wild and crazy stuff, like occult powers almost. But we aren't here to ask questions. So let's get this shit down to the nurse's station, because I want to take my lunch break."

"True that. Oops, I forgot that latest box of scrubs that came in today. Hold up." Footfalls, then a door opened and closed.

Dancing forward with all the fleet-footed grace he had in him, Julian cleared the tunnel and came to a T-intersection. Tracks ran the length, and a one-car tram idled on the rails. A redheaded woman, arms burdened with a huge cardboard box, ambled up to the means of transport. She put her load on the ground, opened a hatch underneath, and slid the box into the compartment.

Saliva flooded Julian's mouth as he readied his mind and body to answer the knock of opportunity. Once the woman entered the vehicle, he ran to the car and joined the boxes.

Surrounded by cargo and a few bags filled with packing peanuts, he slowed his breathing and cleared his head. He could hijack the train, but better to maintain a modicum of discretion and have this pair lead him to their destination. If he had any cover left that hadn't been blown, best to protect those paltry remnants of anonymity, and this option promised speedy results.

The tram started moving and chugged along for a few minutes before stopping. Julian got out, spotted a concrete pillar on the platform, and hid behind it.

"Do you think they put the creepy experiments on level thirteen on purpose?" the woman spoke, an airy hiss sounding off while she talked.

"That's like, so on the nose that I would not put it past them." The guy said. "You think they really have the skull of Satan or whatever it is down here?"

Soft grunts from both people and muted thumps.

The woman said, "I've heard that every beastie they feed to the demon thing drums up a buttload of negative energy, and some scientist made a machine to catch and capture the bad mojo. They want to channel and control all the hate and fear to summon more demons and use them to possess people." More routine loading noises underscored the frightening gravity in the comment. "Probably just an urban legend." Came off like a failed effort to reassure herself.

Julian peeked, catching sight of the employees stacking boxes on pallet jacks. If even a tenth of the madness they discussed was true, the security down here had to be at least as robust as the protections covering the jail and portal room. Or not. This place was topsy-turvy.

Gun drawn, he made a quick call and advanced. "Hi. I'm going to be accompanying you to Medical this evening. Do what I say, and no one gets hurt."

Both employees startled and put their hands up.

"Okay, yeah, no problem." The guy, twenty tops with clean-cut looks, flinched.

"Is there an underground portal?" Julian asked.

"I...I think so," the woman squeaked, her youthful face twisted into a scared grimace.

Not much, but her guess was all he had. "Lead the way."

Pushing the jacks, they scurried without a moment's hesitation.

These two weren't fighters or heroes for their employer, a small victory. The pair led him to a pair of elevators. The woman fumbled at her lanyard, ran a key fob over a black box, and did the facial recognition protocol on one of the mounted consoles.

Reflective doors parted, and the trio stepped in. The man pushed a button for level thirteen, the lowest level, and a long ride transpired in agonizing silence. Julian couldn't get impatient, though, and risk impulsivity. He was almost there. Getting closer.

The stuffy box deposited them in a corridor with a predictable, clinical feel. He jutted his chin at the guy, giving him the signal to lead. Julian might be a hostage taker now, but he was still a gentleman and not about to put a woman on the front line.

Pressurized guilt warped his thoughts while the small group walked. Should he have done more to protect Taylor, rein her in despite the unwavering fortitude of her conviction? He hadn't wanted to act the part of chauvinist pig or controlling jerk by mansplaining why she ought to stay away from Scarab or ordering her to never risk herself for a cause she cared about, but now he doubted his choices. He shook his head. This was not the time for regret.

"Where is Medical?" Best to focus on the matter at hand and chart where these two were taking him. Though they radiated the energy of not being paid enough to stick their necks out, he didn't trust them either.

"Suites thirteen-o-one through thirteen-thirteen," the woman said.

"Rooms within larger rooms." The dude confirmed, turning his head over his shoulder.

"Is each suite protected by facial recognition?"

"Yes." They spoke at once.

"Do you anticipate anyone else being down here besides whoever is working on Taylor?"

They hung a right and passed numbered doors. Addresses started at thirteen-forty, evens on one side and odds on the other, and counted down. A faint electronic whine issued from semi-close proximity.

"On the weekend, I doubt it." The man stopped at room thirteen-o-one.

"You two go in first. I want you to split up and open every door you find. If there's anyone else in there, tell them that you lost a phone and need to check all the rooms. That might buy me some minutes." With any luck, he'd encounter, at most, another low-level lackey and pull off a demand to conscript the person into his plan. "If you spot a gun, say the words 'fresh linens.' A code."

Machines complied with their familiar interplay of light and sound, permitting Julian entry into a nondescript waiting room infused with the chemical smell of new carpet. A vacant nurse's station decorated with a Spiderman bobble head doll and a cup full of pens loomed behind Plexiglass.

"Welcome to Medical." The woman opened a door to an empty examination room.

"Have you seen any of the activity that goes on in here?" Whatever information he could garner, he'd take. One clue or hint beat charging in blind.

"Nope." The man took his face away from a screen and nudged open the final door of his assignment. "We're stockers and delivery people is all. Like Scarab's own private Amazon. All we do is make runs to and from the warehouse. Tonight we were literally just delivering a few loads here."

Julian opened and peered into a room stocked floor-to-ceiling with brown boxes. A laundry bin half full of blue scrubs sat in the middle.

"Sometimes we do the laundry also." The woman looked up at him with big green doe eyes. "All the doors are open. Can we go now?"

He sighed. "Get out. Go home, and don't come back to work for this rotten place. You don't want their stain on your souls."

The employees ran like the Hounds of Hell snapped at their heels.

Julian checked rooms. Supply closet, three empty exam rooms stocked with blood pressure machines and other expected furnishings.

The next one he cased was different and odd enough to trigger a sense of unease in him. The office contained a cheap desk and chair, and a chunky, outdated computer monitor. A faded motivational poster and several portraits of middle-aged men hung on the walls. One man was Taylor's father.

A combination of outrage and excitement pumped him full of chemicals. Speaking of using predictable layouts to his advantage, Julian had enough experience with the madness of this organization that he had no trouble deciphering a clue when he saw one.

With careful hands, he took Jeff's picture down, the gilded frame heavy in his hands, and smiled upon spotting a rectangle the size of a light switch beneath the smiling portrait of the graying senator. Bingo. Under the picture lay a keyboard panel.

Tonight, these freaks had an uninvited guest. Julian keyed in the successful digits they'd used in her father's office, Taylor's social security number, and bam. That door slid right to the side.

A room stared back at him, the space bereft of equipment save for a gleaming white coffin of an MRI machine and what he guessed was a two-way mirror on the wall. In the corner, a simple door with a normal knob beckoned. No more hardcore security. He'd breached the inner chamber, where they must've figured that all personnel were authorized.

His movements methodical, Julian marched over and turned the knob. Unlocked. *I'm coming for you, babe.*

The instant he stepped inside, time hardened into a stunning plane of glass. Bodies floated inside tanks, their sizes ranging from as small as a grapefruit to as large as a football, inchoate things of indeterminate species attached to plastic tubing. Their eyes were fused shut the same as newborn kittens, and none had fur or hair. Distinctly fetal.

Cylindrical tanks lined each side of a long room, noises of bubbling water issuing from them. His rubber soles squeaked against a metal floor as he walked down the aisle of horrors.

One creature twitched in its tank and opened a toothless mouth, its stubby pink legs flailing for purchase before it went still. He kept going. At the end of the line, thick clear strips hung over a doorway.

He walked into another chamber, edges of the plastic tickling his face as he processed his surroundings. In the middle of the empty, steel-floored room, a slender table that looked to be carved from onyx served as the sole inhabitant. In the middle of the stand, a glass box housed a test tube filled with swirling blue liquid, a contained whirlpool operating on its own volition.

Struck with an uncanny and dreadful sense of familiarity, Julian leaned down and looked closer. The shade of blue matched the hues of the energy networks connecting the Other One to the portal.

"That you, Jay?" A mild, unbothered male voice came from the other side of the wall. "We've got the mutant and will begin as soon as we get her on board for her part in this."

A memory turned him to ice yet stoked his fiery impulse to act. *"I dunno, I heard she's a mutant. They can do wild and crazy stuff, like occult powers almost."*

Intense emotions lost out to methodical, goal-oriented clarity. They had Taylor on the other side of this divide and were about to complete a terrible act against her. But the news wasn't all bad. This was his chance, his shot, to get to his love and save her.

"Yeah, it's me." He'd never heard this Jay person speak but banked on the power of suggestion working in his favor.

"Great." The same man said. "Hang tight, and I'll patch you in as soon as we're ready to roll."

Routine biological functions played with the foreboding staccato of war drum beats. Julian watched the wall in front of him, vigilant for a sign. He tightened his grip on the gun and braced himself to enter a new nightmare and pull Taylor from the bleak landscape of death.

TWENTY-ONE

TAYLOR HADN'T DECIDED WHAT WAS WORSE, THE LONG STRETCHES OF solitude, or when the woman in the lab coat, her hair strangled into a ballerina bun, came in to take her vitals or check her restraints.

She'd given up on struggling, her wrists and ankles secured by bolts and chains to the circular altar on which she lay. Her body had acclimated to the cold hardness pressing into her hips and back, so she'd stopped shivering despite the paper-thin hospital gown someone had put on her during the period of unconsciousness.

From her vantage point on the raised slab of black marble, she saw most of the details of the room. The checkerboard floor stood out, the contrasting pattern a disturbing and mysterious intentionality. Antiquated stone fountains on the walls poured continual streams of water into basins. Vaulted ceilings, stone walls embellished with Roman-style pillars, and a faint tinge of smoky-sweet incense frightened her with their esoteric significance.

Time's passage of day into night was meaningless, as the space lacked windows. She didn't know whether Julian had given up looking for her and returned to Peru or died in the process. Either way, she wasn't yet finished. Not with her new friend water in play.

Heels clacked like artillery fire.

Taylor swallowed, heavy in her heart but not yet numb with despair. She eyed the streams of water. The robust flow of liquid ran into those basins but didn't pool or overflow. Which meant drainage. Pipes and plumbing. Water pressure. And liquid amounted to a possible resource for her to shape into a weapon if she located and seized a strategy to use her water magic.

Six sculpted, bronze jugs occupied a snatch of floor space by each of the sinks. A smash to the head with one of those bad boys sure would hurt and stun, but the shackles binding Taylor's wrists mocked any sort of bludgeoning plot.

The woman clattered over, all glasses and red lips and emotionless, expressionless visage. She filled one of the jugs and poured liquid over the altar, wetness pooling tepid beneath Taylor's bound body. Some of the water absorbed into her skin, her pores, merging with her essence in a thrilling union. As the splash trickled off the platform and piddled on to the floor, Taylor rode out a series of surges.

The woman crouched, and metal scraped against metal.

Connection with the water tethering her to optimism, Taylor craned her neck in preparation for catching a glimpse of a knife. "Am I about to be sacrificed? Because that's sure what it looks like."

But when the woman stood, she held a tome, an ancient encyclopedia with a leathery brown cover and tongues of yellowed pages poking out in ratty edges. The anonymous person opened to a section near the back and began to read, "Sister Folly, I, a chaos born disciple, humbly beg you to surrender the fruits of the water witch's womb. Born of human and mated with wolf, allow her gift to serve as fulfilment of your prophecy of awakening. The flesh and blood of her aborted spawn shall join its brethren and fuel you as you rise from slumber and commence your rule over Earth in chaos and pain."

A stark realization washed away the detritus of Taylor's confusion.

"I'm pregnant." The statement of impossible fact scraped a jagged trail up her throat. Her birth control method bragged a low failure rate, but no contraception came with a one hundred percent guarantee. The pregnancy was so early as to be undetectable. Except, apparently, by knowledge of magic.

"You'll read the next part aloud." The drone in the lab coat shoved the book in Taylor's face, assaulting her eyeballs with a mess of arcane symbols in the vein of coiled serpents, looping runes, and text inked in black calligraphy that bled down warped pages.

"I'm not reading shit. What is this?" Water witch, chaos born, Sister Folly. Maybe she could stall for a minute and get this woman to talk.

She fixed a hard stare on one of the fountains and pulled with her mind. As she concentrated, she could see more. See the pulse of liquid flowing in malleable travels, confined by the molding of the pipes that sculpted formlessness into tubes. Networks of encased eels raced, clear tentacles catching light in reflective prism shimmers.

Pressure pounded in her skull. Water throbbed as molecules sought escape from the pipes and longed to come to Taylor. She pulled with her mind, pulled and pulled.

"Just read your part, and we let you go home safe, okay? It's nothing. You'll just feel a little pull in your lower belly, like yanking out a splinter." An impatient, sour look, accompanied the patronizing comment, stoked the already feisty defiance definitive of Taylor's nature.

"Fuck off. You aren't taking my embryo, bitch." Taylor locked her captor's gaze, staring into gunmetal eyes that flared hot and dark with irritation.

If Julian was still alive, she'd make her final choice on whether to end the pregnancy or carry it to term after taking his input into account. Scarab's bullies didn't get a say.

"Sorry, sweetie, you don't have a choice if you want to live. Now read."

Instead, Taylor schooled her breathing into a robust, controlled pattern and drew the water to her. Caught behind stone, it shoved. Trickles ran down the grooves separating stone blocks, glossing the drab building material into a shine. Taylor smiled.

Another person walked into the room, a few inches taller than Taylor and suited in scrubs and a medical mask. Something uncanny about the man...Taylor's world crunched into shock. Her father had entered the fray.

"What is this?" She screamed at the one who had betrayed her, the entirety of the love that had once resided in her heart bleeding away along with the running water. "Why are you doing this? What do you want from me?"

In a hard, angry pull, Jeff yanked his blue germ mask past his chin and stormed up to the woman. "You said she'd be subdued by now and extraction would be complete."

"I can't get her to read the page," the woman said, her tone brittle. "I didn't think her compliance would be a problem, but it is, and since she apparently didn't drink the ionized water before she extracted her chips, I can't launch any mind control programs."

"Talk," Taylor gritted out, straining against her restraints as she pulled close enough to her father to smell his aftershave. "Tell me every single detail of the truth. You've hurt me more than I've ever even begun to imagine. You owe me full disclosure."

A second man in protective clothing ambled in, and Jeff looked at him and pulled a face.

"What did I just tell you? Wait in the damn ante chamber until I buzz you in. I wanted my daughter to have some privacy during and after the procedure." Taylor's father stabbed a finger at a red button beside one of the sinks.

"Huh? I didn't come in through the ante chamber, and we haven't talked since yesterday." Jay Stearns spoke.

Taylor gritted her teeth. She'd hoped to never have to deal with Jay again, but she held a trump card. Leverage came in the form of water magic and the developing life form these people wanted to rip from her insides.

"Then whom did I speak with?" Jeff threw his hands in the air.

Stearns shrugged.

"Save your spat for later," Taylor said. "And start talking, Jeff. Now. Because trust me, I can put a stop to all of this." She mind-winked at the water, and pressurized liquid pushed, pressed, urging the pipes to break.

"Okay." A heavy sigh of resignation wrapped his word in defeat. "My descent into hell began when you were two months old. I gave you a bath. As I dried you off, you started screaming and crying. I set you in the crib, and I saw them. Bruises. Up your precious little back, like a beaded necklace laid over your spine. I took you to the emergency room. The next couple of years were a blur of doctors and hospitals and specialists. Your mother had blown through her inheritance already, and we were up to our eyeballs in debt and leveraged to the hills. Our marriage suffered, but we got pregnant with Donnie because..."

"Because what?" Taylor whispered, astonished but not shocked. The gist came into focus. She'd been subjected to medical interventions leading up to the chips. She had to know why. For closure, for peace. For a shot at saving herself, Julian, and the tiny thing in her womb.

"They said it was leukemia. Terminal. That you wouldn't see your fifth birthday. We tried all of the standard stuff, like the bone marrow transplants. But the cancer was too aggressive."

"Keep talking." The water was urgent now, roaring and booming, so loud in her head that she staved off the urge to shout her speech. All she had to do was give one last mental tug. But not before she drew out the truth at last. "What did you do?"

Bullish anger flashed in Jeff's stare. "I said fuck their prognosis. I researched and dug and dug for solutions. Experimental procedures, clinical trials. Anything to save my firstborn baby girl."

"Hey, McClure." Stearns's hailing came in clipped notes of urgency. "I saw someone walk by about ten feet away. Tall, male, long black hair. I'm thinking unauthorized personnel."

Taylor nearly burst into tears of relief. Julian. He had survived and was coming for her. Not wise to react, though, and negate the element of stealth.

"One second, Jay," Jeff snapped before turning his attention back to Taylor. "Through one of my colleagues at UT, another scientist who worked on the far corners of his field like I did, I found a clinic in Switzerland doing radical stuff with human cells. The idea was to use a synthetic agent smart enough to mimic the body's unique makeup. Inserted in a chip under the skin, it was supposed to suck up the cancer cells, reprogram them, and send them back in as normal. Repeat until the body is cancer free. They were doing far-out stuff with those chips, too, experiments that eclipsed scientific legitimacy. They said those practices were proprietary secrets. I didn't ask too many questions. There were no deal breakers."

Magic. Along with the chips, these rogue scientists had put magic into her body. She'd seen the evidence all around her. "Go on."

"Ten trips to Bern in a single year completed phase one." Jeff glowered at a spot on the sacrificial podium. "Insurance didn't cover jack, and phase one alone cost millions. We maxed out every line of credit we had. So I set out to get the money for your treatments, by hook or by crook."

Spinning with astonishment, she managed to croak out her next words. "How did it end up like this? Literally, here, with me chained to a freaking altar?"

"I turned over every rock I could, looking for a person or organization with deep pockets to invest in my research. To pay me for my work in theoretical physics. Eventually, Scarab, just a private military contractor at the time, bit. I used the initial payout to get you to Bern for phases two and three. So your anti-carcinogen implant was fully installed, operational and working, by the end of your third year. From then it was annual checkups."

"But you still weren't free."

"Hey, McClure—"

"Shut up, Stearns. Anyway, no. Far from it. That's when it all spiraled into total fucking insanity, Taylor. Real looney horseshit. The bit of money left after we paid for the treatments vanished into the pockets of creditors. We went bankrupt, and apparently in my haste to cure you, I hadn't read Scarab's contract carefully. Scarab had me by the balls, and I couldn't give them the additional technology I'd apparently promised. So we started cutting deals. Your mother offered herself up first, agreed to submit to their kitten programming protocol and service rich businessmen on demand. Our marriage was broken beyond repair at this point, so her foray into elite escorting was just business."

Twin streams slid in tandem from the corners of Taylor's eyes as she grieved for her mother, herself, and even her father. They'd made terrible choices to save her life, and despite the indignities she'd endured as of late, she wouldn't forget their sacrifices. "Keep going."

"Soon, what your mother offered stopped being enough. They wanted technology from me, so I got back to work making teleportation machines and time travel equipment. I started to wonder if I could do good stuff with my tech and ideas, as a lawmaker. Atone for my sins, support legislation and companies working here in the U.S. on cutting edge cancer innovation, like the one that cured you. Predict and prevent tsunamis and other natural disasters. Get us into outer space before climate change makes this planet inhospitable to life. In my misguided mind, I thought if I kept appeasing them, I'd build up enough clout or make the right contacts and eventually get commissioned for a passion project. Set things right by contributing a valuable invention to society. I rationalized working for them by telling myself I was getting us out of debt and giving you the best shot possible at a healthy life."

Jeff rubbed his face until the skin reddened.

"And now both of our hands are tied. So to speak."

"Yes. I'm sorry, Taylor. Scarab learned about you, your nanotech treatments, and wanted to take a look. Long story short, these anti-carcinogen chips are one application of the prototype. They had their own scientists working on implants modifying DNA for a super solider program. But you were a special case."

She waited, bound while paradoxically feeling freer than she had in years.

"Your chip unlocked a latent strand of junk DNA, which revealed...a special trait about you. I don't know how to tell you this, but you're a... you might be able to..."

"Shape shift into a wolf? One step ahead of you."

Jeff looked like he was about to be sick. His voice broke with grief as he spoke his next words, "Again, for what it's worth, I'm so sorry. I was going to tell you eventually. But then you took it into your own hands to remove the chips. That's when the wheels came off completely. I lost control." He choked back a sob. "I've totally lost control."

Her empathy was running thin, but at least the puzzle was coming together. "Continue."

"That's when I learned of their eyes project. To take and capture shifters for military use. They threatened me. Said they'd steal you, that they had the tech to do it, and unless I made you into an eye, I'd never see you again. They had this theory that supernaturals and latent supernaturals find each other, making you an ideal scout. The camera chip went in when you were sixteen and under anesthesia to have your appendix out, and six years, later you met Julian, and the programming kicked in. I'm so sorry, Taylor."

There were big pieces of this story missing. "There is no way the plan was limited to me working as a scout and reeling in Julian. This is occult. The book, the altar, this Other One? They wanted us to find each other and have sex so they could harvest the product of our conception. Why? What do they want to do with what's inside of my uterus?"

Jeff's skin paled, and he let out a broken cry. "I don't know, baby, I'm so so sorry. The people at the top, the ones you don't see, hold a hell of a lot back. I just wanted to save you. That's all I ever wanted. And if you go through with this, they promised to release you. What's inside of you isn't a baby. You marched for Planned Parenthood, you know this. It's a bundle of cells, and you get to decide what to do with it. Your body. Your choice. Your conscience is clear."

She wasn't sure what sickened her more, the frantic, pathetic desperation in his tone or the facile, condescending attempt to manipulate her. Taylor gaped at her father with a blend of pity and contempt. "Man, you were so, so close to getting the point about being pro-choice. I've made my choice, and Scarab's insane experiments in blood sacrifice don't factor in to the equation."

He closed his eyes and grumbled. "Just do it, Taylor. For God's sake, quit being stubborn and just do it." He snatched the book from the woman and stuck the open volume in front of Taylor, jabbing a finger against the same portion of text.

"Come on now." The woman laid a soft, frigid hand on Taylor's shoulder. "Spread your legs."

"Kiss my ass." With the strength of a person determined to win a game of tug o' war, Taylor pulled the water. With all the strength inside of her, she pulled, pulled like her life and the potential life of the embryo depended on it.

A caged tsunami howled. In a biblical eruption of tides and waves, stone cracked and jets burst free.

"Sorry, Dad." She aimed one at Jeff, and the clear rope turned on him with snakelike sentience and slammed into the middle of his chest. The force hurled him across the room. His back whacked the wall, hard enough to knock him out but not to deliver a death blow. She repeated the process with the woman and Stearns while they ran around the room shouting panicked nonsense.

As water pooled quickly on the ground, Taylor drew upon the other fantastical skill in her arsenal. Up and out, she coaxed the wolf from her kennel and guided her to the surface. The change happened without pain. Bones broke and reformed with neat clacks, organs drifted around seamlessly and found new spots. The colors of her vision transformed to a varied palette of gray and apprehended more detail around the periphery.

Her center of gravity dropped, and her slimmer canine wrists and ankles slid from the clamps after a few wiggles. She flipped onto her feet and jumped to the floor, the pads of her paws splashing in a couple inches of water. The book floated face up, and she clamped her jaws on that sucker and ran like hell in search of light.

"Babe." Julian's voice, echoing off subterranean walls in the distance. "I smell you. Follow my voice."

And she did, charging with all the power stored in her lean, vulpine muscle. After a long haul, she found him in a big room, some cavernous space with a slight triangular depression in the middle of the dirt floor.

He crouched, hugged her and petted her while moaning tortured sounds of relief. "You made it. Oh, Taylor, I'm so sorry for what you went through, that I couldn't stop it. I thought we'd both be lost forever in this maze. Please forgive me."

She dropped the book and licked his face, assurance that he ought not to feel at fault.

"We need to move." He retrieved the tome. "The Other One is loose and tracking us. As far as I can tell, it wants to collect our pain and feed it to some evil presence underground. I've mapped out an escape route for us that bypasses all doors protected by facial recognition locks. Let's go."

Julian didn't have to tell her twice. Checking their progress with occasional glimpses at the map, he led them through a labyrinth of tunnels, cubby holes, and crawl spaces whose walls packed her tight. She saw dried blood and severed claws smeared on some of the walls and mourned for the ones they weren't able to save. Shifters had suffered and died in this godforsaken place, but never again.

Time to get home to Peru.

Crawling on his belly using his elbows and upper body to propel him forward, Julian came to a metal gate. He maneuvered and wiggled until his boots faced it. One hard kick didn't budge the bars, and she watched with worry, breathing in dust and catacomb funk. But after two more slams, the barrier yielded and flopped to the side.

He slipped out feet first and, once upright and looking up at her through the opening he created, extended a hand.

In a gesture so rich with solidarity, commitment, and love that it froze the flow of time, she laid her furry paw in his big human palm. The two of them, mated and bound. Forever.

The wind sung promises of eternal love, but before rejoicing, they'd better save their asses. Guided by the assistance of Julian's pull, Taylor leapt from the hole and fell five feet.

Her paws hit dirt, and a robust, cooling breeze welcomed her with the sensations of freedom. They'd gotten out alive.

She changed into her human form and craned her neck to the heavens, pinpointing Sirius amidst a resplendent blanket of stars. Julian beside her, Taylor jogged a few feet until she obtained an optimal position right under the star. After catching his fingers and flashing him a triumphant smile, she began to recite the passcode to Peru.

"Latitude coordinates—"

A shrill screech fit for a ravenous zombie clobbered her eardrums first, and pain came sharp and hot in the awful sound's wake. Stunned into a bright world of mindless agony, she glanced down to the source of her misery. Had she been shot?

An ice-white spear protruded from the left side of her chest, slick with the glisten of her blood. While she imagined the scream kept going, the ringing in her ears drowned out the metallic shriek. A stupor took over, dense and thick. She blinked against dark spots. Mouthed words but none came.

"No!" From Julian, followed by another thud of impact.

The spike impaling her flesh crumbled into ashy flakes and fell to the ground. Next thing she knew, she was on her knees, in his arms, halfway lucid and extremely confused, anchored to reality only by his strength and familiar scent.

"What happened?" She spent eons forcing the words out as her uncooperative brain struggled to process.

"The Other One." His statement was grim and angry, laced with the threat of tears. "As soon as I saw it, I threw a punch. No idea why, but it dissolved on impact. But it had already stabbed you by then. Oh, Taylor."

"I'm…" Viscous warmth spilled out of her mouth with her attempt at speech. She was hurt on the inside, bad, and with each passing second, her thinking grew sloppier. "I'm not going to make it."

"Yes, you will. If you can read the coordinates to Peru, you can get us home. There are people there who can help. Who can save your life."

She wasn't convinced. Her head swum, transcendental soup comprised of a mishmash of dreams, memories, and imagination. Her vision faded to black. She held onto her lifeline, her one and only. If she held him as tight as possible, maybe a bit of her spirit would stay with him, and they would never be separated. "I'll love you forever, Julian. Even after I'm gone, I'll love you."

Her grip on life loosened, fingers unfurling around one white string. A red balloon set free to float to the unknown. The bubble got smaller, smaller, smaller. Were there people where she was going? Shifters? Both?

The beginning of a sob eked from him, primal and tormented, but a soothing melody stepped in fast. "I'll love you always and forever, babe. My she-wolf. Warrior woman. I'll visit you every night in my dreams and come join you once my time is up."

With the final, slowing beats of her mangled heart, Taylor mourned for Julian, his heartbreak and sorrow. Mourned for their baby who never even got a chance. Mourned for Salazar, eaten by the jungle. Peace did not come in her final moments. She'd let down too many innocents. She'd failed to become anything other than selfish. Today was not a good day to die.

"Not true." As Julian whispered the assurance, the warmth of his palm pressing against her wet wound. "The most sacred place inside of me honors the most sacred place inside of you. I will always love you, Taylor. And I see your beauty. I feel your beauty."

His touch and words eased her suffering, brought relief to her pain inside and out. She was content, happy, and fuzzy, in the arms of her great love and at one with the universe. In harmony, ready. The end wasn't ugly. Closure equaled perfection. "Thank you."

"Take a deep breath and open your eyes, my love." A touch of joy lilted his gentle encouragement.

She'd been so engrossed in her bliss she hadn't noticed that she'd stopped fading and regained her mental faculties. Taylor dragged her leaden lids upward and blinked at the sight of Julian's serene expression. He petted her hair.

"I'm not dead." She drew in a mega inhale for good measure, and not a nip of pain stymied the effort. Her surroundings remained the same, sandy grass and the oceanic lullaby at night.

"Far from it." Tears streamed down his cheeks, the rivulets of water catching winks of moonlight.

"How?" She glanced down to where she'd taken the hit. A ragged hole ripped her hospital gown where the Other One had gotten her, and spilled blood left evidence splattered on the front, but the injury no longer existed. She gaped at the smooth, undamaged skin beneath the tear and touched the spot for good measure. "How?"

"When I hit the Other One and he crumbled, I felt magic come from my hands. In my intuition, I knew that this power was fundamentally good. So I concentrated as hard as I could on channeling the force, controlling it, and sending it to you. I was winging it, completely flying by the seat of my pants, but it worked."

Holy crap. Julian hadn't gone through the portal and come up empty-handed. He'd picked up healing magic and applied his new ability to save her life. If a shifter's magic reflected a quality of their most essential nature, then Julian's acquisition made total sense. She threw her arms around his shoulders. "I love you. You saved me. Thank you."

"Thank you," he murmured into her temple, rocking her. "You saved me. Let's go home."

Taylor turned to the ocean, a dark mass undulating with rage and majesty in every crest and crash of wave in a seemingly infinite expanse of glory. Her heart and pulse beat in time with those black, lusty waters, and she locked in. "One more thing before we ship out."

Face hot and breath fast, Taylor looked to the sky, where a new half-dollar of a moon shone silver. Two bars of metallic light spilled from the lunar disc and flooded her vision with mercury twinkles.

She pushed, concentrated, until an inverted triangle, red like the first one she'd visualized, ejected from the spot between her eyebrows. The symbol hurdled toward the sea. Water retreated, gathering into a tidal wave as tall as a skyscraper. In the sand left exposed, fish flopped and crabs jumped.

Holding the force in place, Taylor looked once again to Sirius and gave the coordinates. After she finished, she and Julian ascended.

Before they fell backwards into the teleport wormhole, Taylor let go of the symbol. A massive wall of water thundered toward the Scarab base, kissing her toes with cool droplets before slamming into the island and sending the site of suffering and misery to join the Lost City of Atlantis.

TWENTY-TWO

"Ooof." Taylor landed squarely on her ass, knees hugged to her chest, and soaked up relief in the form of jungle fauna songs, fecund smells, and lush darkness.

"Are you okay?" Julian stroked her back, up and down her spine in an assuring check.

Though the impact was bad enough to smart her butt, she hadn't smacked the ground hard enough to jeopardize her embryo. Which she needed to tell Julian about sooner rather than later. "Yeah. Those landings are always a little jarring, but I'm good."

Time to lean into their new life, the least of which would involve logistics like reaching out to Chloe and Angie to explain the move and getting a fix on a location for reliable Internet to complete her degree online. Maybe have someone check her apartment to see if the plants were salvageable.

She had no idea what had happened to her father. He likely had a helicopter or airplane on the island and may have escaped. Or he might have drowned in the tidal wave. She'd proceed accordingly once she figured it out.

Julian would have to arrange to move his paintings and sell his house. Plenty to keep them busy, but they were both intelligent and resourceful if she did say so herself. After all the outlandish tribulations they'd endured, Taylor had the utmost confidence that they could handle trips to button up various details back in Texas. Including finding closure with her family or what was left of it.

"Folks waited up for us." Julian gestured to a spot in the clearing where five dome tents dotted the ground like gumdrops.

"We've got a ride or die crew." They went to the tent in front. "We're back." Taylor crouched as she announced their return in a stage whisper.

Rustles of fabric and a groan replied, followed by the zing of a zipper. The tent flap drooped to reveal Tim, blinking off the dregs of slumber but alert, a scrim of stubble grazing his jawline.

"You guys have got to see this." Awe converted his normally even voice into a drawl. Dressed in the sleep attire of sweats and a Henley, he sprung to his feet and stuck two fingers in his mouth. A shrill whistle sliced humid air and echoed off trees in a haunted melody.

Taylor looked at Julian, curious but not worried. If the news was bad, Tim would have said so. The man didn't sugarcoat or play mind games. As if to convey that he, too, lacked a guess but wished he did, Julian tipped one shoulder in a playful shrug.

Before a single thing even happened, an energetic change flared deep in Taylor, as if a subtle tilt in some hidden frequency turned her bone marrow to quicksilver. An uncanny kind of knowing swirled her perception into a strip made of both hidden and seen worlds. An invisible veil dropped, leaving her flush with a thrill.

Salazar return. A deep, smooth male voice spoke in her head. She gasped, the jungle vivid with life in her mind's eye.

"What happened?" Julian expressed with interest and a trace of concern.

She hadn't even begun to formulate a sensible answer when the lashing whips of a massive force tearing through trees stole her oxygen and dropped her jaw.

A column of moving mass, stretching dozens of feet into the jungle and as fat as an ancient tree's trunk, undulated in primal series of S-curves as it tore a line straight for her. Her mind blanked as the impossible sight hurdled into her field of vision, knocking most thoughts out of her head.

The thing barreling down on her had eyes, a face, and a fearsome presence. A forked tongue larger than two adult arms jabbed out of the distinctly reptilian mouth.

She staggered backward and gripped Julian's hand like only he had the ability to anchor her to what remained of reality.

Julian muttered a partial curse.

Leathery wings crossed with networks of veins flapped, slowing as the giant snake cleared the wilderness and brought its bulk to rest belly-down on the dirt. The beast raised its upper half, cutting a cobra-like resemblance with those wings fanned behind the head, and regarded the trio of shifters with a methodical, predatory gaze.

Adrenaline fried her nerve endings to a crisp.

Salazar return. Salazar kill.

"What? No." Frozen in place, Taylor squeaked out her pitiful resistance as a stew of fright and confusion gunked up any attempt at forming logical thoughts.

Tim laughed, a bemused chuckle.

She managed to grimace at him and throw her free hand in the air. Whatever was going on was scary and no joke.

"Wait for it." Tim steepled his fingertips beneath his mouth.

Salazar pushed his nose toward Taylor, scales the size of Frisbees glossed with a muted sheen.

Taylor say kill and Salazar kill.

"Kill who?" she managed through a mouthful of cotton.

Salazar kill who Taylor say kill.

"Oh." Understanding landed like thunder. Ladies and gentlemen, she had a loyal attack snake at her disposal. Not that she'd take him up on his murderous offer, but it didn't hurt to have a bodyguard of the dragonesque persuasion close by. "No kill now. Salazar no kill. Thanks, though."

Salazar fly. The wings livened up once again, the bladed edges at the ends fanning wide.

Parachutes of snakeskin flared into motion and undulated in a hypnotic pattern, creating a subtle whisper of wind agitated by disturbance.

"Flying is pretty much his favorite thing," Tim said. "He was waiting in this spot when we all teleported back here earlier. I think he'd been looking for you ever since he got big and broke out of his cage and went on his little excursion through the air. I suspected that's what was going on, but at the time, I didn't want to throw another issue in your lap."

"The way you're talking about it sounds like this isn't a big deal to you." Julian bent his thumb at Salazar, who continued to enjoy his wings.

"We've seen it before, yeah. Like I said earlier, latent magic users tend to acquire their powers after passing through a portal. So do their familiars. And now, seeing that you've got a bona fide familiar at your beck and call?" Tim winked at Taylor, trailing off.

She stretched her brow line as high as the lines would reach.

"Congratulations. You, Taylor, are officially a witch." Tim finished the salutation with a slight bow.

She bypassed awe, shock, and denial and rocketed down a smooth path toward acceptance. A few weeks ago, the notion of being a witch would have stretched the limits of her imagination so hard she would have laughed in Tim's face.

The entire landscape of her horizons had changed, of course, dumping her life upside down as her notion of possibilities and limits reversed polarities and flew sideways off the axis.

Slightly overwhelmed by the news and its unknown implication, she tried to sound unbothered and pragmatic, "What does this mean? Do I have to study? Is there some role I play, directions for how to use my magic, instructions?"

Tim glanced at the ground. "You may have found it."

She followed the vector of his tilted face, landing on the old book, and picked up the heavy text with a resolute sigh. "I don't suppose there's an elder here to learn from."

"Nope." Tim walked backwards into his tent, squatted, and rummaged. "I have faith in you, though. You're a good student."

"You've got this, babe." Even in minimal light, the glow of love shone on Julian's face. "You can do anything, and I'll support you in any way I can."

Gratitude filled her. He was right. Together, they could conquer the world. With Julian by her side, she could master magic. Whatever that meant.

Salazar help. Salazar familiar Salazar help. A rough, dry nose butted her shoulder.

"Thanks, buddy." She patted the top of his scaly head, the new duty settling into place amidst her already full to-do list. "Glad to have you back. You scared me."

Salazar sorry. Salazar fly.

"It's fine." she said.

Tim returned from his brief stop in the tent, a shiny object atop a pile of cloth in his hand. He handed over pajamas for Taylor along with two brass keys, newly minted judging by their gleam, each secured to a novelty keychain. One a parrot, the other a llama. "Get some sleep. And the rest of us will take care of cooking breakfast. No hurry in the morning." A wink highlighted his final innuendo.

Taylor wasn't sure which gift conferred the most meaningful blessing, but among Tim's gestures, the general sentiment of reunion, and big changes on the horizon, she accepted plenty. In a swift and whimsical swipe, she snagged the parrot along with the clothes.

Tim turned away while she changed out of her hospital gown.

Julian took the llama and twirled the accessory around his finger. "See you in the morning."

"Yeah." Tim zipped his tent from the inside. "I'm gonna finish out the night here rather than packing out in darkness." He paused and watched them for a second before saying in an earnest cadence, "I'm glad you guys are here. Welcome to the family."

Taylor tucked the magic book under her arm. Family. A word, a concept, once so fraught. Now, though, the meaning behind the label drew her into a caring embrace. Because found family was just as valid as the genetic sort.

With a lazy thumb, Julian stroked the sensitive skin inside her wrist, filling her with pleasure tickles while they strolled to the cabin.

"What are you thinking about?" she asked, knowing that, since this was Julian, she'd get a satisfying answer rich with emotional depth and that self-possessed, calm wisdom of his.

"I keep remembering a time when I was younger." Sticks crunched beneath their feet as they closed in on their shelter.

"What happened?" She stepped up on the stoop.

"I was eleven or so, in this phase where all I ever wanted to do was ride my bike around with these two buddies of mine. We'd get bored and make up words." Memories twinkled like stardust in his eyes, wistful and faraway.

"What kinds of words?" She unlocked the door, taking pleasure in the quiet stillness and scent of cedar, and flicked on the light. Home.

"Mostly for feelings that were blends of incongruous emotions. Such as the combo of relief, guilt, joy, and sorrow felt when a relation you loved but didn't like dies." He sat on the couch, widening his legs and stretching his arms over the top in invitation.

Taylor could think of a few people from her own past to whom such a label applied. She set the book on the coffee table, took her place beside Julian, and gave his leg a gentle kick, opting for banter in lieu of heavy conversation. "You thought that up when you were eleven?"

He caressed her cheek with the backs of tender fingers, regarding her with lidded eyes. "Yeah. There was some heaviness in my childhood. But I was thinking of a different combination while we were standing by the tents with Tim and supercharged Salazar."

"Do tell." She folded her legs underneath her body and turned her sole focus to Julian.

Until recently, she'd never really cared what another person had to say enough to give them her full attention. Others were tedious, and she was the smartest person in the room lording over them. But she could listen to Julian speak for hours, taking in the scope of his intelligence as the enflamed sore of her narcissism healed.

"Excitement, anticipation, and the joy of new beginnings all laced with that inevitable whisper of apprehension that comes from plunging into an unknown."

She rubbed her legs, struck by the coincidental perfection with which he'd timed his reverie. "How apropos."

"Hm?" The jaunty way he tipped his head, along with his mellow energy, let her know his frown was in jest.

No legitimate way to soft-peddle. "I'm pregnant."

His mouth made a hoop as his hand froze midair. "Oh." The brown skin of his stunned face paled to a washed-out tan, and she fretted irrationally that this would not go well. "Oh, wow."

She wrung her hands. "I was on hormonal contraception, the shot like I told you, but apparently the drug was no match for your astonishingly potent shifter sperm."

Healthy valor returned to Julian's complexion, and he smiled at her quip. "I didn't mean to go all dumb on you. I just didn't see that one coming."

"Me neither." Held breath rushed out as a bit of levity lightened the mood. "I want you to know that I want you to be a part of this decision. So please be totally honest with me about what feels right to you, what you want. We have choices."

With one hand laid on top of the other, she crossed her hidden set of fingers. Her preferred choice involved a fetus growing into a baby and then becoming a family with Julian. But his desires needed to mirror hers for a future to work. She refused to trap him. If Julian harbored even the slightest nag of ambivalence, she'd have to make a different choice.

Because parenting was tough enough under the best of conditions, and with the slow-acting poison of resentment infecting the parents? Nope. She'd experienced firsthand the destructive toxicity of growing up in a dysfunctional household wrecked by a bad marriage and refused to inflict the same fate on the next generation.

In a quick and assuring show of conviction, he cupped her face in both hands and gazed deeply into her eyes. "Tell me what you want."

She let her truth flow like water, his kind brown eyes harbors in the tempest of so many huge and profound changes. "I want to have the baby. I want us to be a family."

Integrity surrounded him like an aura made of strength and peace as he simply assured her with his stare.

Her heart broke for how beautiful Julian was, inside and out.

"Then I want that too. And I promise I'll be good to you, and a good father to our baby. Whatever you need, I'm here. I know you haven't had the best example, but our baby will. I've never wanted anything more than I want this, Taylor. I'm complete." He released his hands and pressed a kiss to her forehead in a gesture devastating and precious with innocence, intimacy, and care.

She fell into his arms while happy tears, the liquid evidence of swollen emotions too wild to tame, burst from her truest spaces. "I love you so much. I never knew what love meant until I found you. And now there's like this whole new person inside me, and I love her too. I mean another me, not the baby. But the baby too, obviously. Gah, you know what I mean."

"She's not new," he whispered, making a study of her shoulders, her elbows, the curve of her spine with magic and practiced hands. "She was always there, waiting for the right time to come out. Like your wolf. Same with our baby. They were all waiting for their perfect moment to grace us."

She closed her eyes, at rest against the solidness of his chest, bathed in his heat and scent. "Do you think our baby will be a shifter?"

His hum relaxed her like a chant. "Hard to say. I'm not sure if the ability is a latent or recessive gene, passed through the mother or father or both, or what. I suppose we both have a lot to learn about shifters."

"Yeah. We're really diving in feet first, huh?"

"Starting tomorrow at least." He lifted her in a single, firm haul that made her squeal as her feet gave and she went airborne. "Right now, we'd better dive into something else. Because I intend to keep you up quite late, ensuring that we stumble in to the tail end of breakfast barely able to walk."

"Okay, I'm there for this." She initiated foreplay by kissing his neck until he moaned. An ache swelled her clit and lubricated her passage. In a flash of spontaneity, Taylor channeled her wolf enough to file her incisors into spikes. She nipped a spot just below Julian's ear.

"God, it makes me so fucking hot when you do that." The lust in his speech made the fact evident, as did the oomph with which he threw her on the bed.

Damp and tender, ready, she tore her own clothes off and reclined on the bed, comforter tickling her bare skin. She locked his eyes and spread her legs.

He was at work on his own clothes, shedding the flannel on to the floor and pulling a white undershirt over his head from behind. The agitation mussed his hair, giving him a feral look when paired with the tattoo. Her gaze landed on the bulge pressed into his pants.

At last, the pants and boxers came down, and there he was. She rolled her bottom lip between her teeth and took in his arousal, becoming both predator and submissive prey.

Taylor widened her knees as far as they would stretch, the cool blow of air on the hot secret of her hidden flesh a tantalizing preview. "You want this?"

He answered with a gruff sound, prowling nude up the bed until he aligned their bodies flush with him on top. Hungry eyes cased her face. "I want you, babe."

"You have me. All of me." Body, mind, and heart. She wrapped her legs around his waist and urged him down with the pressure of her hold, showing him with her open and receptive center how much he meant to her.

Taylor had never given herself to another person before, she'd been too insecure and brittle with egotistical fragility to allow herself to be truly vulnerable. She'd had okay enough sex with guys who made sure she came and tried to cuddle and such, but a crucial element had always been missing, a lack she felt intuitively but could not name. Until now. Whole, total trust.

"Forever." He took the kiss he wanted, a passionate lock and probe that spirited her breathing, thinking self to paradise just as his hard cock slid in to fill her with intoxicating pressure.

"That feels so good." A part of her located her primal side, horny and driven by the mating instinct. Another aspect remained human, though, the best of her humanity was felt in the love she gave and received.

He moved on top of her, slow and with scorching eye contact, as she held on to his firm biceps, the strong arms that would protect their family. She didn't even care about an orgasm, this act of theirs meant more than pleasure, but of course Julian saw to her enjoyment.

His hand maneuvered between bodies, the downward journey facilitated by their mingled sweat, and bumped the pads of two fingers over her clit. He used a combination of pressure and motion tactics that had her muscles locking with tension in a couple of minutes, and a long scream tore from her, the relief acting of its own accord the same as possession.

He kept on rubbing her even when his eyes rolled back, and he sped the drive of his pumps to frantic, the selfish plunges were taken in quick succession.

She twitched as he extracted the final drops of the climax from her body, holding him as he buried himself in her and moaned in time with his spasms, breath hot and fast near her cheekbone.

They rode out their post-climactic shock together for a few moments, catching ruined breath. When some time had passed, Julian rolled off her and flopped on his back, catching her hand, and kissing the top before his body went slack.

"What do you think is next for us?" She maneuvered to her side and traced a finger along the cut-glass profile of his jawline.

"I don't know. But I know we're going to make it."

Her gaze floated to the ceiling, where beams and joists supported rustic red logs, as if stars and planets might shine through the building's confines. "What do you think fate is, exactly? The same as destiny? Or is it the will of God or some other form of cosmic intelligence?"

"I think it's a predetermined outcome or prophecy that's given shape based on the conscious choices that we make." His voice grew sleepy as he cuddled and caressed her.

They were both fucking exhausted, obviously.

She snuggled into his warmth, allowing herself a silent and pleasurable detour into the philosophical spaces of her mind before sleep came to collect.

If she and Julian were meant to be, decreed a couple by the workings of this mysterious force, that was one thing. But she supposed he was right about conscious choices shaping outcomes. And from here on out, every choice she made, as a student, worker, community member, partner, and mother, would come from a place of integrity and purpose.

She didn't have to chase money, power, or status to fill the void inside with material markers of success. She didn't have to look down on a legion of flunkies from the apex of some cold, hard perch as a substitute for letting in those who would nurture her for once.

She didn't have to be cold and mean to cover up the hurt and grief quivering beneath the tough act.

She didn't have to chase love, or beg for it, or dance on broken hooves like a resentful prized pony in desperate hopes that one more good performance would cause what she craved to manifest.

The love she desired was in her, with her and all around her—and had come to her once she found in her heart the ability to give what she wanted so badly to get. Only then did the abundance rain down.

Damn, they'd had to suffer for their prize, but Taylor didn't blame fate for putting her and Julian through the ringer. The trials and tribulations had proved it was worth the struggle.

Fate was a ruthless bitch at times, true, but Taylor loved her anyway.

Because a ruthless bitch actually could become a good person, and ruthless bitches deserve love, too.

***

Thank you for reading! Did you enjoy? Please add your review because nothing helps an author more and encourages readers to take a chance on a book than a review.

And don't miss more from Kat Turner in the *Jungle Shifters* series coming soon! Until then read HEX, LOVE, AND ROCK & ROLL, the first book in the *Coven Daughters* series, available now. Turn the page for a sneak peek!

Also be sure to sign up for the City Owl Press newsletter to receive notice of all book releases!

SNEAK PEEK OF HEX, LOVE, AND ROCK & ROLL

Helen Schrader hated witches. After all, they'd gotten her thrown into foster care. But as her thirtieth birthday approached, she sat across from a supposed witch named Nerissa and worked up the nerve to ask her for a spell. Funny how the past refused to die.

Pentagram knickknacks and a crystal ball collection decorated the old lady's living room, along with vintage furniture and a framed art print of three women mixing brew in a cauldron. A bookshelf full of texts on witchcraft, world religions, and philosophy completed vivid testimony to authenticity.

People all over Minneapolis swore the crone could conjure fast cash. The pagans who took classes at Helen's yoga studio spoke of Nerissa in the reverent tones of worshipers.

Perhaps the universe began orchestrating the current turn of events when one of Helen's students walked in on her crying over unpaid bills and handed her Nerissa's business card. Unless her visions from years ago kicked some grand plan into motion.

Did everything happen for a reason?

Though the hardened cynic in Helen scoffed at bullshit magical thinking, an atrophied, softer side not yet demolished by life's cruelty yearned to believe in synchronicity and magic.

Sweat glued her jeans to the backs of her thighs as she adjusted her weight on the sofa cushion. She could stand to do some Zen breathing to calm her nerves. Besides, she'd run out of options to save her business. Her credit was shot, so no more loans. But Light and Enlightened would not become Dark and Forgotten without a final, radical attempt at salvation. Time to take one last shot at rescuing the only permanent home she'd ever known. Throw a Hail Mary pass. She met Nerissa's keen blue eyes and managed a smile.

The universe has a plan. Everything happens for a reason. You've got this.
You are fucking idiot and a loser who is destined to fail.

"You have an impressive book collection." Helen picked a chip in her nail polish as if repetitive motion would banish negative thoughts. "I'm not sure if you got my email about your fee for today. Does twenty dollars work? I'm so sorry I can't offer more."

A lopsided smirk deepened the wrinkles in Nerissa's cheeks. She petted the arm of the leather recliner she sat in and uncrossed her legs beneath a maxi skirt. A knowing tone smoothed the kinks in her low timbre as she said, "Is that why you made an appointment? To discuss literature? Or did you mention the books as a way of confirming my legitimacy?"

Helen drew in a deep inhale and willed the room's sage scent and mellow lighting to relax her before she blundered another attempt at small talk. "Just curious. I've read some of those books. Not the witchy ones, but the Sartre and Nietzsche. 'That which does not kill me makes me stronger' was my motto for awhile. I have an undergrad degree in philosophy. Sorry. I'm rambling."

Yikes, she was a hot and simmering mess. Intelligent aliens were welcome to zap her with a space laser and implant competence into her brain.

Without a word, Nerissa rose. She walked across the living room to the bookcase and ran her finger across spines. "Don't sell yourself short. You have more than an undergrad degree, you started a doctorate. You're smarter than you think, and I can assure you that failure is not in your destiny. Let's have a peek at my favorite book. It's one of the *witchy* ones."

Helen's heart seemed to jump to her throat, and an icy ribbon threaded up her spine. Nerissa must've figured out the facts about her education through research. The other part? Mere coincidence. A nervous laugh bubbled out with her next words. "Is my aura that strong? You practically read my mind."

Nerissa's gray braid swished back and forth as she turned her head over her shoulder. A twinkle in her eye caught slices of afternoon light streaming in through gaps in the drapes.

"There's no *practically* about it. My ability to access your surface thoughts is a sign of our spirit-born connection. I see magic swirled into those beautiful amber irises of yours, too. You are gifted, but we can't step into our deepest truth until we believe in ourselves."

Helen snorted when her stomach went sour. She'd been called a lot of things over the years, but gifted wasn't one of them. Mind reading amounted to an easier sell. This woman was patronizing her due to some ulterior motive. Everybody had one.

"Oh, please. If I was gifted, I'd have more to show for myself by now. Behold, my impressive roster of accomplishments: a pit of debt, a retired stripping career, and a useless degree. Not exactly ticking off boxes on those 'things every woman should have by thirty' checklists."

The self-flagellation lashed Helen to the bone, and her trusty armor of sarcasm didn't protect her from those whip stings. She covered her face and trained her gaze on an area rug, not looking up until the floorboards creaked.

A massive tome in her hands, Nerissa ambled back to her chair and sat. "There will be bigger birthdays if you're lucky. I still remember the sixties. Woodstock. I was the girl in a famous picture, twirling and twirling. I slept with *all* of those rock stars and enjoyed free love."

Heat spread under Helen's breastbone, tightness squeezing her midsection. Was the 'rock stars' comment a sly knock on Helen for falling for the musician ex who cheated on her with every available groupie? A catty little mind-reading trick of Nerissa's?

Whatever. With her life circling the drain, she could not endure head games. Lisa still refused to speak to her. Bad news for a business partner or best friend, let alone both. She had major problems to solve and not a minute to squander.

"Cool. Sounds like fun. I'd like to talk about your services now. My business goes in to foreclosure next week, and my closest friend blames me. I need money. You can do wealth spells, right?"

A grating guffaw rolled out of Nerissa's throat. She opened her volume and leafed. Pages warped from water damage and crowded with words offered coy peeks at possible solutions.

"Patience isn't among your virtues. Hence your tendency to act before thinking and leave projects unfinished. But your drive is noble, and your will is strong. You dare to chase success by any means necessary, which I admire. Takes gumption to sell the spectacle of one's naked flesh to keep the lights on, and don't beat yourself up about the studio. There's a yoga place on every block these days. Lots of entrepreneurial young women such as yourself are losing their shirts teaching Downward Dog."

Helen clamped her teeth down on the tip of her tongue and swallowed a snarky comeback. Not wise to risk alienating the witch. Better to summon tact and diplomacy.

Nerissa hummed a tune while reading.

Helen tapped her foot. She needed to hit the road before traffic became a zoo, and the final notice of foreclosure stuffed in the bottom of her purse wasn't about to dematerialize.

"Finding any good abundance spells?" The fake-casual lilt in Helen's tone prompted her to roll her eyes at herself. She sucked at tact and diplomacy.

"I want to try an experiment." The gray-haired woman flipped to the front of her book and touched a circle inked on the inside of the cover.

"Alright. Sure." Helen snuck a peek at her watch and squirmed.

"This grimoire was an inheritance from my foremothers. My coven daughter will inherit my sacred text from me to learn the spirit witch's craft and begin the work of the six-fold sisterhood. The spirit element is the most cerebral of the six circles."

God, enough with the pointless anecdotes. Nerissa might have all day to meander, but Helen did not. "Whoever she is will be lucky. Like I said, I'm broke as a joke—"

Another laugh from the old witch made for a jarring interruption. "You may be the *she* in question. Here's a free lesson. Your defeatist tendencies stem from fear of finding your true power, so you self-sabotage in an effort to make yourself less threatening. I understand. We wise women have been taught by the patriarchy to hate our gifts."

Helen ground her molars. Aggravation shot through her in a frying jolt. Cash, not a feminist lecture, would solve her problems. She grabbed her purse off the couch and jumped to her feet. "This was a mistake. I assumed—"

Nerissa muttered in some throaty, incomprehensible language. The old woman's eyes rolled back in her head. Blank slates of white remained.

Breath vanished from Helen's lungs. The bizarre sight and sounds boggled her imagination until skepticism intervened. Nerissa's eyeball move could be a trick, a result of training ocular muscles.

"A trick? I don't deal in cheap parlor tricks, dear. Now let's see if you are the one."

A pop sounded in Helen's ears. She blinked a few times as a dazed, sleepy sensation disoriented her. Lost to pleasurable mugginess and an odd feeling of time slowing to a crawl, she didn't snap back to lucidity until she noticed the cauldron painting again.

The painting was upside down. No. Correction. *She* was upside down, hanging in midair.

Blood roared in Helen's ears while she scrabbled unsuccessfully to reclaim control of her faculties. A scream tore its way up her throat but somehow died before erupting. Electric with panic, she flailed, spinning in a dizzy circle. A few chaotic seconds later, she recovered some semblance of her bearings and managed to stay still despite waves of queasiness.

The room returned to focus as blurs of color reformed into bookshelves, furniture, and other familiar shapes. *Almost* familiar. Her perception was weird.

Helen gaped when she figured out was was wrong with her surroundings. The furnishings and Nerissa were below her. She was stuck to the damn ceiling. To make matters weirder, another woman now stood in the spot she'd occupied, someone in jeans identical to Helen's.

Shock slammed into her as a realization dawned. She wasn't looking at a third person. She looked down at herself, her own body, while her consciousness floated above. Brunette waves streaked with blonde highlights tumbled over her shoulders. At least she was having a good hair day, because the out-of-body experience blew her mind. Separation from her physical form had been the last thing she'd been expecting during the visit.

A coil of phosphorescent light spiraled upward from the middle of the open book while the witch chanted, "Coven daughter, come to me. Show us truth and clarity."

Discombobulated, Helen squinted against a glare. The beam bent and twisted into a hoop. The space in the middle of the illuminated circle glimmered. Images appeared. A highlight reel of her life played while she gawked.

Nerissa pulled from Helen's memories and projected them at her. *Now* her mind was blown. What else could this be besides hardcore magic?

"I can help you, Helen, but you need to listen. Can you?"

She ought to get in line and embrace the insanity, or she'd soon be begging Dreamgirls to let her hump their germ-infested pole again. Hard pass on the humping. "Yes."

Helen crashed back into her physical form with a boom, knees weak and mind spinning. Reeling from the loss of control, she plopped her butt on the couch and shook herself out of a daze.

"Did your mother and grandmother have the gift?" The witch's eyes returned to normal.

Mother. The sound of the word was profane, like the filthiest curses flung at her.

What should have carried a connotation of loving nurturance dredged up a memory of the time the mother in question shrieked about original sin while she forced Helen to eat the pages of her diary. Recollections of the incident still scraped her raw with phantom pain. She should have learned to stop talking about her visions after that day. Or after the next morning, spent whimpering on the toilet.

"I didn't know my grandmother. My mother had major issues."

"You never had a mother figure who embraced your gift. Tragic." A soft tremble rounded the edges of Nerissa's words. "The visions began at the onset of your menses and lasted for years, didn't they? Trances? Seizures? Mine showed up at menarche and didn't leave until I mastered my craft."

Wow. One other person on the planet could relate to her secret.

"One foster family returned me because my episodes scared their pet rats. Yep. I ranked below rats." She spoke the words in a jesting tone, but the long ago rejection still made Helen's chest ache with old hurt.

"Rats are inherently nervous creatures. Let your pain go and describe the episodes."

"Speaking in tongues, chattering teeth, muscle spasms. Visions of spinning out of my body and flying through the air, seeing women burning at the stake. Wild times. Of course none of my temp families believed me." Helen shrugged, over-affecting nonchalance as the uncomfortable topic poked at her insecurities. Too weird and too spacey. Dissociative. Broken. Bad girl, crazy bitch.

"Flying through the air. Oh, yes. You are spirit born."

For the first time, Helen settled back in her seat, her muscles loosening, curious to know more. "Okay, so I'm spirit born. What should I do to save my studio?"

"You must choose a path to proceed on your actualization."

"Excuse me?"

"To actualize means to coax your abilities to the surface, where you may direct and control them. The power you possess is dormant and churning in your subconscious, so you endured episodes. When witches repress what we do best, we suffer."

Helen put her hands up, palms facing out. She could accept the idea of having some psychic abilities, but being a witch...the notion stretched the limits of plausibility. "Hold up. I don't think I'm a witch."

A shadow passed across Nerissa's eyes. She leaned forward in her chair, close enough for Helen to smell her rosy perfume. "Are you calling me a liar?"

"No. It's difficult to take in, though."

"Why? You came to me for help, and I'm showing you how to get what you want. But if you've changed your mind about needing money, this can end right here." Nerissa closed the book with a definitive snap.

"I'm not quite convinced is all. What's in this for you?"

"When witches practice, our powers enhance each other. Mine will grow in relation to yours. So while I wish to help you because I care about the spiritual health of my coven daughter and want to see the sisterhood come to fruition, I'm also being a teeny bit selfish."

Outlandish, but what if Nerissa was right? God, the possibilities for turning her life around. She hadn't taken a chance coming to the witch's home only to run out when things got strange. No more quitting, no more failure. Time to nut up or shut up.

"Fine. I'm all in. You were saying. Initiation. Spirit element. Smash the patriarchy with our broomsticks. How do I choose a path?"

"Your choices are Right Hand or Left Hand path. The Right Hand path draws from your internal strengths and abilities, in your case latent color magic. Astral projection and remote viewing would also come from marshalling the Right."

"How does color magic work?"

"The expression is unique to the witch. You'd call out to meaningful colors in your life and weave emotional union with them to perform spells."

"Such as visualizing the color green for money."

Nerissa shrugged. "If you're thinking long-term, sure."

The words "long-term" bounced around in a series of bothersome echoes. Long-term might not suffice. "What's up with the Left?"

"Left Hand powers originate from outside. Think transferring energy into objects in order to manipulate them, or splitting your psyche so as to exist in two places at once. The Left is potent and capable of producing immediate results, but also volatile and dark."

A surge of curiosity charged through Helen. She scooted to the edge of her seat. Potent power and speedy results could save L&E before the bank snatched it away and Helen and Lisa trudged out carrying boxes.

Helen had slunk out of many front doors with tears in her eyes. Never again.

She pursed her lips, though, wavering at what volatile and dark might mean. In all likelihood, something bad. Yet depending on inner strengths didn't seem like the right move, not when one of Helen's dumb mistakes all but catapulted the studio into the abyss.

"Have you chosen?" Nerissa drummed her fingers on the book's cover.

Bottom line, she could not afford to wait. "I choose the Left Hand path."

"There will be a cost." Nerissa rose and offered Helen the grimoire.

"What is it?" Helen accepted, her arms straining under the book's weight.

Nerissa walked to a credenza. Jars filled with liquids in a variety of colors cluttered the top. Helen watched with interest as the old lady rummaged in a drawer.

The elder witch returned with a small sack made of black velvet and a jar half full of clear fluid. She handed over the pouch. "Depends on one's constitution. Could be as trivial as a stomachache."

Helen took the bag, taking a moment to stroke the silky material. She loosened a string and peered in. Crystals in a rainbow of colors sparkled one after the other as if they communicated. "But it could be worse."

"Oh, yes."

"What's the worst case scenario?"

"If the universe decides the darkness wasn't yours to take, it might generate a hex as punishment for selecting the wrong magic. Think karma, but magnified tenfold."

Helen's insides dropped. "Hold up. I don't need more trouble. How would I deal with a hex?"

"Read your book. That's the answer to all of your questions. But first, deploy the crystals. They are sentient and absorbent, and the clear ones are the most pliable and receptive to their witch's will. Give both clear stones away to good people before you undertake your study, as cultivating others' energies will refine your powers. Make sure to set a mental intention before gifting this pair of crystals. Done correctly, this means giving each one precise directions. Otherwise, the hex might begin with dark entities latching on to one or both stones. Once demons establish communion, they can possess crystals."

Yawning, Nerissa thrust the jar at Helen. "Drink this and leave. The Reveal spell I did drained my energy. If I don't get my nap in, my weakened state could compromise you."

Though her pulse accelerated, Helen took the container and unscrewed its lid. She chugged, gag reflex lurching as she downed the sour glop. Her eyes watered, and nausea roiled her insides, but she finished the nasty potion. Go big or go home. "So twenty bucks is okay?"

"We'll settle up down the road." The old woman's eyelids fluttered closed as she sagged in her chair. "Study now."

A rush of pride prompted Helen to straighten her spine. She could be a decent student. Armed with a big book of witchiness and the crystals, she placed her empty jar on a coffee table and sauntered to the front door of the bungalow with her head held high.

The plan: give away two crystals, figure out magic, get L&E solvent, and save her dearest friendship. Doable? Helen smiled and hugged the grimoire to her chest. Hell yeah.

"*Sacrificium.*" A calm, male voice spoke inside of Helen's head. An itchy surge of adrenaline shot to her toes. Though she'd never taken Latin, she sure got the gist—sacrifice.

Her hand tensed on the doorknob, and she glanced at Nerissa. "Did you hear that?"

"No!" Nerissa bolted upright. Her mouth dropped, and her eyes stretched wide, but the show of fear in her expression fled as fast as it came.

Helen's mouth dried. Talk about a bad omen double whammy. "Are you okay?"

Rubbing her temples, the elder looked around the room. "I'm fine. Take care."

Helen jetted to her Mini Cooper. As she fumbled for her keys, a plume of milky smoke erupted in the recesses of her consciousness, vanishing a second after it arrived. She tried to disregard the inexplicable intrusion. Probably just her magic settling in.

She drove to the Minnesota State Fair, but by the time she squeezed between two cars in a dusty makeshift lot, she hadn't managed to forget the creepy voice and smoke.

A definitive slam of her door shoved the unsettling events out of her mind, and she strode to the flapping banner marking the entrance to the fairgrounds.

Today belonged in the win column, damn it.

✳

Don't stop now. Keep reading with your copy of HEX, LOVE, AND ROCK & ROLL available now.

Don't miss more of the *Jungle Shifters* coming soon, and find ALL of the *Coven Daughters* series available now from Kat Turner at katturnerauthor.com

✳

With a business skidding toward bankruptcy and bone-dry bank account, Helen Schrader is willing to do the unthinkable. But what will happen when she hires a witch to cast a money spell?

When the spell sets in motion her own latent magic and her inexperience causes her to accidentally hex her celebrity crush, rocker Brian Shepherd, all that good fortune she hoped for flies out of the window.

Now, Helen and Brian struggle to break the curse and tackle their growing feelings for each other. Problem is, the harder they fall for each other, the deadlier the curse becomes.

But as a dark magic cult with an unquenchable thirst for power closes in on them, the couple will have to face more than just their inconvenient desire. With time running out and danger mounting, can they beat the hex before Brian becomes its next victim?

✳

Please sign up for the City Owl Press newsletter for chances to win special subscriber-only contests and giveaways as well as receiving information on upcoming releases and special excerpts.

All reviews are **welcome** and **appreciated**. Please consider leaving one on your favorite social media and book buying sites.

For books in the world of romance and speculative fiction that embody

Innovation, Creativity, and Affordability, check out City Owl Press at www.cityowlpress.com.

ACKNOWLEDGMENTS

Acknowledgements: Thank you to everyone who has bought, read, reviewed, boosted, hyped, and otherwise supported my stories. Your encouragement is my fuel to keep writing, and I appreciate each one of you more than you will ever know. I hope you enjoy this new series in my paranormal universe. Special thanks to Tee and the team at City Owl for believing in my books. BrocheAroe Fabian, I'm deeply grateful for your thorough and thoughtful sensitivity read. Your incisive feedback and attention to detail helped to ensure that Julian's heritage was handled with care.

ABOUT THE AUTHOR

KAT TURNER is an award-winning author of paranormal romance and urban fantasy as well as the occasional thriller. Her favorite stories to write are those that combine action and adventure with magic, dry humor, and steamy romance if the situation allows. She lives is Kentucky with her family, where she can mostly be found practicing yoga, taking nature walks, or getting lost in the corridors of her own imagination. Kat loves to connect with readers, so don't be shy about getting in touch!

linktr.ee/katturnerauthor

[f] X [o] [d] [g] [BB]

ABOUT THE AUTHOR

ABOUT THE PUBLISHER

City Owl Press is a cutting edge indie publishing company, bringing the world of romance and speculative fiction to discerning readers.

Escape Your World. Get Lost in Ours!

www.cityowlpress.com

facebook.com/YourCityOwlPress
x.com/cityowlpress
instagram.com/cityowlbooks
pinterest.com/cityowlpress

www.ingramcontent.com/pod-product-compliance
Ingram Content Group UK Ltd.
Pitfield, Milton Keynes, MK11 3LW, UK
UKHW040743090325
4899UKWH00066B/1320